C. H. F Routh

Infant Feeding and its Influence on Life

Or the causes and prevention of infant mortality

C. H. F Routh

Infant Feeding and its Influence on Life
Or the causes and prevention of infant mortality

ISBN/EAN: 9783337418571

Printed in Europe, USA, Canada, Australia, Japan

Cover: Foto ©Andreas Hilbeck / pixelio.de

More available books at **www.hansebooks.com**

INFANT FEEDING.

AND

ITS INFLUENCE ON LIFE;

OR, THE

Causes and Prevention of Infant Mortality.

BY

C. H. F. ROUTH, M.D., M.R.C.P.E., M.R.C.S.

FELLOW OF THE MEDICAL, ROYAL MEDICO-CHIRURGICAL, AND OBSTETRICAL SOCIETIES;
CORRESPONDING MEMBER OF THE ROYAL ACADEMY OF SURGERY OF MADRID, ETC.;
PHYSICIAN TO THE SAMARITAN FREE HOSPITAL FOR WOMEN AND CHILDREN;
LATE SENIOR PHYSICIAN TO THE ST. PANCRAS ROYAL GENERAL
DISPENSARY, ETC., ETC.

Second Edition.

LONDON:

J. CHURCHILL & SONS, NEW BURLINGTON ST.

MDCCCLXIII.

LONDON:
T. RICHARDS, 37, GREAT QUEEN STREET.

PREFACE

TO THE SECOND EDITION.

———

WHEN the views first propounded in these pages were put forth, I anticipated considerable opposition. The voice and practice of the profession were against me. I looked for no favour on the part of the press, and I expected the public would not be more propitious. My opinions, however, had been formed after mature thought and reflection, and I felt urged to set forth what I believed was truth, and to expose what I estimated as error. I am thankful to feel my misgivings, in regard to what I have said, have not been verified.

The fundamental doctrines I sought to prove, have been in great measure admitted. The dogma, that it is imprudent to mix two milks, or to allow a mother both to suckle and feed a child

artificially at the same time, now meets with few
advocates. The great mortality of infants is now
no longer attributed so much to hand-feeding, as
to the injudicious manner in which it is generally
conducted. Lastly, the full bearings of the hiring
of wet-nurses upon the spread of illegitimacy,
upon the death of the children so deserted by
their mothers, and indirectly upon infanticide,
are becoming daily more appreciated.

It is true, that in putting forth a second
edition I am anxious to give more development
to the views enunciated, and to make more converts to my opinions; but I have also another
object,—I desire to influence public benevolence
in another and an analogous direction. There
is a sphere of usefulness open, and one in its
accomplishment well calculated to benefit the
masses. I long to see our Foundling Hospitals,
and other analogous institutions, with their large
prospective revenues, extend their philanthropic
operations, and open wider their doors of relief.
There are many honest hardworking mothers
whose circumstances as to money and health prevent them from fulfilling their maternal duties
to the advantage of their children. The over-
crowded and overburdened workhouse is surely

not a fit place for them. Why should not these rich institutions hold out a helping hand to the offspring of these poor mothers, without necessarily neglecting the children of our more frail and unfortunate sisters? It would be a glorious thing to see all these children taken up and fed upon those plain, simple, commonsense principles which the knowledge of the day has developed, and thus rescued in many cases from disease, deformity, and premature death. Some of these rules I have endeavoured to point out; others will become matured in the course of experiment, and I hope the day is not far distant when they will be put into full operation.

Let me be clear, however. I do not presume to say that I have done even a tithe of what may yet be done, for I feel progress will not stop here. But I believe soberly, that the measures I have ventured to recommend are a step, however feebly made, in the right direction. All I can say for myself is that my heart is in the cause, and that the views herein set forth are, so far as I am able to judge, founded on practice as well as science.

Humbly, yet hopefully, I look to my profession

and its many ardent workers to develop more clearly any doubtful points. Confidently and brightly I look to the time when the benevolent public will, by extended and continuous experiment, consolidate our work, and all by common consent carry out our Heavenly Master's injunction, when He said, " It is not the wish of your Heavenly Father that *even* one of these little ones should perish !"

52, Montague Square.
May 1863.

PREFACE

THE influence of injudicious feeding upon infantile disease and mortality has occupied my
attention for some years. Accordingly several of
the divisions of the subject, now given collectively, have from time to time appeared as
separate papers in the medical periodicals. They
are put forth in a more connected form,—it is
hoped also in a more matured shape. Like most
other subjects, however, the question has grown
under consideration, and this must be my excuse
for the length to which these remarks have been
necessarily extended. Possessing, moreover, a
strong affection for little children, and for this
reason much interested in the wellbeing of mothers to whom they are naturally confided, I
have wished to develop the subject in its double

phase. In the hope of effecting this, I have spared no pains in the investigation, and have given myself heartily to the work. I may also say that I have not intentionally allowed myself to be biassed by preconceived opinions: I have honestly sought out truth; in proof of which I may add, that many of the results obtained have taken me by surprise. I was not prepared for them.

I could scarcely have supposed that the ignorance of the masses of the proper manner of feeding infants was so great—that the constituted authorities in the realm could permit so much dishonesty in those who have to provide food for infants; still less that the whole question was so intimately connected with the development of much social evil and moral crime; yet beneath the careless sanction of the community these are gradually yet certainly attaining alarming proportions. Fortunately for me, the public have begun themselves to see the danger. Mothers in high position are exerting themselves to remove this ignorance. Already the Ladies' Sanitary Association has done good service. If the Government be slow in carrying out the work of reformation, those high in authority and connected with it, united in sanitary associations, are bestirring themselves to stem the torrent, and preparing the ground for future legislation.

The medical profession and the clergy, always foremost in works of charity, are heartily co-operating in the work. This is a cheering aspect. Ere long we may hope to see this land, blessed with so much spiritual and general knowledge, also stand pre-eminent for sanitary improvement in this direction. We may soon see the movement ripening, to the salvation of many lives now annually sacrificed before the shrines of ignorance and vice. For myself, I pretend to no knowledge superior to that of my compeers, but I have some zeal to acquire it; and it is impossible for even an ordinary mind to look closely on any subject without obtaining from the very application some useful information.

In the wish to follow in the public wake, and to communicate the lessons I have learnt, I have been led to publish my views. In doing this I may have erred in two ways. Perhaps my style is not so popular as some have wished; still I trust the majority will understand my meaning. Others, on the other hand, perhaps think I have spoken too plainly; but on so important a social question to speak too scrupulously from a mock attempt at prudery, would be puerile. I have a higher game to play than merely to court the popularity of the fastidious. In either case my fault will only tend to bring out, by the clashing of different opinions, that which I should scorn to obscure,—the plain, incontrovertible truth. Notwithstanding, to contribute in any way towards the elucidation of so complicated a question, or to assist in the smallest degree in unravelling laws, which in their future development may insure public weal, is in either case a difficult task; but, from the magnitude of the good hoped for, it becomes a pleasing duty to the active philanthropist.

52, Montague Square.
June 1860.

CONTENTS.

PART I.

MORTALITY AND VIABILITY OF INFANTS.

PART IV.

DEFECTIVE ASSIMILATION.

CHAPTER I.

General remarks on prevalence of abdominal diseases—Defective assimilation—Forms of disease—Three stages—Malignant variety—Post-mortem appearances—Nature of the
disease—Principles of treatment—The dietetic means of
ensuring digestion of nitrogenous, fatty, and saccharine
aliments—Need of pancreatic juice—Vegetable aliments—

INTRODUCTION.

"A CHILD in a house is a wellspring of pleasure."
So said Tupper; and he spoke truly. The mother has suffered in her travail, and the husband
has grieved over his wife's sufferings. But even
in her weakness it is an unalloyed pleasure to
gaze on the little babe that sleeps by her side.
First, helpless to a degree, it commends itself to
her protection; and gradually as the stream of life
acquires power, new feelings of love expand her
maternal heart. Soon the infant by a smile re-
wards the fondling look, and by its little exclama-
tions of pleasure makes her rejoice also. A part of
herself, so long as it continues a suckling, it is
first loved by those who love her, or by those
who see in the little innocent the image of their
own present or expected babes. And thus it
grows daily, and daily by more distinct childish
prattle gives evidence of opening intelligence;
it enlivens all around, and, twining itself round
the hearts even of the sterner sex, it is loved by
all who know it for itself.

B

How different the picture when illness creeps in! How sad the looks are now of those who loved it: the little babe in itself, how changed in aspect! It is sorrowful to behold its now haggard, now excited, restless look, and to hear its pitiful moan. The wellspring of pleasure has become an occasion of grief and despondency, and who knows how soon, like the blighted flowret, it may droop beyond recovery. The mother still tends upon it with unceasing love : self is forgotten in watching over the tender one, but "who can tell whether God will be gracious to the child that it may live?"

It is laid down by Quetelet, that a tenth of the children born die in the first month after birth, and one quarter before the year is completed. This is a fearful fact to contemplate, and one well calculated to alarm parents. In England, in 1860, there were 684,084 births. The number of children that died under one year old was 56,892, so that there was 1 death out of every 12 births; while in London there were 93,414 births, and 7,901 deaths of children under one, *i. e.* 1 in 11. In the city of London, the mortality is fixed at a higher rate by Dr. Letheby.* "Twenty per cent., or just a fifth, of all the deaths in the year were among infants of less than a twelvemonth old.

---

* Thirteenth Annual Report of Sanitary Condition of London.

In the eastern union, the proportion was much
larger; it amounted to one-fourth of all the deaths.
If these facts are examined from another point
of view, it will be seen that in the eastern and
western divisions of the city about 1 in 5 of all
the children born die before they are a year old;
whereas in the central division of the city the
proportion is only 1 in 7. The first of these
numbers is greatly above the average in the
country, and the second is below it. Again,
nearly forty-one per cent. of all the deaths were
among children of less than five years old, and
as children up to this age constitute about one-
tenth part of the population of the city, it is
manifest that they die at the rate of about ten
per cent. instead of rather less than seven per
cent., which is the average for the whole county.
In fact, in the eastern division of the city, the
proportion is rather more than eleven per cent.,
and in the western nearly 14. It is this large
mortality of children which swells the death-rate."*

Now is this mortality a necessary evil? I
believe not; and it shall be my endeavour to
prove that it arises in great measure from *preventible* causes, and the improper manner in
which children, speaking more especially in reference to food, are brought up. Man, it is true,

* *Times*, April 29, 1862.

is born to sorrow as the sparks fly upward; but many of these sorrows are of his own creation.

To prevent by any means the great infant mortality in these realms is a work well worthy of a philanthropist. The first step is necessarily to obtain statistics upon which we can reasonably argue, and from which we may deduce the vital laws which regulate and control this mortality. Unfortunately, however, although there is an outcry everywhere against *red tape* and *routine*, yet both are still very prevalent among ourselves and our medical institutions. Most of the latter, except a few which stand out in honourable contrast, do not give us the benefit of their experience; and thus it is that, in England, much information which, if regularly published, might lead to a just comprehension of many difficult questions in science and in medicine, is lost to the profession. The subject of this work is in this category. The books and pamphlets that have been written on it are *legion*. De Watteville enumerates a hundred and thirty; yet all this foreign and British experience has, after all, effected but little practical good.

To what cause is this failure due? Chiefly to a very general, if not universal, influence. It is a fault with many authors, first, to take up peculiar theories, and then upon these to work out their facts. The direction of these theories is guided by the fashion of the day, or the popularity of particular schools : and thus, as a great variety exists in these influences in different places and at different times, we seldom have data given in one country in such a form as to admit of comparison with those of another. The facts are good, but worked out in a different way, or in a sectarian manner; and so those great truths, which as belonging to the one family of man, should be applicable to all nations, can only be imperfectly deduced—occasionally only glanced at. In other words, we have, as it were, a host of weights, but we possess no means of reducing them to a common *scale*. True, the Registrar-General's statistics of England are invaluable, but in many points they cannot be compared with those analogous tables which set forth the experience of Europe. Even England, Scotland, and Ireland, in this respect, have no common language.

From sheer necessity, therefore, I have been compelled chiefly to use French returns, although of course wishing to make them bear almost exclusively on England and Ireland. Upon this point, however, I wish to say, and that explicitly, for I have been already misunderstood and misrepresented, that from the very nature of the data used, exactitude in the figures given is not to be expected. At most, I can only bring out

results which shall be *true relatively;* and this I
hope I have done. Stating thus much as a caution—I am bound, however, to add that, in many
cases, my conclusions *may* be also *true absolutely.*
Vital statistics, in the present day, are found to
be governed generally by the same common laws;
and, although the actual figure of per centage
does occasionally vary to a small degree, the difference is not by any means so great as it may
at first appear, even where the populations
of different countries are taken. Hence it is
often allowable to deduce from data which we do
not possess for our own country, conclusions
which, nevertheless, are perfectly true when applied to ourselves. Take, for instance, Paris and
London. The mortality may vary by one or two
per cent., but, nevertheless, it is still governed in
the two cities by the same general laws.

With these few remarks, necessary as an introduction, I proceed at once to the consideration
of my subject.

PART I.

CHAPTER I.

GENERAL DIVISION OF CAUSES OF MORTALITY AND VIABILITY.—
CLASSES OF DISEASE.—GENERAL COMPARISON OF THESE, SHOWING
THE GREAT INFLUENCE OF DISEASES WHICH MAY BE PRODUCED
· BY INJUDICIOUS FOOD AND DEFECTIVE HYGIENE.

In the present inquiry I propose in a first part to consider the causes of mortality and viability of infants. In a second, the subject of wet nursing in its physiological as well as social relations. In a third, the general principles and practice of alimentation, and in a last and concluding part, the symptoms and the treatment, dietetic and hygienic, and medical, of such diseases as are likely to shorten life or impair their wellbeing through defective assimilation.

The causes of mortality among infants may, in in the first place, be considered under three heads: First, the actual mortality which prevails in a general population and taken as a whole among infants and young children. Secondly. The especial conditions which favour the increase of this mortality. Thirdly. Those which favour, on the contrary, the viability of children.

First, then, what is the actual mortality of infant population ?

Under the able direction of Dr. Farre, the Registrar General, a series of tables have been devised in which the causes of death are so tabulated and classified as to admit of their being readily understood. These diseases are—

1st. *Zymotic,* or diseases which are either epidemic, endemic, or contagious, induced by some specific body, or by want, or the bad quality of food.

2nd. *Constitutional* sporadic diseases affecting several organs in which new morbid products are often deposited, sometimes hereditary.

3rd. *Local* sporadic diseases, in which the functions of particular organs or systems are disturbed or obliterated, with or without inflammation, sometimes hereditary.

4th. *Developmental* special diseases, the incidental result of the formative, reproductive, and nutritive processes.

Last. *Violent diseases,* or deaths which are the evident and direct results of physical and chemical forms acting either by the will of the sufferer or of others.

In the table given in the appendix, the figures have been reduced to a common scale of 100, to

make the proportion more clear; first, comparatively, to all deaths where the causes are specified;
and secondly, for each group separately, for all
ages ; ages under one, at one, two, and under
five. In a last column I have deduced the average
of deaths under one to births, by which we shall
be able especially to test the influence of injudicious management of children during the first
year of life. (See appendix A.)

The first general deduction is, that the number
of children in England which die during the first
year after birth amounts to 14·3 per cent. from
all diseases. By far the larger number however,
die from *Local* diseases, their number being represented by 6·2 per cent; but when the exposure
to which children are liable is considered this
might *a priori* be expected. The third class of
diseases, however, to which they are most obnoxious
are the *Developmental* diseases. The mortality
from this class may be stated at 4·2 per cent.,
whereas epidemics and endemic diseases carry
only about 2·5 per cent. If we look, however, to
these classes of disease a little more closely, the
inference is, that a considerable number of these
deaths, which are ranged under these several
classes, may in reality have a very close and
direct relation to the nature of food given, and
hygienic regimen followed, and therefore admit
of consideration in immediate connexion with

the developmental diseases. Take, for instance, the *Zymotic* class. This class comprehends four orders. The *Miasmatic* diseases which include all epidemic diseases properly so called. There are, however, mentioned among these, two diseases, which are certainly often induced by bad food and defective hygiene,—dysentery and diarrhœa, in which the digestive organs are chiefly at fault. The next order is the *Enthetic*, which includes syphilitic diseases and their sequelæ. Hydrophobia and glanders may be passed over as having no direct relation to food or hygiene. In the third order, the *Dietic*, however, two diseases have certainly a more intimate connexion, viz., *privation* and *want of breast-milk;* and in the fourth, the *Parasitic*, both *thrush* and *worms*, the former often as a sequela of diseases of digestion; the latter, as the result of injudicious food, have a close affinity to, and are often in fact abdominal diseases.

Among the *Constitutional* diseases in the second order, one of the diseases mentioned is *Tabes Mesenterica*, or consumption of the bowels, and doubtless many deaths generally included under the term *tubercular* have a very close correlation to injudicious food and bad hygiene, and could thus be referred to diseases in the abdominal organs. There are to be found in our profession those who, from experience and pathological research as well as from experiments on animals, would conclude that scrofula, consumption and water on the brain have mainly origin in defective digestion and hygiene.

Among the *Local diseases* there are also some to be referred to similar causes, and many cases of convulsion have their origin in abdominal derangement or disease. All diseases of the organs of digestion belong to the same category; and many cases of skin disease.

The fourth, or *Developmental diseases* of children, have mostly a similar origin. Atrophy and debility have scarcely any other, except when depending on syphilitic taint. The totality of these diseases, exclusive of the fourth class, would raise the cypher of mortality, causes dependent on defective hygiene and injudicious food, to 10·1 per cent.

It is not wished, however, to refer this large proportion, 10·1 per cent., to disease or disorder in the digestive organs. Somewhere about one half would probably be nearer the truth, and inclusive of the developmental diseases, might be estimated at 9·3 per cent. Thus, without insisting upon the exact correctness of the figure obtained, it must be admitted we have good grounds for concluding that defective nutrition and hygiene have a most fatal effect upon children under one. The table in the appendix, however, enables us to come to the same conclusion in another way; that is, by comparing the number of deaths at all ages with those of children under five years old. Ten per cent. of the deaths under one are due to *local* diseases; 4·1 to zymotic; 4·7 to developmental. But if we include, besides, the same diseases before referred to when making the comparison to births, we have 8·5 per cent. more deaths to include. Halving this number as before and for the same reasons, we should have a total of deaths of 8·9 per cent. due to defective nutrition or hygiene.

If we pass on now to disease among children as it occurs in hospitals, the same general conclusion is confirmed.

"If there be one fact more clearly made out by hospital experience than another, it is that of the frequency of *abdominal* disease in children; and whether viewed in their immediate or remote effects, they are by far the most numerous class which we are called upon to treat. Taking the three years of the Clinical Hospital of Manchester, we find they constitute 23·4 per cent. of the number of all diseases; or, if we include those diseases which result from defective nutrition also, they constitute 30·6 per cent. of the whole.

In speaking of the principal causes of mortality among children, Messrs. Muir and Whitehead instance that, "out of 117 deaths, 96, or 82 per cent., occurred in children under two years;

and 93, or 79 per cent., in children affected with diseases arising from *defective or faulty nutrition,* which were partly the direct and partly the co-operative cause of the fatal issue."*

---

* Second Report of Clinical Hospital for Children of Manchester (p. 29).

CHAPTER II.

CONDITIONS WHICH FAVOUR MORTALITY.—FIRST, NATURE OF FOOD PARTICULARLY—WANT OF BREAST-MILK—RESULTS OBTAINED IN LONDON—FOUNDLING AND PARISIAN HOSPITALS—LATE DIMINUTION OF MORTALITY IN FRANCE—EVIDENCE FROM FACTS AND FIGURES THAT OTHER CAUSES ARE IN OPERATION—CALCULATION ON REGISTRAR GENERAL'S RETURN FOR ENGLAND AND LONDON.

THE conditions which favour mortality may be considered under three heads.

1. Those which depend upon the nature of food supplied. 2. Those which depend upon defective hygienic regimen. 3. Those which depend upon the physical and physiological nature of infants.

Among the causes of mortality from the nature of food supplied, a very important one is,

1. *Want of breast-milk.*

It is generally believed that the highest mortality among infants, is that which occurs in foundling hospitals, and this chiefly because the children in these institutions are *brought up by hand* and *without breast-milk.* It may be well, therefore, to consider the experience of foundling institutions on this point, as a preliminary argument to judge how far facts accord with the popular opinion.

Nearly all writers who have endeavoured to explain the mortality of foundlings, have chiefly attributed it to the want of breast-milk.

Years ago, Sir Hans Sloane, in a letter to the Vice-President of the Foundling Hospital, apparently established this fact by showing that the mortality of those suckled compared to those dry nursed was as 19·2 to 53·9 per cent.*

Later writers almost invariably point to the hospitals of Paris, Lyons, Rheims, a place called X, and Parthenay, as examples of the pernicious influences produced by a want of breast-milk. Thus, in Lyons and Parthenay, where the children are suckled at the breast, the mortality is respectively 33·7 and 35; whereas, in Paris, Rheims, and X, where artificial feeding is either extensively or very generally employed, the mortality is respectively 50·3, 63·9, and 80 per cent.

Again, to these more particular results, it is

---

* Quoted at length in Mr. Brownlow's *Memoranda* of that Hospital, pp. 215-16.

Date of Admission	Total.	To wet nurses.	Deaths.	To dry nurses.	Deaths.
March 5, 1741	30	2	—	28	15
April 17, 1741	30	7	1	22	11
May 8, 1741	30	17	4	13	8
	90	26	5 or 19·2 per cent.	63	34 or 58·9 pr. ct.

usual, as a general confirmation to the whole, to add the figures of mortality observed in other European institutions, which are given in the appendix, in which the mortality varies from 40 to 91 per cent.*

A more recent and succinct account by M. de Watteville, who has very ably treated the whole subject, includes all France, and gives the following results, viz.

" In comparing the deaths of *enfants trouvés*, whether with the totality of their number or that of the *expositions*, this is the result obtained. One dies out of seven, from one day to twelve years, or about 14 per cent. ; and the mortality of such children in the first year of their existence is 50 per cent."

There is but one foundling exposed in every 39 births in France, while the number of foundlings in institutions is one to every 353 inhabitants. Again, the number of foundlings *exposed* is one-fourth the entire number of foundlings actually existing in institutions, whence it would follow that the mean duration of life of foundlings is four years. Fortunately, of late years this mortality has been diminishing, and is now, instead of 14·02, as low as 11·30 per cent. These results, however, although evidence that

---

* See Appendix B.

the mortality is lessening, are nevertheless still too high.*

It is not surprising, therefore, that upon statements like these, the conclusion that want of breast-milk is the principal cause of the excessive mortality, should have been so generally adopted. It is manifest, however, on closer examination, that, although these figures may represent the mortality of foundlings, their difference is too great to be referrible to one cause only, and that cause want of breast-milk; for, however hurtful or destructive to life this want may be, it will appear in the sequel that there are many other influences co-operating far more pernicious and fatal.

The institutions referred to are placed in every variety of circumstances, as to climate, cleanliness, food, number of inmates, attendants, size of hospital, etc.; so that although dry nursing may be very prejudicial, other equally prolific sources of mortality must exist, and therefore even upon these grounds to attribute all the fatal results to want of breast-milk, is simply illogical. But this becomes more obvious, when we look more particularly to the details of management in the three hospitals before alluded to.

---

* Thus, for all France, it was for children from 1 to 12 years old,

Year.	Per cent.	Year.	Per cent.	Year.	Per cent.
1838	... 14·02	1841	... 13·30	1844	... 11·33
1839	... 13·37	1842	... 12·60	1845	... 11·30
1840	... 13·25	1843	... 11·35		

Let us note M. Villermé's description.*

"Lyons is apparently, of the great cities in France, that in which most care is paid to foundlings. I have been witness to this in 1825; and I can certify that nowhere else have I seen so much attention, and so wise a care exercised, as in this hospital. So soon as the infant is deposited in the *tour*, it is taken out, warmed, cleaned, its linen changed; and it is given to a nurse, who always *suckles* the child; or it is sent to a wet nurse by a messenger. By whomsoever, however, the child is taken from the institution (and it is generally by the hospital nurse herself), it is never allowed to pass more than two or three days without suckling at the breast. It is necessary that this hospital nurse herself should see the child put into its bassinette at the moment of departure, all precautions being taken to avoid its being chilled in any way. The child's body is almost entirely surrounded by cotton, and hot clothes, always adapted to the season. Finally, the bassinette itself, in which the child is taken away, is surrounded by coverings; and at certain distances, whether the nurse or a messenger carries it, she must stop at some house which has been selected beforehand to accommodate and

* Villermé "On the Mortality of Foundlings"(*Annales d'Hygiène*, vol. xix, p. 47), the same as given in abstract by Dr. West, in his *Diseases of Children.*

change the infant. It was not, however, before 1824, or more particularly 1831, that the hospital administration had so far perfected this department.

" The foundlings of Rheims are fed by the bottle and *petit pot* (and never at the breast) by women from the country, who take them away at the end of twenty-four hours or seven days after their deposition in the hospital. Up to the hour of their departure they are very well taken care of, under the direction of the head midwife.

" The children of the Paris Foundling Hospital are kept longer than those of Lyons and Rheims in the house where they are received, and their nurses (a large number of whom live at great distances) bring them up generally at the breast."

The arrangements, both in Paris and Rheims, appear, from the above account, to be very defective. To keep children, as in Paris, a long time in hospitals, is necessarily to make the children more obnoxious to contagious diseases. Two of these, which produced the highest mortality in the Parisian hospitals, the *endurcissement cellulaire*, and the muguet or diphtherite, were particularly contagious; and unfortunately this contagion would apply equally to all infectious diseases, such as small-pox, scarlet fever, hooping-cough, etc. It is a bad feature, also, to have

20 CAUSES OF

nurses living at a great distance ; and in the difficulty of procuring *wet* nurses, it is to be feared
bad selections are made, perhaps of diseased
females, whose antecedents are not known. At
Rheims, the management is even worse. To
keep many of these infants as long as seven days
on unsuitable diet, and then to send them far up
the country, where they may not be carefully
looked after (since over these nurses there is no
supervision exercised), must be very imprudent.
In Lyons, however, the arrangements made appear to be praiseworthy : but even here exposure
before reception in the hospital is not prevented.

There is another way in which the truth of
this conclusion may be tested, and that is by
figures. I adopted this expedient, and endeavoured to trace out whether there was any one
or more features in the mortality observed in
these three institutions, or even in the same institutions in different years, which might lead us
to suspect, if not actually to establish, the common *cause* in operation. In the hope of deducing
this law, and for the purpose of *comparison*, I
reduced the mortality of these three institutions
to a scale of 1000, and then proceeded to find
out the influence at work in the production of
the several deaths.

This table I do not here reproduce, because
my expectation in this respect has been belied,

and it is elsewhere published in full; suffice it to say that the causes of this mortality are too numerous, and vary so much in different institutions, and even in the same institution at different times, that they require separate consideration. Some of these are doubtless *endemic* to particular institutions; some are *epidemic;* others depend upon the particular class of children sent to the hospitals; or the state of health of their parents, etc.; others are often so peculiar and generally misapprehended, as to necessitate separate study. Writers have already specified many of these causes. A few of them have, however, been overlooked; and thus, although in some respects I may be guilty of compilation, I hope also to bring out some original points, and to make the whole practically useful.

The fact is that want of breast-milk is only one of several causes—a powerful one, no doubt; but still it must be obvious from what has preceded that its injurious effects are much exaggerated.

Every step we take in advance in this inquiry draws us to the same conclusion. Take, for instance, the actual number of deaths attributable to want of breast-milk, as occurring in a general population, and irrespective of foundling institutions altogether. In the year 1860, there were in all England 684,048 births, and 1,002 children registered as having died from want of breast-milk, or 1·4 per 1000. It may be argued, however, and with justice, that this number in no way represents the proportion of deaths due to this cause, particularly as in the Registrar-General's quarterly reports, we are referred to cold, privation; and no doubt under these heads many cases are included which, properly speaking, should be returned under that of death from want of breast-milk. Perhaps, we should include some others, as, for instance, diarrhœa : though I make no doubt, when diarrhœa was present in most of these cases as a symptom, death has been referred to the first cause, want of breast-milk. This is, however, only a supposition; and hence, as it is impossible to measure the amount due to diarrhœa, I am obliged to neglect it. I have, however, to make amends, *included* all deaths from *premature birth and debility* under one year old, which is a large number, but which must needs comprise many who are not thriving under the poor breast-milk given, or the improper food substituted.

Again, as the accounts for London are in these minutiæ more correct from the facility of obtaining information, a more accurate result may be probably got at than from data collected in the provinces. In large towns, also, the cases of death from this cause would be more likely to prevail, than in agricultural districts. Taking, then, for London, the six years, 1849 to 1854 inclusive (see table below*), it follows that out of 473,865 births in six years, 15,241, or 3·2 per cent., died from want of breast-milk in its widest sense; or, out of 73,227 deaths from all causes, occurring to children under one year old, 20·8 per cent. might be referred to deprivation of this kind of diet.*

The great majority of deaths are, therefore, evidently due to other causes.

Mortality of Infants from various causes.

	1849.	1850.	1851.	1852.	1853.	1854.	Total.
From all causes under one year old	12208	10349	11631	12272	12981	13896	73227
Privation	5	2	—	2	1	1	11
Cold	3	1	3	3	4	2	16
Want of breast-milk	174	178	229	240	255	337	1413
Neglect	8	4	—	—	9	3	24
Premature birth and debility under one year old	1232	1241	1470	1537	1475	1518	8473
Atrophy, ditto	874	757	784	827	971	1091	5304
Total	2296	2183	2481	2609	2715	2952	15241
All births	72612	74564	78300	81250	82254	84885	473865

CHAPTER III.

MORTALITY DEPENDENT ON NATURE OF FOOD, CONTINUED.—HAND-
FEEDING AS PRACTISED BY THE MASS OF POPULATION.—CONCLU-
SIONS IN FAVOUR OF BREAST MILK FROM DRS. MEREI AND
WHITEHEAD'S TABLES—FROM BRIGHT'S CASES.—BREAST MILK
FROM A MOTHER GENERALLY AGREES BETTER THAN FROM A
STRANGER—CHATEAUNEUF'S EXPERIENCE—FOUNDLING HOSPITAL.
—PRIVATE CASES.—A MOTHER'S BREAST MILK, HOWEVER, OCCA-
SIONALLY DISAGREES.

It cannot be denied, however, in the second
place, that hand-fed children are much more
likely not only to be weakly and imperfectly developed, but also that the chance of life is much
smaller for them than for children who are suckled
by a healthy mother.

But here we must remark, the argument applies only generally, and has reference more
especially to infants taken as a whole in an entire
population, and who are brought up by hand
upon the most unwise popular principles, indeed,
in many cases upon no principle at all. It cannot apply to cases where judicious food is given
and proper care taken of the children.

In my introduction I had to allude to the little
public good usually derived from hospital experi-

ence to the profession. I have now to direct attention to one of the honourable exceptions, viz., the first, second, and third Reports of the Clinical Hospital for the Diseases of Children, in Stevenson Square, Manchester, prepared by Drs. Merei and Whitehead. These are most able and philosophical documents, no fact being asserted which is not substantiated by accurate statistical researches—such documents as might be yearly produced by every hospital, and confer endless good upon thousands. I shall first, in a short summary, quote a few of these results which bear upon this portion of my subject.

1. The direct and baneful agency of want of good breast-milk may be inferred from the table given below,* from which it appears that the

---

* Results observed in 1,041 Children.

First and second years. Per cent.

1. Children having had breast-milk alone to ninth month or longer, some to fifteenth, eighteenth, or twenty-fourth months.	94 Well developed .	or 62·6
	35 Medium ,,	or 23·3
	21 Badly ,,	or 14
Total... 150		
2. Those who had breast-milk up to sixth, eighth, and ninth months; after which they were partially weaned; about 20 per cent. of them partially receiving for some months longer other food beside the breast.	65 Well developed .	or 57·4
	29 Medium ,,	or 25·6
	18 Badly ,,	or 15·9
Total... 113		
3. Those having breast-milk moderately abundant and bread-food along with it from birth or early ages.	110 Well developed .	or 51
	54 Medium ,,	or 25
	52 Badly ,,	or 24
Total... 216		

larger the supply of breast-milk and the more exclusively it is given, the better is a child developed, and *vice versâ*. Thus, taking the extreme points of the table, we have in the former case 62·6 per cent. well developed, and only 14 badly developed; in the latter case, 10 per cent. well developed, and 64 badly developed.

Again, it is further stated, that among the cases noted during the first Report, there were 34 children who were *marked as having an eminently good development and a strong habit of body*—of these 32 had breast-milk exclusively, and it was generally continued to an advanced period. Thus 4 had it to 18 months and upwards to two years; 7 had it up to the 15th or the 17th month; 7 up to

		Per cent.
4. Children who from birth or the age of two or three months, besides an abundance of breast-milk (as stated by mothers), had received additional food, generally boiled bread and milk, or merely with water, sugar, and arrowroot.	Well deve- 55 loped „ 29 Medium „ 21 Badly „	or 52 or 28·6 or 20
Total... 105		
5. Children who have had from the earliest infancy a moderate or small supply of breast-milk; some for a few months only, others up to nine, twelve, fifteen, or eighteen months, or longer, with other food from birth.	Well deve- 100 loped . 107 Medium „ 191 Badly „	or 26·8 or 26·3 or 45·9
Total... 407		
6. Children fed entirely by hand, and with no breast-milk at all.	Well deve- 5 loped . 13 Medium „ 32 Badly „	or 10 or 26 or 64
Total... 50		

the 12th or the 13th; 7 up to the 9th or the
11th; 3 up to the 6th or 8th; 4 up to the 4th or
the 5th month; of the remaining 2 one had an
abundance of breast-milk from birth, together
with bread and milk; the other insufficient breast-
milk with bread and milk food.

Among those noted in the second Report as
being of very good development—*i. e.* those most
rapidly advanced in dentition, ossification of the
skull, and facility of walking (most of these having
commenced to walk before 12, many at 10 and
11 months)—there were 59, of whom 43 had
breast-milk alone to 9 months and upwards, to
12, 15, 18 months, a few of them even longer;
8 had breast-milk alone to between 6 and 9
months; 8 only received, besides the breast,
other kinds of food before the 6th month. It
may be added, that the respective 59 mothers
were at most not only healthy, but of strong con-
stitutions, and had great abundance of milk.

Out of the 1,548 children affected with various
diseases mentioned in the second Report and
treated in the Clinical Hospital, there were—

					Per cent.
Well developed	·	·	·	585 ...	37·1
Medium ·	·	·	·	462 ...	29·1
Badly ·	·	·	·	451 ...	29·1
Not noted	·	·	·	50 ...	3·2

Of these, 27 per cent. had a full supply of breast-
milk, or at least for upwards of 6 months; 29 per
cent. had a medium supply, with bread or other

food; 38 per cent. had scanty breast-milk and some farinaceous food from birth or earliest infancy; 3 of them had no breast-milk at all from birth or earliest infancy.

2. The valuable notice of deaths occurring at Brighton, given in Appendix C, was kindly forwarded to me by a lady correspondent, and one deeply interested in all efforts made for Improving the Sanitary Condition among the Lower Classes. It can be fully relied upon, and emphatically illustrates the same fact, although brought out from a different point of view.

These 50 cases may be thus classified :—

Convulsions (in 7 Coroner's inquests, verdicts " overfeeding:" several not investigated) · ·	22
Diarrhœa, and other disorders of stomach and bowels	12
Total cases traceable to overfeeding and injudicious feeding · · · · ·	34
Or per cent. · · · · ·	68

The other cases (16 in number) were affected with hereditary, structural, developmental, and epidemic diseases : most probably in these cases death was wholly independent of *diet*. At least, it is remarkable that in those last named 16 cases, the children were in general either fed from the mother's breast entirely, or if brought up by hand, were fed with more judgment than is commonly observed.

The cases of convulsions (Nos. 12 and 15) could not be traced to any cause. They were not hand-fed at all; and probably the attack in each might have been induced by some irregularity in the health or diet of the mothers.

Fed on bread-food without the bottle; some having the breast in addition to bread-food; some having other food, as sago, arrowroot, etc.; dying of convulsions or of diarrhœa   -   •   - 24
Fed entirely from mother's breast   •   - 11
Fed from the bottle -   •   •   - 1
Fed entirely on cow's milk and water   •   - 2

The mortality of those artificially fed is very much greater than that of those fed at the breast, but from the preceding table it is obvious more is due to the injudicious method of feeding the child than to mere absence of breast-milk. Thus both classes of cases prove that breast-feeding is the most encouraging where it can be successfully carried out.

Another circumstance, having direct relation to the food given, and which may tend to explain the fatality is, that—

3. *The mere substitution of a hired wet nurse increases the mortality;* for it should be borne in mind that the chances of life, precarious as they always are in a young infant, are rendered still more so by transferring a child to a wet nurse other than its mother. From a reference to the *Annuaries* of Mortality in Paris, Quêtelet obtained nearly everywhere the same result,—that, in the first three months after birth, twice or three times as many children die as in the other months of the

D

first year. Other authors, he says, have made the same observations; and from their inquiries they have thought to find the cause of this disproportion in the mortality in the habit which mothers have either of suckling their own children or of abandoning them to hired wet nurses. Here is what M. Benoiston de Chateauneuf, in his excellent work on the *Enfans Trouvés*, says on this subject:— "It is true that, to preserve the life of a child, care does everything, and climate nothing, or very little; and Switzerland and Holland are the countries where the smallest number die. Is the explanation of this fact, already offered by Muret, to be found in the habit which all the mothers, at the foot of the Alps as on the borders of the Amstel, have of suckling their children themselves? We cannot say; but we shall only add, that, having been curious to compare the mortality of children at nurse with that of children brought up in Paris, we obtained the following results. Of 100 children suckled by their mothers, 18 die in the first year; of the same number at nurse, 29 die."*

The following facts, for which I am indebted to the kindness of Mr. Brownlow, the efficient Secretary to the Foundling Hospital, direct to a conclusion similar to that arrived at by Benoiston

---

* *Recherches sur la Population, Décès, etc., du Royaume de Pays Bas.* Par A. Quêtelet, f. 18, p. 142-3.

de Chateauneuf. From some parish registers given in the Report of the Special Committee to the Governors of the Foundling Hospital, it appears, also, that the mortality is much greater among those children nursed by strange women, than amongst those nursed by their mothers.*

This table gives a gross mortality of 14·2 per cent. upon admissions ; or, out of 100 deaths, 51·2 will occur among those nursed by their own mothers, while 68·8 will occur among those nursed· by the workhouse nurses. These numbers have, of course, no absolute value, as it is not stated how many children were nursed by their mothers, and how many by workhouse nurses. Still as, out of this number, only 887 were foundlings, and as many as 7,109 were removed to the Foundling

---

* Thus, between the years 1762 and 1770, the annual mortality was as follows from children of and under four years old :—

Admitted :—

Foundlings	-	-	-	877
Illegitimate	-	-	-	5,283
Casual	-	-	-	1,821
Legitimate	-	-	-	19,562

Total · - 27,543

Died :—

Nursed by their mothers	-	-	1,229
Nursed by workhouse nurses	-	-	2,698

Total · - 3,927

Removed :—

To the Foundling Hospital	-	-	525
To their mothers	-	-	3,623
To friends	-	-	2,961

Total · - 7,109

Hospital, mothers, or friends, we may presume this number only were not nursed by their own mothers at the workhouse. Deducting, also, those children who, as sent to the Foundling Hospital, were probably among the number previously included in Foundling Hospitals, we shall have 7,641 children who were probably nursed by the workhouse nurses, giving a mortality of 36·1 per cent. for such children, to 6·1 per cent. for those nursed by their mothers. These numbers are doubtless exaggerated, from the nature of the data, but I think the reasoning adopted will justify our concluding, that the risk of substituting a wet nurse for a mother is great, and that it will certainly increase the probabilities of the suckling's death.

Another fact confirmatory of this view was communicated to me by Dr. Henry Wright, who had it from a lady correspondent. It applies to six twins, *i. e.* twelve children. Six were fed by their mothers, and all did well. Six were entrusted to hired wet nurses; three died; and of the remaining three, two at twelve months were looking puny and delicate, as if they could not live long; the sixth was quite healthy.

From these facts we cannot otherwise than conclude, that bringing up a child on its mother's breast-milk is, without doubt, far safer than entrusting it to another wet nurse. The worst that can be done under ordinary circumstances for a child, is to bring it up exclusively by hand; *at least, in the way in which it is usually done.*

Let me, however, here give a caution. While the rule is very general that pure unadulterated breast-milk from its own mother is the best food that can be supplied to an infant, it is equally true that, in a certain number of exceptional cases, breast-milk does not agree with a child. Thus, from Drs. Merei and Whitehead's tables we find that 14 per cent. of the children did not thrive upon breast-milk, and in 23·3 the development was only medium; while on the other hand, 10 per cent. of those brought up by hand throve very well. Without relation, therefore, to the intermediate classes enumerated in the table, we have at least 24 per cent. who did not thrive upon breast-milk. It is an incontrovertible fact, that some mothers do not possess a milk calculated to benefit their offspring, but to this class I shall again allude.

CHAPTER IV.

MORTALITY IN CONNEXION WITH DEFECTIVE HYGIENE.—INFLU-
ENCE OF HOSPITAL ATMOSPHERE AND CLOSE HABITATIONS.—
REMARKABLE EXCEPTION OF IRELAND.—GREATER MORTALITY IN
TOWNS FOR INFANTS—ENGLAND—IRELAND.—FRENCH FOUND-
LINGS.—FEARFUL EFFECTS OF EXPOSURE.—FRANCE AND ENG-
LAND.—INFLUENCE OF REMOVAL—OF ABUSE OF RECUMBENT
POSITION.—VIOLENT DEATHS AMONG INFANTS.

IF the injudicious feeding of a child is often a cause
of death, so the hygienic conditions in which a
child is placed will materially influence its chance
of life. For instance, infant foundlings are placed
often in very impure air, which, I make no doubt,
greatly interferes with nutrition and healthy development; and has a great deal to do with their
great mortality. As before remarked, the truth
is recognised by all, that hospital aggregation
must necessarily make the children more obnoxious to contagious diseases. Generally speaking,
all the contagious diseases of the zymotic class
before referred to would prove fatal even in a
general population, although to a minor degree,
because the contagious poison is more diluted.
But apart from this source of common mortality,
which should apply equally in both cases, I think

it will be admitted by all those who have had much to do with infant children, that the hospital atmosphere engendered by children congregated together is pecularily offensive and injurious. Even the cleanest children have a peculiar faint soapy odour : when this comes to be mixed with that arising from urinous towels drying by the fire, and from foul motions, it is very abominable ; while the delicacy of infants, and the easy way in which they catch cold, render a certain degree of closeness of the atmosphere imperative ; and certainly, wherever it is possible, it is always kept up. And herein, I think, lies a fertile source of fatality in bringing up infants in hospitals or Foundling Institutions, where of necessity they must be congregated together, except only under a very efficient system of ventilation, which, unfortunately, nurses are very loth to adopt.

Even during the first month of life there is reason to believe that the confinement of a lying-in hospital, so necessary for the mother, increases the mortality of an infant, by at least four per cent.

There is an excellent table for Ireland, setting forth the mortality in *public institutions* for all ages, and from one to twelve months in particular. From this the exact rate of mortality due to hospital confinement might be deduced, if we had a corresponding table of population in public insti-

tutions for the same years; but this last is not
given; so that the table cannot be made available
for calculation. The only tables which bear at all
upon this point apply to the first month, and are
those obtained from lying-in institutions, or from
the statistics collected by accoucheurs of large
hospitals, under whose care the infants, with their
mothers, have remained for the month in hospital.
These tables afford us the means of deducing the
probable mortality in public institutions for one
month. In the summary for all Ireland for ten
years, from 1831 to 1841, for the Irish lying-in
hospitals, this mortality is brought out at 6·1 per
cent. (See table below.)*

Again, from the tables published by different
accoucheurs, we may deduce almost the same per
centage cypher of mortality. (*Vide* table below.)†

In the English table for 1842, where we have
the mortality for early months, compared to births,
the mortality for England is only 4·7 per cent.,
and even for separate counties, except in the case
of the East and West Riding of Yorkshire, it

---

* Total births · · · 35,131
  Total deaths · · · 2,258
  Mortality per cent. · · 6·1

	No. births.	No. deaths.	Per cent.
† Madame Lachapelle	22,243	837	3·7
Dr. Ramsbotham	49,528	2723	5·6
Drs. Hardy and McClintock	6,702	467	6·9
Dr. Arneth (Vienna)	6,608	244	3·7
	85,091	5,311	6·1

does not reach the figure of 6. (See table. Appendix D.)

Yet there appears to be a contradiction to this statement in the case of Ireland. In that country it is notorious that, in many places, the habitations seem to be constructed with the most perfect disregard to all principles of hygiene, and yet the mortality is not generally increased by it.

The writer of the article in the *Quarterly Review*, on Ireland Past and Present, No. 203, p. 78, thus describes the homes of its inhabitants :—

" Any one who has travelled through Ireland, until within the last few years, must have been struck with the miserable condition of the dwellings of the poorer peasantry. They were built of mud; the roof was sunken, and seldom whole. The thatch was black and rotten ; water had saturated it, and grass and weeds grew rank upon it. The window was generally a hole stuffed with hay and rags; and, where glass had been formerly put, there remained scarcely an unbroken pane. The chief access for light or air was the door, which was always open. Close to the door, and generally in front of it, was a fœtid pool, in which foul straw, potato-stalks, dung, and all kinds of abominations, were fermenting and macerating; while *half-naked* and squalid children enjoyed themselves around it. Inside there was as much dirt and discomfort as without; the floor was broken and uneven; the walls were dark from smoke; there was but one room common to the family, their poultry, and their pig. Something like a bed, in which all sexes and ages slept, an iron pot, an old tub, a stool or two, a rude table, and a dresser, with some broken plates, constituted the furniture and all the family possessions."

Here there were contingencies highly favourable to the generation of an atmosphere which, even in rural districts, would be likely to prove peculiarly fatal to infants, and which certainly could not be better than hospital air, and yet the reverse is the case. The mortality of Ireland, as before seen, is calculated upon returns of *population* not of *births*, as there are as yet no returns of births published for Ireland.* The use of this table led me into an error. To obviate this circumstance, and to have the means of making the comparison between England and Ireland more

---

* If we assume that the population for the several ages, *i. e.*, one month, two months, three months, etc., is arranged in the same proportions both in England and Ireland, then, as we know the population for both countries under one year old, it is easy to find by calculation what is the population for the several early periods, one month, two months, three months, etc., before mentioned. By comparison, then, of these numbers with the actual mortality, which we know from the Registrar General's Tables, we can deduce the mortality as compared to the population, and so obtain a figure which we can compare with that from the Irish returns. This has been done: and in this manner we obtain for all England, in 1841, a mortality of 37·9 per cent. for children under one month, while that of all Ireland, for the same class, is only 27·3. So also for the age under one, it is for all England, in 1841, 17·3 per cent., against 12 for Ireland.

easy, the table has been reduced by an approximative calculation to one not unlike the English tables. Let me remark, however, that at most, it can only be approximative.

In the Irish returns, the Census Tables invariably distinguish between rural and civic districts; advantage has, therefore, been taken of this distinction to deduce the relative mortality in both districts.

There is, however, no extant table of the population of Ireland for 1850, so that, *per force* the returns have been calculated on the deaths of 1850 with the population of 1851. This introduces a slight error, still one scarcely of much importance for practical deductions; because such returns will be found, as a rule, only to diminish slightly the cypher of mortality ; since, from emigration and physicial deterioration, the population in the sister island has been steadily on the decrease.

The returns of 1842 for England, compared with those of Ireland for 1851, thus shew that upon the whole, even in well-clothed and well-housed England, the mortality of children is greater than in Ireland. The explanation to this apparent contradiction is, probably, that hazarded by a reviewer of the first edition of this work, that the badness of the atmosphere is, for young children, less fatal only than want of due maternal care or breast-milk, exposure, and other causes. The present

state of the distressed manufacturing districts is
confirmatory on this point. The deaths in Lanca-
shire and Cheshire, even during this season of
scarcity, have been less numerous than when the
workmen were in full employ. No doubt the moderate temperature and absence of epidemics, will
account for some of this low mortality; but maternal care, breast milk, and absence of drugging,
contributed a larger share. This brings me, in the
second place, to consider the mortality of infants
in town as compared with country districts.

The general truth of the diminished mortality
for all ages in the country is shown below; the
mean mortality being 2·462 for towns, against
2·011 for country.* The same result is brought
out by Quêtelet, for the Netherlands. The deaths
being 1 in 36·9 inhabitants for towns, against 1
in 36 for country districts.

The Irish returns enable us very accurately to
determine this point, owing to the division be-

---

* Mortality in town or country according to seasons. England,
1850-60 :—

	Quarters.				
	Winter.	Spring.	Summer.	Autumn.	Mean.
In 125 districts and 32 sub-districts, compri-sing the chief towns	2·635	2·346	2·375	2·494	2·462
In the remaining dis-tricts and sub-dis-tricts of England and Wales, comprising chiefly small towns and country parishes	2·233	2·028	1·759	1·920	2·011

tween rural and civic districts being given. The mean mortality being for children under one, about 8 per cent., and for children under five, about 4 per cent., in favour of rural districts. (See table below.)*

We do not find, however, among the English tables, returns of *infant* mortality in town as compared to country places.

One reason, doubtless, is this : in the English returns, where a distinction of ages is made, even when a town or civic district is spoken of, the population always includes a small number of families engaged in agricultural pursuits. Again, when rural districts are spoken of, reference is made to an entire county ; the returns thus necessarily include many families engaged in manufacturing pursuits, and town residents. So far there is an error, which should not be overlooked;

* Percentage of Deaths to Population of each age in Ireland.

Date.				Under 1 year.		Under 5 years.
1850-1	...	All Ireland.	Civic Districts	15·4	......	8·4
,,	...	,,	Rural ,,	8·4	....	4·2
,,	...	Ulster.	Civic ,,	12·3	....	6·9
,,	...	,,	Rural ,,	6·9	....	2·6
,,	...	Connaught.	Civic ,,	15·4	......	7·7
,,	...	,,	Rural ,,	8·6	......	5·0
,,	...	Leinster.	Civic ,,	15·6	......	9·3
,,	...	,,	Rural ,,	9·01	......	4·3
,,	...	Munster.	Civic ,,	15·1	......	8·4
,,	...	,,	Rural ,,	11·0	......	5·6
1850		All Ireland.		6·0	......	
		Mean.	Civic ,,	14·7	......	8·1
		,,	Rural ,,	8·3	......	4·3

and no calculation made can be otherwise than approximative. It has, however, been so made ; and
as far as it goes it justifies the same conclusion as
that deduced from the Irish tables. Taking five
particularly rural districts (see table below)* the
mean mortality to births is 12·1 per cent.; and
selecting five large towns for comparison, the
mean mortality is 15·2, thus making the mortality
3·1 per cent. greater in towns. This result is,
however,· to be received with some restrictions.
If some of our largest manufacturing districts
were taken, the mean mortality would be much
greater, 18 per cent. at least, while in some towns
it is as low as 9 per cent., and in some counties
as high as 14 per cent. The general average is
all we can rely upon.

It would have been satisfactory to have deduced
the same general conclusions for foundlings bred
in town as compared to those bred in the country.
Unfortunately, however, after long inquiry, I do
not find this distinction made in any work on
foundlings which I have seen ; nevertheless, I

---

* Mortality to 100 births of children under 1.

Rural Districts.			Town Districts.		
Extra Metrop.,	Surrey	12·1	Dover	- -	14·1
Ditto	Kent	12·5	Canterbury -	-	14·
Rutlandshire	- -	11·1	Peterborough	-	16·3
Devonshire	-	12·	Exeter	- -	15·3
Essex -	- -	12·8	Bristol	- -	16·2
	Mean -	12·1		Mean -	15·2

have attempted to deduce it from some figures given in the general statistics of foundlings in France, published by authority of the Government. But here, as in the former case, the data being insufficient, I am unable to obtain more than an approximative result. The relative mortality, however, between town hospital foundlings and those placed in the country thus comes out more strikingly than we might have supposed. Thus, in five years,

Out of 52,883 town hospital foundlings, the mortality was 72·2 per cent.
Out of 122,110 country ditto, the mortality was 11·5 per cent.

This conclusion proves that town residence for children is not so salubrious as country residence, and as a corollary, that foundling hospitals, if established at all, should always be placed in the country.

The effect of exposure and removal are fertile causes of mortality among children, and their influence is well brought out in connexion with foundling hospitals. The returns from these afford ample means of measuring the mortality from this source.

Effect of Exposure.—On comparing the French returns before referred to, the percentage mortality of exposed children, as compared to that of the ordinary foundlings, was 13·4 to 72·4 for exposed children, and only 3·6 to 26·5 for found-lings.*

Upon this point, as explanatory of the great mortality in the building, Mr. Brownlow speaks admirably in his very interesting work *(Memoranda of the Foundling Hospital)*. He says: "This practice of transporting children from remote towns was condemned by a distinct resolution of the House of Commons, and a Bill was ordered to be brought in to prevent it; but this Bill was never presented; so that parish officers and others still continued to carry on their illicit trade, by delivering children to vagrants, who, for a small sum of money, undertook the task of conveying them to the hospital, although they were in no condition to take care of them, whereby numbers perished for want, or were otherwise destroyed; and even in cases where children were left at the hospital, the barbarous wretches who had the conveyance of them, not content with the gratuity

---

* Exposed Children.

In the Departments			Highest.		Lowest.
Where it was highest	-	-	83·3	to	60
Where it was lowest	-	-	19·2	,,	0
Mean	-		72·4	to	13·4

Foundlings.

Where it was highest	-	-	50·	to	20
Where it was lowest	-	-	5·	,,	0
Mean	-		26·5	to	3·6

(See this table in full at p. 3.)

they received, stripped the poor infants of their clothing into the bargain, leaving them naked in the basket at the hospital." (P. 173.) Indeed, Mr. Wrottesley, in his report to the House of Commons, states, what is almost too horrible to believe, "that parents brought their children in a dying state, for the purpose of having them buried at the expense of the hospital."*

Mr. Brownlow makes, a little further on, the following very pertinent remarks: "It has been truly said, that the frail tenure by which an infant holds its life will not allow of a remitted attention even for a few hours. Who, therefore, will be surprised, after hearing under what circumstances most of these poor children were left at the hospital gates, that, instead of being a protection to the living, the institution became as it were a charnel-house for the dead? It is a notorious fact, that many of the infants received at the gate did not live to be carried into the wards of the building; and, from the impossibility of procuring a sufficient number of proper nurses, the emaciated and diseased state in which many of these children were brought to the hospital, and the cruel conduct of some of those to whom they were committed (notwithstanding these nurses were under the superintendence of certain ladies, sisters of charity), the deaths amongst them were so fre-

---

* *Report* of 1836.

quent that out of the 14,934 received, only 4,400 lived to be apprenticed out, being a mortality of more than 70 per cent." (P. 175.) These children were doubtless deprived of breast-milk. To attribute their death, however, to this cause only, would be manifestly unjust.

Effect of Removal.—Under this head we have conflicting opinions. From Mr. Wakefield's tables, it appears that 57 per cent. of all infants who had been brought from a distance of more than fifty miles died in the hospital, whereas the mortality among other children did not exceed 48 per cent. —a difference of 11 per cent. from this cause alone. M. Gaillard brings out the same point by comparing the mortality of foundlings deposited in the town and hospice of Poitiers, with that of infants at Lyons, who were merely removed there from the Maternité. During six warm months, seven of the former died to six of the latter; during six winter months, nineteen of the former died to ten of the latter. At Poitiers most came from a distance, whereas at Lyons they were chiefly supplied by the city itself. This appears natural. A child brought a long way very soon after its birth, the mother probably too ill to accompany it, fed in the interim in a very improper manner, weakened by hunger and fatigue, is placed, no doubt, under very unnatural and unfavourable circumstances; yet it is a question how

far, in practice, this rule applies. We learn from
M. de Watteville's book* that this mortality cannot be due to the transport, since in other cases,
where the children are not very ill, and not exposed, the mortality is actually decreased. Thus
—out of 32,608 children, excluding 8,000 who
were taken out of these institutions by their
parents, only 13 died during the journey, and
209 only in the month following their removal
—a cypher of mortality positively below that which
obtains in such institutions. No doubt want of
care, and neglect of infants in removal, will increase the mortality; and in this way we may
perhaps explain the different results obtained.†

"These unfortunate children in general have
already been injured while yet in their mothers'
wombs; a very large proportion suffering, from
their birth, from defects of body which, later in
life, quite unfit them for labour. And then, it
should be added, want of care in infancy, whether
in a hospital or when put out at nurse, contributes
a great deal to make them weakly and obnoxious
to disease."

---

* *Statistique des Etablissemens et Services de Bienfaisance,*
p. 23.

    † Out of 8,879 children, aged from 1 day to 2 years.
      ,,   12,110   ,,   2 years to 6 ,,
      ,,   7,661   ,,   6   ,,   9 ,,
      ,,   3,958   ,,   9   ,, 12 ,,
          ——
        32,608

4. *Influence of the Recumbent Position and Want of Exercise.*—In the *Union Médicale*, November 2nd and 23rd, 1852, there are two very able papers by M. Hervieux, on the abuse of the horizontal position at the Hospice des Enfants Trouvés, and its influence on the mortality of the newly born infants. The following is an abstract :—

The *nursery* of this hospital is sixty feet long by twenty wide, and from twenty to twenty-five feet high. Light is introduced by eight windows, besides a painted one. The temperature is kept up by a large fireplace in the centre, around which persons can sit at ease, besides two large stoves at each extremity; so that the heat is equally diffused. Dry oak boards, covered by carpets, constitute the flooring; and the walls always appear very dry.

The *linen* is very clean and white; altogether, everything that could be desired, in the way of neatness and cleanliness, is carried into effect.

In this room are eighty-four cots to receive infants. Nine women are engaged in feeding and cleaning these little creatures, which is done four times a day, 6 A.M., 9 A.M., 12, and 4 P.M. The food is given in the *spoon*. Besides these nine day nurses, there are two night nurses employed in the same way all night. Thus, including the most restless and the quietest children together, it may be assumed, on an average, that each child is taken up six times a day. To clean and feed a child would occupy about twenty-five minutes in the hands of inexperienced nurses, ten or fifteen in the hands of those more experienced. Thus, the children, on an average, are held twenty minutes—6 × 20 = 120; so that each child has only two out of twenty-four hours exercise or movement. Now, what is the effect of this? A child, under natural circumstances, even if fed, generally lies upon the bosom of its mother or nurse; here it obtains artificial heat; and, in the hands of others, through the shaking, petting, etc., gets ample exercise. Thus the heat of body is maintained. But, short of this exercise, the temperature of the child's body will fall; the extremities will cool; the circulation become slower; the respiration will be embarrassed; all the major functions will fail; the cellular tissue will harden; the visceral organs will become congested; some will die by "scleroma," others by passive pneumonia (which is, after all, only proof of congestion of the lungs); some of serous effusion or hæmorrhage in the head or spinal cord. These are simply the results of *cold* superadded to those of *starvation*.

Now, in order to prove that these children are starved, M. Hervieux proceeds to speak against the system of feeding infants only at regular hours. Looking at the case of many infants who keep sucking thirty to forty times a day, and who are very often kept constantly to the breast, MM. Natalis Guilliot and Lamperière, of Versailles, have shown that infants absorb in the twenty-fours from 48·1 to 60·4 oz. Such children thrive wonderfully; and hence to stint and feed a child so precisely by rule—a child who, in the earlier two or three years of life, gains half the height and weight he will acquire in all his life, is little less than absurd.

This large amount of food has been objected to, as giving rise to gastric derangement; but if no such diseases are to be found in towns, among the rich and those poor who, when they can do so, almost always overfeed their children, this objection cannot be correct. To their credit be it said, the milk will often be provided for the child, though they themselves want the common necessaries. A child wants good food and air; but this will not suffice; he requires to be moved about; to go out in the open air and sun; and to be properly attended, in a hygienic as well as a dietetic manner. M. Hervieux therefore recommends that, instead of nine, there should be at least thirty-six nurses to tend the children.

It is lamentable to have to speak of neglect, privation, and even infanticide, as a cause of mortality among children. From the Registrar-

General's report it would appear that, for the year 1860, 61·5 per cent. of all the persons poisoned, suffocated, and murdered were infants under one year old, *i. e.*, that out of 1,678 persons dying from the above causes, 1,030 were infants under one—a lamentable figure, and one to be well noted, because occurring in this so-called Christian land. I do not mean to say it is not as bad, and it may be worse, in other countries, but the tale it tells is not the less sad. I shall have again to refer to this point in connexion with wet-nursing, and therefore do not dwell upon it now, although it was necessary to mention it here in its order.

CHAPTER V.

ON SOME PECULIAR PHYSIOLOGICAL RELATIONS WHICH INFLUENCE THE MORTALITY OF INFANTS.—MORTALITY GREATER IN EARLY PERIODS BOTH FOR FOUNDLINGS AND CHILDREN IN A GENERAL POPULATION.—SEASON.—INFLUENCE VARIES WITH LOCALITY IN PUBLIC INSTITUTIONS AS COMPARED WITH PRIVATE RESIDENCES. —THE MORTALITY IS GREATER FOR MALE CHILDREN THAN FOR FEMALES.

IT has been shown by all writers that the mortality of children is always greatest during the early periods. The data before given for Lyons, Rheims, and Paris, prove this to be true for foundlings. De Watteville fixes the mortality during the first year at fifty per cent. The same fact is set forth in the table given below from Bordeaux and Lyons.*

---

* At Bordeaux, out of 928 foundlings of the same age, the deaths in twelve years, as given by M. de Watteville, were as follows:—

Year.		Deaths.		Per cent.		Remaining.
1	......	480	......	51	......	418
2	......	112	......	28	......	336
3	......	37	......	10	......	299
4	......	14	......	5	......	285
5	......	13	......	5	......	272
6	......	4	......	3	......	268
7	......	2	......	1	......	266
8	......	7	......	3	......	259
9	......	3	......	1½	......	256
10	......	4	......	2	......	252
11	......	3	......	1½	......	249
12	......	4	......	2	......	245

It is also the case with children of a general population, although to a less extent. Thus from
Quêtelet's researches, it appears that in the Southern Netherlands the rate of mortality for children
from 0 to 5 years is very much greater for early
years† than for those which follow. And this is
true for whatever country selected.

When we come to consider the question of the
mortality in early months of the first year, this
appears to be far greater. Burdach gives a table
of the mortality in the several quarters of the

Thus the average annual percentage of mortality was 10; or 73
per cent. on twelve years.

At Lyons, out of 8,053 children, from birth to twelve years, the
deaths were—

Year.	Deaths.	Per cent.	Remaining.
1	 3098	...... 37·10	 4955
2	 1114	...... 22·41	 3841
3	 383	...... 9·47	 3458
4	 157	...... 4·50	 3301
5	 84	...... 2·54	 3217
6	 57	...... 1·77 •	3160
7	 39	...... 1·20	 3121
8	 23	...... 1·05	 3033
9	 20	...... ·64	 3008
10	 26	...... ·84	 3012
11	 15	...... ·49	 3027
12	 8	...... ·28	 3019

5031

Thus the average annual percentage of mortality was 8; or 62
per cent. in twelve years.

Years.				Deaths.
† 0	•	•	•	100,000
1	•	•	•	77,507
2	•	•	•	69,470
3	•	•	•	64,799
4	•	•	•	61,899
5	•	•	•	59,864

first year.* From this, deaths appear to be three or four times more frequent in the first quarter than in the second, and so on diminishing as the child grows older.

The same fact is brought out by Mr. Acton in his paper on Illegitimacy.† Out of 336 illegitimate children born in St. Marylebone, St. Pancras, and St. George, 110 died under three months.

It may, therefore, be said that the younger a child is, the greater is the chance of death; or, to state the proposition otherwise, every day in early infancy gained by a child renders the probability of duration of life greater. Quêtelet expresses his views on this subject in the following terms :—" To have a just idea of the great mortality of infants soon after birth, it is sufficient to note that, in towns as well as in country districts, there die during the first month after birth *four* times as many children as during the second month after birth, and almost as many as during the entirety of the two years that follow

---

* Mortality in different quarters of the first year. (*Burdach Physiologie*, vol. iv, s. 523, p. 387.)

	Brussels.	Brunswick.	Berlin.	Hamburgh.	Paris.	Vienna.
Mean Term	1 in 17	1 in 10	1 in 16	1 in 21	1 in 24	1 in 17·6
1st 3 Months	,, 8	,, 3	,, 7	,, 11	,, 8	,, 7·4
2nd ,,	,, 23	,, 13	,, 19	,, 27	,, 51	,, 26·6
3rd ,,	,, 25·07	,, 21	,, 23	,, 30	,, —	,, 31·8
4th ,,	,, 25·12	,, 41	,, 21	,, 26	,, —	,, 28·

† *Statistical Society's Journal*, December 1859.

the first year, although even then the mortality is very high. The tables of mortality prove, in fact, that one-tenth of children born die before the first month of life has been completed." This mortality is so great, especially for male children, that from the first year after birth the number is reduced to one-fourth.

The subjoined table, also from Quêtelet, which relates to the mortality of Brussels, makes it during the first year of life 1,034 deaths in the first month, against 3,538 for the whole year, or 29·2 per cent. See table below.* So that more children die in the first month than in any of the remaining months of the first year. In Paris, and for the year 1823,† the corresponding numbers are in the proportion of 1,764 to 693, or 59·2 per cent.

We observe the same thing for children of the early months in the returns for England. I have taken as an example the year 1842. By reference to the table annexed, in which I have taken indifferently several counties, the same truth obtains. In England, out of 100 children born, while for

* 1st Month	... 1034	7th Month	... 162
2nd ,,	... 890	8th ,,	... 152
3rd ,,	... 231	9th ,,	... 140
4th ,,	... 185	10th ,,	... 150
5th ,,	... 156	11th ,,	... 142
6th ,,	... 156	12th ,,	... 140

† *Annuaire du Bureau des Longitudes pour 1826.*

the whole period of one year 15·2 per cent. children will die, 4·7 will die the first month, 1·7 the next, and so on. This law will be seen by reference to Appendix D to apply to all counties indifferently.

The same fact is brought out in a different manner for the first and following months in the arranged table, from which it appears always to be greatest in the first month, in the civic districts of Connaught reaching the high figure of 38·8 per cent.

To account for this great mortality, various inquiries have been made. Many of these instituted in foundling institutions will be found to apply, although in a lesser degree, to children generally, and as such it may be of advantage to consider some of the causes in operation in these institutions.

Influence of Season.—It results from the inquiries of the Registrar General that the mortality varies greatly with the temperature. A fall of the mean temperature of the air from 45° to 4° or 5° below the freezing point (32°) of water, destroys from 300 to 500 lives in London. It produces the same results on a larger scale all over the country.* The return (see table before given, chapter iv, p. 40,*) where the percentage

---

* *Eighth Report of the Registrar-General*, p. 37.

mortality for town and country is given, proves it
to be highest in *winter* when *cold* is most prevalent.
This is chiefly true for cities well-drained and for
dry country soil. Summer, however, may be
most fatal to inhabitants of *marshy* districts or of
cities which are badly drained. In Rome, as
formerly in London, the old words of Celsus still
apply—" Saluberrimum ver est, proxime deinde
ab hoc hiems, periculosior æstos, autumnus longe
periculosissimus"—because as the temperature
advances, and autumn comes on, dead vegetable
and animal matter undergoes rapid decomposition,
the living animals are infected, and where the *Mias-
mata* are concentrated in cities or in undrained
lands, remittent fevers, dysentery, plagues, and
malignant maladies are generated.

Among the most pernicious influences to young
children, however, we may include cold. The
change of temperature from 45 to 4 or 5 below
zero as before stated, producing an increase of
mortality in London alone of 300 to 500. As out of
100 deaths, however, from all specified causes,
nearly 24 occur to children under one, and 36 to
children under five, the great increase of mortality
to children by cold is thus at once made obvious.
Indeed, it is a household word amongst us, which
takes its origin from the Registrar General's returns, that a very cold week always increases the
mortality of the very young and very aged. We

cannot, however, come to a similar conclusion for children if kept in public institutions. It is true, the Abbé Gaillard pointed out this contingency in the case of the Foundling Institution at X. Thus, in November and December, 1829, out of 29 children, 19 died in the first month after admission; whereas, in July and August of the same year, there died only 11 out of 25 admitted. But we learn from the Irish tables that, in *public institutions*, the greatest number of deaths take place in *spring*, the least in autumn. It appears that, the deaths being 100 in all seasons, 30·8 will take place in spring; in summer and winter it will be about the same—27·1; while in autumn it will be least, only 14·3.

The corollary to be drawn from the above facts is, that as children in public institutions are not allowed out-door exercise, so long and so frequently as those of a general population, it is wise in very cold and changeable weather to restrain this pastime within reasonable limits.

Another peculiarity to be mentioned under this head, is the greater mortality of male as compared to female infants, although more boys are born than girls. M. Quêtelet states, the birth of boys as compared to girls for Belgium for the years 1815 to 1829, to be a mean of 1000 boys to 944 girls in towns, or 938 girls in cities. From tables which he has drawn out, he finds that the number

of still-born children in towns is double that of
still-born children in rural districts, and that for
three still-born males, there are only two stillborn females, and that even after birth for the
two following months the proportion of males
that die as compared to females is about four to
three—for the fourth and fifth, it is five to four;
afterwards as six to five, although after the eighth
or tenth month the mortality for both sexes seems
to be equal. The same general conclusions apply
to all countries, though the exact cypher of mortality may vary a little.

CHAPTER VI.

CONDITIONS WHICH FAVOUR VIABILITY.—TABLES OF VIABILITY UP
TO FIVE YEARS.—POSITIVE INFLUENCE OF BREAST-MILK, DESPITE
INJURIOUS HAND-FEEDING COMBINED, PROVED BY FOUNDLING
HOSPITAL RETURNS.—CASE OF WALES.—POSITIVE BENEFICIAL
INFLUENCE OF LIGHT, IF NOT TOO STIMULATING.—OF SOME
COLOURS.

IN Quêtelet's work, *Researches on Reproduction
and Mortality of Man at Different Ages,* we have
a table given us of the viability of man. This
table is calculated upon that of mortality, the
inverse rates of each number placed opposite to
the age may be considered as the relative degree
of the viability of man at different ages, or, in
other words, of his relative chance of life. I have
annexed it for reference for five years.*

* Age.	Degree of		Age.	Degree of	
	Mortality.	Viability.		Mortality.	Viability.
Month.			Year.		
First	960	1	First	115	9
Second	273	4	Second	77	13
Third	200	5	Third	60	17
Fourth	168	6	Fourth	27	37
Fifth	135	7	Fifth	21	48
Sixth	127	8			

Many of those causes which have been enumerated as favouring mortality, are precisely those which, if avoided, are best calculated to favour viability. Thus, abundance of breast-milk, especially from the child's own mother; the exclusion of other food, especially that of a vegetable character, as we shall see more distinctly in the sequel; the purity of the atmosphere in which they live, especially in country districts; eschewing travel or exposure in cold weather, the abuse of the recumbent position; and violence,—are all circumstances which tend to favour the viability of an infant. Many of these causes have been fully considered before in their relations to death, yet it may be of advantage to allude to some of them in a more positive manner in their relation to viability.

And, first, in regard to breast-milk. We have seen from Drs. Merei and Whitehead's tables, that feeding a child on breast-milk exclusively, produces a good development in 63 per cent., medium development in 23 per cent., and bad development in 14 per cent. Nor, further, is there any advantage when the mother is in good health, and has abundance of milk, in feeding an infant on extra food besides. On the contrary, the results then obtained are only 52 good, 28.6 medium, and 39 bad development. Lastly, and as opposed to these results, injudicious feeding

F

by hand produces 10 good, 26 medium, and 64 per cent. bad development.

By reference again to these tables, and by uniting the third and fifth classes together, which include children who have had breast-milk in moderate abundance *with* other food, from birth or early ages, which we are bound to assume from general experience was injudicious, the results are 35 good, 25·7 medium, and 39 bad, development.

Between the cases where children are fed by hand, and those in which they are assisted by artificial food, there is a great and manifest difference. If, therefore, with injudicious feeding with moderate breast-milk the results are so favourable, the *wonderfully preservative influence of breast-milk* must at once be admitted.

But we may bring out this truth still more forcibly.

a. When we consider the gross ignorance of those who take care of children, *injudicious feeding* is too mild a phrase. The food supplied acts in many cases little better than a slow poison. This I shall be able to show in the sequel when speaking of babies fed with aluminized bread pap, and the vegetable aliments usually supplied.

b. Actual experiment in this direction, and on a large scale, has been carried out by the London

Foundling Hospital, and the returns prove that the plan is eminently successful. In this hospital, the children are sent into the country to wet-nurses, for the most part married women, with a baby of their own to suckle besides; and these women keep them during the period usually allotted to suckling, and for some time afterwards, and so bring them up. They are afterwards brought back to the hospital. Now it is manifest in such cases, that by far the larger majority of women are quite incapable of nursing two hearty children at the same time exclusively upon the breast. Indeed, the exceptions in which this can be done, without very serious injury to the woman, I conceive are very rare. Clearly, therefore, other food is given; and if so, knowing the little knowledge such women usually possess of what is proper food to give, we may well rest assured that the hand-feeding pursued is not always judiciously carried on. Notwithstanding these disadvantages, the results prove again how strong is the preservative influence on life of breast-milk, even when partaken of only in partial quantities.

The following is the mortality, as given us in Mr. Brownlow's book, before referred to.

Out of 100 children under five years of age, received at two separate periods, viz., from May 1835 to May 1837, and from May 1837 to March

1839, Mr. Brownlow shows the following was the mortality :—

	1st Period.		2nd Period.
Deaths in first year of their age	12	...	9
Deaths in second year of their age	5	...	10
Deaths in third year of their age	2	...	2
Deaths in fourth year of their age	0	...	0
Deaths in fifth year of their age	1	...	0
	20		21

The causes of death were—convulsions in 9 ; diseases of membranes of the brain, 5 ; water on the brain, 4 ; inflammation of bowels, 4 ; inflammation of lungs in 3 ; malformation of chest, 3 ; diarrhœa in 3 ; croup, 2 ; scarlet fever, 2 ; hydrocele, atrophy, bilious vomiting, scrofula, hooping-cough, teething, and breaking a blood-vessel, of each 1.   Now, making all allowance for a country residence, which we have seen before exercises a favourable result upon hand-feeding, the results are very satisfactory.

The same conclusion may be brought out in another way.   It is not generally known, but it is nevertheless almost universally the practice in Wales to feed children from birth, besides giving them the usual breast-milk.   Now it were natural to suppose, that if such a course of action were injurious to children, the mortality among infants would be greater in this part of Great Britain than in other counties.   The reverse, however, is the fact.   From the table given in Appendix D, for the year 1842, which has been indifferently selected, because the deaths in the Registrar-General's reports for that year were given for the early months, the mortality is actually less out of seventeen counties, taken also indifferently, if we except Dorsetshire and Devonshire.* The efficacy of this plan is, however, more obvious for the later months. The child so brought up, if he weathers the first quarter, has more viability. Thus fewer upon the whole die under one year.

In reference to the number of cases dying from want of breast-milk, the table, also given in the Appendix, gives also a lesser mortality from this cause in Wales. This is an important conclusion to arrive at when we consider the injurious quality of food given, to which I must again refer, and is strongly illustrative of the preservative influence of breast-milk.

Secondly, in reference to light. If close and ill-ventilated apartments are injurious to children, so is absence of light. We are all cognisant of

---

* Proportion of deaths to 1,000 births in England, London, and several counties, taken indiscriminately, from want of breast-milk, in the year 1860 :—

England	-	- 1·4	Dorsetshire -	- ·3
London -	-	- 4·6	Devonshire -	- ·3
Oxford -	-	- 1·2	Monmouthshire	- 1·4
Cambridge	-	- 1·1	South Wales -	- ·2
Durham	-	- 1·05	North Wales -	- ·08
Norfolk	-	- 2·4	York, West Riding	- ·4
Kent (extra metropolitan)	1·3		York, East Riding	- 2·03
Surrey (ditto ditto)	3·9		North Riding -	- ·5

the salutary influence upon plants which light exerts. Deprived of light, they become pale, emaciated, lose finally all colour, and elongate without keeping their consistence, and lose all their usual properties. The ordinary chemical changes in the plant do not occur. The same is true with animals; whether in the obscurity of a cell, in dark habitations, in caves or mines where the light of the sun does not penetrate, man loses his strength and colour; his flesh becomes soft and flabby; and this habit, if long continued, degrades him to that point that he cannot bear the light of the sun but with pain.

The above remarks, in part extracted from De Bureaud Riossey's work on the *physical* education of women, are extended at length to illustrate the importance of light to children. Dr. Milne-Edwards' experiments on the development of tadpoles in the dark and in the light, are alluded to. An animal which, in the first stage of its existence, has the character of a fish, with a tail, branchiæ, and no limbs; and in the second stage no character of fish, no tail, no branchiæ, and four limbs, afforded an excellent subject for these experiments, and it is well known that the results proved that these changes, if not absolutely prevented, were singularly retarded by the privation of light. The infrequency of deformity among the Chaymos, the Caribs, the Mexicans, the Peruvians, is ascribed by M. Humboldt to the free action of light on their bodies, rather than to any peculiarity by which their life is distinguished from that of the inhabitants of more civilized countries, and it is certainly probable that the use of what the French call *insolation*—a free exposure of the body to the sun and air—might, as suggested by Dr. Edwards, be advantageously had recourse to in scrofulous affections and other maladies of degeneration.

" It is presumed by some physiologists, that the frequent and free exposure of the body to the atmospheric air in the fine climate of Greece tended to the development of the exquisite forms which yet live in ancient works of art. The traveller in Ireland, if acquainted with the condition of the poor in our large manufacturing towns, may usefully compare appearances, resulting on the one hand, from habitual residence in dark habitations; and on the other, from almost constant exposure to sunshine and air. The manufacturer's younger children leave the cellar or the garret, but only for the narrow court or damp, neglected, back street; but the Irish cottager's child, although born in even greater poverty, runs about as soon as it can run at all in the open air of a temperate climate, not at all overburthened with clothing. The pale, unhealthy, scrofulous character of the manufacturer's child is too well known, whereas it is impossible to imagine finer examples of childish beauty and grace than are beheld at the doors of Irish cabins."*

In fact, light is a very effective stimulant, and, except in diseased states of the body or where the light to which an animal is exposed is excessive, it materially increases the vitality of the animal.

Dr. Laycock, in his work on the *Reflex Function of the Brain,* has alluded to some of the influences of light on the nervous system. How it maintains activity and tone, and prevents sleep is well known. This influence is subject to the law of diffusion. Sometimes it acts powerfully. Jungken was acquainted with two persons who were instantaneously seized with asphyxia if light were excluded, or awoke in a state of suffocation if their taper had gone out. A case of this kind is mentioned in Dr. Forbes's translation of Laennec. In these instances the incident excited impression of light, maintained the activity of the respiratory ganglia—prevented them in fact, from going to sleep. The diffused influence of light will produce an opposite effect. Observation 86, Bordeu's *Recherches sur le Pouls,* is that of a very aged female on whom a single ray of the sun, or the light of a candle, excited an abundant sweat, so that she was obliged to be always in the dark.† A bright surface will often suffice also to induce in a person

---

* *British and Foreign Medical Review*, vol. v, p. 404.
† *Ib.*, xix, p. 308.

affected with hydrophobia a characteristic paroxysm.* These are examples of diseased action, and useful as illustrations of a common law. Exposure to excessive light, on the other hand, is injurious. Headaches, apoplexies, and even mania, may be produced by *insolations*. There is a need, therefore, of moderation. Light so used will do good, and promote viability, because the strength of the child is also improved thereby.

The influence of *colours*, which is due to a modification of light, is also important, though the full effects of them are not yet made out. Under a yellow-coloured glass plants will not thrive, and it has been stated that school boys kept in rooms painted yellow are sufferers. It is well known also, that the yellow-coloured glass is taken advantage of by photographers because it does not admit the chemical rays. Here is, probably, therefore, the reason it is unhealthy.

The colours of porous bodies have been shown by the arguments of Dr. Stark, to exert a decided influence over the absorption of odours, the dark colours being most efficient. He has suggested, therefore, by a fair analogy, that colour may modify also the absorption of contagious effluvia.†

---

* *British and Foreign Medical Review*, vol. v, p. 201.
† *Ib.*

CHAPTER VII.

I HAVE before alluded to injudicious food given in the absence of breast-milk, in its relation to mortality. I have now to consider food when given, in its relation to viability. It may then be broadly stated, that animal food is indispensable to a child in the earliest periods of life. I may so far anticipate here in a few words what I purpose speaking of more fully in the sequel, when speaking of alimentation. Food, as is well known, to be capable of supporting life, must contain three substances in due proportion:—1. Plastic or nitrogenous matters, to nourish the fleshy or muscular parts of the body. 2. Calorifiant or combustible matter, *i. e.* hydro-carbons, to supply the respiratory process, to keep up animal heat, and to provide fat for the body. 3. Mineral matters, or salts, to supply the bones, and hold in chemical union, combination, and action, the solids and liquids of the body. Among the first class are fibrine, albumen, or casein; among the second, fats and oils, sugar and starch; among the third, lime, potash, soda, magnesia, in union with phosphoric, sulphuric, hydrochloric acids, and many others. Some one or more of these are contained in all aliments in beautiful combination, and so they are found capable of supporting life. Singly, however, or as a simple substance, these plastic, fatty, or mineral matters cannot do this; starvation, in modified forms, being always observed to follow their employment when given alone.

Milk contains these elements in combination. There are casein, the plastic ingredient; fat and sugar, two combustible substances, and the several mineral matters needed. As such, if good in quality and given in sufficient quantity, it will support life for an indeterminate length of time. The proportions in which these substances are contained in other aliments vary, but it should at least be 10 of plastic to 30 or 40 combustible, and the mineral should vary from 1·5 to 6 or 7 per cent.

Now the whole analogy of comparative anatomy proves that all young animals require animal food for some time after birth, because (a) this is generally supplied by the parent, or by some adventitious animal structure. (b) The infant itself is

so anatomically and physiologically made as to be
capable of digesting animal food only.*

(*a*) The following facts, chiefly taken from Burdach, will illustrate the first proposition. In many
species of mollusca, and especially in gasteropoda,
in many insects, and among the batrachian rep-
tiles, the mother produces, together with the egg,
what is called a *nidamentum*, which nourishes it
for some time after its birth. Certain insects
even feed upon the external envelopes which surround them, as in the case of the *stratismys
chameleon.*

The yellow substance which surrounds the abdominal walls in some animals, or which is en-
closed in the central abdominal cavity, is an
auxiliary of this kind. Its presence explains the
fact that spiders and snakes, for instance, remain
some time after birth without requiring any other
kind of food. The raw food which the greater
number of birds give to their young is exclusively
animal, hence the more readily attainable and
digestible. The northern ducks and the petrels,
with their nests situated on high rocks near the
sea, easily procure this food, and they always
return to their nests richly laden with fish. The
sparrows nourish their young with insects and
worms, which they find everywhere in abundance;
and hence certain rapacious birds, which require

---

* See Burdach's *Physiologie.*

a greater amount of animal food for their young, become at the breeding season particularly audacious in order to procure it.

Some of the sparrow and crow tribe bring the nourishment in their beaks, emptying it into those of their young. The rapacious birds, on the contrary, bring it in their claws, place it before their young, and tear it in small pieces for them. The heron and the pelican bring the fish in the pharynx, which is dilated to a large pouch below the bill; and the pelican applying its lower jaw against its own breast, allows its young to eat out of this pocket as out of a plate. Among some species of vultures and dark-winged eagles, the crop seems to serve as a reservoir for the food intended for the young. Approximating to a higher degree of maternal co-operation, the female does not give nourishment to her young till she has in part digested and assimilated it. The bees and wasps are of this class, and swallow some pollen, and then disgorge it mixed with honey. Among pigeons, the greater number of grallatores, some palmipedes, and many sparrows, the mucous membrane of the œsophagus is dilated into a crop, well supplied with vessels, into which the grain which is difficult to digest is first conveyed, and then softened under the chemical influence of a fluid analogous to the gastric juice of the stomach. When half digested, and converted into a kind of chyme, it is subsequently disgorged into the beak of their young. This modified chyme it is which is popularly called pigeon's *milk*. The male assists in this operation as well as the female. Finally, in mammalia we arrive at the production exclusively by the mother, of milk, which bears in its composition considerable resemblance to the diluted yolk of egg, and in some respects to the *nidamentum*. It will be seen from the preceding review, that the food which is required by the young is essentially animal; and even in those cases where the birds themselves are granivorous, or vegetable feeders, they either supply their young with animal food exclusively, or else with vegetable food so semi-digested in, or intermixed with, the animal fluids, that for all purposes it may be regarded as animal food.

Gradually as the young animal becomes older, this exclusive dependence upon the maternal supply ceases. Among pigeons, for instance, after three days the young bird begins to partake of other food also. The reindeer at the end of some days begins to eat grass and lichens, and the calf in about three weeks can no longer live exclusively on its mother's milk, but requires other food. Still the dependence of young animals upon the food which they directly obtain from the mother in the natural state, is very

close. In the case of the *simia rhesus*, that animal attaches itself to its mother's nipple, and
remains in this position for fifteen days, in sleeping as well as waking, never leaving one breast
but to attach itself to the other. To endeavour,
therefore, to nourish any young animal exclusively on vegetable food, is contrary to the entire
law of nature, and especially so in man, where
the parental relations are so much closer, and
maintained for so much longer a period.

(*b*) The infant itself is so anatomically and
physiologically constructed, as to be capable of
digesting *animal* food only.

A very little reflection would have convinced
any observer, that if among *herbivorous* mammalia the young require animal food, this is, *à
priori*, a strong argument against the use of vegetable food in *omnivorous* or *carnivorous* animals; yet even upon this point our medical
authorities are not agreed; many vegetable compounds are both recommended and taken. Apart
from the common-sense view of the question, let
us look to the physiological construction and anatomical arrangement of the alimentary canal of a
child. Upon these points Burdach, in his *Physiology*, speaks graphically. It is remarkable that
suction is the only faculty for the prehension of
food which the child possesses at birth, and even
this is soon lost if not practised. The jaws are

not so constructed as to permit active movements, nor the gums to bear pressure. The
hard palate is but little developed : although the
cavity of the mouth is sufficiently wide. There
is, moreover, no saliva secreted for the first two
months, so that no species of preparatory change
can take place in it, as, for example, in the conversion of starchy matters into sugar, through
the agency of this fluid (saliva). The mouth is,
therefore, merely an organ of transmission and
suction. The lips are large, and the tongue and
pharynx, uvula, and soft palate, are well developed, to secure these ends.* The stomach in
infants is a small tube-shaped membrane, dilated
in the centre, one extremity ending in the œsophagus, and the other in the pylorus, resembling
in this character that found in carnivora through
life. In position, also, it lies more parallel to
the trunk; the large and small curvatures and
muscular structures being but very little developed. The liver at birth is unusually large, the
pancreas perhaps not more developed than the
salivary glands ; the intestinal tube is much
shorter, and the large intestine approaches more
nearly in its length to the small. The cæcum
(in which, moreover, it is believed a sort of additional digestion occasionally occurs) is very

* Burdach, p. 434.

small. The peristaltic motion is more rapid. All these are evidences that food taken will be kept for a shorter time in the canal, and therefore should be in the condition most favourable for digestion.* Lastly, in no other of the mammalia is there, in the first periods of life, such a complete absence of teeth. In man they appear latest, and are longest in obtaining their full development. In fine, comparing these appearances with those observed in herbivorous animals, viz., well-developed salivary glands, compound stomachs,—sometimes four in number; muscular gizzards,—as in some birds, long intestines, large cæcum, etc., it is manifest they are the exact opposites to what we find in young infants. As the child grows, the peculiarities which are permanent in herbivorous animals gradually present themselves. The stomach assumes a more horizontal position, the *valvulæ conniventes* become well developed, the peristaltic motion of the intestines becomes slower; in fact, all the changes calculated to retard the food in its progress, and thus to expose it more completely to the solvent juices for digestion, occur. All this proves indubitably that animal, not vegetable food, is the proper diet for an infant.

Secondly, in reference to the hygienic relations

---

* See West's *Diseases of Children*, pp. 402, 403.

G

of the child as a fed animal, to make that food profitable to the infant, we have to consider the conditions necessary to the proper exhibition of the food given. In chap. iv, it may be remembered, I laid great stress on the abuse of the recumbent position of children, so well explained by M. Henrieux, and so fearful a cause of their mortality. The effects produced were cold and starvation (see p. 49). Decidedly, therefore, in any plan adopted to bring up a child by hand, these effects must be especially combated against and avoided.

1. In discussing the conditions to be observed in giving infants their food, I would lay down the two following rules as essential to the preservation of the child's health.

(*a*) That, in early ages especially, a child should be kept warm, artificially or naturally, especially during the time it is being fed.

(*b*) That a child should be made to take at such periods the semi-erect, which is the natural position.

I believe that the comparative anatomy and physiology of mammalia entirely prove that attention to these two rules is a necessity.

(*a*) *Warmth required by an Infant.*—The records of mortality prove indisputably that *cold* is very deadly in its influence upon children. We have already seen that whenever a week is more severe than the preceding one, instantly the Registrar-General's returns show an increase of deaths; and this especially among the very old and very young. It is of the latter only that I have to speak. The whole bearing of comparative anatomy goes to prove that heat is indispensable for the preservation of new-born and very young animals. The common sparrows, ortolans, and swallows, are born quite naked; other birds almost so, as in the case of linnets and magpies; but then their nests are very warm. Among the gallinaceous birds, the *grallatores*, and some of the *palmipedes*, the young are covered with a species of down, which, albeit transitory and succeeded by feathers, is notwithstanding very warm. It is observed that this down is preserved longer on young birds which are obliged to remain in the nest a long time, and are unable to seek abroad for their food; as, for instance, in the goose; and the parent birds themselves are provided with similar down on the belly between the feathers, which only disappears some time after incubation. Many of the young, besides this down, are provided with a thick coating of grease, to preserve them against external cold. This is the case among the *procellaria*. But even among the mammalia, the first coating is not like that which follows, although also transitory. The hedgehog has a fine velvety hairy coating; the seal, a long soft hair. Added to this, as has been well shown by Edwards, the calorifying power is always imperfect in the very young. Birds and mammalia, which are born naked, have little proper heat, and derive it chiefly from the parent. The animal heat of young sparrows withdrawn from their mother (the temperature of the atmosphere being 64° Fahr.), fell in one hour from 87° Fahr. to 66°; and, when the external atmosphere was 71·6° Fahr., it fell to 73·4°. The same result has been observed in dogs and rabbits. But one fact is remarkable here, especially in reference to its application to a child. It is not the *difference of the external covering which is the cause of this fall:* external furs may be put round the young to keep them warm, and yet the loss of temperature is the same. This is not the case with older birds; for in these, even when all their feathers are cut away, the heat is retained. The maternal heat is all that a young bird needs the first day, since the umbilical vesicle of the egg still supplies it with food. It is interesting to note, that these young animals, although they lose skin heat so readily, and become, as it were, insensible from cold, will yet regain it, and recover, on being artificially warmed. This power, however, is lost in proportion as the animal becomes older, and more able to generate heat itself.

The mother's nest, among those animals which

are born naked, is invariably both deeper and warmer than amongst those who have the warm covering. This is remarkable with birds; but, even among mammalia, in proportion as the young are born more or less naked or blind, so do the parents take greater or less precautions, and make their beds or nests warmer. Less care, however, in this respect, is taken among mammalia which generally have their young in summer. In some instances, where a nest is not so readily made, the heat is maintained by a persistent connexion between the mother and young. In the kangaroo tribe (the connecting link between the oviparous and viviparous animals), there is a pouch to keep the animal warm attached to the abdomen, where the young kangaroo remains with the mother's nipple persistently in its mouth for seven weeks. But in a higher class we have the *simia rhesus*, which, for a fortnight after birth, fixes itself to its mother's nipple, and never leaves one but to take hold of the other. All this indicates, apart from the necessity for food, an equally great necessity for the maternal heat.

The application of these facts to man is most important. The infant is born naked. It is true, his eyes are open, but, according to Burdach, for the first month he is, as it were, blind; perhaps able to distinguish light, but that indistinctly. Heat only is essential to him at first, and he will rapidly lose it on exposure. The proverb, " Can two lie together, and not have heat ?" should be proved in the case of every infant and its mother. Temporary separation may be, and should be, recommended, for then, owing to the power of the infant of again recovering its heat near the mother, no harm is likely to follow, but the separation should not be for long. These remarks apply generally to the young animal at all times, but especially at meal times. During digestion, there is a continual flow of blood towards the alimentary canal; and hence the sensation we experience of feeling cold after dinner, which a familiar proverb among us has interpreted as a *sign of a good digestion*. It is only after this is complete, that the blood resumes its position more on the external skin, and the sensation illustrated by another proverb, " *The south wind blows after dinner*," is brought about. But, as the means of producing heat in the infant itself are very limited, and its meals are frequent, so it requires that the artificial heat from its mother should be often given to it : therefore, during meals, a child should be kept warm.

(*b*) *Position of a Child while taking Food*.—This is not less important to a child brought up by hand. " The child," says Dewees, " should not receive its nourishment while lying. It should be raised, which will not only become a pleasanter position, but it also diminishes the risk of strangulation."* The semi-erect position which the child adopts in sucking is not only favourable, as affording it the readiest means of partaking of its mother's heat, but there is besides an anatomical reason. The stomach is placed more perpendicularly as to position. There is but feeble muscular power in it; and the cardiac opening is less able to contract and retain food taken. Thus, in any other position of the child but the semi-erect, the milk taken is likely to be brought up again, and lost to the child. Yet it is strange that, in feeding children by the bottle, nurses are usually in the habit of laying the child on his back on their knees, often with the head lower than the trunk, so as precisely to favour those accidents which it is desirable to avoid. To correct this abuse, with the assistance of a very intelligent chemist, Mr. Cooper of Oxford Street, I had a bottle constructed, to which his new stop-cock was applied. This last is so constructed as to prevent the child from taking down air with his food, and thus those pains from flatulence, so common in children, and often so distressing, do not occur. This bottle, which is shaped like a female breast, has two openings in it: one, which is for the use of the child when very young, has no stop-cock, but a

---

* *Diseases of Children,* chap. v, p. 178.

tube and a small nipple of India-rubber; the other, to be used when the child is older, has stop-cock and tube also, but a larger nipple. It may be worn by the female in the position of the breast, or across the chest, kept in position by a handkerchief or band, and if next the skin, it is kept warm, if need be, all night or day. The child, on taking the food out of such a bottle, is placed in the normal position, and at the same time kept warm by the female.

There is another way in which it may prove useful. Mothers often tell us that the child will not take the bottle: and the reason is obvious. It is not likely that a child, accustomed to the semi-erect position and maternal heat, will readily assume the new and recumbent position, at once a less pleasant one from habit and so much colder. With the mammary bottle this source of difficulty is obviated. I remember well an instance in a child, who, from the serious illness of the mother, had to be weaned. No means whatever adopted could prevail upon this child to take the ordinary bottle; but it readily used the mammary one. There is one objection to such bottles, and it is this, that being made of glass they are hard and resistant. Could such a bottle be devised made of some soft waterproof material such as India-rubber deprived of all odour, there is no doubt that a child could be easily deceived, and it would afford an excellent way of assisting a mother through some difficulties. The ordinary O'Connel Bottle, and all others made upon that principle, if the nipple is kept close to the warm breast, and the child's sucking powers are not weakened, is a good substitute for the time being. In due time the child will get more accustomed to its use and the pious fraud need not be continued.

PART II.

CHAPTER I.

LACTATION.—QUANTITY OF MILK NORMALLY SECRETED.—THREE
KINDS OF WET-NURSES:—FIRST, THE HEALTHY NURSE: SECOND,
A NURSE AFFECTED WITH GALACTORRHŒA: THIRD, A NURSE
AFFECTED WITH DEFECTIVE LACTATION.—ALSO THREE VARIETIES.

THE several points before discussed, bring us to
this conclusion as the one of paramount importance in infant feeding. We must endeavour to
give a child, as much as possible exclusively
breast-milk, and this leads us necessarily to the
consideration of lactation. A proper cognizance
of this function both as regards mother and child,
is manifestly of the greatest moment if we wish
to put a child in the most favourable condition
for living. We have, then, to consider the varieties found among wet nurses; but as the classifi-
cation depends upon the amount of milk secreted by a woman—it is well, as a preliminary, to
define what is the quantity of milk normally
secreted by a healthy woman, and which will suffice for a healthy child.

Dr. W. Henry Cumming* has estimated the amount ordinarily furnished to be from one and a half to two quarts daily, or from four to five pounds; and in those cases where two children are suckled by a mother, about four quarts or eight pounds. He also states that an infant three months old will take from 48 to 64 fluid-ounces daily, in six or eight half-pint doses. So that he estimates the quantity of milk taken in the first year to be from 1000 to 1300 pounds.

I believe this is somewhat an exaggerated statement. A three months' child generally thrives very well on four or at the most five meals a day, the quantity taken each time amounting to a half-pint. This would fix the quantity at two pounds to two and a half, *i. e.* thirty-two to forty fluid-ounces. A quart and a half would therefore be the utmost a good nurse need produce for one child. A younger child, one to two months, may need to take his meals more frequently,—it may be every two hours except when asleep,—but then the quantity consumed does not exceed, as a rule, as I have often assured myself, two wine-glasses or three ounces every meal. This would raise the quantity taken in twenty-four hours to thirty-six ounces—a quart and a quarter. A child above three months may take about forty-

* *American Quarterly Journal of Medical Science,* July 1858; Ranking's Retrospect. 28, 275.

eight ounces daily. I should think it, therefore, fair to assume as an average, forty ounces of milk daily for a year—and this will bring up the amount to about 912 pounds of milk. The outside would be 1000. Let us, therefore, take this higher number for the purpose of calculation.

According to Becquerel and Rodier's analysis, taking the mean of three experiments, the child consumes during the first year about 111 pounds of dry solids, of which 44 pounds are sugar, 30 pounds casein and extractive matters, butter 25 pounds, and salt about 2 pounds—of which last about 22 ounces are phosphate of lime.

A child may thus gain in the first year from 11 to 16 pounds in weight, implying less than 3 pounds of dry solids, and yet have a large residue of from 95 to 100 pounds " to be expended in the production of heat, and in the activity of an energetic vitality." A child thus nourished, will be well developed as far as teeth and bone are concerned, and will be able to resist cold and disease.

I have thus far followed Dr. Cumming's argument, and occasionally expressions, though I have altered the figures to what I believe, from my own experience, to be the average of English women.

Dr. Cumming believes that few women can satisfy the requirements of even a weakly child, as a strong vigorous fat woman always loses weight while suckling her child. The milk draws away more than the stomach of even such a woman can replace, and the balance is taken by absorption from her previous accumulation. He endeavours to prove the same conclusion by comparing a wet nurse to a milch cow. " A woman weighing 130 lbs. will give daily 4 lbs. of milk containing about 5 ounces of dry solids. A cow weighing six times as much, 780 lbs., will give 20 pounds of milk containing 30 ounces of the same. It should not then surprise us," he adds, "that so many mothers fail to supply enough food for their infants;" and finally, he concludes, "that physicians should give serious attention and thoughtful consideration to a plan offering a substitute for human milk scientifically correct, and practically successful."[*]

Upon his data, which are all too high, it would be difficult to come to any other conclusion. But Drs. Merei and Whitehead's tables prove the reverse. Those children thrive best who are fed exclusively at the breast, and therefore some women must have milk enough. If they become thin under it and become weakly, it is that they need assistance. And this is one of my objects in dwelling so much upon the subject of infant feeding.

---

[*] *American Quarterly Journal of Medical Science*, July 1858; Ranking's, 28, 275.

In practice we meet with three kinds of nurses. First, those who fortunately are sufficiently numerous, have a healthy lactation, and who are capable of fully performing their duties as mothers. They are generally healthy women, matronly looking, and in good fleshy condition. The breasts are large, but the size is due to the number of lacteal tubes and not to the deposit of fat in and around them. The veins over the bosom are tortuous and well marked, the nipple protrudes well, being either of a dark colour or pinky red, according as the patient is dark or fair. The areola is well developed with more or fewer glandular follicles around, which become whiter when the areola is stretched. There is plenty of milk. Whatever the woman takes seems not only to nourish her, but to increase the flow of milk, which is rich in quality. The draft regularly recurs after every meal, and, whenever the child comes to be suckled,—and it thrives well on the milk which it obtains from her. From Drs. Merei and Whitehead's first and second Clinical Report of the Children's Hospital at Manchester, the following analysis of the amount of milk secreted, may be deduced. Of 952 mothers examined as to their sanitary condition in the hospital, there were 629 strong and healthy or 66 per cent., and of this number 420 or 66·7 per cent. had abundance of milk to six months and upwards, some even to two years.*

The second class is that in which the women are affected with galactorrhœa or excessive flow of milk, they being themselves weak and unhealthy; and this class includes varieties—(a) where the lactation is abundant, and does not seem very sensibly to weaken the mothers; and (b) where the lactation being excessive, or it may be only moderately abundant, and yet does exhaust the patient; (c) where the milk escapes too readily from the breast.

In the first variety, the appearance of the breast may be the same as in healthy lactation. It is, however, usually large, and the veins are scarcely so

* Supply of breast-milk in 952 women.

	Actual Number.	Had abun. milk 6 mts. & up. some ev. to 2 yrs.	Had medium quantity of milk.	Had scant. quant. of milk, a few noue.
Strong and Healthy	629 or 66· per ct.	420	114	95
			209	
Proportion per cent.	100	66·7	18·1	15·
			34·8	
Delicate and Sick...	323 or 33·9 per ct.	88	69	166
			235	
Proportion per cent.	100	27·2	19·2	27·4
			46·6	
Total	952	508	183	261
			444	
Proportion per cent.	100	52·3	19·2	27·4
			46·6	

blue. The quantity of milk is excessive; but it is very watery in quality, and the child, although occasionally fat, has its flesh less firm, and is generally remarkably pallid. The women affected with this variety are generally women who have begun to bear late in life, and are usually of a weak or leuco-phlegmatic habit. In their appearance they do not materially depreciate. The quantity of milk is so speedily increased by a high regimen that they generally avoid it, and thus after a time the child becomes weak, and obnoxious to tubercular diseases, more particularly water on the brain, and is generally very excitable and liable to convulsions.

In the second variety, there is an excessive or moderately abundant flow of milk. The mother herself is the chief sufferer. All she takes seems to go to the formation of milk, which acts as a drain upon her system. Dyspeptic troubles soon creep in; the appetite is bad, food seems to disagree with her, and she becomes less able to supply the milk required. This secretion seems finally to be obtained from the very waste of her body. She becomes thinner and thinner, and weaker daily, till perhaps fainting fits supervene; gradually, there being no source from which the secretion of milk can be kept up, it ceases, and lactation becomes impossible. At this stage, the case is one of defective lactation, and symptoms present themselves which belong to the second variety of the third class, under which head it is best considered.

The remarkable circumstance is, that all this while the child often thrives well. The milk secreted has been comparatively good, and such mothers have often such heavy children that they have not the physical force to carry them. Serious functional, and sometimes organic, lesions, and diseases of the womb and chest are not uncommon in cases of this kind. In an able paper by Dr. Ashwell,* this has been well shown : still in these cases Dr. Ashwell lays down distinctly the proposition, that, "although lactation to be morbid need not be long, and that evil consequences may ensue occasionally after a few weeks of suckling, still these symptoms occur more frequently when the period is protracted beyond nine months"—(p. 60). This is so far a ground for comfort to a mother who is anxious to try her utmost (as I think it is always her duty to do) to suckle her child, and thus give it a better chance of life.

Drs. Merei and Whitehead have enabled us again, from their tables, to estimate the probable percentage of these women. " Out of 952 mothers examined as to their sanitary condition, 323 were delicate or sick, and of these 88, or 27·2 per cent.,

---

* *Guy's Hospital Reports*, v. 1840.

had abundant milk." The third variety of galactorrhœa, I have generally observed among weak
and delicate women, although it may be found
among the more healthy. The milk flows out-
wardly suddenly and in large quantities after
some emotion in which the child is concerned,
and especially if the child comes to the mother.
It flows so rapidly that the infant is well-nigh
choked as the milk comes into its mouth, and
overflows all round it, completely wetting the
mother. Usually between the periods when the
child takes it, the milk keeps oozing out. The
breast as it were, like an incompletely closed
tap, leaks. Upon the whole, the quantity of milk
secreted is below the normal standard, and such
cases are rather remarkable for the watery character of the fluid. The disease here is one of
weakness, analogous to that which occurs in weak
persons of both sexes in incontinence of other
secretions, and arises from a relaxed state of the
whole system, especially of the outward openings
of the lactiferous tubes.

The third class is defective lactation. The tables
of Drs. Merei and Whitehead above quoted, prove
that among healthy mothers, as we should naturally expect, only 16·5 per cent. will be affected
with defective lactation, whereas, among weak
and delicate women, the number will reach 46·6
per cent. But when we come to compare the

cases of defective lactation among themselves, as to the causes of the insufficient supply, the figures tell a different tale. I have here taken two tables of Drs. Merei and Whitehead from the First and Second Report (see below*); and these prove that the number of women affected with defective lactation, is unexpectedly large. The affection is, therefore, far more common than is generally supposed.

My experience is pretty nearly the same, although I cannot yet as satisfactorily reduce my results to figures as Drs. Merei and Whitehead have done. For convenience, however, I may speak of them more generally as follow :—

There are three varieties of defective lactation —1st. One arising from a state of hyperæmia, or from over-feeding. This is the rarest variety, and by far the most remediable. 2nd. One accompanied by a weakened or anæmic state of the body, contributing about 11 per cent. of the number of

*	First Report.	Second Report.	Total.
	p. c.	p. c.	p. c.
Mothers going out to work	32 or 24·9	152 or 29·7	181 or 28·7
Constitutional debility			
Suckling irregularly and immoderately	22 or 17·	132 or 25·8; 39 or 7·6 = or 33 4	193 or 10·
Illness or disease in mothers..			
Advanced age			
Destitution, want of sufficient or suitable food	19 or 14·7; .. = 52 or 10·2		71 or 11·0
Domestic troubles			
Natural scantiness of secretion, without obvious reason......	58 or 43·4	136 or 26·6	192 or 30·2
	129 or 100	511	640

cases.   This is improperly supposed to be the
most frequent variety, and it is among such examples that the effects of hyper-lactation, and
the termination of the second form of galactorrhœa, are most generally observed. The third
variety is by far the most common, amounting to about 30 per cent. It usually obtains
among middle-aged women, or those who have
married at a late period in life, or who may
be rather masculine in form and character. It
commonly happens in these cases that during
suckling periods the secretion of milk is never
properly established, or, if present, soon disappears. As in cases of obstinate constipation of
the bowels, so here, there is difficulty in secreting milk, although the body itself is well developed and the physical powers good. These
three varieties require separate notice and treatment.

1. *Defective lactation from hyperæmia or ple-
thora.*—This is a variety which I have chiefly
observed among *hired wet-nurses* selected from
the poorer classes, and admitted into wealthier
families. It is a peculiarity of many of our London poor, indeed of domestic servants generally,
that when obliged to support themselves, or put
upon board-wages, they live as it were upon the
smallest quantity of food possible; but when feeding at the expense of a master or mistress, the

amount they devour often surpasses all moderate imagination. They, in fact, gormandize. If in such instances a wet-nurse is given all she asks for, she will be found often to eat quite as much as any two men with large appetites; and as a result she becomes gross, turgid, often covered with blotches or pimples, and generally too plethoric to fulfil the duties of her position. The plethora, as first induced, is of the sthenic variety; but it soon assumes an asthenic character; and as the immediate result, the breast no longer secretes its quantum of milk. There may be good milk secreted, but it is in small quantity, and this quantity diminishes daily. The breast may also enlarge, but it is from a deposition of fatty tissue in and about it, as in other parts of the body. The veins on the surface become less apparent, always a bad feature in a suckling breast, till finally the flow of milk ceases altogether.

Defective secretion from anæmia, or privation, or exhaustion.—This, as I have before stated, is generally believed to be the most common variety. But this is a mistake. From the tables before quoted, it appears that in Manchester they constitute about 14·7 per cent. of all the cases accompanied with defective lactation. Drs. Merei and Whitehead have offered another table,* show-

---

* *Second Report*, p. 10.

ing that there was not that close relation between
a deficiency of milk secreted, and the degree of
comfort enjoyed or aliment taken by their patients;
so far as these could be measured by the amount
of their wages.* This insufficiency of milk, however, is here taken relatively to the infant; the
mothers, perhaps, might have had an abundant
supply, had they not separated themselves from
their infants during part of the day to attend to
their trades. But this circumstance, of course,
more frequently happens with those engaged in
the less lucrative trades.

The reason which has led probably to the belief
that these cases so frequently occur, as compared
with other varieties, is, that they are precisely
those which come most commonly under treatment. Thus, in Drs. Merei and Whitehead's
Reports, we find it stated, under the head of "suckling mothers' diseases," in the first year 43 cases;
30 of bronchitis, diarrhœa, etc., and 13 of anæmia
lactantium; in the second year, 53 cases, nearly
all of constitutional debility and deterioration of
milk from hyperlactation; and in the third year,
79 cases, more than 60 of which were affected
with anæmia lactantium; nor is it surprising that

	A full supply of breast-milk.	Medium breast-milk.	Insufficient breast-milk.
*			
Upwards of 18s. per week	120	60	122
Less than 18s. per week	122	72	112

such cases should be common among those examples of poverty which crowd our cities. Insufficiency of food must produce insufficiency of milk. The symptoms of this variety are well marked. The face of the patient betrays a haggard and starved look; it is remarkably pallid; the eyes are preternaturally bright, and with dark marks beneath them; there is breathlessness, with pains along the back; frequently copious leucorrhœa; and the patient generally complains of a sinking sensation at the epigastrium, and of exhaustion. It is extraordinary how, in some of these cases, the little children themselves keep up a remarkable amount of fat in their appearance; but in such cases, though not by any means in all, I have frequently traced the source of this *embonpoint* to the fact that those children were also fed artificially. The most fearful symptom, however, to which these women are liable is loss of sight, and frequently of memory; and in the lower orders, where the want of food, required to compensate for the drain which has been made, is got with so much difficulty, the recovery of the sight and of the mental integrity is a very long process, extending often over years. I know one case in which this recovery, notwithstanding a long-continued chalybeate treatment, with good food which was procured, failed to restore complete integrity as at first over a period of two years. Dr. Ashwell, in his paper before alluded to, on hyper-lactation, enumerates several examples of this re-sult; in addition, he shows that epilepsy, and even insanity, may result from women oversuckling their infants. I cannot say that my own experience confirms the occurrence of similar symptoms in women who, having an insufficiency of milk, have still persisted in nursing their children. I have seen many examples of weakness and anæmia to a marked degree, but none of these more severe results; and the reason is obvious: where de-fective secretion of milk first arises from debility, the complete suspension of the secretion will follow long before these mental and bodily symp-toms to any marked degree can occur.

3. The third variety is the most common. A natural scantiness of secretion, not due to want, occupation, constitutional debility, advanced age, etc., constitutes thirty per cent. at least of all cases. But I would include under this category many of those cases which occur in women of more mature age, probably included in the tables under the term "advanced age," but which cer-tainly cannot be fairly so designated. I would also include under this heading many of those cases of defective lactation produced by irregular suckling, and going out to work, because neither of these cases may be included under those of hyperæmia or anæmia.

CHAPTER II.

DISADVANTAGES TO A HEALTHY WOMAN IF SHE DOES NOT NURSE.
—SORE BREASTS — NIPPLES. — DEVELOPMENT OF CANCER, OR
OTHER UTERINE DISEASES.—A DISEASED OFFSPRING.

SHOULD a healthy woman suckle her children? This, and the disadvantages which are likely to result to herself if she does not, are what we have next to consider.

"La femme," says Burdach, "éprouve un sentiment voluptueux en têtant son enfant;" and naturally so. It is always delightful to perform a duty, how much more a maternal obligation! Is there a more delightful occupation for a mother than to watch the little babe hanging upon her breast, so helpless, and yet so fondling, nestling so closely to her, and feeding so contentedly upon her milk? Is there any means by which love can be more riveted between two beings in such intimate and close relation? "Can a woman forget her sucking child?" And when every day brings new pleasures, and ripens on both sides the mutual affection,—when the child thrives well, and, as if in tender gratitude, lies smiling upon the mother's lap, what a comfort, what a happiness for the mother! It is scarcely credible, yet a painful evidence of our fallen nature, that there are to be found those who can so far forget themselves, and their responsibility before God and man, as to transfer to others the performance of those duties, nay, who will even conceive them irksome, because for a time they interfere with their pleasures and gay occupations. Could the brute creation speak, they would cry " shame" upon such, and all nature united would re-echo the cry upon such egotistical and cruel parents.

But this is not all. The mother will not only suffer moral punishment: in this matter the chances are that she will find if she sows to the flesh, she has of the flesh reaped corruption. Not only may her own natural feelings and those of her offspring towards herself become blunted and callous, but she may also be the victim of immediate bodily suffering, perhaps ultimately of loathsome disease.

Painful distension of the breast, fever, and very painful abscesses may occur, which, by weakening the system, lay the foundation of exhaustive diseases, such as anæmia, indigestion, and even consumption. The less selfish mothers fare better. Young,* quoted by Ferris, gives the cases

---

* *De Lacte*, p. 7.

of 2,400 women in different lying-in hospitals; two only of such had milk sores : and Nelson, in his *Essay on the Government of Children*,* instances 4,400 cases, of which four only had milk sores, and "these had no nipples, or had had formerly sore breasts."† All these women suckled their own infants.

But it may be worse than this. It has been said that cancer is the ultimate result. Haller, Ferris, and Sir A. Cooper all adhere to this opinion. The late Dr. W. Hunter also believed that a very considerable proportion of those unfortunate women who are afflicted with cancer of the breasts are such as refuse to nurse their own children.

I am aware this opinion is not quite confirmed by recent inquirers. Mr. Birkett has favoured me with an analysis of 485 cases of cancer which he has made, and which have come under his personal observation. Of this number there were 389 married women, and only 96 single women.

This proves that the disease is more common among married women. Most of these belonged to that class of life in which the mothers usually suckle their own infants, so that it is difficult to show that the disease is mainly produced in those who suckle least. However, this opinion appears

---

* Page 52, in a *note*.   † Ferris *On Milk*, p. 12.

to be the most probable, from the observation of
the high authorities before quoted.   For it remains to be seen whether all Mr. Birkett's cases
not only suckled, but did so regularly and for a proper term.   It is known that at least twenty-eight
per cent. of these women usually go out to work,
and neglect to nurse their children properly.   The
question must, therefore, be still considered *sub
judice*.   Still, Haller's opinion is certainly more
in accordance with theory, if we compare the appearance and condition of those mothers who do
not nurse their children, with those who do.   The
former, as a rule, deteriorate in every way.   Their
nutrition is defective and perverted—a condition
highly favourable to the development of cancer.
On the other hand, suckling mothers acquire proportion, size, and health, a condition in which
cancer seldom if ever occurs.   The exceptions are
only found in those cases where either suckling is
carried on to excess, or where poverty and want
forbid the taking that quantum of food necessary
to the proper performance of this function.   Nothing tends so much to develope women as suckling.

But if there be any doubt as to the influence
of not suckling upon the production of cancer,
there is none whatever on its influence in the development of other disease of the womb often of
a very severe and painful kind, of long duration,

and it may be, incurable. Owing to the sympathy which exists between the breast and the womb, if the function of one of these organs be not properly fulfilled, the other is sure to suffer. The immediate effect of suckling is to cause the womb to contract. Hence the reason that sucking a breast when a woman is flooding often causes the flooding to cease by directly exciting the wished for contraction. When pregnancy has terminated, the volume of the womb is still large, and, unless it becomes lighter, it will by its weight have an increased tendency to fall out. This is particularly the case with a weakly patient, especially if she maintains the erect or semi-erect position too soon after her confinement —or walks out when still in a weakly state of health; and this is the common cause of prolapsus. Hence the need of the constant maintenance of a contracting influence upon the womb, to promote its absorption and diminution of size, and this is what suckling brings about gradually but effectively. The organ becomes reduced in volume, and finally acquires a healthy standard. But if this condition be not arrived at, then the womb remains large and heavy. Bearing down sensations, back-aches, and copious leucorrhœa result, due to inflammation of the lining membrane of the womb or endometritis, and congestion of the organ, and ulceration of the cervix, etc., with all

the painful consequences. Thus, for a moment
of selfishness, a life may be made miserable.
Another result is apt to follow if suckling is not
practised. Women will have children too rapidly
for their strength, and thus another cause of
endometritis is brought into operation.   Aran
believes that out of 100 cases of uterine disease,
at least 62 were due to abortion in pregnancy re-
curring too frequently.   Out of 100 other cases,
70 had not suckled their children. Scanzoni, moreover, attributes displacement backwards, or retro-
flection of the womb, to a similar cause. Fifty-four
women affected with this disease had 86 children,
only 57 of whom were suckled by their mothers.
In these, the volume of the uterus was not diminished by suction of the breast, and hence the
womb fell back by its own weight.*   In another
place, the same writer states that, out of 196
women affected with uterine flexions, only 56
had suckled their children. It would be difficult,
perhaps, to find for a woman a severer punishment than this last affection, if combined with
local inflammation.   It is not unusual to see her
ere long a confirmed invalid, and, what is worse,
years of suffering may be the result. In the mean-
while, matrimonial life becomes unbearable. She
can no longer attend to her duties. She has paid

* Scanzoni, p. 75.

a severe penalty for a selfish disregard to a law in nature, and she must esteem herself fortunate if cured after months, it may be years, of suffering.

But more than this. If a woman bears children too frequently and too rapidly, which is a likely occurrence if she does not suckle, or does so for too short a period, *disease* may be thereby generated in her offspring. According to Dr. Jenner (and my own experience is so far quite confirmatory of the opinion), frequent child-bearing is the common cause of *rickets* in the children that are born latest, and deformity in the child may be the result. But even if the extent of mischief done does not amount to rickets, the offspring will very probably prove diseased and weakly— and it is to be feared that the mother may not have the felicity of seeing her children attain the age of maturity. The laws of nature are irrevocable, and no woman can afford to maintain a code of her own, in defiance of them, with impunity.

CHAPTER III.

CAUSES AND TREATMENT OF GALACTORRHŒA.—CAUSES—A PECULIAR
TEMPERAMENT—A MENORRHAGIC TENDENCY — PATIENTS WHO
SUFFER FROM BREAST SYMPTOMS DURING THE CATAMENIA—
SUPPRESSION OF SOME HABITUAL EXCRETION—OVER-SUCKLING—
HYPERTROPHY OF BREASTS—TREATMENT: DIETETIC; MEDICINAL;
IODIDE OF POTASSIUM; BELLADONNA; COLCHICUM; IRON—OTHER
REMEDIES.

If it be undoubted that, in the case of a healthy
woman, it is her bounden duty and for her good,
that she should suckle her children, it must be
admitted that there is more room for hesitation
in the case of a woman affected with galactorrhœa
—but even in these cases much may be done, if not
entirely to cure our patient, yet to preclude the
arrest of wet-nursing altogether.

The causes of this variety have not been so
well studied, but a few may be mentioned—(a)
In the first place, a peculiar temperament—a pale
face, or, if not pale, a white skin, with almost
hectic flush—a sort of congestion of the cheeks,
which would rather give evidence of plethora or
overfulness of blood, but which, in fact, arises
from the very opposite influence, and a general
tendency to local determinations of blood to parts.

however, goes, I give very much the preference to *conger-eel soup*. It is not generally known, but I am told it forms the stock of turtle and many nourishing soups; and for this reason our French brethren, who have so much taste for "potages," import these eels in immense quantities from this country, and particularly from Jersey and Guernsey, where they abound. As a soup it is peculiarly nourishing, and very readily improves both the appetite and the strength. Like lentil powder, the stomach will often retain it when it will reject all other kinds of food. Mr. Jones, of Jersey, speaks highly of it, and gives a case in which when all other means had failed, it checked vomiting after chloroform. Its comparatively low price also renders it very easily obtainable by the poor.* Crabs, as a remedy for increasing the flow of milk, are of very old date. They are recommended by the author of *Gynæciorum*,† who also prescribes with the same object, a bluish coloured fish *(glauciscus)*, taken in its juice, and a variety of smelts *(smarides)*, taken with fennel sauce and boiled in milk.

Certain kinds of solid food and flesh have been

---

* Three pounds of conger eel and two calves feet, with two quarts of water. Boil gently until the first is reduced to rags, then strain, and add sweet herbs and asparagus or peas, a pint of milk, a piece of butter the size of a walnut, with a little flour to thicken. When used as a galactagogue, use fennel in lieu of sweet herbs, and haricot beans in lieu of the peas and asparagus.

† Page 634, A.

M

recommended by eminent authors, in preference to those commonly in use. Aetius enjoins the use of fine bread, the legs of swine, tender birds, and the flesh of kids. Indeed, swine's flesh is generally preferred to other kinds of flesh, and among these it probably claims the most favourable mention, after the varieties of fish already alluded to.*

Secondly, there are several vegetable aliments which act in a similarly favourable manner.

First among these stands *revalenta*, only another name for the ordinary *lentil powder;* but pea-soup and bean-soup have also a marked effect in improving the flow and richness of milk. The lentil and bean, however, are preferable to peas, where they are as easily procurable. Besides the better taste, the first is slightly aperient, and the latter does not produce flatus either in the mother or child, which peas are apt to provoke.

There can be no doubt that some of the culinary plants usually taken are preferable to others. Women popularly ascribe peculiar galactagogue properties to turnips ; and the Commission appointed to investigate the subject spoke very favourably of potatoes. To a certain extent I

---

* (From Galen.) Sunt autem hæ aves C. conia (swan) vespertalis, noctua apis, et quæ baccis junipero pascuntur, unde nominantur Germanis quam olifer turtorum genere adnumerant. . . . . Quam merito ejus ramenta jusculis adjiciuntur utpote saluberrimæ etiam puerperorum. See also Ægineta on some kinds of game.

think it must be admitted this popular belief is founded in truth. It is, however, among those numerous edible fungi which infest our pasture lands that those plants are to be found which are chiefly concerned in increasing this secretion. Their richness in nitrogenous matters may probably be the cause of this, as before stated. I must content myself with mentioning only one of these, the *Elaphomices granulatus,** or *Boletus (Lycoperdon cervinum)*, or deer balls, which if taken increase the milk. The question as to which of the varieties of mushrooms influence most favourably the secretion of milk, opens a wide field to further experiment and observation.

As to *drinks*, the greatest diversity of opinion prevails. When I come to speak of a kind of food administered to cows, I shall have to notice the effect which refuse slop from whisky distillers has in increasing the quantity of milk of cows to which it may be given. Upon the same principle it is that ale and porter have so high a reputation as milk generators. From Aetius downwards all authors recommended them, and there is no doubt of their efficacy with many nurses. Many of these will tell you that they cannot do without it. To stout, and double stout especially, the

---

* Redwood, p. 563.

preference is given, and in my own experience I have found the double stout of Barclay, Perkins, and Co. most efficacious in many cases. The use of such beverages, however, is frequently abused. Apoplectic tendencies of a slight character are induced : although I have never seen anything like the result which obtains in animals fed on the exciting food before alluded to. If the porter, however, be taken too copiously, it soon ceases to exert the same beneficial effect upon the breasts, the function of which becomes less active, till, at last, it is entirely suspended. What is true as a physiological law in other points, that continued excitement of the same kind exhausts nervous energy, is true also for the breasts. The exciting influence should vary in character as well as degree ; and in this manner the exhausting tendency is counteracted. Fortunately, we have in an analogous bland fluid—I allude to milk from the cow or goat—a liquid peculiarly adapted to produce milk readily in the suckling mother; and if in such cases the stout and milk are given alternately to the extent of two or three tumblers of the latter, to one of the former, or if they are drunk in combination (a beverage more agreeable to the taste than would appear to the imagination), a less exciting and more nourishing food and drink is thus provided for the mother, which will often enable her to perform with much ease to herself her maternal duties.

Another kind of drink which was much praised by the ancients is *sweet wine*. Aristotle, it is true, forbids it; Oribasius, Aetius, Avicenna, Paulus Ægineta, and a host of others, on the contrary, recommend it. My own experience, I must say, except in those cases where there exists such debility as to necessitate the employment of stimulants, is in this country against our ordinary wines; or spirits, indeed, of any kind. I do not say a wineglass or two may not be indulged in; but the habit does not increase the flow of milk.

Much more efficacious are some of those soups usually made, and which have been already alluded to.*

---

* Old recipe from *A Rich Storehouse in Treasury for the Diseased*. By A. T. London: 1596. 1. A very good medicine to increase milk in a woeman's breasts, ch. clii, p. 31 :—Take Fennel Rootes and Parsnepe Rootes, and let them be boiled in broth, which must be made of chickins. Then let the patient eat the same rootes with Fresh Butter, which must be new made, as possiblie it may be gotten, and this will cause great store of milke to encrease in any woeman's breastes. This hath been often proved. 20. Ch. 153. Take rice and seethe it in Cowe milk, and creeme some wheaten bread therein, it must be such as is cleane without rie, and put into the said mylke some Fennel seed, beaten into fine powder, and a little sugar, to make it sweet, and this is known to be exceedingly good. 30. Ch. 154, p. 31, b. Take a good quantity of greene wheate, which groweth between Michaelmas and Easter; you must take both of the blades and rootes, and stamp it very well, and straine it through a fine linen cloth into some posset ale, and put therein a little fine sugar, and this will encrease great store of mylke in woeman's breastes, within the space of three or four days. This hath been proved.

CHAPTER V.

TREATMENT OF DEFECTIVE LACTATION CONTINUED.
MEDICAL.

MEDICINAL TREATMENT.—REMEDIES :—LAVER—BORAGE—LETTUCE—SOW-THISTLE— ROCKET — CASTOR-OIL LEAVES—TAPIOCA—PARTRIDGE BERRY — CYTISUS—MILK-WEED—MALLOW—GITH—PULSATILLA—COMMON SALT — CRYSTAL—SAKEIK — FESIRE—IRON AND COD-LIVER OIL.

MEDICINAL TREATMENT.—I proceed to speak now of those medicinal remedies which have been recommended. Paulus Ægineta, in speaking of these, says, "That medicines for the formation of milk are possessed of some efficacy, I am well aware, and yet I do not recommend them in all cases, for they greatly waste the body." This opinion seems to have been very generally acted upon in modern times by those who were acquainted with such remedies; but the fact is, by far the majority of practitioners make no use of galactagogues, because they do not believe in their existence.

I think the consideration of these different remedies is best taken according to their natural orders. I should premise, however, by saying, that my experience is necessarily limited to a few of these only; I have not been able as yet to try all, nor even the majority; and from the difficulty of identifying plants spoken of by different authors of past centuries, with those under a different name in the present day, the experiments may in some cases have been conducted with the wrong plant. Again, preference has generally been given to those which were found most efficacious and most frequently named, and unmistakably defined by ancient as well as modern authors. All, however, I have met with, are here subjoined in a tabular form :—

1. *Algæ.*
Porphyra lacciniata, laver (Galen).

2. *Boraginaceæ.*
Echium vulgare, bugloss. Borago, borage.

3. *Caryophilleæ.*
Saponaria vaccaria, cow basil (Redwood).

4. *Compositæ.*
Lactuca sativa, lettuce ; sonchus arvensis, common sow-thistle.

5. *Cruciferæ.*
Eruca sativa, garden-rocket (English Phys. enlarged).

6. *Euphorbiaceæ.*
Ricinus communis, castor-oil plant; Jatropha curcas.
Janipha manihot, Tapioca, or cassova plant.

7. *Ericacæ.*
Gaultheria procumbens, winter green-box berry.

8. *Labiatæ.*
Ocymum (basilicum) ? Melissa asinos, basil thyme.

9. *Leguminosæ.*
Cytisum scoparium. Coronilla juncca (milch vetch). Cicer.

10. *Malvaceæ.*
Malva sylvestris, marsh mallow.

11. *Rosaceæ.*
Quinquefolium vulgare, or Potentilla, creeping cinquefoil.

12. *Ranunculaceæ.*
Nigella sativa, or melanthium (Gith); Anemone pratensis,
pulsatilla.

13. *Umbelliferæ.*
Pimpinella anisum, aniseed; Anethum fœniculum, fennel;
Anethum dulce, dill; Apium sativum, parsley; Daucus carota,
carrot. (Galen.)
Common salt, sarkeik, fesire, iron, and cod-liver oil.

Boraginaceæ.—Echium vulgare, viper's bugloss.
Flowers blue; July; biennial; found on sandy
and chalky soils. Roots opening, and said to be
slightly astringent. (Redford:) "The seed drunk
in wine procureth abundance of milk in women's
breasts."*

I have tried this remedy in the shape of a
strong infusion; but I could not trace in any of
the cases any effect as a galactagogue.

Borago Officinalis.—Common borage. Flowers
blue; June and July. Biennial. Borage and
bugloss. "The seeds and leaves are good to
increase milk in women's breasts."†

Of this plant I have no experience.

CARYOPHYLLEÆ.

Saponaria Vaccaria.—Cow basil, vaccaria. Seed
heating, diuretic; this plant is said to increase

---

* Culpepper's *English Phys.*, p. 368.
† *Ibid.*, p. 39.

lacteal secretion in cows fed upon it. (Redwood.) Galen speaks very favourably of it.

I have tried this remedy in a few cases only as a strong infusion, and I think I can speak favourably of its effects. In my hands the patients seem to have remarked that the quantity of milk produced under its employment was materially increased.

COMPOSITÆ.

Lactuca sativa.—There are many varieties. Has been substituted for opium to check diarrhœa; allays cough and diminishes rheumatic pains. Leaves refreshing, slightly anodyne, laxative, anaphrodisiac. The milk it yields constitutes, when inspissated, lettuce opium, or lactucarium. (Redwood.) "The juyce of lettice increaseth milk in nurses."*

I have no experience of this drug.

Sonchus Arvensis.—There are several varieties of this plant. The corn sow-thistle, sonchus ciliatus, or oleraceus, common sow-thistle; s. lævis, or smooth sow-thistle; s. asper, or prickly sow-thistle. In their effects they are described as possessing properties like those of lettuce. Culpepper speaks of the plant as follows:—"The

---

* Culpepper's *English Phys.*, p. 142.

decoction of the leaves and stalks causeth abundance of milk in nurses, and their children to be well coloured. It is good for those whose milk doth curdle in their breast."*

I have also used this remedy in a few cases, and in my results I should place it in the same category with saponaria, which it closely resembles in its action.

CRUCIFERÆ.

Eruca sativa.—Rocket. South of Europe; said to be antiscorbutic, diuretic, flatulent; seeds acrid, stimulant, exciting the stomach, and a good substitute for mustard. Culpepper speaks of it,— "The seed also taken in drink taketh away the ill scent from the armpits, increaseth milk in nurses, and wasteth the spleen."

Of this plant also I have no experience.

Avicenna states there are two varieties, one wild, and the other cultivated. When the seed is boiled into a decoction, and put, instead of mustard, as a poultice, it causes the milk to abound.

EUPHORBIACEÆ.

Ricinus communis, oil-bush, Palma Christi. Castor-oil plant. India. Seeds are purgative, yield oil by boiling and expression. Root in de-

---

* *Op. cit.*, p. 344.

coction diuretic; leaves with lard used externally as an emollient poultice.

The galactagogue properties of castor-oil leaves were known to the Spaniards of Peru and Chili. M. Frezier, Engineer in ordinary to the French king, in his narrative of a voyage to those parts, performed during the years 1712-13-14, stopped for some days at San Vincente, one of the Cape de Verde islands. In his description of that island he states, that among other plants he saw there the *palma Christi* or *ricinus Americanus*, by the Spaniards in Peru called *Poterilla;* and they affirm that the leaf of it applied to the breasts of the nurses brings milk into them, and applied to the loins draws it away.*

The employment of castor-oil leaves as a galactagogue in this country dates since 1850. In a paper read before the British Association, at Edinburgh, in 1850, and afterwards published in the *Lancet* of same year,† Dr. McWilliam brought the effects of this plant before the profession. " The leaves of this plant in Bonavista in the Cape de Verde Islands are known as the *bofareira,* which is in reality the ricinus communis of botanists, and occasionally the leaves of the Jatropha curcans, both belonging to the natural order of Euphorbiaceæ. Two kinds are known

---

* Dr. McWilliam's Letter, p. 488, vol. ii, 1850.
† Vol. ii, 1850, p. 294.

in these islands, the *red* and the *white*. They are both varieties of the same plant, but the red is avoided by the natives, the former being said to be galactagogue in its properties, the latter eminently emmenagogue. In cases of childbirth, where the appearance of the milk is delayed (a circumstance of not unfrequent occurrence in those islands), a decoction is made by boiling well a handful of the white bofareira in six or eight pints of spring water. The breasts are bathed with this decoction for fifteen or twenty minutes. Part of the boiled leaves are then thinly spread over the breast, and allowed to remain until all moisture has been removed from them by evaporation, and probably, in some measure, by absorption. This operation of fomenting with the decoction, and applying the leaves, is repeated at short intervals until the milk flows upon suction by the child, which it usually does in the course of a few hours. On occasions where milk is required to be produced in the breasts of women who have not given birth to or suckled a child for years, the mode of treatment adopted is as follows:—Two or three handfuls of the leaves of the ricinus are taken and treated as before. The decoction is poured, while yet boiling, into a large vessel, over which the woman sits, so as to receive the vapour over her thighs and generative organs, cloths being carefully tucked around her so as to prevent the escape of the steam. In this position she remains for ten or twelve minutes, or until the decoction cooling a little, she is enabled to bathe the parts with it, which she does for fifteen or twenty minutes more. The breasts are then similarly bathed, and gently rubbed with the hands; and the leaves are afterwards applied to them in the manner already described. These several operations are repeated three times during the first day; on the second day, the woman has her breasts bathed, the leaves applied, and the rubbing repeated three or four times. On the third day, the sitting over the steam, the rubbing, and the application of the leaves too, with the fomentation of the breasts, are again had recourse to. A child is now put to the nipple; and in the majority of instances, it finds an abundant supply of milk. In the event of milk not being secreted on the third day, the same treatment is continued for another day; and if then there still be want of success, the case is abandoned, as the person is supposed not to be susceptible to the influence of the bofareira.

Women with well-developed breasts are most easily affected by the bofareira. When the breasts are small and shrivelled the plant then is said to act more on the uterine system, bringing on the menses, if their period be distant, or causing their immoderate flow, if their advent be near."

Dr. McWilliam gives the cases of three women (occurring under the notice of Drs. Almuda, Sir George Miller, and Consul-General Rendall) in whose breasts milk was induced by the employment of the bofareira. In all these cases pregnancy had occurred some years previously.

Dr. Tyler Smith has made some experiments upon the use of this plant. He tried the effects of the leaves in five cases, in three of which it proved successful. In one it produced a copious flow of the catamenia, in another of leucorrhœa. From his experiments he believes that the castor-oil leaves, applied externally, have distinct galactagogue effects. He followed out in his experiments the description given and quoted above from Dr. McWilliam's paper, but did not apply the steam of the decoction to the generative organs; nor does he appear to have given it internally.*

I believe I am the first who has used castor-oil leaves and stalks internally as a decoction in this country. I was led to do so from having frequently observed that suckling women, after taking a dose of castor-oil, noticed that they secreted a larger quantity of milk—a result which I certainly cannot entirely attribute to the removal of accumulated fæcal matters; because I have not seen the same full effect from the use of other

* *London Journal of Medicine*, vol. ii, 1850, p. 951.

purgatives. Dr. Tyler Smith* alludes to this effect having been noticed by others, although, he adds, it may do this by moderating febrile excitement. It occurred to me, therefore, that in defective lactation, the exhibition of castor-oil leaves and stalks in a decoction might produce, or more directly cause a flow of milk. I have now given the remedy in several cases, and I must say I have not been disappointed. The flow has been remarkably increased. Four objections, against its use, however, should be mentioned. 1st. Some patients complain while taking it of a sensation in the eyes, not exactly amounting to pain, but accompanied with dimness of sight. I do not think this effect, however, is due to any peculiar effect of the castor-oil plant. I have only noticed this symptom in weak women; and I rather attribute it to the forced flow of the secretion, an effect exactly analogous to that which is observed in nurses who have suckled too long, when the child takes the breast. 2nd. A second is, that the dose after a time requires to be much increased, as the remedy appears to lose its effect. A temporary suspension, and the substitution of another galactagogue, remedies this inconvenience. 3rd. The third objection is a more serious one, but one which I hope in time will be remedied—

---

* *Ibid.* p. 954.

the difficulty of procuring the leaves or stalks in sufficient quantity. It appears that they are not imported into the country, and all those that can be obtained are produced in Botanical gardens. The larger number come from the gardens of Mr. Butler, of Covent-garden; but then the supply is but small. I have, however, found this remedy so important as a galactagogue, that I hope ere long it will either be imported or grown in larger quantities, so as to be used much more extensively.

The last objection applies to an occasional effect observed after its administration. The roots in decoction were before said to be diuretic. The leaves in decoction are occasionally so also. I have heard of two examples. In the one, so far as I could hear, a large quantity of water was daily passed under its influence, and it did not appear to produce any increase of the secretion of milk. In this case, however, I am not aware if the breasts were kept warm. If not, it is conceivable that an effect similar to that observed with diaphoretics should occur. These remedies, it is known, will not act as sudorifics if the surface of the skin is kept cool, but as diuretics. If an analogous explanation applies to galactagogues, it points out the importance of keeping the breasts very warm when the decoction of castor-oil leaves is given internally. Moreover, we are led to this mode of management by noting the manner in which the remedy is employed in Bonavista. Hot fomentations of the leaves are there always applied locally to the breast. Where this diuretic effect is produced, it is well therefore to smear the extract of the leaves over the breast in the same manner as belladonna extract is sometimes used, with a warm ordinary poultice outside it, and this combination will probably fulfil all the indications in the treatment. In the second case, both the secretion of the kidney and the milk were much increased, and to such an extent as to make it obligatory, for the sake of the patient's strength, to discontinue it. I am not aware (as both of these cases occurred in the practice of others) whether hot fomentations were also applied to the breasts. The breasts as a rule should always be kept warm, when this remedy is given; and when the diuretic effect is produced, not only kept warm with poultices, but well smeared over with the extract.

When the castor-oil leaves are given as an infusion to women *who are not suckling,* I have observed two effects, both of which seem to denote its specific action. First, it produces internal pain in the breasts, which lasts for three or four days. Then, secondly, a copious leuchorrhœal discharge takes place, after which the effect on the breasts entirely disappears. During the existence of the pain at the breast I make no doubt that if a child

had been applied, the suction would have determined the lacteal secretion. This, however, is an
experiment to which I have never found a patient
willing to submit herself, and so have not been
able to prove it.*

In two instances only have I seen anything
like emmenagogue effects upon women. One
was a hospital case, in which intense uterine congestion existed, and in which, with a view of
deriving to the breasts,'I administered the remedy.
In this case, after giving the *liquor* for two or
three days in ℥ij doses, an attack of menorrhagia
supervened. I may say that the patient had been
labouring under uterine disease for years. The
menorrhagia soon ceased after the remedy was
suspended. My friend, Mr. Robinson, of Devonshire Street, had another case in which he gave
the remedy. Mrs. E. M., æt. 31, was confined Oct.
2nd, 1862, after eighteen hours labour, of a moderately sized female child, healthy, etc., and without
any unusual symptoms. At the end of two weeks,
finding there was but very slight flow of milk,
after regulating the bowels and using a mode-

---

* Avicenna mentions a particular plant, under the name of
Albetaflores palmarium, or Albata, which causes the secretion of
milk when taken to be much increased. Is this the Palma Christi?
It is also spoken of by him as Bussura, *i. e.* (Palma) Besser and
Beda, which he has not further described, because, he adds, "they
are well known." It appears to have been a plant in his time in
very common use.

This remedy is prepared and sold by Mr. Greenish, 20, New
Street, Dorset Square, W.

rately generous diet, I prescribed for her ℥i of
the liquor palmæ christi three times a day. The
fourth day after taking it she complained of bear-
ing-down pains in the womb, loins, and thighs,
and very considerable hæmorrhage. The remedy
was therefore suspended, a slight aperient was
given, and the symptoms subsided in three or
four days. The remedy was now again given,
and the hæmorrhage again recurred. It was now
attributed to the palma christi, and astringents
with sedatives substituted with good effect. At
the end of another eight days, the palma christi
was again given, but only twice a day; but in
three days I was again obliged to suspend its use
for the same symptom. The patient ultimately
got well on *tinctura ferri sesquichloridi.*

These cases prove that the remedy should not
be given in cases where there is disease or irritation of the womb. In a class of .cases of an
opposite character, chlorosis and anæmia, in both
of which there was a wish to provoke the cata-
menial flow, the remedy failed altogether. Except pains in the breast, as before stated, and an
occasional leucorrhœal flow, these were the only
symptoms observed. Nothing like a sanguineous
discharge was ever noticed.

The following, however, may be taken as a
good typical example of the mode in which the
liquor palmæ christi usually acts in ordinary cases:

A lady had seven children. For the fifth she had so little milk that she was obliged to give the child up entirely to a wet-nurse. With all the others, however, the milk had disappeared after the second month, and generally the quantity of milk secreted was very small. She was recommended to take the liquor palmæ christi. It was soon found to act specifically on her mammæ. If she missed a dose or two there was a sensible decrease in the quantity of milk secreted. By its continued employment, however, in doses of a dessert spoonful three times a day the quantity of milk needed was maintained. She had suckled her present child for the last eleven months, and had all along continued to have a sufficient supply for it.

Another plant, belonging to the order Euphorbiaceæ, is the *Janopha Manihot*, the *Tapioca* or *Cassava* plant. I extract the following account of it from Livingstone*—

" There are two varieties of the Manioc or Cassava, one sweet and wholesome, the other bitter and somewhat poisonous. The latter is more speedy in its growth than the former. Very little labour is required for its cultivation. The earth is thrown up into oblong beds about three feet wide and one foot high, in which pieces of the manioc stalk

---

* Page 207 and 286.

are planted at intervals of four feet. In from ten to fifteen months the roots are fit for food, but there is no necessity for raising them at once, as the roots do not become dry and bitter till three years. When the roots are taken up, a piece or two of the upper stalks are replaced in the hole and a new crop is thereby begun. The plant grows to a height of six feet. In a dry soil it takes two years to come to perfection, requiring during that time one weeding only. It bears draughts well and never shrivels up under it as other plants do. When planted, however, in low alluvial soils and well watered, it will come to perfection in twelve or even ten months. Every part of the plant is eatable, even the leaves may be cooked as a vegetable. When the bitter plant is used, the people get rid of the poison by steeping the root four days in water, when it becomes partially decomposed. It is then stripped of its skin, dried in the sun, and pounded into fine white meal, closely resembling starch. This meal is mixed with as much boiling water as it will absorb, and in this state forms the ordinary porridge of the country. It is, however, both unsatisfying and unsavoury; no matter how much a man may eat, two hours after he is as hungry as ever, while in point of flavour I can only compare it to starch made of diseased potatoes. The well-known substance tapioca, is extracted from the plant by pouring water over the grated root, and this disengages the starch from it, which subsides, and is then dried over a slow fire, the mass being kept in motion during the process and thus forming itself into globules with which we are familiar. It is the staple article of food in Africa, and is sold at the rate of 10 lbs. for 1d. throughout the interior of Angola.

" The leaves of this plant are given to milching goats, and their milk is thereby much increased. This, like the palma christi, is another plant the leaves which should be imported to enable us to judge of its galactagogue effects."

Of the various plants which succeed in my list, except those mentioned among the *umbelliferæ*, I have no experience. One only I have tried, the *cytisus;* but my trials have been so limited that I cannot speak of its effects at present. I shall content myself, therefore, with their mere enumeration, and the properties they are alleged to possess.

ERICACEÆ.

Gaultheria procumbens. — Winter green box berry, chequer berry, partridge berry, mountain tea, North America. Leaves, Galtheria, Ph. United States, used for tea. Fruit contains an aromatic, sweet, highly pungent volatile oil, which is antispasmodic and diuretic; a tincture has been useful in diarrhœa. Coxe states that the infusion is useful in asthma. It is used in North America as tea. The brandy in which the fruit has been steeped is taken in small quantities, in the same way as common bitters. It has been employed as an emmenagogue, and with the view of increasing the secretion of milk; but its chief use is to impart an agreeable flavour to mixtures and other infusions. It is employed as an infusion, and also in the form of an oil, which is more used in regular practice than the leaves. Instances are on record of deaths resulting from the use of the oil by mistake in the dose of one ounce. On examination after death, there were strong evidences of gastritis.

LABIATÆ.

Ocyminus.—There are several varieties. Album, Toolsie tea, dried leaves used as a substitute for tea. Juice in one-drachm doses given for colds. O. Basilicum, Basilicum; sweet basil, strong scented, emmenagogue, gives the peculiar flavour to Fetter-lane sausages. According to Anstie, assuages childbirth pains. O. Cavum, sudorific, anti-gonorrhœal. O. Cuspum, anti-rheumatic remedy, etc.

It is probably the O. Basilicum, which has been by some believed to be the basil spoken of as a galactagogue.

Avicenna speaks of this plant as the Bedareng, which is known as well as its oil to be the beneficial ingredient of oil of marjoram. Its water and leaves increase the secretion of milk.

Mellissa Acinos.—Syn. acinos vulgaris, basil thyme, and mellissa chenopodium, wild basil; supposed also by some to be the basil meant by older authors as a galactagogue.

LEGUMINOSÆ.

Cytisus.—A large number of ancient authors speak of this remedy as an effective galactagogue. I do not find the variety, however, further specified. " A decoction of the young tops of cytisus scoparius is said to be diuretic and cathartic, even to animals who browse upon them. The flowers and seeds, used as a pickle for table, are cathartic, and are sometimes roasted as coffee. C. Laburnum, seed and bark poisonous, narcotic, acrid, leaves diuretic, resolvent."*

Johann Nardius speaks of the cytisus as a galactagogue, if given in the food of animals. The remedy, indeed, is as old as Hippocrates.

I have used the cytisus scoparius once or twice. I cannot say I have noticed galactagogue results.

It is not impossible, however, that the cytisus that is here meant is in reality altogether a different plant from the cytisus we now know. The

---

* Redwood.

following passage from Aetius Tetrabiblos* seems to favour this view :—

" Tythymalli and those medicines that are called galactides, or galactagogues."

"*Halimon sive Halmyris.*—Some eat the seeds of the fruit of halimon, and having cooked them serve them. The plant gives strength to milk and to the seminal secretion. A drachm of the root drank out of water, quiets convulsions, and tormina, and both attracts and increases milk." The dictionaries give the following meaning to halimon :—"*Halimon i.* n. ἅλιμον ; some kind of *marine fruit:* ab ἅλιμος maritimus."† " Et *cytisus* necatur eo, quod *halimon* vocant Græcii. Alii *halimon* (lege halimon) olus maritimum esse dixere soldum, et unde nomen ἅλμιρος, salsus, genus nitri."

It may be that some kind of sargossum or sea laver—perhaps the *ulva lactuca, sea lettuce, or lettuce green laver,* both edible varieties of sea-weed—is meant. It is remarkable, too, that the author of Gynæciorum enumerates among his recipes to increase the secretion of milk—" Lac vaccinium bibat ; aqua salsa valida vel marinæ fomenta et post vino calido."‡

Avicenna has likewise alluded to this plant

---

* Page 71. † Plin. l. 17, c. 24, ad fini ex Theophrast. Hist.
Plant. l. 4, c. 24. ‡ Page 78.

under the name of "*Melha*." "This," he states, "is the *halimus* which resembles *hauserigi;* its leaves, like olive leaves only wider, are eaten as vegetables. The expressed juice causes milk to abound."

Coronilla Juncia.—Syn. polygala vera. Milk vetch. This herb in decoction increases milk.

I believe this is the same plant which is known and sought for in London by many suckling mothers—indeed it is kept for that purpose by herbalists. It is usually obtained from Gravesend, and known more popularly as the *milk weed.* I have used it largely, and I must also speak very favourably of it. Second only to castor-oil, and of about the same efficacy as the fennel, it is more readily available for most persons. I have also used the leaves of this remedy as a decoction, and have found it very efficacious. I have not tried the roots or the seeds. Probably the medicinal effects of these parts of the plant would be even more marked, and in winter they would be more readily procurable than the fresh leaves.

Cicer Arutinum has been said by some to exert a galactagogue effect. "The seeds are heavy, but wholesome, and may be roasted for coffee, farina resolvent." .

MALVACEÆ.

Malva sylvestris. — This plant, so commonly

known, marsh mallow, is stated by Culpepper to be a galactagogue. " The leaves boiled, used by nurses, procureth them abundance of milk."* This effect, I presume, is due to its nutrient qualities, rather than to any peculiar medicinal effect.

Avicenna speaks of a variety of *Malva* as a galactagogue under the name of *cubeze*, " which is a wild kind of malva, as the *muluchia* is a domestic variety. Cubeze, he adds, is a species which is known as the muluchia *arbaca;* and this is the *althœa*, popularly the *Jewish vegetable*, not the *luxinquum*, which is a different species, and is *red*. The leaves and flowers make the milk to abound."

ROSACEÆ.

Quinquefolium Vulgaris, or *potentilla reptans.* Creeping cinquefoil, five-leaved grass, said to be a galactagogue.

RANUNCULACEÆ.

Nigella sativa.—Gith, fennel flowers, devil in a bush. Nigella arvensis, or melanthium sylvestra. Seeds acrid, oily, attenuant, used as a spice. Paulus Ægineta recommends sweet gith as a galactagogue.

---

* *Op. cit.* p. 150.

Anemone Pratensis. — Pulsatilla. This plant has been recommended by Avicenna.

UMBELLIFERÆ.

Five plants in this order are commonly recommended: — the *Pimpinella Anisum; Anethum Fœniculum*, or fennel; *Anethum Dulce*, or *Graveolens*, dill; *Apium Sativum*, or parsley; and *Daucus Carota.*

All these plants are too well known to require description. All older authors, from Hippocrates downwards, speak of them. The *fennel* (marathron of the Greeks), indeed, seems to be the staple ingredient of most of the remedies employed to promote secretion of milk. Ægineta recommends the root and fruit of the fennel boiled in ptisan. Aetius recommends the leaves of the *dill*. Ægineta also directs that the fruit of the *carrot* should be given in such cases. My experience of these several plants has been confined, in a medicinal point of view, to the fennel. I have used rather extensively the infusion of fennel seeds, and of all those plants which I have tried, I consider it as second only to the *ricinus*. It is remarkable how materially it increases the flow of milk in those who take it, sensibly producing the draught in many women who have been strangers to this sensation to any extent for weeks. In one respect it differs, not producing the same amount of dimness of sight which the castor-oil leaves do ; at least patients have not complained to me of this effect when taking it. The appearance of the children has been also particularly good under its influence.

There are two other specific galactagogues, which must here be alluded to. One is *common salt*. The other is a substance spoken of by authors of the last century as *chrystal*.

Common salt.—We are pretty well aware of the effects of common salt upon the body in proper quantities : one of the most important of these, according to Liebig and Boussingault, is to improve the glossy and smooth appearance of the coats of animals. Nardius, in his *Analysis of Milk*,* has the following remarks on it :— "Albertus says that insular cattle are larger because of the saltness of their pastures ; the salt, moreover, having a quieting (taming) effect upon them, so that they yield an abundance of milk. Whence it happens, that in seaside places, where cattle feed on salt pasturages, they are more prolific ; their flesh is more tender ; their milk more abundant, and richer in cheese. The learned Mercurialis, it is true, controverts this opinion ; but still he admits that a moderate use of salt does increase milk." Moreover he adds, " that

---

* *Op. cit.*

sheep will fatten upon salt drinks; and that, for this reason, it is customary to give to them, every fifth day, salt, in the proportion of about 200 pints for every 100 sheep." So also the poet testifies:—" Let the lover of milk bring frequently to the managers of his cows, cytisus, lotus, and salt herbs. These last they love best, and the effect will be to swell out their breasts. Moreover, having partaken of these they will drink more, and so a larger flow of milk will be provoked."*

The last substance to be mentioned is *Chrystall*, differently spelt as *Christal* or *Crystall*. I find this substance used in several receipts of old farmers and numerous works of the last century, and then much in vogue as a galactagogue. " Take crystall, and beat it into fine powder, and mingle it with as much fennel-seed, likewise beaten in fine powder, and a little fine sugar. Let the woman use to drink hereof somewhat warm, with a little white wine, and this will cause great store of milk to increase in her breasts : yea, it will restore her milk again, though it be clean gone from her."† Whether, from what has been premised on common salt, it may be supposed Rock Crystal is meant, I do not know. In some of the old

---

* Nardius, *Analysis de Lacte*, p. 153. Collection of Pamphlets, 1650-1652, Brit. Mus.: *Rich Storehouse Treas. for the Diseased.* By A. T. 1596, chap. 155, pp. 31-36. † *Ibid.*

medical dictionaries, the *crystallus* is further designated as "crystallus mineralis, potassæ nitras fusus sulphuris paucillo mixtus." Also, as " sal prunellæ." Nicholson, in his *Dictionary of Chemistry*, describes the Crystal Mineral as follows :—" In the ancient dispensatories we find a formula for making a salt of this name, by fusing nitre, projecting a little sulphur thereon, and afterwards casting it into little cakes."* On this supposition, nitre would possess properties not at present attributed to it. I have not, however, with the view of testing this surmise, tried the remedy.

Two other plants, used as galactagogues by the Arabians, are mentioned by Avicenna,—*Sakeik* and *Fesire*.

" *Sakeik*, called *Sakaik* (alnaman), is a rose, vehemently red. If its flowers and stalks are boiled with decoction of barley and eaten, they make the milk to abound.

" *Fesire* is the *hezargiesum* or *hezar chasen*, otherwise the *vitis alba*. The juice of this drunk with a decoction of wheat insures the flow of milk."

I cannot close the category of medicines to be given to a suckling woman without referring to two other remedies in more common vogue—*iron*

---

* Nicholson's *Dictionary of Chemistry*, 1808.

and cod-liver oil. I have already shown that in reference to the first of these many learned writers* have asserted that iron often exerts a repressive influence upon the lacteal secretion, and facts apparently in confirmation of this opinion, chiefly occurring when patients take chalybeate waters, have been given. However, I have explained this error at page 127, and that these effects are rather due to ill-timed administration, or to the preparation of iron given. Any remedy which will be likely to induce constriction generally of the system, we should expect would be à *priori* detrimental. Besides, if we look to the appearance of a woman who has long nursed, and may be said to be exhausted by the process, we shall notice some well-marked symptoms which indicate at once the remedies to be employed: general pallor, amounting often to anæmia, debility, languor, copious leucorrhœa, pain in the back, headache, increased by the erect and relieved by the recumbent position, and general emaciation. All these symptoms are clearly those of want of red globules in the blood, and precisely those which experience proves most readily subside under the exhibition of iron. Few having to treat such a case would hesitate to give it. The use of iron here, if given *pari passu* with the

---

* *Bull. de Thérap.*, Dec. p. 554, *Med. Times and Gaz.*, January 23, 1858, p. 96.

nursing, would have prevented, or at any rate delayed, the occurrence of exhaustive disease. So also the emaciation is often painfully remarkable after nursing. In milch cows (as I have before said)* it is this very emaciation which deteriorates the value of the animal so much after two or three months, as to make it a losing concern for a farmer to keep a milch cow at all. Among milch cows, it is only by giving highly combustible food (oil cake) that this result is obviated. Why not apply the same rule to the human female? It is with the intention of fulfilling this indication that I have given cod-liver oil. Of the preparations of iron I usually give the iodide, especially when there is any strumous disposition to contend against, or the syrup of the superphosphate, which from the excess of phosphoric acid, so important to both mother and child, is peculiarly applicable; sometimes, where there is excess of acid, or gastrodynia present, the sesquioxide or carbonate—the more astringent preparations I entirely discard. In addition, I give a teaspoonful dose of cod-liver oil twice a day after breakfast and dinner. Indeed, the usefulness of these two remedies, as ascertained by observation in cases where intense debility and anæmic symptoms with emaciation were wont always to make

---

* Page 149.

their appearance from the third to the seventh month of suckling, cannot be doubted.

Having on subsequent pregnancies attended such cases, and given them during their suckling periods both iron and cod-liver oil, beginning as early as the sixth week after delivery, and sometimes even earlier, and continuing the remedies up to the period of weaning, I have been gratified on finding at the end of that period that these distressing symptoms of debility and emaciation never recurred: on the contrary, the patients were unimpaired in health, strength, and looks, and the children were far stronger and larger than those which preceded them. Perhaps it is the dread of physic and a disregard to the artificial life women lead in towns, which are in great measure the causes of the common prevalence of symptoms of hyper-lactation.

As a *resumé* of the foregoing remarks, it may be concluded that defective lactation is in many cases a curable affection; and that under proper treatment the mother may be enabled to fulfil her maternal duties, not only without injury to herself, but with great advantage to her offspring. These results, if fully carried out by future experiment—which may be looked for with great interest, and I must also say, with full confidence —are of great importance.

CHAPTER VI.

CIRCUMSTANCES UNDER WHICH A MOTHER SHOULD NOT SUCKLE.—
SPECIFIC DISEASE IN THE MOTHER—WHEN THE MOTHER'S MILK
DISAGREES—WHEN THE MOTHER CAN ONLY SUCKLE WITH ONE
BREAST—WHEN THE MILK IN BOTH BREASTS IS DISEASED—IN
EXHAUSTION FROM HYPERLACTATION—SORE NIPPLES.

FROM what has been said it will be gathered that, in many cases, a mother may be so treated by hygienic, dietetic, and medicinal means as to be put into a condition favourable to suckle her infant. But if she cannot do so entirely, she may be assisted by artificial food, judiciously selected and given to the child. The principles of alimentation in such cases, *i. e.*, the rules which should guide us in bringing up a child by hand, either entirely or when it depends in some measure upon a small quantity of breast-milk from its mother, belongs to the third part of this work. We have now to consider under what circumstances a mother should not suckle her infant.

A specific disease in the mother.—It is stated that where disease of the parent exists, such as *scrofula,* to an unusual degree, *consumption, mania, cancer, syphilis,* and other dangerous here-

ditary diseases, it is not wise to let a child derive
its nourishment from this source of contamination.   I am bound to admit the full force of this
objection, which is doubtless valid in the greater
number of cases.

Consumption is so prevalent a disease, and one
so likely to be increased by oversuckling, that
for the mother's sake it is well not to allow
her to suckle to the same extent as a healthy
mother, both for her own and for the child's
good.   Yet even in such cases we must not
lose sight of the healthy influence of suckling,
to which I referred (at p. 104) ; and if it be
her own child a mother has to suckle, it may
after all be better to let her do so if it be done
within reasonable limits, and especially if she
be assisted by artificial food also given to the
child.

To a maniacal patient, or one likely to have a
violent paroxysm, no one would think of trusting
a child.   But too little attention is perhaps paid
to the existence of cancer in a family, as a draw-
back to a mother suckling her child.   In the year
1860, 2,100 men and 4,857 women died of this
disease in England, and the malady seems on the
increase.   The proportion of deaths from cancer
to deaths from all other specified diseases was, in
1860, 1·3 per cent. In 1841 it was only ·8 per cent.,
showing a very material increase, which bears no

proportion to the increase of population. In *scrofula* and *syphilis,* perhaps (both of which diseases are often very amenable to treatment), the objection to suckling does not always hold. The mother must be treated, and the remedies which cure her will equally cure the child. This is especially true in the case of the syphilitic taint; for it should also be remembered that in putting such a child to a wet-nurse, we must of necessity also contaminate her, and she will in a little while be scarcely in a better condition than the parent herself. The case of scrofula is precisely one of those in which the child, in addition to the breast-milk it receives from its mother, can be also artificially but judiciously fed, and the mother, thus enabled to rally in her own health, because the drain upon her is diminished, can be so cared for as to produce, if not a large quantity, at least a sufficiency, of good milk for her infant.

Evidence that the mother's milk does not agree with a child.—In some cases the milk of the mother disagrees with the child. It may produce diarrhœa, insomnia, it may be convulsions. This is more especially the case in very impressionable women. In some, as we have seen before, it will produce death. In the Vienna puerperal fever, the death of the child was often the first indication that the mother was about to sicken with the fever. But commonly, other unhappy effects, although fortunately very short of those before-mentioned, will be produced. We have seen in Drs. Merei and Whitehead's tables that 24 per cent. of the children who received abundant breast-milk alone, to 15, 18, and even 14 months, were badly developed, and did not thrive well; as many as 23·3 per cent. having only a medium development.

No doubt, therefore, if it be clearly shown that the mother's milk disagrees, this is a legitimate reason for not allowing her to suckle her child; but this conclusion must not be arrived at hastily, for even here treatment sometimes will effect a good deal. Change of air, change of food on the part of the mother, wine, some artificial food, or medicine to the child, will often prove beneficial; a week or two of perseverance and attention in these respects will frequently remove all source of irritation. Those cases, I must say, which have resisted such measures, have occurred either in a very early or a very late period of nursing. In the former instances, the simple substitution of a wet-nurse seldom suffices alone. So much treatment is required besides, that it is often a difficult question to determine how much is due to treatment, and how much to the wet-nurse. Still, I must admit, that in a few cases the salutary effect of the change is very obvious. In later periods of suckling, *i. e.*, after eight months, weaning often proves as effective as the adoption of another wet-nurse.

3. Where a mother can only nurse with one breast, either because the nipple in one is defective, or from one breast having been the seat of abscess, some have maintained that the mother is wiser not to suckle her own child. This, I believe, is altogether an error. The one breast which remains healthy performs all the duty, and the amount secreted is fully equal to the requirements of the child. Sometimes, without known cause, a child refuses to take the breast of one side. The mother frets, and is unhappy, imagines it to be perverseness in the infant, and probably fears an abscess in the neglected breast. Only the last of these contingencies requires attention, and will, no doubt, if treated upon the principles before laid down when speaking of galactorrhœa, p. 125, soon pass away. The mother should not fret. Let the secretion of the full breast be drawn by a pump, or by some kind Samaritan, and after a few days, if the child be applied, it will often take it readily. It sometimes occurs that there is a peculiar taste in the milk of one side as compared with the other, which explains the dislike on the part of the infant. Dr. Hartman instances a case where this anomalous lactation occurred.

" An infant, whose mother was in good health

and had borne several children, exhibited a healthy appearance for the first five weeks after its birth. The alvine evacuations then became copious, fluid, and discoloured, and the child lost flesh and strength. After the usual remedies had been vainly administered for a fortnight, the mother remarked that the child did not take the right breast willingly, and so much did the unwillingness increase, that at length the mere application of the nipple to the infant's lips occasioned loud crying. On examination, it was found that the milk of the right breast had a distinctly *salt* taste, whereas the milk of the opposite breast was of the ordinary sweetness; no difference of consistence or colour was discoverable. From that time the child was only allowed to suck the left breast, and in a few days all diarrhœa and sickliness of appearance vanished. It is not a little singular that while the mammary secretion was thus unnatural, the health of the mother remained unimpaired."*

4th. Sometimes the milk is diseased not only in one, but in both breasts. The nature of this disease has been ably ventilated in a paper on "Saccharine fermentation in milk within the breast of the mother," by Dr. Gibb, from which I here epitomize.†

---

* *British and Foreign Medical Review*, vol. xii, p. 432.
† *Archives of Medicine*, vol. ii, No. 3, 1861; Ranking's *Half-Yearly Abstract*, vol. xxxiv. p. 254.

Vogel announced the discovery of *vibriones*, a species of animalcule, in human milk, in 1850. These he clearly proved were developed within the mammary gland itself. He believed it to be due to fermentation in the milk, by general congestion and increased heat in the breasts, connected with general excitement of the sexual system. This view was disproved, because the milk was neutral, not acid, and it was argued that the fermentation evolving lactic acid would immediately destroy these infusoria. Dr. Gibb's attention was first called to this disease, from the circumstance of an infant, aged 7 weeks, being brought to him in an extreme state of emaciation, although the mother herself was the very *belle idéale* of a healthy nurse. The child had been healthy and plump at birth, but was now never satisfied with its mother's milk, and was ravenous, though spoon-fed besides. In other respects, no active disease, such as diarrhœa, diuresis, or diaphoresis, could be found about it to account for the atrophy present. The mother's milk was therefore examined. It had a specific gravity 1032, was rich in cream, and neutral, with a large quantity of sugar. So far it seemed normal. Examined, however, microscopically, seven hours after withdrawal, it revealed myriads of living animalculæ, *vibriones baculi*—or, as Dr. Gibb terms them, *v. lactis*. The next day the milk was examined the moment after being drawn. The vibriones were found as before. The breasts were free from congestion and heat, but there was much sexual excitement. From subsequent inquiries, Dr. Gibb has found that in the milk of females, we occasionally find two genera of animalculæ. These occur in women whose general health is disordered from various causes during lactation; where there has been immoderate suckling; or lastly, where there has been but a very small quantity of milk secreted, quite insufficient for the requirements of the child.

In some persons in whom, at an early period of lactation, the supply of milk was abundant and rich, and where the constitutional symptoms were similar to those mentioned, the two varieties of animalculæ have been found, but not in the same individual. These creatures consisted, first, of the true *vibrio lactis*, resembling little red, minute hair-shaped bodies, similar to those found in some of the other fluids of the body; and, secondly, of *monads*, which he finds to be far more frequent and common than vibriones, their diameter varying in different specimens of milk, from the three-thousandth to the five-thousandth part of an inch. The production of these creatures is due to a saccharine fermentation in the sugar, which then becomes a fit nidus for their development; the amount of lactic acid so formed, not being at first in sufficient quantity to overcome the neutrality of the milk. This kind of milk, however, after exposure, becomes môre rapidly sour than healthy milk.

In the case first quoted by Dr. Gibb, the child ultimately did well. It was not weaned at once, but gradually; being fed judiciously for a time, while taking a diminished quantity of its mother's milk.

I cannot believe that this disease is altogether accidental. I have not seen, nor have I heard of it, among the upper classes. It is rather to be looked for among the poorer classes, and especially among those who are remarkable for want of cleanliness in their persons. We may expect to find such individuals generally unhealthy looking, and badly nourished, in many respects, resembling that class of persons who have worms, or are liable to scabies or other epizootic diseases,—*i.e.* where there is a deficient vitality, or peculiar idiosyncrasy.

Not admitting for one moment the dogma of spontaneous generation, I believe that the ova of these creatures must be obtained from without. Among the lower orders it is not unusual to find the nipples in the reverse of a cleanly state, particularly as the prejudice obtains among many that it is dangerous, and favours inflammation or abscess in the breast of a suckling woman to wash it. These parasites once breeding externally, their passage upwards into the lactiferous tubes is an easy matter, as in other animal cavities. This suggestion, and probable explanation, directs to the treatment. The breast, and the nipple especially, should be washed frequently with luke-warm water and soap, and as often as the child has sucked so often should the ablution be repeated. If, after several trials, the animalculæ do not diminish in number, the child should then be gradually separated from its mother, and judiciously fed. In this manner a cure will soon be effected.

5th. In some women the deficiency of milk resists all measures : such cases are happily but few in number. If, however, after repeated attempts we cannot provoke flow of milk, this is a circumstance which justifies the mother in not persisting to act as a wet-nurse.

6th. The same conclusion applies in the case of women who are utterly exhausted by oversuckling. If, in these cases, want of good food is also combined, as is the case with many poor women, it is hardly possible to conceive how they can continue to suckle. In a few, where it can be given, the attempt may be made to assist the child by artificial food as well; but in every case where the exhaustion does not exist to a marked degree, and where the mother is comparatively healthy, but only weak, I hold it very wrong to prevent her from fulfilling to the utmost that is compatible with her state, her maternal functions. How long she is to persist, and how she is to be assisted, must depend upon the decision of her medical attendant.

7th. The last circumstance to which I shall allude under this head, and which has been urged as a reason for not allowing a woman to suckle her child is the presence of sore nipples. In this affection, there is fissure of the nipple, similar to that which occurs in another part of the body. In some cases the pain becomes so acute as to amount to actual agony—against which the powers of forbearance of even the most devoted mother must succumb.

In mild cases, to wash over the part with gum, will often suffice. In my own practice, however, the ordinary Friar's balsam has appeared to exert the most salutary influence. It can be applied readily by means of a camel's-hair brush three or four times a day, and infants do not seem to dislike the taste of this drug, as that of solutions of caustic or tannin, which are sometimes applied. Occasionally, however, in more severe cases even after this application, the child's mouth, especially if the child be a strong one, cannot be tolerated. Here a glass-shield and artificial nipple must be used, and the infant must suck from the latter. In the employment of this, however, some precaution is oftentimes necessary. The glass should fit the nipple as exactly as possible, and should especially not be too deep. Otherwise if the mother's nipple be (by the suction made on the artificial nipple) pulled upwards too far, the fissures are again put on the stretch, and the effect is equally painful. It must needs, also, be made gradually and by some kind Samaritan, before the child is applied. Once the cavity of the shield and artificial nipple is filled with milk, the child may be allowed to suck, and he will often be able to do so with but little discomfort to the mother. Again, the shield and artificial teat may be filled with warm water, a little sweetened, and applied in this state to the mother's nipple before the child is allowed to suck. In very bad cases, again, it is well to use belladonna, as before stated, p. 125, to the breast, to facilitate the flow of milk. The same precautions being observed in regard to the nipple as before insisted, to prevent poisonous results.

The chief and the best course in such cases to pursue is the preventive. Many women, previous to attaining the age of twenty-five, have only the conical-shaped virgin breast, and the nipple is not sufficiently drawn out to admit of its prehension by a child, particularly during the first days of life, when its powers of suction are not strongly developed. Hence much annoyance is sure to occur to the mother during the very early period of lactation. If suction, temporarily, by an older child be practised, or if pumps be used, the nipple is very likely to become fissured, and then ere long suckling will be so painful a process as to be greatly dreaded. But those nipples may be and should be *prepared* for their function. For two months or so prior to delivery they ought to be carefully sponged over night and morning with some astringent lotion, such as oak-bark, or spirit such as eau de Cologne, to overcome the delicacy of the skin. The nipple should also be brought out by the use of the breast-shields. Of these, four kinds are made: wood, gutta-percha, glass, or metal. The two last are to be preferred. In one case, I saw the ordinary glasses for leaking nipples used with the greatest advantage: the nipples being brought out very readily by them. This was a lady who had had the greatest difficulty to suckle her child, and then could do so from one breast only, owing to the manner in which the nipple of the other breast was drawn in. Using the glasses before spoken of, she was able to suckle her second child with the greatest comfort from both breasts.

CHAPTER VII.

REASONS WHICH INFLUENCE SELECTION OF A WET-NURSE FROM
AMONG FALLEN WOMEN—BENEVOLENT AND SELFISH.—DIFFICUL-
TIES OF SELECTION—INJURIOUS INFLUENCE ON A HOUSEHOLD—
IT IS AN INCENTIVE TO CRIME—WORKHOUSE EXPERIENCE—IT IS
AN ENCOURAGEMENT TO INFANTICIDE.—RETURNS.—MR. ACTON.—
REGISTRAR-GENERAL.—DANGER FROM SUBSTITUTION OF A WET-
NURSE FOR THE CHILD'S MOTHER—DANGER FROM NURSE'S MIS-
CONDUCT.

WE pass on now to those cases where it is imperative to employ a wet-nurse. It is usual in
our profession to select a fallen woman. Now
let us well consider—

First, *The reasons which induce the selection of
a wet-nurse from this class.*—These may fairly be
included under two heads: *benevolent* motives
towards the hired wet-nurse; and *selfish* considera-
tions of personal advantage to the hirer. Among
those who are actuated by the first feeling we
find many. In our profession it is one which has
been strongly, yet I think unwisely, urged by a
high medical authority; and there are not want-
ing other members of the profession who side
with him.

A fallen woman, it is urged, is, as it were, an outcast of society, shunned by the virtuous, and if sometimes courted by the vicious, it is only to urge her more greedily into crime. She is generally attractive. Her attractions have been her snare; and the vanity which has caused her to fall once, and the difficulty of curbing strong passions once roused, make her an easier prey. Surround such a person by a virtuous family, let benevolence be shown to her, let her recover a respect for herself, and in the kindly attentions received, and those she tenders to the child she now suckles, and under the happy influence of religion, you may stop her downward course—you may arrest the tendency to a repetition of the offence—you may preserve a useful member to society, and thus save her from ruin. These I admit are powerful motives, the more to be regarded because purely unselfish; and wherever the woman has fallen but once, been perhaps deceived by a too confiding disposition, and hitherto has borne an irreproachable character, their full force cannot be denied. But such cases are few and far between. The end, in the greater number will, I fear, seldom be found to have justified the means.

But, in many instances, the principle which rules those who select from among this class of wet-nurses is more purely selfish. With many

P

it is that lower wages will be required; or that from her isolated position, if she comes, she is more likely to remain than a married woman. Her love for her child is the only attraction which will take her away; and it is known that after a time, so strong is the affection of a woman for the child she suckles, that her love for this last will in time exceed that which she bears to her own child, and so she will cling to the foster-child and forget her own. Again, there are no conjugal affections or domestic duties at her own house to draw her away. A fallen woman who is obliged to seek employment as a wet-nurse is generally abandoned by her seducer, and so, if she be selected, and suits, she will be more likely to remain. I pass over the unnatural act (if not a moral crime) thus committed, in leading away a woman to forget her own offspring, which the Creator intended she should love and nourish.

Secondly. *There are great difficulties in the selection of a fallen woman* as a wet-nurse. It is believed that a diseased woman will produce diseased milk, and that if the disease be hereditary, it will as certainly be communicated to the child suckled, as if the wet-nurse herself were the child's mother. Hence, in the selection of a nurse we avoid *syphilitic, phthisical, cancerous, epileptic, weak women,* as well as those in whose parents insanity or any other mental eccentricities exist, or have existed. Unfortunately, however, the history of these cases, at least in London, is almost *always obtained from the applicant herself.* Now it is manifest that an adept in such cases (particularly if the disease is only latent) may deceive any medical man. He asks if she has had syphilis. She denies it. Yet she may have uterine syphilis, so well described by Mr. Langston Parker. Delicacy forbids a more complete investigation. Moreover, external examination in most of these cases is limited to the breast, which may, even in a case of uterine syphilis, appear quite healthy. To prove that this is not merely a theoretical opinion, but one founded on fact, I will relate a case :—

A woman became a patient of mine. She represented herself as married. I found out subsequently that she was single. She denied having ever had syphilis. Atrophy came on in her infant, and a very suspicious roseolar eruption around the thighs. I demanded an examination, and found an indurated uterus and a specific ulcer within the os, extending towards the external os uteri. The child died; but there can be no doubt that had I not trusted her, and had she been properly examined, and that at an early period, the child's life might have been saved. But fallen women may also deceive you in a host of other

ways.   A common deception relates to the age of
their milk.

On one occasion, when I was seeking for a
wet-nurse, a woman presented herself to me ;
she had, she said, been confined three months,
was married, and had had two children before.
The milk appeared good, and I selected her.   It
turned out she was unmarried, had not had a
child for a twelvemonth, and to keep the infant
now in her charge quiet, drugged it.   Another
woman, who had just been delivered, stated she
had only been seduced some ten months back.
I found out she had cohabited with a *roué* for
two years, and had had two miscarriages previously, and so on.   These examples are sugges-
tive, and prove how small is the dependence that
can be placed in the class of women we are
alluding to ; and if they are deceitful as to *present*
faults, why should we trust them as to their antecedents, and immunity from disease acquired in
earlier life ?

Thirdly. *The influence of a wet-nurse upon a
household* is another reason why a fallen woman
should not be selected.   If it may be operative
for good sometimes in reclaiming her, it may, if
the woman be a bad character at heart, be operative also for evil on the mistress, the master, but
particularly on the other servants, especially so if
in the principles of any there are sympathizing

dispositions. These women often "speak unad-
visedly with their lips," and have frequently
doubtful peculiarities.

As to the effect upon a mistress of a household
in a country where the purity of our wives is
unimpeachable, and their virtue proverbial, the
tendency to corruption by conversation with such
women is fortunately very rare, and I believe seldom, if ever, occurs. To dwell on this point is
therefore unnecessary. Still all will admit that
too frequent association and companionship of
the better classes, even with virtuous domestic
servants, is nearly always prejudicial. A lover
of low company in our ranks of life is soon regarded as an interloper in better company, and
one to be avoided. Let us also bear in mind
that the intimacy of a mistress with her child's
wet-nurse is of no ordinary kind. It is close,
and for the time, constant. It is fostered, in
great measure (at least in the beginning), by the
maternal love which overflows with gratitude
when she beholds her once weakly child thriving
upon the milk of the hired wet-nurse. Such
alliances (more dangerous where the nurse is the
only nursery attendant, as in the case of newly-
married couples with small means) are, to say the
least, an unfortunate contingency. And surely,
if it be right to prevent our wives from visiting
ladies of doubtful reputation, it cannot be right

to admit fallen women to their intimacy, and this in their very houses. If it be true that " ce n'est que le premier pas qui coûte," surely it is better to avoid taking it.

The same reasons apply, although less forcibly, when we come to speak of the masters of households. Not to allude to those endless petty annoyances which so commonly arise in connection with hired wet-nurses of this class, it may suffice to remark that the records of medicine, the annals of our Divorce Courts, and the history of the social evil, prove that married men are not exempt from error in this direction.

But, it is chiefly amongst the women-servants in an establishment,—those who in their station are on equality with the wet-nurse,—that the danger is greatest. In the *Dublin Quarterly* there is a review of Dr. Stranger's book.* From this review I epitomize the following sad story. It is the case of an honest, hard-working, but poor servant, attracted by the splendour of a passing courtesan on horseback. She is sad, not, alas ! at beholding a fallen creature, but because she compares her own comparative poverty, and unassuming garments, and hard toil, with the courtesan's gay habiliments and luxurious mode of life. Gently chided by her mistress, who has

---

* On the *History of Prostitution in New York*.

also been a silent spectator of the scene, she acknowledges her error with tears. Yet in a year or two that misguided girl has launched into a similar course of vice in New York. A little while longer she is placed prematurely on her death-bed. One look has sufficed to tempt her from the right path ! !

But the wet-nurse, in her favoured position, is a daily and more lasting picture. Covetous people there are, and not a few have strong passions. " What a difference of wages ! what superior food is given to her ! She rides in the carriage as a lady visitor. She is more considered than any other servant in the establishment. What prevents my doing likewise ?" True religion and innate modesty will triumph, it is true, over these whisperings of the Evil one ; but all have not these, and ours is the guilt in putting the stumbling-block before them.

I trust I am not misunderstood. I make these observations entirely believing that the worst effects produced are only of very exceptional occurrence. I know that nowhere in this world is the purity of the domestic home so great as in these realms. But it is because faithfulness and virtue are so estimated among English women, and because vices such as those alluded to are held aloof from and reprobated ; because, as yet, no looseness of morals, as on some parts of the

Continent, is tolerated in good society, that I speak. I would pity, I would relieve, and I would let the good and strong-minded of both sexes do their best to reclaim these poor fallen sisters, nay, I would bless them for doing so; but let it be done by seeking for them other employment less dangerous and objectionable, and not in employing them as wet-nurses, and familiarizing our households with the spectacle of vice rewarded.

Fourthly. What holds for the household applies equally to the community. *It is an incentive to crime.* If fallen women are preferred to married, if we give better wages to them than to other virtuous female servants, if we pass over their fault lightly, and allow them to occupy a superior position in households, we may rest assured we are only adding fuel to fire ; we are favouring the passions of the frail sisterhood; and by giving lucrative employment to some who may be willing victims, we are encouraging the base seducer in his course of infamy. Already some of the advertisements in our daily papers, where women hold out their shame to a premium, prove that it is an incentive even now in full operation.

Let us take, as a confirmation of this point, the following return from our workhouses, extracted from the *Times* of June 11, 1862 :—

" FEMALE ADULT PAUPERS.—Yesterday morning the following curious return was issued of the female adult paupers in the workhouses of the several unions and parishes of England and Wales, classified according to character :—Single women pregnant with their first child, 569; single women who have had one child, 2,847; single women who have had one child and are pregnant again, 292; single women who have had two children, 1,711; single women who have had three children, 877; single women who have had four or more children, 782; idiotic or weak-minded single women with one or more children, 470: total, 7,548. Women whose out-relief has been taken off on account of miscon- duct, 327; women incapable, from syphilis, of getting their own living, 543; prostitutes, 790; girls who have been out at service, but do not keep their places on account of misconduct, 383; girls brought up in the workhouse, and who have been out at service, but have returned on account of misconduct, 373; widows who have had one or more illegitimate children during their widow- hood, 680; married women with husbands in the workhouse, 1,698; married women with husbands transported or in gaol, 258; married women de- serted by their husbands, 2,131; imbecile, idiotic, or weak-minded women and girls, 5,160; re- spectable women and girls incapable of getting their living on account of illness or other bodily de- fect or infirmity, 5,300; respectable able-bodied women and girls, 2,267; respectable aged women, 11,615: total, 39,073."

From this table, if we include the widows of immoral character, we have as many as 8,220 women of bad character, or 21 per cent. of the whole number, or nearly one-fourth of all our female paupers. Is this not retribution? and has it not arisen from our not sufficiently discouraging immorality?

Fifthly. But we are doing worse. *We are, perhaps, encouraging murder, at least, authorizing the death of the nurse's child.* Upon this point let us hear Dr. Bachhoffner. He is reported to have spoken before a meeting of the Vestry of St. Marylebone as follows:—

" He had already said, that of 1,109 illegitimate children born in the rectory district, 820 had been born in that house; and of that number there had been 516 deaths of illegitimate children registered during the same period, or 46 per cent. In St. Mary's district there had been registered 592. In this district Queen Charlotte's Hospital was situated. The number of deaths had been 109 children, or 18 per cent. In All Souls district, out of 145 illegitimate children born, there had been 87 deaths, or 53 per cent. Out of the 592 illegitimate children, nearly 400 had been born in Queen Charlotte's Hospital. In Christchurch the case was worse: of 223 births of illegitimate children, there had been in the same period 209 deaths, or 93·7 per cent., up to the age of 3 years. In St. John's, out of 140 births there had been 129 deaths, or 87 per cent. These last two were the " dry-nursing districts ;" and speaking from 16 years experience as district registrar, it was a remarkable fact, that usually within three or four weeks of the registration of the birth they were called upon to register the death of the same children, the cause being mesenteric disease, diarrhœa, inanition, and other diseases resulting from the mode of feeding and deficient attention to the children. In the Cavendish Square district (a moral district), there were 40 births and 36 deaths, or 96 per cent., the worst of the whole.*   But when we speak of stillborn children, returned as such, the case may even be more horrible."

It is known that in some parts of the immoral community of this professedly Christian land, the mere existence of burial clubs proves a sufficient inducement to heartless parents to sacrifice, by poison or otherwise, their infant children, whom perhaps they have known for a few years and actually loved. It is manifest that when an infant is in the way it may as easily, and perhaps more easily, be got rid of by neglect as by more direct measures.   For *stillborn* is often only another

* *Lancet*, vol. ii, p. 415-16, 1859.

word for *infanticide*, since so many infants are returned under that title to avoid registration. " Who is there (as the *Lancet* remarks in a leading article for Oct. 22), that having any experience of the society in which we live, will not ask with a shudder, what security our laws or our administration provide against the concealment of *infanticide* under the word *stillborn* ? How do we know that these illegitimate children have died without foul play ?"

In a letter from Mr. Costen he writes me, that " in the St. Pancras Infirmary out of 200, which is the average number of women confined there yearly, about 174, or 87 per cent. of these are unmarried, including prostitutes suffering from syphilis and its effects, servants, etc.; 8 per cent. of the children are stillborn ; 5 per cent. die before they are one month old." Now the usual number of stillborn in a population is much less. From Dr. Barne's London Maternity Reports we find, that the normal proportion of stillborn births, out of 10,561 labours, was 308, or only 2·9 per cent. Now why this disparity ?

As the women leave the workhouse after the month, no further details as to these children could be supplied to me by Mr. Costen. Several of the more healthy women go out as wet-nurses, but their children do not remain in the Infirmary. In fine, all vital statisticians—Burdach,

Farr, Quêtelet—agree as to this greater mortality among illegitimate children. *Want of experience* and *dry* nursing will explain part of this mortality, but to be accurate we must put down a large figure to infanticide. It was the opinion of Mr. Wakley, the late coroner for Middlesex, that at least two hundred infanticides in London annually escape detection. If so, why hold out greater incentive to the crime ?

Mr. Acton, however, should be heard upon this point also. He gives us a table of deaths of children under one year of age returned as having occurred in England and Wales in 1856 from violent causes.

Injury at birth	104
Poison not distinguishable	7
Opium	13
Laudanum	40
Godfrey's Cordial	19
Drowned	16
„ found	48
Strangled	14
Suffocated	223
„ by food	8
„ by bedclothes	206
„ overlaid	69
Murder	5
Manslaughter	2
Accident	6
Injury	14
Infanticide	52
	846

Now note here Mr. Acton's remarks : " It is a frightful list ; no less than 846 babies are recorded officially as hanged, strangled, poisoned, suffocated, and so forth, during the year 1856. The great majority of these *we are justified in assuming were the illegitimate offsprings of first falls in virtue.*" Is it possible? and yet we can recommend those who may be murderesses as wet-nurses in virtuous families!

I am not inclined to go the whole length with Mr. Acton: yet infanticide has a fearful reality in this country. Here, again, let us quote the *Times* :—

"INFANTICIDE IN LONDON.—Infancy in London has to creep into life in the midst of foes. We hear often of the impoverished or poisoned air of close alleys and rooms unfit for habitation, and now the coroners have just told us in their official returns that 67 infants under two years of age were murdered last year in the metropolis. 150 more were 'found dead,' a large proportion of them left exposed in the streets; how many of these were 'persuaded not to live' must remain a secret till the disclosure of all secrets. Of above 50 others we learn that they either lost their lives through the misconduct of those who should have tended them, or that their deaths are attributable, wholly or in part, to neglect, want, cold, or ex-posure; the mother of one was only $13\frac{1}{2}$ years old. More than 250 infants were suffocated, very generally in bed, and in upwards of half these cases there was no evidence how the suffocation was caused, or the juries did not state in their verdict that it was accidental. 1,104 deaths of infants in London in 1861, under two years old were such as to demand a coroner's inquest upon them. The age is the same as in the massacre which Christendom annually remembers, but the size of this great metropolis causes it to out-Herod Herod."

The Registrar General's returns for 1860, already quoted,* tell the same tale in another way.

Taking deaths from poison, suffocation, and homicide, there died 1678 persons, but of these 1030 or 61·5 per cent. were under 1 year old, and on all ages under 5, 1156 or 68·8 per cent.

It is well to note in this return that the majority of children that die, are precisely those who need wet-nursing. For the ages 1 and 2, etc., the numbers are only 54·28. Why this great difference? Has hiring wet-nurses not a good deal to do with it?

In justice, however, to Mr. Acton I should say, that he believes it is because these women, so long as they are burdened with their children, cannot find employment, that infanticide among them is so common ; that if they were more generally employed as wet-nurses the crime would no longer occur so frequently, because the motive for

---

* See Appendix A.

it would be removed. This is, however, a mere gratuitous assumption. Have they not all the employment *according to the demand* in the way which can be given to them already? Are not they, as a class, already employed and recommended by all the faculty? unless, indeed, it is wished to oblige our wives not to suckle our children, purposely to give these women greater opportunities of employment. But suppose we did, and the infanticides did not occur so frequently, (which position, however, remains to be proved,) if a woman is abandoned enough to commit infanticide what other crime will she not be ready to commit so soon as a temptation sufficiently powerful occurs? and if so, where is the security in confiding our children to such women? I believe but few of these frail sisters are bad enough to commit infanticide. Those that are, are criminals, and dangerous in more ways than one. They must be dealt with as such, and not put in positions of trust. The larger majority of them, if their antecedents are known to be good, may be employed, but not as wet-nurses. It is not lawful to do evil in order that good may come.

Sixthly. There are dangers to the foster-child itself, which may be classed under three heads. The first applies even to the best of wet-nurses, viz., that the mere substitution of a wet-nurse for the mother of the child increases the chance of its death. The second, to the inexperience of all women with their first children. The third, to the great fear of misconduct of many of these fallen women.

1. *The mere substitution of a hired wet-nurse increases the mortality.* This point has already been referred to (p. 30), and I therefore need not do more than mention it here.

2. *There is danger from the wet-nurse's inexperience.* It may be urged, that when we are quite certain that a woman has fallen but once, and that she has previously borne a good character, and that her antecedents are well known, the objections above made do not apply, particularly if full medical examination be made before the engagement. True; but then with delicate children— and these are generally the class which require suckling by a hired wet-nurse—it is important that the nurse should have *experience* in the management of children. Women who have fallen for the first time, in most instances, have *none.* Nothing can be more amusing than to see a man, who is quite ignorant and unaccustomed to children, take up a child and nurse it. But among women a novice is equally uncomfortable to look at, and the result, unfortunately, is far more sad to the infant. I remember meeting an example which made a great impression upon me. A lady

Q

was very ill, and the child had to be taken away from her and from the care of the monthly nurse. It was given into the charge of a married woman, but who had herself had no children, and was therefore inexperienced. The child began to droop, and became ill and thin to a degree. The moment, however, the monthly nurse was able to resume her attention to it, the circumstances of food, lodging, clothing, etc., being the same, the child began to thrive, and eventually did very well. A woman upon her *first fall* is not likely to understand the management of children, unless she has been a nurse before—a rare exception. If employed at all, she must be as carefully looked after as the child, by the mother, or by another nurse. It may be urged in reply, that the same objection applies to the employment of a married woman with her first child, and the objection is a valid one; but then the fallen woman is selected because she is a first transgressor, the married woman should be chosen among mothers of many children. Indeed, all who have had much to do with delicate infants must be conscious how exceedingly important it is to have a good nurse, and one who understands children well. It is by far the most important element in bringing up a child.

3. *There is danger from misconduct on the part of the wet-nurse herself.* There are some faults

which women of this class are especially liable to commit. One is *drugging*, the other is *starving*, an infant. A great number of women do not like to lose a good place, and they have often so little morality, that sooner than lose their situations, or in the hope of keeping them as long as possible, they will not hesitate to sacrifice the life of the child. I will cite a case. I engaged a wet-nurse for a child about six weeks old. The woman's milk was, from her account, about six weeks older. The breasts appeared full; the milk itself was rich in milk globules, and answered to the usual tests—it was pronounced good. I subsequently found that this woman had had two illegitimate children, and that she had very little milk. The deceit practised by her when she appeared for examination before me was similar to that adopted by dealers with the cows they wish to sell, *i. e.* not milking them for some twenty-four hours before sale, so that the udders shall appear full. To keep the child easy it was regularly drugged with some opiate after the breast had been given. The parents were deceived; milk upon which the baby slept so well was supposed to suit it. The child, however, began and continued to lose flesh, till in fact it was reduced to so great a state of weakness that it became questionable whether it could live many minutes. The nurse was changed, and after some time it did recover, but with difficulty.

Here is another instance. A gentleman selected, under medical advice, a fallen woman as a wet-nurse for his weakly child. After some days she disappeared. He set off to seek the fugitive, and found she had gone back to the man with whom she had formerly cohabited. However, as her milk agreed well with what had been before a weakly child, he prevailed upon her to come back. Some months afterwards he found out that every night she used to spend her time with the cabmen of a stand in the neighbourhood.

A more common fault is illustrated by the following case. I engaged a wet-nurse, also a fallen woman. The milk suited in every way at first. Subsequently the child did not seem to thrive. It was always crying, although pacified when put to the breast, but apparently never satisfied. I examined the milk frequently, microscopically and chemically. I always found it good, nay, even unusually rich; but I soon discovered it was insufficient in quantity. This was detected by offering the child food immediately after it had been suckled, and finding that it partook of it with avidity. Had this not been found out the child would have died of starvation. These are only a few of the tricks practised by wet-nurses selected because of their want of morality. But there are various accidents of a similar nature likely to occur when infants are given into the charge of women without principle.

But, again, as a justification of their employment, it has been averred that, first, many married women are quite as bad. Secondly, it is said that many of these fallen women are persons of good constitution, and of favourable age and previous excellent character; and it is conceived that if proper care be taken to select those *free from disease*, in the great majority of instances they would be found very suitable wet-nurses, and very good domestic servants.

Upon the first of these points I am not ready to cavil. It is sometimes a true proposition, but then their shame is not openly and unblushingly proclaimed; the example offered, is not the same glaring encouragement of vice; the evil is not prominently displayed. Still, if we know a married woman to be vicious, who could recommend her engagement? The possibility of doing harm by employing a married woman is no reason for doing more harm by engaging a fallen woman.

Secondly. It is all very well to talk of fallen women being excellent characters, save and except in the one sin by which they fell. This may be true for small towns and country places, where everybody's antecedents are known. It is only true for London and very large towns as an exception. For how are wet-nurses procured? They are generally wanted in a hurry; application is made at a lying-in hospital, and the matron kindly furnishes the names of several, one of whom is usually selected. But these are not generally women whose antecedents she knows. They are persons who apply to her for a wet-nurse's situation, and whom she recommends in consideration of a small fee, because the age of the milk suits. But she is very often deceived. Some of these women are found on subsequent inquiry to have fallen more than once (p. 213), and to have had much experience in evil ways, although they may not have been upon the streets. Many of these have at one time or other of their lives suffered from those syphilitic diseases peculiar to their class. A few may have contracted habits of swearing, intoxication, and dishonesty; and there are some who, if the occasion again offered and proved remunerative, would gladly revert to their bad habits. What dependence could any one have on such a woman that she would care properly for a child? It is true that sometimes even the most degraded may be restrained in their vicious course by strong affection for the little innocents that hang upon their breasts; and the power of religion can even soften the heart of the most depraved creature upon earth. But to hold out a premium for crime upon the bare chance of such a conversion, is fraught with the greatest danger, and is only, after all, doing evil *palpably*, in order that good may come out of it *possibly*.   Except, therefore, in a case of *extreme necessity*, and where the life of the child can only be saved by employing a wet-nurse, and where none other can be found but a fallen woman, I hold it is a gross moral and social wrong to employ such a woman as a wet-nurse.

I would not, however, in regard to this unfortunate class, wish my words to be misconstrued. Woman is to me always an object of interest ; and, even in her most degraded state, she is an object for christian pity and reformation.   Many are rather sinned against than sinning—the victims of villains who have deceived their too confiding love.   If we are assured of this ; if the woman be one of a class not previously depraved, the peculiar circumstances of the case may be taken into account, and it may be allowable to select her as a wet-nurse ; and then if she is carefully watched while attending to the child, and her own child is also well looked after, we are giving that woman an opportunity of gaining an honest livelihood, and once more reclaiming a lost position in society.   But I know from experience, that where you have to do with a woman of bad character (particularly if she has been confirmed in her vicious habits—if she be a harlot in taste and habit), do what you will, you cannot obtain from her reliable information, either as to her own antecedents or those of her family, or as to any peculiar taint with which she may have become infected: and thus you may be doing irretrievable injury to the little babe which you require her to suckle.

It is not likely that a woman who has obtained her livelihood by the sacrifice of every principle of virtue will hesitate to assert the most deliberate falsehoods, when by so doing she will obtain a remunerative occupation, and one which may place her (albeit nominally a servant of a wealthy establishment), in the highest possible position to which a woman in her station of life can hope to attain. If this be so, it only points out the immense importance of selecting a wet-nurse who shall be as healthy in *mind* as she is in *body*. If, therefore, fallen women are to be employed as nurses at all, let them do the menial work in large hospitals or prisons, under proper kind surveillance; but a virtuous household is not their proper domicile.

A curious point here presents itself for inquiry, —Are mental peculiarities of a good or bad kind transmitted through the milk of a wet-nurse, as well as bodily infirmities? This is an all-important inquiry. As it borders, however, on the metaphysical, and is extremely difficult or doubtful of proof, I think it wise not to discuss it here.

CHAPTER VIII.

THE PHYSICAL QUALIFICATIONS OF A WET-NURSE TO BE SELECTED —1. SHOULD HAVE GOOD MILK : CHARACTERS OF GOOD HUMAN MILK—2. HEREDITARY PREDISPOSITION GOOD—3. AGE NOT TO EXCEED 30.—4. NEAR THE AGE OF MILK OF MOTHER—5. MELAN-CHOLIC TEMPERAMENT—6. MILK IN SUFFICIENT QUANTITY.

THERE may be a state of health present in the mother which renders the selection of a wet-nurse essential. If she is weak or pale, or hysterical to a degree ; if there be copious leucorrhœa, but par-ticularly if there be headache and a sensation of sinking at the epigastrium, or if the sight become impaired,—the mother should desist. This de-fect in the sight will become blindness if the nursing is prolonged,—a blindness often per-sistent, and the least curable. Moreover, as shown by Drs. Merei and Whitehead, such milk is not only injurious to the child at the time, but does not contain sufficient nutriment for its pro-per development. As such, it is noxious. Then, again, the child's mother may be dead. Or, lastly, the child, after an abortive attempt to bring it up by hand has been made, is in a state of dangerous atrophy, diarrhœa, etc. In such a case there must be a change; and we may have to select a wet-nurse. In this choice we must have due regard, lest we injure the child to be nursed, to her physical as well as mental qualifications.

To the latter, however, I do not here recur. But in reference to the former, I believe that to make a judicious selection is one of the greatest difficulties which a medical man has to encounter, because so very much depends upon the person chosen.

The physical qualifications of a wet-nurse may be summed up under the following heads :—

1. She should have good milk.

2. Her hereditary predisposition should be good.

3. Her age should not exceed 30.

4. She should not have been confined many weeks before or after the child's mother.

5. She should be of the melancholic temperament.

6. She should have not only a good quality, but also a sufficient quantity of milk.

As a corollary, we may add, that when a wet-nurse cannot be given to a child exclusively, a married woman suckling another child may be employed to assist the artificial feeding.

1. *She should have good milk.*—This point will be best treated by considering what the cha-

racters of good human milk are. One of the best evidences of a wet-nurse's good physical constitution is, the secretion of an *abundance* of healthy and nutritious milk. Good human milk has an average specific gravity of 1032, varying from 1030 to 1034. It is always strongly alkaline ; this alkalinity it usually retains from five to six days, after which it becomes acid. To the taste it is sweet, much more so than cow's milk. When allowed to stand, it will be seen to separate into two portions. The superficial very white substance, known familiarly as *cream*, consists chiefly of the oil-globules, which, being of a lower specific gravity than the other portions of the milk, rise to the surface. The more transparent subjacent liquid, known popularly by the name of *skim* milk, when the cream has been removed from its surface, consists of casein, sugar, and salts, held in suspension or solution in a white, opaque liquor.

The agitation of the superficial portion, or cream, breaks asunder the oil-globules, which in this state constitute *butter*. If the subjacent portion, after the cream has separated from it, be kept any time, the sugar contained in it becomes converted into lactic acid, which gradually precipitates the casein as a curd. Rennet, or the mucous membrane of the stomach, and most acids, have the same effect. The fluid which now re-

mains, technically called *whey*, contains still in
solution a large quantity of sugar and the salts
of milk, which are readily separated by evaporation. When looked at through the microscope,
milk is found to consist of a colourless fluid, the
liquor lactis, in which are floating a number of
bodies :—(*a*) *oil-globules*, similar to those found
in all parts of the body. (*b*) The proper *milk-
globules*, smaller in size, varying from 1-95,00th
to 1-700th of an inch. These also appear to be
oil-globules, from the fact that they reflect light
strongly; but, from the difficulty experienced
in dissolving them in ether, they are evidently
covered with a layer of something else, which
surrounds them as a capsule. (*c*) There are a
great multitude of *small granules*, or *granulated
corpuscles*, floating amongst the milk-globules,
most abundant in milk secreted at a very early
period. The *liquor lactis* holds in solution the
casein, though some observers believe that the
external layer of the milk-globules is also made
up of casein.

Years ago, M. Devergie devised a rough way of
testing the quality of milk by the quantity of these
large globules. He found that milk might be divided into three classes :—1st, that having large
globuled milk ; 2nd, that having small globuled or
pulverulent milk ; 3rd, that having milk of me-
dium-sized globules. Out of 100 women, 17 had

the first variety of globules, and in 10 of these 17, lactation increased their number. Twenty-two had the second variety, and out of these 22, 17 had the richness of their milk increased by lactation. In his opinion the more numerous the large-sized globules, the richer the milk.*

According to the latest analyses by Becquerel and Rodier, the composition of human milk may be stated as follows :—

	Mean.	Maximum.	Minimum.
Specific gravity - - -	1032·67	... 1046·48	... 1025·61
Water - - - - - -	889·08	... 999·98	... 832·30
Solid constituents - -	110·92	... 147·70	... 83·33
Sugar - - - - -	43·64	... 59·55	... 25·22
Casein and extractive matters - - - -	39·24	... 70·92	... 19·32
Butter - - - - -	24·66	... 56·42	... 6·66
Salts by incineration -	1·38	... 3·38	... ·55
	1000·00	1000·00	1000·00

There exist in addition certain *volatile principles*, which may be obtained by the evaporation or distillation of milk, and to which in great measure is probably due the odour of new milk. I shall have occasion again in the sequel to refer to these several principles in detail. It may suffice here to make a remark in reference to two of these principles,—the extractive matters, and the volatile principles of milk. Of the first, it may be stated here, that most of those peculiar changes

---

* Sur la valeur de l'examen microscopique du lait dans le choix d'une nourrice. *British and Foreign Review*, 1844.

which render milk so detrimental do not occur so much in the casein, sugar, butter, or salts, as in the *extractive matters*, concerning which, to our regret, it must be added, in the emphatic words of Lehmann, so aptly used by Becquerel and Vernois, " we know absolutely nothing."

The same is true with regard to the volatile principles, the nature of which has not yet been determined by chemical inquiry, although several experiments for that object have been made.

It will be seen that the extreme limits of health exhibit a very marked difference, and hence one great difficulty in selecting a wet-nurse.

2. *Hereditary Predisposition.*—In the inquiry made as to the hereditary predisposition of a wet-nurse, the greatest care is required.

Medical men are, in this situation, invariably guided by the principle, that diseases which are known to be hereditary from parent to child, can be also conveyed to a suckling through a wet-nurse's milk.   Hence, it is usually the custom to reject those affected with any taint of consumption or tubercular disease, syphilis, or other similarly communicable maladies.

The great extent to which the former of these affections prevails may be gathered from the fact that the proportion of deaths from it, to 1000 deaths from all diseases, is 154·5 for males, 172·3 for females, and 163·4 for all persons.   Syphilis is not generally fatal to the mother, but its consequences on the life of a child are very deplorable. It is known that a woman thus tainted will consecutively bring forth stillborn children, or have a succession of miscarriages; but it is not as generally known, or at least enforced, that even the healthiest children will, if they partake of this milk from a syphilitic nurse, gradually become atrophied, and die.

Simon mentions a case of a young woman who contracted this disease after the birth of her first child, and who, in consequence of improper medical treatment, *carried the disease about her for years.* Her children continued pretty well till they reached the age of six months, then became highly scrofulous, and died in a state of general marasmus; and yet this woman's milk, when analysed, appeared to be quite healthy, and even rich. Donné, from several examinations of the milk of syphilitic women, concluded that no difference could be found in either the chemical or microscopical characters of such milk. Meggenhofen, however, found that it was *acid* in reaction.

It is sometimes, as I have before said, very difficult to make out syphilitic disease, although present. I have already alluded to Mr. Langston Parker's opinion, and given a case as an example (p. 207). This points out the necessity of full examination wherever the slightest suspicion of contamination exists.

Again, sufficient caution is not usually taken in the case of cancer. I have before said, that of late years *cancer* has been on the increase (p. 192). The disease is known to be hereditary; and therefore is it necessary to be doubly cautious in making a selection where any blood relative of the nurse has laboured under the malady. What is true of cancer I would equally apply to *insanity*. This is also an hereditary disease, the taint of which, even if not actually transmitted as insanity, often develops itself in after life, in analogous, although milder, affections. Extraordinary peculiarities, eccentricities, strong dispositions to crime or sexual indulgences, more frequently a deficiency in intellectual power, are apt to follow—evils greatly to be deplored, and therefore, if practicable, to be avoided.

3. *The age of a nurse should not exceed thirty.*— I would further venture to state that it should not be much under twenty-five. I have already shown elsewhere* that the age of the highest sexual development in a female is twenty-six, at which age she is in the best condition to fulfil her maternal duties. After thirty this power slowly deteriorates; and before twenty-five she can scarcely be said to have completely acquired that physical health, which has been weakened

---

* *On Procreative Power. London Journal of Medicine*, 1850.

during the progress of puberty and the changed position which she has been made to occupy in society. It is but right to add, however, that we do not find the milk itself very much altered, chemically or microscopically, between the ages of fifteen and forty. Still, at the extremities of the scale, the differences are obvious. In the very young, the butter, casein, and solid matters generally—excepting the sugar, which exists in diminished quantity—are on the increase; in the older women, there is a larger proportion of water and sugar; the amount of butter and casein is diminished, although the latter is still in excess as compared with the normal condition; from which it may be inferred, that the milk of a very young person is less digestible, and therefore less to be recommended for a delicate infant.

4. It is usually said that *the wet-nurse selected should have been confined as nearly as possible about the same time as the mother of the child for whom the milk is required.*—Too much stress, however, should not be laid on this contingency; for it should not be forgotten that the constituents of milk not only vary in relative quantities in different animals, but even in the same. So liable are they to vary, that the different circumstances of life may materially affect them in the same individual. Indeed, Parmentier and Deyeux have shown that the milk of women of the same age,

R

confined at the same time, and submitted to the same influences, was always different—in fine, that the milk of the same animal, obtained at different times, varied greatly.* All that we should look to is, that the milk be good, and that the age of it be not too far removed from what the child's mother's milk was; for milk materially changes in its composition as the period of lactation is prolonged; and thus the female, although possessing very excellent milk, may yet supply a fluid which will prove injurious to the suckling.

The effects of age on milk are summed up as follows by Becquerel and Rodier. The specific gravity varies much. The proportion of *water* increases from the fifth to the sixth month, and from the eleventh to the twelfth; it diminishes from the first to the second, and from the eighteenth to the twenty-fourth. The *solid matters* increase in a marked degree from the first to the third. The *sugar* decreases during the first month, but increases from the eighth to the tenth month. The *butter* increases considerably up to the sixth month, and then considerably decreases from the fifth to the sixth, and from the tenth to the eleventh month. The *salts* undergo a slight increase in quantity from the first to the fifth month, then correspondingly de-

---

* Burdach, *Physiologie,* s. 520, p. 356.

crease. These changes are really most important to trace, because they are indices as to the
substitute which, bearing a proper proportion to
the amount and quality of nutritive matter required, is best fitted for a child whom it becomes
obligatory to wean, or for whom another diet is
imperatively called. It must be confessed, however, that the constituents of milk vary so much,
that it is very difficult readily to estimate its
goodness from their present quantity. Its composition varies also, within the limits of health,
so much, that we have often no better method of
testing it than trial with the child, when, if it
agrees with it, we may conclude it is good. " It
may, however, be stated as a rule, that if the
butter is in excess, the milk is poor in quality,
excepting in syphilis and phthisis, particularly
when the latter is accompanied with diarrhœa,
and in mental disturbance. In the former it may
fall to 9·12 per cent.; in the second, to 12·7; in
the latter, to 5·14; the normal proportion being
26·6. Thus in acute diseases the mean is 29·8;
in chronic, 32·6; in acute enteritis, 31·5; in acute
pleurisy, 54·2; in acute colitis, 54·2. In nurses
of feeble constitution it is 28·78, as compared to
25·96 in those of robust constitution. In very
young nurses it varies from 15 to 20, 37·8, and
so on."*

* Op. cit.

5. A wet-nurse of a melancholic temperament should be preferred.—The milk of a brunette is generally richer in solid constituents than that of a blonde; for which reason the former are preferred as wet-nurses. The following analyses, quoted from Simon, were made by L'Héritier:—

	Blonde, aged 22.		Brunette, aged 22.	
	1	2	1	2
Water - - - - -	892·	... 881·5	... 853·3	... 853·
Solid constituents -	108·	... 118·5	... 146·7	... 147·
Butter - - -	35·5	... 40·5	54·8	... 56·3
Casein - - - -	10·	... 9·5	... 16·2	... 17·
Sugar of milk -	58·5	... 64·	... 71·2	... 70·
Salts - - - -	4·0	... 4·5	... 4·5	... 4·5
	1000·0	1000·0	1000·0	1000·0

These are extreme cases; but the average ratio of solid constituents lies from 120 for a blonde to 130 for a brunette. There is yet another reason why a brunette is to be preferred. Blondes usually belong to the sanguine or scrofulous temperament. A fair skin, with brilliant colour, light blue eyes, very light or red hair, are usually present in such cases. The digestive powers are weak, and an unusually irritable manner is a frequent accompaniment. As a consequence of this sanguine and more passionate character, the milk of blondes is very apt to become altered under mental excitement. In extreme cases it has been known to produce the death of the infant; but it almost always produces serious results. In the case of a recently delivered woman, who was in a state of considerable fever induced by a fit of passion, the child after partaking of her milk was seized with vomiting, diarrhœa, and convulsions. This milk was examined by Simon; it had an alkaline reaction and a strong animal odour, when boiled. After twelve hours it developed a large quantity of sulphuretted hydrogen; and yet the casein, sugar, and butter had not undergene any change in quantity or quality.

Brunettes usually belong to the bilious or melancholic temperament. In disposition they are more gloomy and dull than blondes. The milk is richer; and a precocious child is, as it were, restrained by this milk from over-excitement in its mental manifestations. Its body has time to be formed and to develope itself before it is exhausted by undue psychical excitement, and a stronger child is the result.

Among the brunettes there is to be found another variety, closely connected with the sanguine. The eyes may be very dark, even black; the complexion also dark; but with this there is a transparency in the look; the eye is unusually bright; the veins appear vividly blue through the skin. Such persons have all the vivacity of character common to the sanguine, and are to be avoided for similar reasons.

Intermediate between the sanguine and melancholic is the lymphatic or phlegmatic temperament. It is the reverse of the sanguine. It is accompanied with weak pulse, languid circulation, cold extremities, and pallid skin.* There is deficiency of red blood, of vascular action, of tone; and the proclivity is to watery fluxes and other chronic affections. Such persons are not calculated to make good nurses, and should therefore be scrupulously avoided.†

Lastly, the nervous temperament is to be rejected. This is characterized by agitation and trepidation of manner. There is an exaltation in the nervous phenomena, and a general tendency to nervous and hysterical diseases.‡ When we remember that a child is eminently impressionable, and has to go through an excitable period in teething, to exalt a nervous tendency cannot be wise. Deyeux examined the milk of a woman who was liable to frequent nervous attacks. He found that, simultaneously with these attacks the milk became transparent and viscid, like albumen, and did not resume its normal condition till some time afterwards. To expose a child to such variations is most injudicious.

6. *She should have not only good milk, but it should be in sufficient quantity.*—This is very im-

---

* Druitt's *Vade Mecum*.   † Williams's *Principles of Medicine*.
‡ *Ibid.*

portant; for upon no point do I think we are so
liable to be deceived as upon the quantity of milk
supplied. Hervieux, whom I before quoted (p. 49),
states the amount consumed by a child in twenty-
four hours to be sixty ounces. Forty ounces is
probably nearer the truth (p. 88); but still, when we
consider that a child has in the first year of its life
to acquire not far from one-third of its full growth
and size, we must consider that it requires, at the
same time as it has to supply waste and wear, a
large quantity of food to meet the emergency.
Quêtelet, from his calculations, considers that, as a
mean, a child grows in length, in the first year of
life, males from 20 inches to 26, females from
19 to 24½ inches; the weight in the former increasing from 6 lbs. 13 oz. to 20 lbs. 7 oz., and
in the latter, from 6 lbs. 3 oz. to 18 lbs. 14 oz.
These data do not clearly set forth the extent of
food required. We may, however, infer this from
experiments made upon animals. The philosophical Boussingault has shown that a calf increases—

	lbs. per diem.
During the period of suckling	2·4
Under 3 years old	1.5
Above 3 years old	·2

From this we may conclude that the greatest
amount of growth and consumption of food takes
place at the suckling period. This increase of
weight, however, bears a direct ratio to the quantity and quality of food supplied. Boussingault

has admitted, what might be presumed at first sight, that an animal of great size, *cæteris paribus*, will require a larger amount of forage. Again, in regard to the quality; in winter, usually, cattle which are not set aside to fatten are stinted in their food, and fed almost exclusively on straw. Straw is an aliment which, compared to hay or other kinds of fodder, is deficient in both combustible and incombustible element. Hence, towards spring the cattle are thin, and yield but little milk, and have lost much strength. If these results happen to a full grown, they will, *à fortiori*, occur to a growing animal. The following table from Boussingault gives this statement. It will appear that, for every hundred pounds of living weight, neat cattle require—

	lbs. of hay.
For simple sustenance	0·7
When labouring (Pulsh)	2·0
When in milk (Pulsh)	3·0
Ditto (Perrault)	3·12
Ditto, large cows (Boussingault)	2·73
Growing rapidly (Boussingault)	3·08

An infant, therefore, requires proportionally a much larger quantity of food than an older child, or a man. Strange to say, farmers, who are generally libelled as deficient in intellect, have found out this truth, which many persons in London, who keep boys as pages instead of employing men-servants, appear still to ignore. If they can do so, farmers always refuse to employ growing lads when grown men are to be had, having found out that, although their wages are lower, they more than compensate for this advantage by the larger quantity of food they consume.

The following, however, is one of the disadvantages of a wet-nurse. The breast often appears large and full of milk, but whether owing to an increase of adipose tissue between the lacteal ducts, or to the peculiar conformation of the breast in some women, is not noted. But the milk, although it is found, when examined chemically or microscopically, to be particularly rich and good, is often *insufficient in quantity.* And some nurses are so anxious to keep their situations, and so devoid of honest principle, that they will keep their fatal secret, and if it be not discovered, the child will die. Yet it is a fraud which, from what I have before said,* can be easily detected. The child cries frequently; its sleep is disturbed; it becomes thin, and generally pines away. Let the child be watched; and, the moment it has had the breast, and the nurse has left the room, offer it artificial food. The avidity with which it will attack this, the quantity it will consume, and the sleep of quiet and comfort which will almost instantly succeed, will reveal the fraud, and oftentimes be the means of saving the child's life.

---

* Page 224.

PART III.

CHAPTER I.

ON SOME GENERAL DEDUCTIONS IN REFERENCE
TO ALIMENTATION MADE FROM THE COMPOSI-
TION OF MILK AND ITS SUBSTITUTES.

SALINE INGREDIENTS— OF MILK.—PHOSPHATE AND CARBONATE OF
LIME—USES. — PHOSPHATE OF SODA. — PHOSPHORIC ACID. —
IMPORTANT RELATIONS OF CHLORIDE OF POTASSIUM.

THE remarks before made upon the need of
maternal warmth and of the semi-erect position
for a child, have, I conceive, shown

1. The advantage of employing some kind of
mammary bottle for a child who is to be artificially fed, and of letting the child recline against
the body of the person so feeding it (pp. 78-84).

2. That the recumbent position, and continued
judicious exercise to obviate cold and starvation,
are imperatively required (p. 49).

3. That the child is by formation and all analogy
of comparative anatomy, constituted to receive
in early ages animal food only (p. 75). But there
are other general principles to be brought prominently forward, which are made at once obvious

by the consideration of human milk in its component parts.

The nutritive properties of milk depend on the combination of three alimentary substances, which may be classified as—first, the *combustible*, or those subservient chiefly to respiration and the fattening of the body, which are two in number, namely, the fatty portion in butter, and the saccharine portion, the sugar of milk ; secondly, the *nitrogenous* or *plastic ingredient*, subservient to the development of the fleshy and parenchymatous portions of the body, the casein ; lastly, water, and the *mineral ingredients*, phosphates, chlorides, carbonates of lime, soda, potass, etc., for the purposes of the solution and the solution of substances.

The *combustible* materials. Two of these—namely, fat and sugar—enter into the composition of human milk.

Fat.—Important as are the relations of the mineral ingredients in the organism, those of the fatty matters are perhaps more so. Amongst fats, as they occur in the body, we have stearine, margarine, oleine, phoceine, and butyrine, all compounds of oxygen, carbon, and hydrogen, united in such proportions that one portion of the elements constitutes a fatty acid, fixed or volatile, whereas the other portion, plus water, constitutes *glycerine.*

A fat, however, does not consist of fatty acid and glycerine, but of fatty acid and oxide of *lipyl*, which last has the composition formerly ascribed to glyccrine (C_3H_2O), and in its separation from the fatty acid appropriates the water.

In this way these several fats may be considered —margarine as margarate of oxide of lipyl, oleine as oleate of oxide of lipyl, etc.

The importance of fatty aliments for a young child is very great. A healthy child is almost necessarily fat, and a sickly child almost as necessarily thin. Now the substances which produce fat in digestion are, first (with great waste, however, of the substances so used), nitrogenous ingredients; secondly, with a very great saving in the amount of aliment employed—alcoholic or fermented liquors, fatty or oily, saccharine and starchy matters. To two of this last class only, the fatty and saccharine, which exist in large quantities in milk, we can properly here refer. Milk, indeed, contains a larger quantity of fat than any other animal fluid. An average of 2·9 per cent. of fat has been found in a woman's milk.

Fat is needed particularly as the nucleus in the cell-growth, around which the albuminous or nitrogenous matter is deposited. A deficiency, therefore, of fatty matter in the food will lead to atrophy, because there may not be a sufficiency of it in the system to supply the nuclei. This must be the case, unless other matters convertible into fat are taken to supply this ingredient. Besides the mechanical services which fats render the animal organism, they take part through their chemical metamorphoses in the most varied animal processes; they take an active share in the digestion in the primæ viæ, and preside generally over all the processes by which the fluid nutrient substances are converted into the solid substrata of the organs.

The formation of the colourless blood-corpuscle seems also to owe its first impulse to the metamorphosis of fat, which thus serves as the most important auxiliary in the formation of blood. Special attention should also be given to the fact that no animal cell and no fibre are formed independently of the presence of fat, although the concurrence also of albuminous substances is required. But even if fat is taken as aliment to be absorbed, *i. e.*, assimilated, it must be in a free state as a fatty acid; for fat, as such, will not be absorbed.

As before stated, fats consist of a fatty acid and oxide of lipyl. In the adult it is the pancreas which effects this separation into these proximate constituents. We all know that if this change does not occur the fat passes off unchanged by the bowels; and, as Bernard has shown, the expulsion of fat is one of the truest indications of diseased pancreas. In the infant, judging from the want of development of the salivary glands, the pancreas probably does not suffice to the complete performance of this function. It is here that we remark one of those wonderful adaptations of nature. First, in butter we have excess of a free fatty acid; therefore rendering the assimilation of it possible without the assistance of the pancreas; secondly, in the large proportion of *phosphate of soda* in the human milk we have another way in which it can be formed into an emulsion, and so taken up in the system.* It is important to notice that as phosphate of soda is probably absent in *cow's* milk, this may be one of the reasons why it occasionally disagrees when given to very young children.

Again, as in the adult, while excess disagrees, a small quantity of fat favours digestion. The effects of a diet too exclusively fatty, present many resemblances to those changes induced by one too exclusively saccharine. Magendie fed dogs upon olive-oil and water. All the phenomena were the same. During the first weeks there was comparatively little difference, then weakness and loss of power supervened, and finally death took place. With butter the effects

---

* See remarks on Mineral Ingredients further on.

were the same; the dog died on the 36th day, although afterwards, in pity, meat was given on the 32nd day. One eye ulcerated, and the urine was destitute of *phosphates* and *uric acid*. Generally speaking, however, this ulceration was not common. In combination with other aliments, excess of oleaginous food appears to exert a beneficial effect, particularly in cold countries. In Iceland, where all circumstances considered usually favourable to the development of the scrofulous diathesis are present, the inhabitants enjoy a remarkable immunity from it, without any other assignable cause than the peculiarly oleaginous character of the diet usually employed.*

Fatty matters are occasionally accumulated in the blood. Several cases are on record in which the blood was quite white, in consequence of excess of fat. In some cases it was chyle, unchanged. Short of this, milky serum is not very unusual from this cause. The face and general appearance of such persons are very greasy and oily looking, quite the character of what Dr. Gibb terms "the atheromatous constitution."

The proportion of butter required for an infant, taking human milk as the average, is 1 part in 2·8; or, taking solid constituents, as much as 1 in 3.

---

* Carpenter's *Physiology*, p. 383.

2. *Sugar* exists in the body in two forms—
First, as *Sugar of liver, or diabetic* sugar, which
is identical with the *grape sugar,* as it occurs in
the grape; and second, as *sugar of milk.* It is of
the last only we have to speak particularly, and it
has several very important bearings. In alkaline
blood it certainly assists to dissolve the carbonate
and phosphate of lime. Even if some salt of
lime be present, the sugar may, as in the chick,
combine with the alkali or lime in the alkaline
fluid, and then dissolve the carbonate of lime as a
compound of sugar with lime or soda. This was
shown by Barreswill.*

But sugar is capable of being transformed into
fat in two ways: first, by undergoing a kind of
vinous fermentation, the atom of sugar being decomposed into carbonic acid and a substance poor
in oxygen; or, secondly, by a kind of *butyric*
fermentation, hydrogen, carbonic acid, and a compound poor in oxygen being found, which last is
one of the known fatty acids. In all these cases
a peculiar ferment is developed, which is capable
of separating the oxygen from the hydrogen.
The *lactic* precedes the *butyric* fermentation, and
of all nitrogenous bodies it is with *casein* especially that this change is effected. This, doubtless,
is one of the reasons why casein is the nitrogenous

---

* Day's Lehmann, chap. iii, 220.

aliment found in milk. The butyric fermentation, like the lactic, requires the addition of equivalent quantities of alkalies for its perfect accomplishment.*

" But in every case the deposition of fat within the animal body betrays a certain deficiency of oxygen, showing that the amount of oxygen respired is insufficient to allow the complete separation of the sugar into water and carbonic acid."†

Another important use of sugar is, that it is essential to the formation of milk. Sugar is not secreted by the mammary gland. The sugar is probably merely separated by the gland from the blood in which it exists. It is not readily detected in the blood; but this is probably due to the rapid manner in which it is excreted. Certain it is, if an animal is fed on starchy or saccharine matters, the quantity of sugar is considerably increased. It is upon these grounds that a milk containing more sugar and more closely resembling human milk, can be obtained from a cow or goat, if either be fed on beet-root in excess.

Allusion has been already made to the effects of a diet exclusively saccharine. Magendie fed dogs exclusively on sugar and distilled water. During the first seven or eight days they were sufficiently brisk and active; in the second week they began

---

* Day's Lehmann, i, p. 282. † *Ibid.* iii, p. 221.

to lose flesh, although all along the appetite continued good; in the third week they became feeble and lost their appetite. Films also appeared in the eye, followed by an escape of its humours. From six to eight ounces of sugar could up to this time be taken ; now, however, they could only consume three or four. Debility increased till voluntary movement was impossible, and death resulted from the thirty-first to the thirty-fourth day. General atrophy of muscular structure, and signs of inanition in the intestines, which were pale, empty, and contracted, were well marked on a *post-mortem* examination. These results may be expected in a minor degree where children have their food either too much sweetened, or if the breast-milk contains too large a proportion of saccharine matter compared to the other ingredients—a state which I have detected in some wet-nurses with very thin milk. The proper proportion of sugar in milk should be 1 part in about 2·3, or taking solid constituents only, 1 in 2·6.

II. *The Nitrogenous Aliment.*—Liebig states, " In the same way as in the egg, the *albumen* of the blood holds the first place in the powers of formation of the fœtus, to which it is conveyed from without. By its elements it takes a share in all processes, it determines growth, and also the production and amount of all organized tissues in the young as well as in the adult frame. . . . Only those substances are, in a strict sense of the word, nutritious articles of food which contain either albumen or a substance capable of being converted into albumen."

In milk "we find it in the shape of *casein*, a substance which, like albumen, contains sulphur and nitrogen, and the absence of every other nitrogenous compound in milk renders it perfectly certain that from casein alone the chief constituent of the young animal's blood, as well as its muscular fibres, membranes, etc., are formed in the first stage of its life."*

From the experiments of Guillot and Leblanc it appears to be a normal constituent of blood in man and other animals, at least so far as the examination of seventy specimens of blood in men, women, oxen, cows, rams, sheep, etc., justifies the inference ; but the quantity is notably increased during pregnancy.†

Casein differs from albumen in not being coagulable by heat, but it is precipitated by all acids, even acetic and lactic acids, which have no effect upon albumen. The addition of water to milk favours the separation of the casein, and renders it harder and less digestible.

One advantage, however, which casein has over

* Liebig's *Letters*, p. 247–8.
† *Comptes Rendus*, 1850, xxxi, pp. 520–585.

albumen, among many others we have dwelt upon, is that it facilitates more readily than any other nitrogenous body, the butyric fermentation of milk where the lactic fermentation has been already induced. It is doubtless in assimilation converted into albumen and fibrin wherever so required ; for instance, the albumen which accumulates around the fatty nucleus of the cell-growth.

Dogs fed on casein exclusively live for a long time, but become weak and thin, and lose their hair. Its quantity in human milk varies, *c. g.* 20 to 40 per cent. in 1000 parts, or in reference to solid constituents, 1 part in 5 to 1 part in 10.

In speaking of these several alimentary substances it may be stated, that "after an animal has been fed for a long period on one kind of aliment, which, if long continued, will not support life, allowing him his customary food will not then save him, but he will die as soon as if he had continued to be restricted to the one article of food which was first given."* A variety is therefore essential to the maintenance of health. It is perhaps because in artificial feeding due regard is not paid to this variety that the third stage of defective assimilation is induced, from which recovery very rarely, if ever, occurs.

It follows as an important corollary from the

---

* Baly's Müller's *Physiology.*

foregoing general remark, that if inferior milk be given, or if artificial animal food be prepared from milk in an improper manner, the same evil results will follow, because excess or defect in one or more of the ingredients will be given. It becomes, therefore, important to look at the question in the point of view of the proper and wholesome admixture of food.

Thirdly, of the *saline ingredients*. Their due appreciation will set forth some very important principles in alimentation, and also give us a key to the quality of substitutes required when artificial food is given.

The salts of milk are not the least important of its constituents. They are stated in the annexed table for human and cow's milk :—

Mean of two Experiments.

Cow's Milk.		Human Milk.	
Phosphate of lime	2·84		0·706
Phosphate of magnesia	1·06	Carbonate of lime	0·069
Phosphate of peroxide of iron	·07		
Chloride of potassium	1·63	Other salts	0·053
Chloride of sodium	·29		0·098
Soda	·43	Sulphate of soda	0·074
	1·000		1·000

Schwartz in his *Journal*,* enumerates the following salts in 100 parts of human milk.—Soda, resulting from the decomposition of lactate of soda, 0·03; chloride of potassium, 0·07; phosphate of soda, 0·04; phosphate of lime, 0·25; phosphate of magnesia, 0·05; phosphate of iron, 0·001.

First, of the *phosphate of lime*. This salt, especially when combined with carbonate of lime, is most useful in the process of alimentation. It is on their combined agency that the solidity of the skeleton depends. Moreover, it is a peculiar property of phosphate of lime to make carbonic acid more soluble in the blood. Its administration, whether in a separate form or in aliment to a growing animal, is thus peculiarly indicated. Deformity of every kind in the skeleton may depend on an insufficient quantity of this salt in the blood; for it should be remarked, first, that not only is it useful because it is itself appropriated to the system; but, secondly, phosphate of lime when present in a fluid (which in the present case is milk, and by subsequent assimilation becomes blood) has the property of enabling that fluid to take up more carbonic acid. Now when carbonic acid in its turn is in excess, it dissolves carbonate of lime. Hence, the quantity of carbonate of lime held in solution in the blood is thereby made greater, and is in this way from time to time more easily and largely deposited in bone. Chalk, or carbonate of lime, is insoluble in distilled water; but in proportion as this becomes saturated with carbonic acid, so a larger quantity of the chalk is taken up—a property never to be lost sight of when it is wished to strengthen a growing child.

Secondly, the *phosphate of soda* has an alkaline taste and reaction like the *carbonate*, and its solution in the presence of free carbonic acid takes up as much of that acid as carbonate of soda does; and, like it, only more easily, gives it off by agitation *in vacuo*, or by evaporation, without losing its power of again absorbing carbonic acid. Hence it follows, that in adults the change of carbonic acid combined with alkali by phosphoric acid, which occurs when animal food is taken in lieu of vegetable food, and *vice versa*, has no pernicious influence, because it gives rise to no alteration in the essential properties of the blood. The process of sanguification, of the production of heat, and of secretion, are carried on alike under the influence of the predominating alkali, as before stated.*

But phosphate of soda seems to possess another useful property in the economy. The fatty acids, stearic and margaric, are converted into emulsions in the chyle through its agency, so as to allow of their easy assimilation in the system. This peculiar property, discovered by Dr. Marcet and lately exemplified by Dr. Thudichum before the Medical Society of London, is of immense importance in

---

* Liebig's *Letters.*

the explanation of the digestion of fatty matters, and is another reason for supplying food rich in phosphoric acid and soda, which is especially the case with animal aliments, to growing and weakly children; fat, as before stated, being the nucleus around which albuminous matters are deposited.

Thirdly. In the uses of *phosphoric acid,* viewed particularly as an acid, and in regard to alimentation, there are several very interesting points. The blood is *alkaline,* and, as opposed to this, flesh is *acid,* the acidity being due to phosphoric acid; and this is true for other solid portions of animal food, but for muscle especially, which contains an excess of phosphoric acid.

Fourthly. In muscle, and in soup made from muscle, we have also excess of *chloride of potassium* in lieu of chloride of sodium. Now there is considerable analogy in this respect to milk which contains an excess of chloride of potassium, although it also contains some chloride of sodium. (See Table below.*)

* *Composition of ashes of flesh.* (Keller.)	When boiled there enter into the soup.	*Composition of ashes of milk.* (Com.)
Phosphoric acid ...... 36·60	26·24	Phosphate of lime ...... 50·7
Potash .... 40·20	35·42	Phosphate of magnesia 9·5
Earths and oxide of		Phosphate peroxide of
iron .... 5·69	3·15	iron .... 1·0
Sulphuric acid ...... 2·95	4·95	Chloride of sodium...... 5·0
Chloride of potassium 14·81	14·81	Chloride of potassium 27·1
(Liebig's *Lett.,*p.428)		Soda .... 6·7
100	100	100

No doubt this large excess of the potash salt in milk answers many of the purposes of chloride of sodium in the economy. But chloride of potassium enjoys the peculiar property, in common with carbonic acid, of dissolving carbonate of lime, or chalk. The advantage, therefore, of giving to the infant this salt for the purposes of the skeleton, and in supplying to the muscular system a salt essential to that structure, must appear at once obvious.

The excess of potash salts generally, but of chloride of potassium especially, which last, as in muscular flesh and milk, so greatly exceeds in quantity the chloride of sodium, is very remarkable. Dr. Andrew Clark has also informed me that potash salts are always in excess in cell-developments, even when the growths are morbid—a fact of great importance, although often overlooked, as showing that those animal foods which contain an excess of potash salts should be preferred as aliments for growing children.

While, however, these facts are admitted, it is important to oppose a mistake usually made, in speaking of chloride of potassium. Robin and Verdeuil have properly insisted upon the impropriety of confounding this salt with chloride of sodium, or common salt, in all its agencies upon the animal economy. Although it is true that they may mutually be substituted for each other in plants, they cannot always be similarly substituted in the animal body, particularly in the young animal. We have said that chloride of potassium exists in large quantity in muscle; it is found also in small quantity in blood. The reverse is true as regards chloride of sodium. This proves a peculiar antagonistic power in these two salts. It is remarkable also to notice, in connexion with this opposite action, the fact that muscular tissue which contains a large excess of chloride of potassium has an acid reaction, whereas blood which contains a large excess of chloride of sodium has an *alkaline* reaction. Now this correlative antagonism cannot be purely accidental. Nay, its constant occurrence proves that it is intended to fulfil some wise purpose, although we may not fully appreciate it. It is also curious to note that the potash salt, so needful to cell-growth, is in milk (the food *par excellence* for babies, in whom growth is so rapid and continuous) conveyed not as a sulphate, phosphate, or carbonate, but as a *chloride*. This preponderance of chloride of potassium and phosphoric acid in milk is also remarkable in a portion of the blood. I allude to the blood-globules; a coincidence the more remarkable, as the blood-globules are eminently concerned in nutrition. Upon this point I quote Lehmann's remarks.

"Although we are able to calculate the quantity of the *mineral* constituents in the blood-cells, the questions still remain to be answered,—whether there are certain salts which especially accumulate in the cells, and if so, which they are. These questions have also been answered by C. Schmidt, for he has discovered that the fluid of the blood-cells (*i. e.* the water contained within the blood-corpuscles) contains in addition to the organic matters a preponderance of *phosphate* and *potash* salts; so that, consequently, the phosphate of potash and the greater part of chloride of potassium pertain to the blood-cells, whilst the chloride of sodium, with a little chloride of potassium and phosphate of soda, is found in the plasma, *i. e.* the serum and fibrin. In the plasma the organic materials are combined only with soda; while in the blood-cells the fatty acids and the globules are combined both with potash and soda.

" C. Schmidt, in analysing a specimen of food which contained 396·24 p. m. of blood-cells and 603·76 p. m. of intercellular fluid, found 1·353 of chloride of potassium and 0·835 of phosphate of potash in the former, while there were 3·417 parts of chloride of sodium, besides 0·267 of phosphate of soda and 0·270 of chloride of potassium, in the latter. Schmidt has examined and tabulated the relations between potassium and sodium and between phosphoric acid and chlorine in the blood-cells, and in the intercellular fluid in several of the mammalia. (See Table below.*)

"These results coincide with those of Nasse, who found most phosphates in the blood of those animals which were distinguished for the abundance of their blood-corpuscles, namely, swine, geese, and hens; in sheep and goats, on the other hand, in whose blood he found comparatively few corpuscles, he also found the least phosphates. On another occasion Nasse has expressed the opinion that the phosphates must be principally contained in the blood-corpuscles."†

It is also worthy of remark, that as metallic chlorides exist in extraordinary quantity in the gastric juice, and in the saliva also, as chlorides of sodium, but especially of potassium, this may be probably another reason why chloride of potassium is provided in excess in milk, which is the natural food of young infants, in some measure

* 100 PARTS OF INORGANIC MATTER.

Genus.	Blood-cells.		Plasma.		Blood-cells.		Plasma.	
	Potassium.	Sodium.	Potassium.	Sodium.	P. O.	Chlorine.	P. O.	Chlorine.
Mean of 8 experiments .	40·89	9·71	5·19	37·74	17.64	21·	6·08	40·68
Dog.............	6.07	36·17	3·25	39·68	22·12	21·88	6 65	37·31
Cat	7·85	35·02	5·17	37·74	13·62	27 59	7·27	41·70
Sheep..........	14·57	38·07	6·56	38·56	8·95	27·4	3·56	40·89
Goat	37·41	14·98	3·55	37·89	9·41	31.73	5·90	40·41

† Lehmann, translated by Day, ii, p. 188.

to compensate for the absence of saliva, usually present in adults.

"When, however, the functions of the blood-globules are considered, it is manifest that as in their constitution they on the one hand possess a remarkable correspondence with muscle in the large quantity of potash salts, especially chloride of potassium, and on the other hand a like correspondence to nervous matters in the large quantity of phosphuretted fat contained within them, it appears reasonable to conclude that they are especially destined to elaborate materials for the nervous and muscular tissues, whereby the fleshy organism and vital activity of the nervous and muscular systems are strengthened. Coupling this fact with the larger quantity of blood-globules in animals of high animal heat. and in youth, their excess in dynamic fevers and ple-thora, their diminution in weak persons and low fevers, and generally in all cases where the system is badly nourished, we cannot fail to perceive how intimate is the relation between the process of nutrition and the quantity of blood-globules, and as a consequence the important relation in this process of phosphates and chloride of potassium."* These are all reasons why chloride of potassium should exist in such large quantities in milk to supply an ingredient so much needed by a young and growing animal.

* *Op. cit.*

CHAPTER II.

OF THE VARIOUS KINDS OF ANIMAL MILKS TO BE SUBSTITUTED FOR
HUMAN MILK.—COMPOSITION OF HUMAN MILK AT DIFFERENT
AGES.—ASSES' MILK.—GOATS' MILK.—COWS' MILK.—DIFFERENCE
OF MILK, TOWN AND COUNTRY, SUMMER AND WINTER, MORNING
AND EVENING.—RESULTS OF VARIOUS FOODS IN ITS COMPOSITION.

THE preceding remarks place us in a better position to consider the efficacy and nutritive qualities
of substitutes for human milk, by which it is
wished to maintain the functional integrity and
growing powers of a child.

(*a*.) The simplest of these is clearly milk from
another animal. Of this fluid three kinds are
usually spoken of: *ass's* milk, which is said to
come nearest to human milk; *cow's* milk; and
goat's milk. I will speak of each of these varieties
seriatim. Before doing so, however, it will be
well to set forth in a tabular form the relative
quantities of the solid ingredients and the water
contained in human milk, at periods of three
months for the first year, and of six months for
the second year: so that we may be enabled
thereby to judge of the amount up to which each
of these ingredients should be brought, and which

is best adapted to the age of a child, when we substitute for its mother's milk that of the ass, the cow, or the goat.*

Ass's Milk.—It has usually been said that ass's milk is the nearest to a woman's milk ; but I believe this to be an error. It contains, certainly, more water, but only about half as much casein and butter, about twice as much sugar and salts. In the Appendix I have given five analyses of ass's milk, of specific gravity from 1023 to 1039.

---

* COMPOSITION OF HUMAN MILK.

Table calculated from one given by Becquerel and Rodier.

	Specific gravity.	Water.	Solid constituents.	Sugar.	Casein with extractive matter.	Butter.	Incinerated salts.
1st Quarter	1032·50	877·33	122·67	42·30	33·39	34·94	1·73
2nd "	1031 81	893·14	106·86	43·71	37·95	23·89	1·37
3rd "	1033·07	890·83	109·17	43·67	40·89	23·40	1·21
4th "	1031·24	892·98	107·03	45·79	36 89	23·03	1·29
12 to 18 mhs.	1032·05	891·34	108·66	43·92	36·98	26·44	1·32
18 to 24 "	1030·81	876·55	123·45	41·33	37·32	43·47	1·33

COMPOSITION OF ASS'S MILK.

	Simon. Milk 1 yr. old.	Peligot. Mean of sev. anal.	Chevallier and Heuri.	Lehmann.	Vernois and Becquerel.	Human milk.
Water	907·00	904·7	916·3	795·0 to 789·1	890·12	889·08
Solid constit. ...	91·05	95·3	83·5	205·0 to 210·9	109·88	110·92
Butter	12·10	12·9	1·1	12·1 to 12·9	18·50	34·61
Casein	16·74	19·5	18·2	16·0 to 19·0	35·65	39·24
Sugar, with extractive matters & salts	62·31	62·9	—	(with extractives.		
Sugar	—	—	60·8	68 0 to 62·9	50·46	26·66
Salts	—	—	3·4	— —	5·24	1·38

I shall endeavour to show in the sequel how it is that this milk so often disagrees.

Goat's milk.—In many parts of the world the goat is the substitute for the cow as the provider of milk to the population. The objection usually made to it is its disagreeable odour, from the presence of *hircic* acid. Observers differ greatly as to its composition, as may be seen from the table at p. 271, partly given by Simon.*

The analysis by Boysson gives a composition not unlike human milk. Mayer, indeed, says that goat's milk is preferable to cow's milk, because it resembles more than any other milk that of a woman; and this is doubtless true, particularly if we compare with it the milk of very young women. It is certain that many children thrive very well on it in Ireland, Malta, Switzerland, and other mountainous countries. One advantage which the goat possesses over other animals that yield milk, "is the greater impunity with which she sustains the various vicissitudes of the weather. She will sleep readily under a powerful sun, without suffering; she will remain unaffected, if exposed to rain or storm; she will bear a great amount of cold, although to this last she is more susceptible. Experience, however, has proved that the goat, as well as the cow, will yield a

---

* Simon's *Animal Chemistry*, vol. ii, p. 65.

larger flow of milk if fed in stables upon proper fodder; but then great attention should be paid to the cleanliness of the stable, and the removal of all offensive matters. The best milk afforded by the goat is that which it yields about two months after kidding. The peculiar odour and taste of goat's milk, from the presence of hircic acid, and which is not always very agreeable to those who taste it for the first time, is an objection; but persons soon get accustomed to it, and come to like it. This smell, however, is not *essential* to goat's milk, being chiefly present, and then most strongly, when the goat is allowed to associate with the ram; and is greatly diminished if the animals are kept clean, and especially if washed from time to time. It is also far less marked in those goats which have no horns: in the milk of these there is little more odour than in that of the cow.*

INFLUENCE OF KINDS OF FOOD ON GOAT'S MILK.

	Fed on straw and trefoil.	Fed on beet-root.	Normal (mean).	Human milk (normal).
Specific gravity ...	1031·10	1026·85	1033·53	1032·67
Water	858·68	888·77	844·90	889·08
Solid constituents	141·32	111·23	155·10	110·92
Butter	52·54	33·68	56·87	34·61
Casein & extractive matters...	47·38	33·81	55·14	39·24
Sugar	35·47	38.02	36·90	26·66
Salts..............	5·93	5·72	6·18	1·38

* Parmentier.

T

It is interesting to notice here a fact established by Becquerel and Vernois; that is, that the character of the goat's milk, like that of the cow, may be regulated by the *quality* of the food supplied. If a highly nourishing and rich milk is desired, it is best to feed the animal on straw and trefoil; but if a light milk is required, beet-root is preferable. This difference is set forth in the table, p. 269, to which I have also appended the composition of human milk, for comparison.

Cow's Milk.—This is the substitute for human milk best known in these regions. The absence of unpleasant odour, and the greater ease with which it is obtained in Great Britain, are advantages in its favour. In appearance it is of a bluish white colour, almost tasteless, specific gravity varying from 1030° to 1035°. Its microscopical characters are about the same as those of human milk, excepting that the milk-globules are more abundant. Its chemical composition is given on the next page.

Now it is clear, comparing this with human milk, that—1. The quantity of water is less in that of the cow; 2. The solid matters are in greater quantity; 3. The sugar is less in amount; 4. There is more casein; 5. And more butter; 6. The salts are also in excess.

It is quite manifest that, if the above analyses are to be depended upon, a simple dilution of this

ANALYSES OF GOAT'S MILK.

	Chevallier and Heuri.	Clemm.	Boysson.	John.	Payen.	Stipriaan. Liuscius, and Bondt.	Lehmann.	Douné.	Vernois and Becquerel.	Human Milk.
Water	868·0	865·175	892·8	849·3	855.0	744·0	886 to 884	819·4	844·90	889·08
Butter	32·2	42·507	29·9	11·7	40·8	45·6	33·2 to 42·5	-48·6	56·87	34·61
Casein	40·2	60·321	52·9	105·4	45·2	91·1	40·2 to 60·3	43·8	58·14	39·24
Sugar	52·8 }	44·065 {	20·7	28·4	—	43·8	40 to 53	91 2 (with ext.)	36·91	26·68
Salts	6·8 }								6·18	1 38
Residue of whey..	—	—	—	—	58·6	—	—	—	—	—
Cream	—	—	—	—	—	7·5	—	—	—	—

ANALYSES OF COW'S MILK.

	Simon.			Herberger.		Lecanu.	Bousin-gault.	Chevallier and Henri.	Poggiale (10 cows).	Playfair (9 cows).	Vernois and Becquerel (30 cows).
Water	857	861	823	862·0	853·0	868	874·0	870·2	862·8	—	864·06
Butter	40	38	55	37·5	38·9	36	39·0	31·3	43·8	49·0	36·12
Casein	72	68	67	67·0	69·8	56	34·0	44·8	38·0	41·6	—
Ditto, & extractive matter..	—	—	—	—	—	—	—	—	—	—	38·03
Sugar	28	29	51	26·3	31·3	40 }	53·0	47·7 }	52·7	—	55·15
Sugar, & extractive matter..	62	61	13	7·2	7·0					—	
Fixed Salts	—	—	—	—	—	—	—	6·0	—	—	6·64
Earthy salts	—	—	—	—	—	—	2·2	—	2·7 }	—	—

milk will not suffice. Water may be added, to diminish the relative quantity of casein and butter to the normal figure it attains in human milk ; but it will also reduce unduly the amount of sugar ; and thus, at the outset, we meet with a difficulty in its employment.

As with the goat, however, so with the cow,— the food supplied, and the circumstances under which it is given, will, in great measure, modify the character of the milk yielded ; and there are also some other differences quite compatible with health, referring to the circumstances in which cows are placed, which materially affect the nature and yield of milk.

(a) Country Milk and Town Milk.—The former is stated to be preferable to the latter. The reason is, no doubt, that the cows are less crowded together, and the milk is less watered.

Becquerel and Vernois have also proved the truth of this popular opinion from their experiments. See Table below. (The mean figures only are given.*)

* Influence of Season.

COMPOSITION OF COW'S MILK.

	Paris.		Country.
Specific gravity	1033·10	......	1033·72
Water	869·78	......	857·80
Solid constituents	130·42	......	142·20
Butter	33·66	......	38·85
Casein and extractive matters	53·66	......	57·00
Sugar	37·07	......	38·99
Salts	6·03	......	7·36

This difference is not, however, due to the mere exposure to country air, because experiments have proved that when cows are fed on hay, with oats or barley-straw, or the ordinary culinary roots with a certain quantity of wet bran, a similar milk is obtained from them in towns.

(b) Summer and Winter Milk.—Owing to the difference of nutriment given, the composition of these two milks is not the same. The principal difference observed in winter is a diminution of the water, and among the solid constituents an increase of the butter only; both the casein and sugar are slightly diminished. In summer there is more water; but what is remarkable is, that among the solid constituents the casein, sugar, and salts are diminished, and the butter is considerably increased.

(c) Milk, however, does not vary according to the season only, but according to the period of the day during which it is secreted.

In 1851, Dr. Hassall, in his report on the adulteration of milk, proved this. While ten samples of morning milk from different cows yielded collectively 77½ per cent. of cream, or an average of 7½ for each cow, the same number of samples of afternoon milk yielded 96¼ per cent., the average being 9¼. The curd amounting in the first case to 693, in the second to 810 grains. But milk varies more during the same milking, that last drawn being much richer than that first drawn, the latter yielding 61⅔ per cent. against 141⅓ per cent. of the former.*   More lately, Professor Boedecker, however, has completed a series of experiments, to elucidate this point, and he has arrived at the result that the milk of the evening is richer by 3 per cent. than that of the morning, the latter containing only 10 per cent. of solid matter, and the former 13 per cent.   On the other hand, the water contained in milk diminishes by 3 per cent. in the course of the day; in the morning it contains 89 per cent. of water, and only 86 per cent. in the evening. The fatty particles increase gradually as the day wears on.   In the morning they amount to 3·17 per cent.; at noon to 2·63, and in the evening to 3·42 per cent.   This circumstance, if true, would be very important in a practical point of view.   Let us suppose two pounds of milk to yield only the sixth part of its weight of butter; then the milk of the evening may yield double that quantity.   The caseous particles are also more abundant in the evening than in the morning—from 2·24 they increase to 2·70 per cent., but the quantity of albumen diminishes from 0·44 to 0·31.   The serum is less abundant at midnight than at noon, being 4·19 per cent. in the former case and 4·72 in the last.

(d) Results obtained by various kinds of Food, and by Beet-root in particular.—Dr. Playfair ad-

---

* *Lancet,* 1851, p. 322 and 258.

duces an example of a cow fed on much nitrogenous matter, in which not only was the amount of nitrogenous matter or casein in the milk increased, but also the butter. Certainly the yield of milk is increased by much of that stimulant diet which is occasionally administered after a time to cows, such as refuse slop from whiskey distillers, and which is known to be given largely in America, and for which cows acquire so depraved an appetite, that they will not afterwards take their ordinary food.* Other less exciting food has the same result. Thus, Parmentier and Deyeux found that cows fed on the leaves and stalks of maize yielded more milk than when fed on ordinary fodder. Moreover, the milk was extremely sweet. The milk obtained from cows fed on potatoes and common grass was much more serous and insipid. That from cows fed on cabbage was disagreeable to the taste. Hermanstadt found also that fresh aliments caused a larger quantity of sugar to appear in the milk than dry food. Mr. Curwin found† that coleseed when given to a cow was far the most productive of milk *(Brassica Napus. Rape);* and in this respect was superior to Swedish cabbages and Kohl-rabbi.

Among the most approved fodders for cows are

---

* Hassall. † *Treatise on Milk,* 1825.

sainfoin, Spanish, and ordinary trefoil; but there are a vast number of other annual plants among the graminaceæ or leguminosæ, which, if cultivated and given to the cows, would prove exceedingly useful. Indeed, Anderson assures us that cows fed upon trefoil, in addition to grass, yielded a superior kind of butter to that afforded by cows fed upon this famed pasture only. The ancient faculty of medicine in Paris appointed a commission in 1771 to trace the effects of various roots on the milk of cows. These reported the potato to be particularly useful in increasing the quality and the flow of milk; also, that its administration to the mothers of thin, weakly children, had led to the rapid improvement of these latter in every respect.

The effect of several varieties of food is set forth in figures in the table given below,* compiled

* AFTER CHEVALLIER AND HENRI.

	Ordinary fodder.	Beet.	Carrots.
Water	870·2	868·8	866·7
Casein	44·8	37·5	42·1
Sugar of milk	31·3	27·5	30·8
Butter	47·7	59·5	53·0
Salts	6·0	6·8	7·5

AFTER VERNOIS AND BECQUEREL.

	Summer food.	Winter food.	Normal Human milk.
Water	859·56	871·26	889·
Casein and extractive matters	54·7	47·81	39·24
Sugar of milk	36·38	33·47	26·66
Butter	42·76	42·07	34·61
Salts	6·80	5·34	1·38

from one quoted by Dr. Hassall from Chevallier and Henri, and from another given by Becquerel and Vernois. Chevallier and Henri's cows were fed on the ordinary fodder—beet-root and carrots. The winter food of those referred to by Becquerel and Vernois was daily one bundle and a half of trefoil or lucern, weighing from 12 to 13 pounds; half a bundle of oat-straw, weighing from 9 to 10 pounds; and at the rate of 55 pounds of beet-root per week, half in the morning and half at night, with two buckets of water daily for drink. The summer food was green trefoil and lucern, Indian corn, barley, grass, in no fixed quantity, in amount, however, estimated at from 99 to 100 pounds per week. At night, in returning from the field, the cows were given in the stable from 11 to 13 pounds of grass daily. Drink as in winter.

These tables prove that if cows be fed on carrots, the casein and butter are diminished, but the sugar increased in quantity; whereas, if fed on beet-root, both the casein and butter are much diminished, and the sugar is much increased. Here, as in the case of the goat, a milk is produced, which, except in the excess of the salts, is very like woman's milk.

It is manifest, therefore, that a great deal depends upon the manner in which cows are fed. Generally this is done in the cheapest possible way, because milching cows so deteriorate in value after eight or nine months use as such. I am told that cows purchased for £18 to £20 at the beginning of a season, will sell at a loss of £6 to £8 at the end of it; they look so small and meagre. This mode of feeding cows is after all only evidence of great shortsightedness in the owner, since the deterioration may be easily prevented. A very intelligent gentleman in Nottinghamshire has informed me, that if the cows are fed upon a steamed food composed of chopped hay, bran, malt culms, and rape-cake, not only will they produce an extra quantity of milk, but keep throughout the milching period in first-rate condition; in fact, they will at the end of the six or nine months look as well as they ever did.

CHAPTER III.

OF SOME OF THE OBJECTIONS TO THE USE OF ANIMAL MILKS.

ASS'S MILK: EXCESS OF SUGAR AND SALTS.—GOAT'S MILK: ADVAN-
TAGES FROM ITS EMPLOYMENT.—COW'S MILK: DIFFICULTIES IN
ITS EMPLOYMENT — ADULTERATION CHIEFLY WITH WATER —
ACIDITY. — MEYER'S EXPERIMENTS. — UNHEALTHY SHEDS FOR
COWS.—REVOLTING FILTHINESS OF SOME IN LONDON.—NECESSITY
FOR PARLIAMENTARY INTERFERENCE.

ASS'S MILK.—To the excess of salts is probably
due the purgative effect of ass's milk occasionally
noticed in adults who take it. The saline matter
amounts as a minimum to twice, as a maximum
to four times, as much as in human milk. Now if it
be a fact, as is usually stated in books, that ass's
milk is the best substitute for woman's milk (but
there are no conclusive experiments to prove it),
do children fed on it exclusively, invariably thrive?
Answers to these questions are important desi-
derata; but till the problem is solved, the substitution of ass's milk cannot be urged merely
because it contains more sugar than cow's milk,
or because it proves wholesome food to invalid

adults. In many adults, cow's milk in any quantity produces nausea and vomiting. It is usually well borne on the stomachs of infants, although it may disagree otherwise. But to make up the requisite quantity of casein and butter, twice as much of ass's milk would be needed. The quantity of sugar, as well as the *salts* thus taken, would be greatly in excess. Would not scrofula be developed as a result? And what good effect on the brain and bones would the excess of the salts produce? We know that sugar is not of itself capable of supporting life when it is given singly. Besides the debility which supervenes, abscesses form on the cornea, which penetrate internally, so as to let the humours escape. Finally death occurs. The *post mortem* appearances are —general atrophy of the muscles, contraction of the stomach and intestines, etc. These experiments, chiefly instituted by Magendie, however cruel and revolting, are not without their practical importance. Although it may be urged that no children are fed exclusively upon sugar, and that therefore the objection does not apply, still we often meet with a class of cachectic patients, eminently scrofulous, with morbid tastes for sweets. In these, strumous ophthalmia, with ulcers on the cornea, make their appearance. Is it not reasonable to conclude that these morbid products are due to a diet too exclusively saccharine? and have we not some grounds for fearing that very similar results would occur if we ventured to bring up children exclusively upon ass's milk?

But more than this: it has been shown by Lehmann and Elsasser, that *fat* exists in most of the fluids secreted by the body, and assists digestion along the whole course of the alimentary canal. The solution of food, although delayed by *excess*, is hastened by a moderate quantity of fat. So also, in early or fœtal development it is the fat-globule which attracts, as it were, the albumen or nitrogenous elements around it, acting in the cell-growth as the nucleus around which parts grow. Moreover, the fats of the blood are also deposited in the blood-globule—the portion in the blood generally admitted as most concerned in the nutrition of the body; and this is doubtless one of the reasons why cod-liver oil proves often so useful. To attempt, therefore, to feed a child exclusively on food poor in fatty matters, as ass's milk, is evidently unphilosophical.

It has been stated by Mr. Lobb, that, by adding two and a half per cent. of *cream* to ass's milk, a very good substitute for human milk would be procured with great ease. "The expense of ass's milk," remarks Mr. Lobb, "would put it out of the reach of the poor." He might have added, the expense of *cream* in towns would have the same effect. The suggestion, however, is a good

one, because in the country it might be easily
procured.

In many parts of Great Britain, asses are to be
obtained at a very cheap rate. I am told five
shillings are in some places, in winter, gladly
accepted; and I believe thirty shillings is the
usual price. If, therefore, ass's milk can be
successfully modified by the addition of cream, a
herd of these animals would prove most useful to a
foundling hospital, not only in providing milk for
the infants, but in affording a ready method of
exercise; while as beasts of burden they would
prove valuable, particularly if situated in a country
neighbourhood or by the sea-side. To determine,
therefore, the practical usefulness of ass's milk,
in combination with cream, would be no small
matter, and would be fraught with immense advantages. Theory, on the other hand, condemns
its use when given on scientific grounds, and,
until its usefulness is proved by practice, I feel
bound to oppose the popular prejudice.

Goat's Milk.—The table given at p. 271 shows
that the milk from a goat, if she has been fed
upon beet-root, very closely resembles in chemical
composition that of a woman, only that it is richer
in sugar and salts. It certainly comes much
nearer to human milk than ass's milk. Indeed,
as evidence that practice confirms theory in this
instance, I may cite experience in Ireland. In

that country, I am informed, the foundlings of Dublin were very many years back sent to the mountains of Wicklow, to feed upon the goats' milk. As the children grew older, the goats came to know them, and became very tame; so that the infant could go to the goat to be suckled by it, as it would to a human wet-nurse. The children throve, I am told, remarkably well. The same results, I am informed, have been observed in Malta.

It is therefore to be much regretted that an animal so easily kept and obtained should not be more generally employed. If our Foundling Hospitals were to have establishments in the country, where goats might be kept in numbers, there would be no need for exclusiveness in admitting cases, infanticide might cease, and the hundreds of babies now sacrificed to the murderous system of dry-nursing, might be saved to their parents and the nation.

Cow's Milk.—The disadvantages met with in the employment of this variety of milk are well known to most of us; they are disadvantages dependent upon its bad quality, and are very serious in their results, and very difficult to overcome.

A few of these I will consider *seriatim*. They are—

1. Adulteration of cow's milk.

2. Its acidity, dependent upon stall-feeding.

3. The effect upon milk produced by keeping cows in unhealthy sheds.

1. *Adulteration.*—The most painful part of our experience in towns is, that pure milk cannot be procured; it is almost always adulterated. In the excellent work of Becquerel and Vernois, the *Annales d'Hygiène*, it is said to be adulterated in Paris by the following substances :—water, glucose, flour, starch, dextrine, infusion of amylaceous matters (rice, barley, bran), yolk of egg and white of egg, sugar, gelatine, liquorice, boiled carrots, broken-down calves' brains, serum of blood, several salts, bicarbonate of soda, chalk, turmeric, emulsion of hemp or almond seeds, etc. We do not, however, find that in England these are commonly employed, but adulteration by water is extensively practised. Dr. Hassall, out of 26 samples of milk, found that 11 were adulterated with water in the proportions of from 10 to 50 per cent.

Dr. Sanderson, the medical officer of health for Paddington, found out of thirty-two specimens of the milk examined by himself and Dr. Alfred Bernays of St. Mary's Hospital, that in all, except one, the quantity of water was greater than it was in pure milk. In twelve instances the quantity of solid constituents was only half as great as it ought to have been, in a few only one-fourth; many specimens contained less than 6·5 or 5·8 per cent., a few, 3·5 instead of 12·98, as in pure healthy milk.

Dr. Hillier, the medical officer of St. Pancras, examined twenty specimens of milk, and found that the quantity of water added varied from 25 to 50 per cent. That supplied to the workhouse was one of the poorest. Instead of a gallon containing nearly 9,000 grains of *solid* matter, it contained only 5,425 grains, or two-thirds the proper quantity. Dr. R. D. Thompson found in Marylebone, that the gallon of milk, in seven samples, weighed as a mean 71,680 instead of 72,415 grains, which amounts to the withdrawal of 1·44 oz. of solid matter, well calculated to nourish the body, and substituting for it water. Dr. Hyde Salter and Mr. Hunt, from the confessions made to them by milkwomen, their patients, state the quantity of water usually added is one gallon of water to two of milk. What sort of food can this be for an infant, especially if diluted, as it almost invariably is, by the purchaser, and often afterwards by medical direction? Is it to be wondered at that children fed on such weak milk do not thrive?

2. *Acidity.*—Cow's milk, except the animal has been fed exclusively upon grass, is almost always *acid* in stall-fed cows; human milk is always alkaline; hence another reason why cow's milk disagrees with many children.

U

The experiments of Dr. Mayer of Berlin are particularly conclusive upon this point. He says that for a considerable time he had been in the habit of examining the milk supplied to house-holders in Berlin, and testing it by litmus paper, according as the cows were fed from brewery slops or brandy lees, gardeners' produce, or in the country. In every instance, except one, he had found the milk decidedly sour.

(*a.*) Of cows fed with brewers' lees, red pota-toes, rye bran, and wild hay, in five instances the milk was slightly sour, in one very much so.

(*b.*) Of forty cows fed with potato mash, barley husk, and clover and barley straw, in ten which were examined, the milk was sour, in three very sour.

(*c.*) From among fifty cows, fed on potato husks, barley husks, and wild hay, five were exa-mined, and in all the fresh milk was sour.

(*d.*) From fifty-two cows, fed on potato mash, husks, wild hay, and rye straw, out of twelve se-lected for examination, the fresh milk of all was sour.

(*e.*) From six cows, fed by a chief gardener on coarse beet-root, red potato, bran mash, and hay, the fresh milk was slightly sour.

(*f.*) From five cows, fed by a cow-feeder on lukewarm bran mash and hay, in four the fresh milk was quite neutral, in one it was decidedly alkaline.

The whole of these experiments were made in the winter season, when the cows were necessarily stall-fed, and they confirm the truth of the general opinion, that the fresh milk of stall-fed cows is almost invariably acid. Dr. Mayer does not believe that this acidity is due to want of exercise, so much as to the unscientific manner in which the cows are fed; and he particularly objects to the potato mash, which he considers the cause of the acidity. The milk of the cows of gardeners and cow-feeders is usually praised by the Berlin women as being particularly good. But Dr. Mayer has observed that it often gives rise to diarrhœa and cutaneous eruptions in children; which, he supposes, is due to the cows being fed with the cabbage, turnip, and potato refuse. The very worst milk is that supplied by cows fed on potato refuse from brandy distillers; the best among the stall-fed being that obtained from the cows of cow fatteners, which feed on hay and grass in stalls. By substituting the milk of the latter for the former, he was often enabled to arrest at once the intestinal derangements previously referred to.

3. *Effect on Milk produced by keeping Cows in unhealthy Sheds.*—The supply of good and selected food is, however, only one part of the management needed to insure good milk from milk-bearing animals. Excessive cleanliness should in

every way be enforced.   Upon the subject of the cleansing of cow-sheds, Messrs. Parmentier and Deyeux remark :—" Nothing contributes more to maintain the good quality and quantity of cow's milk than scrupulous cleanliness in the shed.   If the refuse matters are left about and removed only at long intervals, the cows lying amid all this mess are always weak ; the udders are hot; and the milk, so susceptible of acquiring a bad odour, soon contracts a bad taste, of which it is with difficulty again deprived.   The great reputation of the cows of the Prevalaye is due to the remarkable cleanliness in which they are kept, which also enables them to yield an abundance of milk, and to be particularly free from disease."

A very slight glance at what is revealed to us in Dr. Hassall's book as to the unhealthy localities and ill-ventilated sheds in which cows are kept in London, will convince any man of common sense that the cows in such localities cannot be healthy, and that their milk must also prove occasionally very detrimental.

I have, in the course of a large dispensary practice, visited some of the wretched inhabitants living either in the immediate neighbourhood, or over these sheds.   On one occasion I remember having to cross through the shed to get to the small upper room above it, where lay a child infected with fever.   The puddles of liquid and fæcal matters through which I was forced to pass, and the abominable odour pervading the apartment, I have not yet forgotten; and yet from this cow-shed a large proportion of the neighbourhood was supplied.

The character of disease which attacks the wretched inmates of the small, close cottages just around it is always low, if not typhoid. Many examples are given in Dr. Hassall's book of the wretched, filthy, and offensive sheds in which cows are kept. A common sewer would be in many cases equally pure. These facts are well known to most medical and to many general readers of the *Lancet*. I shall, however, content myself with very few quotations. The first from the *Lancet*, which retails Dr. Normandy's experience, and some others included in the reports of the Officers of Health of later date.

In the Report of the Commission on Adulterations (quoted by the *Lancet*, ii, 1855, p. 551), Dr. Normandy states he was lately in the neighbourhood of Clerkenwell for the purpose of examining a well in that locality, when he met with a sight which prevented him from tasting milk for six months afterwards. He there saw from thirty to forty cows in a most disgusting condition, full of ulcers, their teats diseased, and their legs full of tumours and abscesses; in fact, quite horrible to look at; and a fellow was milking them despite of all these abominations. This was by no means an exceptional case, a great many dairies being in the same condition. The milk in consequence provided was really *diseased milk*. This state of the poor animals must have been produced by the manner in which they were kept.

In speaking of cow-sheds, Dr. Hillier says of St. Pancras, that there are ninety-two such establishments, some well placed, with good drainage; twenty-two are not near inhabited dwellings; others quite underground; twenty with inhabited rooms above them; some surrounded by noxious exhalations. Their size is often very insufficient; the cubic space for each cow is sometimes as low as 230 feet; 1,000 to 1,500 being not at all more than cows require. The drainage is very bad in twenty or thirty. Very few are efficiently ventilated; whilst from forty to fifty are as bad as they can be in this respect. Forty of the sheds are kept in a most filthy condition. Seven sheds are without water supply. The manure is kept too long in seventy-six cases; in sixty-three, there is no suitable pit for it; in scarcely any is the place covered over. Occasionally the manure heap is immediately under the windows of dwelling houses, and in some instances is made the receptacle for the contents of human *retirades*. The grains on which the cows are fed are usually kept until they are sour, and give out an offensive smell. In seventeen sheds the cows drank distillers' wash, which was kept in uncovered receptacles, and was very offensive. In addition, there is often vegetable matter lying about the yard in a rotten state. In fifteen of the sheds pigs are kept as companions to the cows. Some of the animals are very clean, being curried and attended to in the same way as horses. In many instances, on the contrary, they are fearfully neglected, and their coats are either one entangled mass of filth, or else are free from hair, owing to a diseased state of the skin. In a leading article in the *Lancet** we read,—"If we may credit, and we are not disposed to question the statements of Professor Gamgee, who some time ago visited several of the London cowhouses, cows are found having abscesses on their udders discharging pus into the milk-pails, and others suffering from various diseases." The filthy state in which some cowhouses were found in 1857 by Dr. Lankester,* in the aristocratic district of St. James's, is also evidence of a most disgraceful state of things, formerly very generally prevalent.

The deaths from diseases of cows are enormous. One cowkeeper, out of a large number, lost in one year ninety; another, who keeps fifty

---

* Nov. 1862, p. 508.   † *Report* of 1857, district of St. James's.

cows, lost three hundred in six years; another, with from four hundred to five hundred cows, considered it not bad luck to lose two cows weekly from disease. Insurance prices tell a tale. *Country* dairy cows are insured at sixpence to sevenpence halfpenny in the pound; *London* dairy cows, at eighteen pence to two shillings in the pound; so that they consider the risk on town cows three times as great as on country cows. Dr. Sanderson in his report says the mortality of cows in Paddington was three hundred and four in 1856. In a large proportion the drainage and ventilation were deficient, and fatal disease had prevailed to a frightful extent among the animals kept. No less than 19 per cent. of the whole number of cows had died in three months; in one case all the cows died.

So much for a few dainty spots in this great town. But is it better in other parts of England, or in other great towns? When diseased cows—many of which, to use a common term, are in consumption, or whose bodies are one mass of ulcers and abscesses—are the animals selected to provide milk in our large towns, is it wonderful that so many children brought up by hand die in towns, while so few comparatively die in the country? No wonder, then, as Dr. Merei says, is it that cow's milk is so depreciated among the working classes. That gentleman states, that of all children fed on other articles besides bread (and the number, from another table, appears to be 602 out of 722), only seven, or 1·1 per cent., received cow's milk without bread or other admixture; twenty-seven, or 4·4 per cent., used it with arrow-root or sago, partly with flour.

There can be no doubt, from the general foregoing remarks, that if the subject were more closely studied, cows and goats might be so cared for and so fed as to yield a quality of milk which would be found most serviceable to children brought up by hand. The milk obtained from cows fed upon beet-root, with a very small dilution of water, might be brought so closely to resemble human milk as in all respects to perform the same services. But every day's experience proves that nothing but the most stringent measures can effectually remedy the abuses that prevail. *Parliament must interfere:* and in what better cause could it do so than by compelling all cowkeepers to sell good milk, to strengthen the bone and sinew of its people, and preserve the lives of thousands of helpless babes? Till this is done, our best efforts, it is feared, will prove nugatory.

It is one of the greatest advantages of the New Metropolitan Act, that we have medical sanitary officers now appointed, and men of undoubted eminence in their profession to superintend these matters, and to correct the abuses. Herein Lord Llanover has deserved the gratitude of thousands : herein is to be found a great cause of the present and future diminution of infant mortality.

CHAPTER IV.

OF OTHER ANIMAL SUBSTITUTES — CREAM —DESICCATED MILKS :
MOORE'S AND GRIMSDALE'S—EGGS—BONE SOUPS AND JELLIES—
—BEEF-TEAS—SWEETBREAD-TEA—RAW MEAT—CAUTION IN EM-
PLOYMENT OF LATTER.

THE difficulties which surround the employment of cow's milk, in the state in which only it is procurable, have led to ingenious contrivances for its modification. Thus—

Cream as a Substitute.—I have before said that there are some cases in which no wet-nurse can be found to suit a child; and in these, moreover, milk in its several forms may be tried, but the efforts to bring up that child upon milk will fail altogether. In many of these cases, it is observed that there is a great quantity of acid produced in the stomach of the child, and the same effect results when it takes saccharine matters. It is in such instances that the mixture of one part of cream to three of water proves often very beneficial. I have known of a child reduced almost to a state of complete atrophy, gradually recovering its good looks and strength on this change of diet. Cream in composition contains pretty nearly the same ingredients as milk, except that the casein is diminished, and the fatty matters considerably increased. In this manner, the absence of sugar is compensated for by the excess of fatty matters; and thus the fluid produced is sufficiently rich, both as a nutritive and as a calorifiant aliment. The addition of water diminishes the density, and makes the mixture more digestible. If to every half-pint of this mixture half an ounce of lime-water be added, the tendency to the formation of acid is removed, the solubility of the casein and the emulsion of the fatty matters are insured, and both these last become more assimilable.

Something like a substitute may be found, however, in the employment of *desiccated milks,* to which if water in proper proportions is added, a milk presenting all the peculiarities of good rich milk is produced. Two of these kinds are known in London—Moore's Patent Concentrated Milk, and Grimsdale's Patent Desiccated Milk. In a communication received from Mr. Moore, through a late friend, that gentleman stated that his milk could be manufactured at 1s. 4d. per lb., which would be equal to one gallon of pure milk. The milk is, I understand, merely evaporated at a temperature under the boiling point. It appears to possess many advantages.

The other preparation, Grimsdale's Desiccated Milk, is not in the form of extract, but rather of powder, of the same bluish white colour as milk. This has rather a gritty feel to the finger, and, when put on the tongue, a strong milky taste; and it mixes readily with boiling water. It is sometimes acid, sometimes alkaline. From calculation, one ounce of the powder requires 6·4 oz. of boiling water to make it of the same strength as milk. I have no experience of its uses or advantages. The objection to it seems to be, that it needs boiling water for its solution; nor am I aware if it is in its preparation evaporated to the consistence of an extract by heat above or under 212° Fahr.

Other Substitutes for Milk. Eggs.—It would appear natural, from the lessons comparative anatomy and chemistry give us, that where milk could not be procured, *eggs* would afford a good substitute. Indeed, in composition the egg presents several points of analogy to milk. It is true we have albumen in the place of casein; but these two substances, for all practical purposes, may be considered as identical. The white of the egg is albumen in a very pure state, with about 22 per cent. of water, and 0·65 per cent. of salts. The yolk, with 52 per cent. of water, and 1·52 per cent. of salts, contains as its albuminous compound a substance called *vitelline*, very like albumen in composition, but coloured by an oil containing phosphoric acid, and in its ultimate composition being a little richer in hydrogen and oxygen. Moreover, Barreswill has determined the presence of sugar in the white of egg. It has an alkaline reaction, which is due to the presence of carbonate of soda. The yolk, on the contrary, contains little or no alkali, and its emulsive character is to be ascribed to the presence of a substance very like pancreatic juice. The proportion of white of egg to yolk may be stated as 60·6 to 39·4 and 58·4 to 41·6.

By reference to the subjoined table* it will at

---

* *Composition of Egg* (Gobley).

				Yolk.
Water	·	·	·	51·3
Vitelline	·	·	·	15·7
Margarine and Oleine	·	·	·	21·3
Cholesterine	·	·	·	0·4
Phosphorous body 7·2 ⎫				
Oleic acid 1·2 ⎬	·	·	8·4	
Phosphoglyceric acid ⎭				
Cerebric substance	·	·	·	0·3
Salts ·	·	·	·	2·3

				White.
Water	·	·	·	77·15
Albumen	·	·	·	22·2
Salts	·	·	·	0·65

The salts raised to 100 parts contain, according to Polack,—

			Yolk.		White.
Chloride of potassium	·	·	—	...	42·17
Chloride of sodium	·	·	—	...	14·07
Potass	·	·	6·57	...	16·09
Soda	·	·	8·05	...	1·15
Lime	·	·	13·28	...	2·79
Magnesia	·	·	2·11	...	3·17
Sesquioxide of iron	·	·	1·19	...	·55
Phosphoric acid	·	·	66·70	...	5·79
Carbonic abid	·	·	—	...	11·52
Sulphuric acid	·	·	—	...	1·32
Silica	·	·	1·4	...	2·04

once be seen, that in the quantity of phosphoric acid, and of chloride of potassium, only to a larger extent, egg resembles milk and flesh, and, as such, must possess similar properties in nourishing a child.

The white of egg, however, should be given as nearly as possible raw, or, if warm, only heated to 130° Fahr. Beyond this temperature it coagulates, and then becomes much more difficult of digestion. If the egg be put in boiling water for two minutes only, except a thin external layer of albumen which will have been coagulated, it will be warmed throughout. Cow's milk contains 5·5 of casein per cent. and white of egg as much as 11·1, yolk 1·5—together 12·6. Eggs should, therefore, be diluted; and, with a little sugar of milk added, would form a very fair substitute for milk.

Bone Soups and Jellies have been recommended as aliments for children. The opinion at present almost universally entertained is, that gelatine, the chief ingredient in such soups, etc., although a nitrogenous substance, is, like hair, innutritious. It is unassimilable by children, as well as by older persons; and it only overloads the blood with nitrogenous products, which render this fluid impure and unfit for the purposes for which it is required. Still, as an emulcent in cases of irritation of the bowels, or for the exhibition of wine or particular remedies, jellies may be useful, occasionally, just as arrowroot may be given in similar affections.

Next in order, as substitutes for milk, are beef-teas; and of these I shall speak of three kinds only—Liebig's Beef-tea, a beef-tea made with artificial gastric juice, and Hogarth's Essence of Beef. Meat possesses this advantage over vegetable food—in a given weight it contains more nutritious matter. An essence or extract of meat thus contains, in a still smaller weight, all the nutritive properties essential to the maintenance of life, and, if mixed with a little fat, all the nutritive and combustible properties to be desired. Unfortunately, a complete extract of meat, entirely soluble in water, cannot be made, owing to the insolubility of fibrin.

Liebig's Beef-tea.—When flesh is finely lixiviated with cold water, all its soluble matters are removed, and a perfectly tasteless, inodorous residue is left, which in every case is white like fish. The solution remaining is highly coloured, and consists of lactic and inosinic acids, creatine, creatinine, and a nitrogenous organic acid, which forms a pellicle on the surface like casein, though differing from it in many other respects. There are several other ingredients not very clearly made out, besides chloride of potassium, phosphates, especially of the alkalies, a little lime, and more magnesia.*

It is this solution which is to be evaporated to dryness, and constitutes the best *extract of meat*. In doing so, however, as the albumen in it coagulates at 133° Fahr., and the colouring matter at 158° Fahr., and would above this temperature be precipitated, it is advisable to evaporate it in a sand bath, at 120°; in this manner all the nutritive, combustible, and mineral matter will be retained. To this extract more or less water may be added, according to the strength of the tea required. It is well to use on these occasions the flesh of young animals in preference to old. In the latter case the albumen will vary from 1 to 2 per cent., while in the former, it will be as high as from 12 to 14 per cent.

The extract prepared by Mr. Roberton, of Manchester, and obtained in the form of a dry powder, is the best I am acquainted with. However, except in cases where haste is required, there is scarcely any need of using any extract, since the beef-tea itself, prepared by lixiviation in water over night, is more easily obtained. This, also, should not be heated above 120° to 130°; nor even boiled. If more body is required, a little flour or fine oatmeal may be added to the

---

* See Appendix F.

X

tea, so as to thicken it; in which state also finely divided meat may be added, and so suspended in it. Lastly, a little lime-water may be mixed with it, to remove any excess of acidity.

A beef-tea has been recommended which promises to have some advantages even over Liebig's. I allude to one made with a prepared or artificial gastric juice. We are all aware that the digestion of nitrogenous matters is chiefly effected in the stomach, and this through the instrumentality of a fluid called "*the gastric juice*," which possesses the particular property of dissolving very speedily all azotized aliments. This *artificial* gastric juice can be readily prepared by digesting the mucous membrane of the stomach of any animal in dilute hydrochloric acid. The best proportion for making the latter is three drops of the strong acid to one ounce of water. By exposing this mixture to a gentle temperature of 70° Fahr., we obtain a fluid possessing all the properties of gastric juice. If beef-tea be first prepared on Liebig's plan, and then after a few hours' maceration in cold water the artificial gastric juice be added, and the temperature raised to 70° Fahr., some of the fibrin will be taken up as well as the albuminous matters before in solution in the supernatant water; and a beef-tea much richer in azotized food—in fact, an *artificial chyme*—will be obtained. *Pepsine*, the active principle which exists in the gastric juice, used singly, acts upon fibrin but slowly. But, as before stated, the juice of meat contains lactic acid. When pepsine and lactic acid are conjoined the solution of the fibrin takes place very quickly. For cases of defective or weak assimilation, the advantages of such a beef-tea are very obvious.

The same result can be obtained by addition of the liquor pepsinii, or the essence of rennet, in both of which we have the principal ingredient of gastric juice, which in cases of defective assimilation is so much required.

Another method, of which I have no experience, yet which theoretically appears very plausible, would be the addition to beef-tea, or to milk, of a solution of *sweet-bread*, or a pancreatic tea, or broken down pieces of the sweet-bread itself. It is known that fatty matters are saponified by the secretion of this gland, which is always contained, in some proportion, in the substance of the gland itself, which may, therefore, be substituted for it. The secretion also converts starch into sugar, and probably also exerts a solvent action upon azotized matters. I shall, however, again refer to this point in the sequel.

Hogarth's Essence of Meat.—Of the composition of this material I can say nothing, except that I believe it is a concentrated solution of meat-tea —in fact, a meat-tea reduced by the evaporation of its watery ingredients to the consistence of a syrup. I can, however, confidently speak from experience of its utility. It is certain that children who have been reduced to a state of great weakness by hand-feeding, or improper diet, occasionally recover, and that almost marvellously, under its influence. I have used principally the essence of beef. Its taste is much liked; and in doses of five or six teaspoonfuls daily, with a very little water, it is well digested by children. Indeed, it is often borne in infants affected with exhaustive diarrhœa from weaning, when milk and farinaceous food disagree.

This result may probably explain the success occasionally obtained by the administration in exhaustive diarrhœa, of raw meat, which is but a step further in the same direction. " In these circumstances," says Dr. West,* " there is still one article of food—raw meat—which, strange as it may seem, is often eagerly taken, and always perfectly well digested. Professor Weisse, of St. Petersburg,† first recommended its employment in children suffering from diarrhœa after weaning; and it has been since then frequently given by other physicians in Germany in cases of long standing diarrhœa. The lean either of beef or mutton very finely shred may be given in quan-

---

* *Diseases of Children*, p. 498.
† *Journal für Kinderkrankheiten*, vol. iv, p. 99.

tities at first of not more than two teaspoonfuls four times a day to children of a year old, and afterwards, if they crave for more, a larger quantity may be allowed. I have seldom found any difficulty in getting children to take it; often, indeed, they are clamorous for it; it does not nauseate if given in small quantities, nor does it ever aggravate the diarrhœa; while, in some instances, it has appeared to have been the only means by which the life of the child has been preserved. With returning convalescence the desire for this food subsides, and the child can without difficulty be replaced on its ordinary diet."

Upon this point more lately some very important facts have been recorded by Dr. F. P. Leverett, of South Carolina, in an article reproduced as an abstract in the *Dublin Medical Press*.* As the subject is most important, I may be pardoned for giving this abstract almost in full.

"In the fall of 1855, Dr. Caspar Lewis introduced the use of raw beef into the children's ward of the Philadelphia Hospital, to which he was the attending physician and lecturer. He had the fillet of beef as free from fat as possible, scraped with a knife, so as to obtain the pulp, as

* May 9, 1860; *Charlestown Medical Journal*, Sept. 1859.

Weisse, of St. Petersburg, recommended. This he seasoned generally with salt, sometimes with sugar, so as to tempt the children. He gave of this pulp at first a teaspoonful, three or four times a day, and gradually increased the amount as the child's fondness for it increased. It required but a few days in any case to get the child to take it with readiness, if not avidity; some even relished it from the first. Many of the students who attended Dr. Morris's clinical lecture in 1855, witnessed the great benefit which many of the children derived from this remedy, then new in our country. Weisse some years previously recommended its use in the diarrhœa of weaned children, but to the comparative inattention it received in Europe may be assigned the reason of its being almost unknown to us. Dr. Morris mentioned to Dr. Leverett, that it had been suggested to him by his friend Professor Thomas, of Baltimore, who had used it with great benefit for one of his children suffering with chronic diarrhœa."

There are several cases related in the paper above referred to, in which raw meat was given with the greatest advantage. Their consideration, however, more properly belongs to the *treatment* of defective assimilation, and will occupy our attention when we come to discuss that portion of our subject. It was necessary to mention this remedy in this place, as a most important mode of cure, and one often eminently successful when all other means have failed. The objection to it is one to which Dr. Leverett in the above paper also refers, namely, that raw meat, often at least on the Continent, contains the ova of tape-worm, and hence those who take it in this state become affected with this parasite. A case of this kind has lately occupied the attention of medical observers; and as raw meat is likely now to become from its manifold advantages a frequent remedy, it is as well to refer to it in this place by way of caution.

"On January 12, 1860, a robust maid-servant was admitted into the Dresden Hospital. She had been indisposed since Christmas, and confined to bed since New Year's Day, complaining of depression, lassitude, sleeplessness, loss of appetite, and thirst. These symptoms persisted on her admission. There was considerable pyrexia; the abdomen was painful and tympanitic, and although neither splenic tumour nor roseola were present, the case was put down as one of typhoid fever. A remarkable affection of the whole muscular system now rapidly supervened, consisting in extreme painfulness of the extremities, with contraction of knee and elbow joints, and œdematous swelling, particularly of the legs. The pain was so severe that the patient was continually moaning. Pneumonic symptoms now appeared, and death took place on the 27th inst., preceded by an apathetic condition. The *post mortem* examination showed in the internal organs merely an atelectatic condition of the left lung, with numerous small lobular infiltrations, bronchitis, and hyperæmia of the mucous lining of the ilium. The muscles, however, which showed a greyish red colour and a slightly freckled appearance, were found, on microscopic examination, to harbour vast numbers of *non-capsulated trichinæ*. The par~ sites were living, some coiled in spirals, others with extended bodies, and all (as Professor Virchow was the first to show, in a fragment of muscle which was forwarded him for examination) living in a sarcolemma of the primitive fibrils. They showed various stages of development. They were diffused over all the striated muscles of the body, with the exception of the heart, and that in such vast numbers that, under a small magnifying power, as many as twenty were counted in the field of vision simultaneously. The muscular substance was otherwise fragile, homogeneous, and non-striated, and showed numerous transverse fissures. The intestinal mucus was found to be swarming with mature trichinæ of both sexes; and the remarkable fact was elucidated, that female trichinæ are viviparous, the central portion of the bodies being observed to be full of well-developed embryos.

" Inquiry being directed to the probable source of trichinatous infection, it was ascertained that on December 21, four days before the patient was taken ill, two pigs and an ox had been slaughtered on the establishment of her master. Some smoked ham and sausage, prepared from the meat of one of the pigs, were fortunately obtained, and on examination proved to be full of trichinæ. The parasites had a shrunken appearance, otherwise unchanged; reassumed a normal appearance on addition of water, but showed no signs of vitality. It is particularly worthy of remark, that to the naked eye the ham appeared quite healthy. It is very likely that the deceased had partaken of some of the raw meat. The butcher of the establishment (butchers notoriously indulge in raw meat) had also been taken seriously ill a short time afterwards, and had been confined to his bed for three weeks with severe muscular pains, his whole body being semi-paralytic, etc. This complaint was ascribed to rheumatism at the time, but Professor Zenker correctly surmises, that an immigration of trichinæ not sufficiently extensive to prove fatal, may have been the cause of attack, and that capsulated trichinæ would be very likely discernible in his muscle."*

It may be stated that muscles are liable to two kinds of parasitical infection—commonly found in the abdominal muscles of sheep, and often present in the rabbits of London. One of these is the *cysticercus*. The muscle is covered by a number of small bladders. On opening one of these, a small animal, bladder-shaped also, with a prolonged portion, at the extremity of which is the head, is observed. The other variety is the *trichina spiralis*, above alluded to. This creature is generally confined to the voluntary muscles, and is occasionally found in animals who during life have been apparently in good health. The muscles affected with this parasite are more fragile than usual; and to the naked eye, instead of looking red and clean, have a freckled appearance, or here and there a greyish aspect, which it is at once obvious is not due to an intermixture of fat. Looked at more closely, numerous transverse fissures are found on the surface, together with a number of white spots or vesicles, which are oval-shaped, and opaque at each extremity. Within each vesicle is a *worm* coiled upon itself. This is the *trichina*.

Meat about to be given *raw* should, therefore,

---

* *Medical Times*, June 1860.

from prudential reasons, be carefully examined: if it appear grey, and there are any spots on the surface, it is a suspicious specimen. A small magnifying power will at once, however, clear up the doubt. Fortunately in this country beef is seldom, if ever, infected with these parasites, and it is this variety of meat which is usually prescribed in a raw state.

CHAPTER V.

MODE OF CORRECTION OF IMPURE MILKS, AND OF PREPARATION
OF ARTIFICIAL MILKS TO RESEMBLE HUMAN MILK.

IN the foregoing chapter sufficient has been said on the use of the various kinds of milk in their natural condition. Let us now consider the questions—1. The correction of inferior milks, so as to adapt them for the sustenance of infants; 2. The preparation from strong and rich milk of a compound resembling human milk.

1. *Correction of inferior kinds of Milk.*—The correction of milk depends, in the first place, on the means we have of determining its purity. Practically, however, except in the laboratory of the chemist, we can do no more than to judge of the amount of its dilution with water, which is, after all, the usual adulteration practised in this country. To determine this amount of water, two ways, among many others, require mention here: that devised by Dr. Minchin, and that by Dr. Merei.*

* *Dublin Medical Press*, Aug. 8, 1860; Ranking, vol. xxxii, p. 9.

Dr. Minchin's method depends upon the translucency of the milk. A certain amount of transparency exists with the purest milk; but in proportion as it is more or less translucent, so in proportion are we able to test the amount of dilution. The instrument he has devised is made of brass, in the form of a shallow oblong vessel, capable of containing about an ounce of fluid; the depth of the vessel is made to increase gradually by means of a slab of white enamel, fixed in a gentle slope from one end to the other. The slab is graduated throughout its entire length. Upon this the milk is poured till the vessel is filled, and a cover of plate glass is then put on; this should be done by giving it a sliding motion, to exclude air-bubbles.

When the vessel full of milk is thus covered, the degree of dilution possessed by a sample under examination is estimated by the number of degrees on the enamel, which can be read through the glass cover; for the glass being in contact with the edge of the enamel plate at one end, and separated from it by a gradually increasing interval towards the other, the intervening stratum of milk is made to assume the form of a thin edge. If the fluid under examination be of a rich quality, abounding in oily and caseous particles, it will possess such an amount of opacity that only a few degrees can be discovered on the subjacent enamel when the instrument is held opposite the light. If, on the contrary, the specimen be of inferior quality, whether from innate poverty or the admixture of water, the diminution of opacity thence resulting will be evinced by the enamel scale becoming visible through a deeper part of the fluid, or at a greater distance from the commencement of the scale: the degree of transparency, therefore, can be measured by the number of lines visible through the fluid."

2. The method of Dr. Merei is equally simple, and depends upon the quantity of cream that can be separated from a given quantity of milk. If we take a tube nine inches long by half an inch wide, graduated into sixteenth parts of an inch, and put into it about two ounces of milk and the same quantity of water, and expose it to a temperature of 50° to 60° Fahr. for about eighteen or twenty-four hours, the cream will be found to have separated, and will be observed as a whiter, more opaque substance, floating on the surface of the milk. If this stratum above the milk amounts to seven or eight of the graduated degrees, that milk is essentially good and rich, and contains about six and a half to seven and a half of butter. Medium milk will contain only five or six degrees; the worst kinds, only three degrees; and the inferior qualities supplied to the

poor (skim milk), only two degrees. Here, then, is a ready means of measuring quality.

Now, experience has shown that such poor milk causes more gastric disorders than rich milk; nay more, that to obviate this result it requires a greater dilution than rich milk, notwithstanding its poverty. Dr. Merei attributes this to the preponderance of casein, which is one of the chief causes of gastric disorder. This casein, it is observed, is both *harder* and *coarser* in cows than in human milk. This is, no doubt, one cause; but there is another which, I think, applies, and which is mainly due to the dishonesty of milk-dealers. The cowkeeper has already watered his milk, to separate a certain amount of cream from it. The retail milk-keeper has very frequently done the same. The butter has thus been already taken out. Lactic acid has formed, and what butter remains in the milk is scarcely now contained in perfect combination as an emulsion, but is disintegrated, or, as it were, in imperfect mechanical suspension only. The casein is perhaps in the same state.

Dr. Merei's experience, in the method he adopts to improve inferior milks, seems to point also to this view of the case.

In case of feeble children, with bowels previously deranged, he recommends that, instead of diluting the milk with water, we should add a

decoction of arrowroot, made with one teaspoonful of this substance to three-quarters of a pint
of water, this quantity to serve for the admixture
of the whole day's supply. In more severe cases,
the arrowroot may be increased to two teaspoonfuls. This arrowroot is not given as an aliment,
but as a softish substance to soothe mechanically
the irritation of the intestinal mucous membrane.
Langenbeck, indeed, believes that in such cases
the granules of starch intersperse themselves between the particles of casein, and thus in great
measure prevent the formation of hard indigestible
curds.

The mixture Dr. Merei gives consists of three
or four pints of this thin decoction of arrowroot to one part of new milk slightly boiled,
and in the twenty-four hours amount of food thus
prepared he adds about one to two tablespoonfuls
of *cream*. Children will digest well from a pint to
a pint and a half of this mixture in twenty-four
hours, according to age. As they grow older,
he increases the proportion of milk, but not of
the cream. If an infant be under four months
of age, tolerably strong and regular in his bowels,
and has to be bottle-fed, a mixture of first quality milk with water, in equal proportions, will
suffice; after four months, one part of water
to two of milk, if given at a temperature of
90°, agrees well. For children liable to diar-

rhœa, a very thin and weak infusion of aniseed tea, instead of water, may be substituted. Where the gripings and diarrhœa are severe, it is well to combine a teaspoonful, three or four times a day, of dill or peppermint water and water in equal parts, with lime water and a trace of opium to allay the irritation."*

The above has been very generally the plan upon which I have acted in these cases, with two exceptions. The ease now-a-days of giving cod-liver oil to infants, and its cheapness as compared to cream in towns, have led me usually to prefer the former, which doubtless acts in the same way as cream in supplying an oily but highly assimilable combustible aliment. I have, also, usually combined sugar of milk, both because, it exists in cow's milk in smaller quantity than in human milk, and it favours a butyric fermentation.

The advantage of sugar of milk is not merely due to its sweetness, and because it is the sugar which sweetens milk in its normal state; but I have found on trial that it allays the morbid irritation of the bowels, and will often check diarrhœa.

I believe this is due chiefly to its undergoing fermentation less readily than ordinary sugar;

---

* Extract from a private Letter.

and certainly the alkalinity of milk which is rich in sugar, as that of the woman, does not so readily become acid as cow's milk.

The acidity of milk is best corrected by lime-water, in the proportion of one to two tablespoonfuls of lime-water to the half-pint of milk. In cases of diarrhœa this quantity may be increased. The advantage of giving sugar of milk with the lime-water is further shown by its facilitating the solution of lime, especially the hydrate, and so in this manner favouring assimilation. In cases where the bowels are constipated, the acidity is best corrected by magnesia, as much as will cover a four-penny piece, or more, as the case may be, and in this way a purgative salt is produced which relieves them. If the gastric disturbance which a particular milk induces, is very great, then chalk may be substituted for the lime-water, in five to ten grain doses. This will also be dissolved in the sugar of milk. Where, however, the tongue is very red, and there are other evidences of gastritis, the carbonates of soda or potash are to be preferred.

2. *Preparation from rich or strong milk of a compound resembling human milk.* My attention has been called to this preparation by Mr. Harry W. Lobb, a gentleman who for some time past has closely studied the subject. In p. 133, in his little brochure on *Hygiene,* he gives us the follow-

ing method of preparing Professor Falkland's milk for infants. I subjoin it here in full.

" One-third of a pint of new milk is allowed to stand until the cream has settled; the latter is removed, and to the blue milk thus obtained about a square inch of rennet is to be added, and the milk-vessel placed in warm water. In about five minutes the curd will have separated; and the rennet, which may again be repeatedly used, being removed, the whey is carefully poured off, and immediately heated to boiling, to prevent its becoming sour. A further quantity of curd separates, and must be removed by straining through calico. In one quarter of a pint of this hot whey is to be dissolved three-eighths of an ounce of milk sugar; and this solution, along with the cream removed from the one-third of a pint of milk, must be added to half a pint of new milk. This will constitute the food for an infant of from five to eight months old for twelve hours; or, more correctly speaking, it will be one-half of the quantity required for twenty-four hours. It is absolutely necessary that a fresh quantity should be prepared every twelve hours; and it is scarcely necessary to add, that the strictest cleanliness in all the vessels used is indispensable."

The above is a very ingenious process, but it is open to objection in one or two particulars.

a. Messrs. Parmentier and Deyeux have shown that there is a disadvantage in boiling milk. When eight pounds of milk obtained from cows fed on grass, cabbage, potatoes, and maize, respectively, were distilled, eight ounces of a colourless fluid were obtained. That from those fed on grass was aromatic; on cabbage, offensive; on maize and potatoes, quite inodorous. Hence they infer, that if this volatile principle constitutes in any way one of milk's constituent parts, it must be wrong to deprive milk of it, or to expose it to those circumstances which favour its separation. Experience with infants has also shown me, that boiled milk is seldom so well borne as milk simply warmed by the addition of hot water. To this volatile principle I shall again recur.

b. The objection has been made by Mr. Lobb, that in Dr. Falkland's process scarcely enough casein is removed. The former has another method of preparing this artificial human milk, which he calls *mincasea*, which I here subjoin:—

" Half a pint of new milk is set aside for the cream to separate, which latter is removed; and to the blue milk half a teaspoonful of prepared rennet is added; this is placed over the fire, and heated until the curd has separated, when it is broken up with a spoon, and the whey poured off. In winter, three drachms of powdered sugar of milk are added to this warm whey; and the whole is mixed with half a pint of new milk. In summer, three drachms and a half of sugar of milk are added, and with the new milk are all boiled together."

There is another formula given by Mr. Turner, a homœopathic chemist, of Manchester. Although I disbelieve the dogma of homœopathy, I am not above taking a lesson from an adversary. His formula is very simple. "Dissolve one ounce of sugar of milk in three-quarters of a pint of boiling water, and mix with an equal quantity of good fresh cow's milk." This process is simpler than Professor Falkland's and Mr. Lobb's, and, as such, I prefer it, and would fain recommend it, except that I should prefer water of a temperature of 160° Fahr. to the boiling water. The most ignorant nurse might prepare it easily in any part of the country where good milk can be procured.

The disadvantage which applies to this process in towns, as I have before stated, is the difficulty which attends the procuring of good milk. The same objection applies to many other places, as on board a ship.

In Appendix F, I have annexed a series of formulæ which I have hitherto used in private practice and in the Cripples' Home Infant Nursery. These may be useful as a guide and reference, and, so far, as a means of preventing intestinal mischief.

CHAPTER VI.

HAVING now considered the animal substitutes for human milk, we have to consider another important class of substitutes, *i. e.* those from the vegetable kingdom, and at the outset two questions present themselves for consideration,—

(*a*) Is the chemical constitution of vegetable food such that we may safely employ it as a substitute for animal food? and if so (*b*), at what period should it be given?

(*a*) As I have elsewhere said, animal food is, as it were, the essence of vegetable food, and far more digestible. But there is another peculiarity possessed by animal food. Liebig, as we have already stated, has shown that the blood in the body is preserved alkaline in carnivorous animals through the agency of the *subphosphate of soda;* whereas, in the case of herbivorous animals, the salt which maintains the alkalinity of the blood is the *subcarbonate of soda.* This last result, however, only applies in the case where the food consists exclusively of the lowest grains, roots, green vegetables, and fruits, the ashes of which contain carbonates; because if lentils and the higher cerealia, as wheat, oats, etc., be employed, since their salts are nearly the same as the salts of blood, the subphosphate of soda is also found in the blood.

But more than this; in meat, and the higher cerealia, not only have we a larger quantity of mineral ingredient, but we have also a large quantity of plastic or nitrogenous element. The hydrocarbonaceous, calorifiant, or combustible element contained is also in fair proportion, so that any of them may then be safely used. Still there is a very great disparity between these vegetable substances among themselves, and as compared with animal compounds. In order to make this clear, I have annexed the following table, compiled from Professor Liebig and Dr. R. D. Thompson, in which the amount of nitrogenous or plastic matter being expressed by 10 in all cases, the relative amount of combustible or respiratory material is given for purposes of comparison.

Proportion of ten plastic to the following quantities of respiratory matters in the following articles of consumption :—

Veal -	- 1	Rye Flour -	- 57
Hare -	- 2	Barley	- 57
Beef -	- 17	Maize	- 70
Lentils	- 21	Potatoes, white	- 86
Beans -	- 22	East Indian rice	- 100
Peas -	- 23	Dry Swedish turnips	110
Fat mutton	- 27	Potatoes, blue	- 115
Cow's milk	- 30	Rice	- 123
Linseed	- 30	Buckwheat flour	- 130
Fat pork	- 30	Arrowroot -	- 260
Human milk -	- 40	Tapioca	- 260
Wheat flour -	- 46	Sago	- 260
Oatmeal	- 50	Wheat starch	- 400

The respiratory ingredient in these vegetable substances with large figures being chiefly starch (such as if digested at all becomes converted into sugar), would, as proved by Magendie's experiments, lead to the development of scrofula, from deficiency of plastic or nutritive ingredient. But from the non-development of saliva at an early period, it is to be feared that even this change would not occur. And this seems, often at least, to be the case. In a paper published on the *Diet of Infants*, Dr. Stewart, of New York, in speaking of the Parisian hospitals, says,—" It is the custom at these and similar institutions, whenever an infant is sick, to withdraw him altogether from the breast, and to substitute for the milk some farinaceous substance, made fluid by boiling arrowroot, gum, and rice-water, or a thickened preparation of rice, known as *crême de riz*, and other preparations of a similar kind, forming the diet of a sick infant. In the reported cases of the Foundling Hospital, and those for the reception of sick children, prescriptions of this nature form a very important part of the treatment, as will be seen by referring to the different treatises in French on the diseases of children." "The attention of M. Guillot having been directed to the changes which the food given to children underwent, and to the excessive mortality among them, he instituted a series of investigations in a number of cases of death, with special reference to the state of the contents of the bowels. He was struck with the uniform similarity,—a jelly-like substance being present in the bowels, and in some instances lining both the small and great intestines. This was subjected to the test of the tincture of iodine, which produced an intensely blue colour, thus proving it to be starch."*

This jelly-like substance is sometimes tinged with blood. Its presence, however, in the bowels of a child proves that starch is not digestible, at least in the early periods of life, which is, in fact, what we might have anticipated. In adults it is

---

* Dr. Stewart on "Diet of Infants," *Dublin Journal*, 1845, pp. 141-2.

converted into sugar; but if this change is not effected in the child, in whom one of the principal organs that bring this about does not act at all, or at least very imperfectly, the presence of starch in the bowels in any excess must be detrimental and injurious.

But more than this. From the absence or great diminution of sugar, which assists, as before seen, in dissolving the carbonate and phosphate of lime, these ingredients are not taken up in sufficient quantities in the blood for the purposes of the economy. Hence a tendency to rickets is established. These ingredients are not assimilated. There is, moreover, a deficiency of sugar for the respiratory processes, and a loss of animal heat, the oily matters only remaining to supply this want by conversion into sugar. Whether this is easily accomplished in a child has not, so far as I know, been proved by experiment. Practically judging from the injurious effects of a diet too exclusively starchy, there is reason to doubt it. Yet how frequently, and even by medical men, is arrowroot ordered in cases of diarrhœa as the exclusive diet!

I cannot conceive anything more injurious than this popular arrowroot feeding. I believe it is a cause of the death of many infants. The following example, one out of many, received from an authentic source, will suffice to prove this. A poor woman had had five children; all had been brought up artificially on arrowroot, and all had died. A sixth in due time was born, and she was strongly urged by a kind friend to try nourishing food, such as milk, beef-tea, etc., instead of the arrowroot. This she agreed to do. Meeting her accidentally some time afterwards, this friend inquired about the infant. The reply was, " Oh! it is dead; but it is no fault of mine, as I fed it on the best arrowroot that could be procured." So strongly rooted is the popular prejudice in favour of this starchy ingredient, which contains only 10 parts of plastic matter in 260 of combustible matter, instead of 10 in 40, as in human milk (see table, page 324), and therefore never can suffice to nourish a child, especially a weakly one.

A favourite substitute, also, for human milk is *barley*—or more properly what is known as *patent barley*. Here, again, we have a flour comparatively poor in nitrogenous material. But, besides this, it contains *dextrine*, a substance which even in the adult is difficult of digestion, and *à fortiori*, must be so in an infant. Its starch corpuscles are less soluble in the gastric juice, the milk is slightly acrid, and it is somewhat laxative.* When barley paste is washed, the milky fluid

---

* Hassall on Food.

deposits not only the starch, but also a protein matter, supposed to be *insoluble* casein.

Next in esteem with the public is *pap*. Now pap is given very early. I have seen it given to a child from birth. It seemed to thrive upon it at first; but in about a month's time the child, which was of enormous size, sickened, and recovered only after much difficulty. Unfortunately the popular prejudice in favour of white bread proves often a cause of death. Magendie's experiments made with dogs have set this point at rest. A dog fed on white bread, wheat, and water, did not live more than fifty days, whereas a dog kept on soldiers' *brown* bread did not suffer. The explanation in this case can be satisfactorily given. It is to be found chiefly in the relative differences of the saline constituents of wheat, as compared with those of milk.

The objections to pap may be classed under three heads—

1. The disadvantage of wheat-flour, given in bread, is due to the absence of two salts, both of which, as we have already seen, are very auxiliary to nutrition (pp. 257 and 260)—(*a*) to a marked deficiency in chloride of potassium; (*b*) to the decomposition of the free phosphoric acid, and, perhaps, the phosphates, into insoluble and therefore useless salts to the economy;—(*c*) and to its mechanically distending the stomach.

2. To a diminution of the quantity of cerealin

contained, and which thus interferes with the proper digestion of the grain.

3. To the adulteration of bread with inferior kinds of grain.

First. (*a*) If we except those of the pea and bean tribes, most of the edible flours are deficient in the same way. *There is no chloride of potassium in wheat, etc., and consequently, in bread. But, more than this, the phosphoric acid is partly, often considerably, neutralised in its effects.* (See note below.*) Englishmen like to use white bread, which, independently of containing less nutritive matter than brown bread, as I.have fully shown elsewhere, contains *alum.* This adulteration is known to make inferior flour, and flours generally of a bad colour, white, and equal in appearance to flour of superior quality; and, secondly, it enables flour to retain a larger quantity of water, by which means the loaf is made to weigh heavier.† The bread is also less liable to crumble as it gets stale.

Accum, quoted by Hassall, states the smallest quantity of alum that can be employed to produce this white appearance is 4 ounces to a sack of

---

* Composition of ashes of wheat by Erdmann, exclusive of peroxide of iron, 1·33 per cent. and silica and sand, 3·37 per cent.

Alkaline phosphates for 2 mo.	49·13
Earthy ditto for 2 mo.	23·13
Free phosphoric acid	27·69
	100

† Hassall.

240 lbs. Dr. P. Markham states 8 ounces to be the usual quantity employed, and Mitchell found that in the 4-lb. loaves he examined the amount of alum varied from $34\frac{1}{2}$ to 116 grains in each. 114 grains would amount to 20 ounces to the sack.* Out of 28 samples of London bread examined by Dr. Hassall, in all alum was found, in smaller or larger quantities. The injurious effects of alum cannot be too strongly urged. Alum forms with phosphoric acid, as Liebig has shown, an *insoluble salt*, and so prevents the phosphoric acid from being appropriated to the economy. The blood becomes incapable of performing its duty, and hence children fed on it deteriorate, and in the end will die. And herein is the explanation of the frightful amount of disease observed in pap-fed babies. The phosphoric acid, so essential to them, is in great measure lost. The brain and nervous system, and the bones are arrested in their development; and hence also one reason for the great comparative success in bringing up children by hand in the country on home-baked bread, which contains no alum, and which, although of darker colour, provides phosphoric acid in an assimilable state to the child.†

* Hassall.

† From an analysis by Erdmann, given below, it would appear that 100 lbs. of ashes of wheat contain—

Alkaline phosphates	46·48
Earthy ditto	21·87
Free phosphoric acid	26·19

(b) It is not necessary, however, that the *whole* phosphoric acid should be lost in order that the white bread pap should disagree. The experiment of Magendie, before alluded to, proves that a dog fed on white bread did not live longer than fifty days, dying at the end of this period with all the signs of inanition; and we must expect that the same rule before quoted, which applies to other animals, will hold good here, namely, that after continued restriction to any one kind of aliment which cannot singly support life, a return to ordinary food will not save life. The power of general assimilation has been lost. Moreover, a pap-fed child, because obliged to use the spoon, cannot be brought again to suck the bottle or the breast. He has lost the instinctive power of suction from want of habit. So the habit of digestion of particular kinds of food once completely lost is never again acquired. I believe

---

But as 100 lbs. of wheat only contain 1·83 lb. of salts, and since 80 lbs. of flour will make 100 lbs. of bread, the 100 lbs. of bread will contain—

	lbs. Avoir.	grs. Troy.
Alkaline phosphates	·69	4830
Earthy ditto...............	·319	2233
Free phosphoric acid	·37	2612

But as a sack of 240 lbs. contains from 4 to 20 ounces of alum, *i. e.* from 1·7 oz. or 743·7 grains, to 8·3 oz. or 3621·2 grains, it will contain 82·3 to 391·3 grains of alumina. Looking now to the composition of phosphate of alumina, $Al_2 O_3 PO_5$—*i. e.* $(2 \times 51·44) + (3 \times 71·44) = 317·2$—we have enough alumina to saturate 184·1 to 853·6 grains of phosphoric acid.

one reason many pap-fed children among the lower classes live spite of the pap they take is this :—the little infants, fortunately for themselves, are often spoilt; they keep asking for what they see on the table, and besides the pap, pieces of meat, herring, cheese, etc., which form the usual food of the parents, are given to them; and so that which in the better ranks of life would be considered unwholesome, and therefore would be withheld, is the providential means of saving their lives, because the food is then not exclusively pap, and the phosphoric acid needed is obtained from other sources. Again, the reason why some kinds of baked flour agree so well is, that phosphate of soda is added, and so in the excess of phosphoric acid given the bad effects of the alum are neutralized.

(c) But there is another way in which pap proves injurious. It more often, perhaps, than is recognised, is the immediate *cause* of death. It has long been known that bread and milk, if given to canaries in full quantity, swells in their stomachs, and thus, pressing against the heart, impedes its action, and often causes their death. The same result sometimes occurs in the infant. At pp. 28, *vide supra,* I have enumerated several fatal cases in which the coroner's verdict assigned over-feeding with pap as the cause of death.

2. A diminution of the amount of *cerealin* which should be normally contained in grain and does not exist in ordinary pap, again explains much of its indigestibility, and this depends chiefly on the manner in which the bread is made; and here I must follow Dr. Dauglish* in his remarks on the subject.

Pure *white* bread is made from the flour of the interior of the grain of wheat. This flour is much the whitest. That nearest to the outer skin is much darker, and makes brown bread; but, whereas the former is comparatively rich in starch and poor in gluten, the reverse is the case with the latter. Hence one reason why bread made with entire grain, even in its interstices, and exclusive altogether of the bran, is darker than ordinary bread. But more than this, the flour which adheres to the bran, and which amounts from 10 to 12 per cent. of its nutritious matter, was, till lately, supposed to be *gluten.* This portion of the grain has now been found by M. Mege Mouries to consist chiefly of a vegetable ferment, and metamorphic nitrogenous body, which he has called *cerealin*, and another body called *vegetable casein.*

This *cerealin* in its native state acts as a most energetic ferment and solvent in an aqueous

---

* Ranking's *Retrospect,* vol. xxxii, p. 1.—*Medical Times and Gazette,* May 12, 1860.

solution, on starch, dextrine and glucose, producing the lactic and even butyric changes, *but not the alcoholic*. But it is especially active on gluten, and lactic acid has been developed, when in the presence of these three before-named substances. Thus, its action upon gluten exactly resembles that of pepsine on fibrin. Singly, it acts but slowly upon the gluten, but if conjoined with lactic acid the solution of it takes place very rapidly. As a proof that cerealin is a most active digestive solvent of gluten and starch in flour, the experiment of Mr. Stephen Danby, of Leadenhall Street, may be mentioned. He found that when 2 grains of dry cerealin were added to 500 grains of wheaten flour and the whole digested in half an ounce of water at a temperature of 90° for several hours, 10 per cent. more of the gluten and 5 per cent. more of the starch were dissolved, than when an equal quantity of flour, to which this extra proportion of *cerealin* has not been added, was experimented upon.

M. Mouries states that the activity of cerealin is destroyed at a temperature of 140°, but Dr. Dauglish has found that it is simply suspended by the heat required to cook bread thoroughly. Cerealin, like pepsine, is soluble in water, but not in alcohol; hence bread or flour cakes made without fermentation are easily soluble, whereas those subjected to alcoholic fermentation are not.

The activity of cerealin is destroyed by *most acids*, and by *alum* in particular. Hence, another reason why aluminized bread is indigestible.

The non-fermented and aerated bread of Dr. Dauglish possesses an advantage over that usually sold, because it contains this ingredient *cerealin* unchanged, and is therefore more digestible.

This fact may be used to explain many popular customs.   Many nations, indeed the majority, live on unfermented foods or breads. The Hindoo and Chinese on rice; the American Indian on maize; the Irishman on potatoes; the Scotchman on oatmeal; the African often exclusively on manioc bread, and thrive well and maintain their strength. The Frenchman lives on his white bread, which has fermented; hence one of the reasons why he cannot compete in heavy work with the Englishman, who lives on flesh.   His bread is not sufficiently nutritive, and does not contain enough *cerealin* to dissolve all the gluten. Panification generally, and where the bread rises well, has another advantage, which is also in measure brought about by roasting or baking grain. The inhabitants of the Mediterranean live on vermicelli and macaroni chiefly, also non-fermented. But here there is this difference—these substances are first dried, and so made more porous, and thus *a greater surface is exposed to the digestive juices*.   Gluten, when prepared from flour in the ordinary way and deprived of its cerealin is, from its compactness, very indigestible. Only the surface is affected by the digestive fluids. One of the objects of baking grain and flour, as in the use of baked flour for our nurseries, of macaroni, or raising it into a spongy mass as bread, is to divide the material, and expose a much larger surface of it to the penetrating digestive solvent. If, as in the case of aerated bread, this can be done without fermentation, so much the better.

The above explanation prepares us for understanding the reason that if bran tea be mingled with the food of badly nourished children, they thrive on it; so also where non-fermented or so-called digestive breads are used. There is excess of cerealin, and so the breads are easily digested.

Dr. Dauglish tells us the aerated bread has been found most efficacious in many instances. " Private gentlemen have sought interviews with him to record the history of their recovery to health after years of suffering and misery by the simple use of this bread as diet. Children that have been liable to convulsive attacks from an irritable condition of the alimentary canal and nervous system have been perfectly free from them, immediately the new bread was substituted for fermented bread. And cases are now numerous that have been communicated by medical men of position in which certain distressing forms of dyspepsia, which had remained intractable under every kind of treatment, have yielded as if by magic almost immediately after adopting the use of the aerated bread."

My own experience is generally confirmatory of this opinion. Although it must be admitted that occasionally aerated bread is scarcely light enough for some persons, it is certainly, as a rule, more digestible, and eminently more satisfying to the appetite. It was exclusively used in the Samaritan Hospital and gave great satisfaction, and was only suspended when it ceased for the time to be made. This contingency, however, fortunately no longer exists.

The principle upon which the so-called light or digestive breads are made, is to add to a mixture of carbonate of soda and flour, a quantity of cream of tartar, or some equally unobjectionable and pulverulent salt, so that on the application of moisture or heat a neutral salt may be formed, and carbonic acid set free, this last by entangling the particles of dough causing the bread to rise. Arguing upon these premises, and looking to the uses of the phosphates in the animal organism, Professor Horsford, of Philadelphia,* has recommended an acid phosphate of lime, a dry and pulverulent salt, which, after its action with moist carbonate of soda, leaves phosphate of soda, a

---

* Ranking's *Half-Yearly Abstract*, vol. xxxii, p. 7.—*American and Chemical News*, etc.

blood constituent, and phosphate of lime, an essential constituent of blood and bone. In his own hands, and those of his friends, it appears to have answered beyond expectation. Dr. Samuel Jackson, Professor of the Institute of Medicine, in the University of Pennsylvania, speaks also most highly of its effects. Practically, I have no experience of it; but, speaking theoretically, it appears devised upon scientific principles. One advantage which it possesses is that it enriches *white* bread with phosphate of lime, which, as Dr. Jackson states, existing more abundantly in the bran, is usually rejected in most kinds of white bread, and thus lost to the economy.

3. Another fraud extensively practised in London, is the large admixture of *rice-flour* in bread. This, I believe, is not generally known. Its great whiteness and its great power of absorbing water, are properties peculiarly well known to bakers, and not only to ordinary bakers, but to many of our hypocritical workhouse-poor feeders. I have been informed by a wholesale corn and flour merchant, that there is a species of rice-flour which is expressly kept for the purpose of adulterating bread, and which is largely employed in some of our London workhouses. In this way the nutritive power of the bread is considerably diminished, although the calorifiant power is increased, the proportion of the former to the latter

being, instead of 1 to 7, as it ought to be in wheat-flour, increased to 1 in 10 or 11, producing precisely the same results in the human frame as those which follow the employment of a diet too exclusively saccharine, viz., scrofula, atrophy, and all its dependencies, so commonly observed in some of these large establishments.

Among the vegetable substances, that which comes closest to milk in its composition is, without doubt, *lentil powder*, or, as it is called for the purposes of obtaining a better sale, *Revalenta Arabica*, containing both phosphoric acid in abundance, and chloride of potassium ; it also includes casein, the same principle which is found in milk. Moreover, its nutritive matter is to its calorifiant matter in the proportion of 1 to $2\frac{1}{2}$, milk being in that of 1 to 2.   No wonder, therefore, that under its influence many children affected with atrophy and marked debility have completely recovered. I have given it with the very greatest advantage in such cases, and, so far as I may judge from my own experience, I should conclude that practice fully carries out the result which, from a knowledge of the composition of lentil powder, we should have been led to anticipate.   Lentils have also a slightly laxative effect, and therefore in many instances, where the child is of a constipated habit, they are to be recommended.   Peas and bean meal in this respect resemble lentils ;

the former, however, is objectionable, because it produces flatulency. The latter is not generally obtainable; still the bakers take advantage of this fact in regard to the beans, and usually, where wheat by partial germination has lost some of its nitrogenous element, or where the flour used is poor in quality, add a proportionate quantity of white bean flour to restore it to its proper nutritive value.   •

3. The only advantage which another popular kind of food seems to have (I allude to what is called *baked flour*) is, that it contains a smaller quantity of water, which has been expelled during the heating process, and in this respect it comes to resemble more closely, because more concentrated, an animal compound. Moreover, by the baking, the starch granules are rendered more separable, and as before stated, p. 336, the gluten is reduced to a more porous state, and more readily acted upon by the gastric juice, and as an aliment, therefore, is more nutritious and digestible. Again, from its greater capacity for absorbing moisture it is somewhat more astringent, and less likely to produce diarrhœa, which indeed it often checks; but the absence of chloride of potassium and fatty matters in it, both so essential in growth and cell-development, is, I think, a fatal objection to it. Hence, if it be given, it should, to supply fat and chloride of potassium, be mixed with milk.

Baked flour enters into the composition of most of the ordinary foods for children. The best combination which I have seen, and heard most favourably spoken of, is the *vegeto-animal food* prepared by Mrs. Wells, in which it is mixed with sugar of milk. Now, as the salts of milk are usually left in its preparation in combination with it, the food prepared contains a sufficiency of phosphoric acid and chloride of potassium. When flavoured with a little spice, it forms a very agreeable food for infants : so far as I have tried it, I am satisfied as to its effects being beneficial. One advantage it possesses, common however to all properly contrived mixtures, when these are already mixed in due proportions, nothing is left to the discretion or whim of nurses, who, when not too disposed to spoil the child's food by excess of sugar, are so often careless in preparing it ; so that in the hands of the most ignorant it may be safely used.

Among the best bread compounds made out of wheat-flour, that which from my own experience I should recommend (because I have seen it frequently attended with beneficial results to children, who were evidently losing flesh and strength under other ordinary foods), is *Robb's biscuits.* This kind of food is almost always readily digested, and infants seem to relish it wonderfully.

There is one more variety of child's food to which I must allude, because it seems to be prepared upon really scientific grounds. I mean *Yorkshire food*. I am informed it is in common use in the north of England and in many families in London, and that the experience of those who employ it is that their children will often thrive on nothing else. This statement, however, is doubtless exaggerated.

It is prepared by taking three pounds of baked flour, half an ounce of phosphate of soda, and a quarter of an ounce of carbonate of magnesia. Three teaspoonfuls of this mixture are rubbed up with a little cold milk or water, and reduced to a pulp; to this pulp a cupful of milk or water is then added, and the whole warmed. This soon thickens and constitutes the food. It will be seen that two advantages are offered by this mixture. First, excess of phosphoric acid is supplied; and, secondly, the disadvantage usually resulting from artificial food, namely, constipation, is avoided.

There is a vegetable compound in use among the inhabitants of these islands, which has some advantages even when given to children, and that is *tea*, and what is remarkable is its close resemblance to juice of flesh. The equivalent of tea as a nutritive substance, is very high, considerably higher than the best cereal grain. The exhausted leaves, after tea is made, contain also from 12 to 14 per cent. of casein. In juice of flesh we have creatine and creatinine present, two animal compounds which, according to Liebig, closely resemble the active principle of tea, —*theine*. The richness of tea in albumen, fibrin, and probably casein, is also remarkable. The large quantities of potash and phosphoric acid, likewise, is worthy of note.*

According to Mulder, the portion of soluble matter which hot water extracts from black tea varied in six specimens from 29 to 38 per cent. From the same number of green teas, from 34 to 46 per cent. Peligot found that the mean quantity obtained from the dry commercial article was from black tea 38 per cent., and from green tea 43 per cent. in each kind, and he estimated the amount of nitrogen to be 4½ per cent. Thus, from 100 parts of tea, supposing it entirely extracted by hot water, 6 per cent. of theine would be contained in the decoction. In domestic

---

* *Composition of Tea* (Java and Hyson)—Knapp.

			Salts.		Infusion of Tea.
Ethereal oil	...	·75	Potash	...	47·45
Chlorophyl	...	2·14	Soda	...	5·03
Wax, resin, and gum	...	15·09	Lime	...	1·24
Tannin ...	...	15·76	Magnesia ...	...	6·84
Theine ...	...	·53	Oxide of iron ...	...	3·29
Extractive	...	20·75	Phosphoric acid	...	9·88
Apothein	...	3·78	Sulphuric acid ...	...	8·72
Muriatic acid, extractive		20·59	Silica	...	2·31
Albumen	...	2·65	Carbonic acid ...	...	10·09
Fibrin (in part casein ?)		22·64	Oxide of manganese	...	·71
Salts ...	...	5·20	Chloride of sodium	...	3·60
			Carbon and sand	...	1·09
		100			100

economy, however, the entire quantity of theine is never extracted, about one-third being left behind in the leaves.*

Liebig has directed attention to the good results which attend the employment of tea among our labouring classes, as a nutritive agent, and he concludes that this is owing to the resemblance it bears to the juice of flesh in its chemical composition. More lately my friend, Dr. Edward Smith, has investigated the effects of tea upon digestion.

These experiments have proved—First, That tea has the power to increase the transformation of other food, and particularly of such as contains carbon. This is probably due to the gluten which tea contains, and which acts as a ferment. Secondly, it increases the function of the skin, as is seen by the perspiration which often follows : its use thus correcting one of the disadvantages of milk and cream. "If any one will notice," adds Dr. Smith, "the effect of a bason of milk when taken alone, he will find that the hands and the exposed parts of the skin become hot and dry,

---

* 100 Parts of the following Teas afford—

	Gunpowder.				Souchong.
Water ...	... 10	...	... ...	...	... 8
Extractive	... 47 with { volatile oil } ·5				... 43
	{ theine } 6·				
Exhausted Leaves	43 containing casein 14	...		...	... 49

and will at once appreciate the fact that the addition of milk or fat to tea has the effect of preventing the increase of perspiration, and thereby the cooling of the body." Speaking generally, Dr. Smith believes " that the essential action of tea is to promote all vital actions, and to increase the action of the skin."* It is necessary, however, that there should be a supply of food upon which it may act, otherwise the increase of vital action will waste the body. This is one way, therefore, in which it may prove beneficial as a corrective of milk, or rather as an adjunct.

It would occupy too much time to speak of the various kinds of children's food made and sold. I do not doubt there are several of great value ; but it is no part of my intention to make an examination of each of these. I lay down general rules, which I believe are founded on a scientific basis. Their application to other aliments is best left to others.

(b) At what period may vegetable food be given ? *My reply is, not before the eighth month :* and for these reasons. Man belongs to the omnivorous class ; there must, therefore, be a time when vegetable food may be safely given. There is no doubt a relation between the period of time occupied in incubation or gestation, and the

---

* "On the uses of Tea in the Healthy System."—*Journal of the Society of Arts*, February 15, 1861.

time when an animal is so far developed and grown as to partake of herbivorous food without danger. Thus, if a granivorous bird occupy three weeks in incubation, a mammal nine months in gestation, we should, *à priori*, expect the offspring of the former to be sooner capable of maintaining life independently of its parent than the latter.

Again, the same thing would apply to an herbivorous animal provided with a stomach fitted for digestion of vegetables, *i. e.*, a compound stomach, which would be sooner independent than a carnivorous animal, with only a membranous stomach, even though the period of gestation were the same in both. Thus, in the cow and in the human female gestation has the same duration; but in the offspring of the former, the calf, we have the compound stomach of herbivora; in the child we have the simple membranous stomach of carnivora, and so the former depends less upon its parent, and attains soonest independent existence and maturity. But the best test of capability of independent life in man is the *dental apparatus*. The appearance of the teeth is the index that a child is maturing rapidly, or the reverse; or whether it is or it is not in that condition when vegetable food may be safely administered.

The order of appearance of teeth is variously

stated: and the earlier do not agree with the more recent tables,* as Drs. Merei and Whitehead have shown. From their results, "excluding those cases with only medium development, and reckoning those only with a favourable and those with unfavourable development, they conclude that in the former, in 128 out of 161 children (or 79 per cent.), the first teeth appeared before the 8th month was past, in 38 at 8 to 9 months, in 12 after the 9th, and in 3 after the 12th; while in the great majority of children with unfavourable development, namely, in 71 out of 119 children (60 per cent.), the first teeth were cut at 8 months and upwards, in 46 from 9 to 12 months, and in 16 even after 12 months, and only in 48 (44 per cent.) before 8 months."†

Upon these data, it would appear that the eighth month is about the earliest period that vegetable food may be borne. The teeth which appear, are not of value because they are then capable of mastication, but simply as evidence that changes have occurred in the organs of digestion, which have progressed *pari passu*, and that the salivary and pancreatic glands, the intes-

---

* Anterior incisors ... ... 7th month
  Lateral do. ... ... 9th „
  Anterior molars ... ... 12th „
  Canine ... ... 18th „
  Posterior molars ... ... 2 years.

† *Report of the Clinical Hospital*, p. 14.

tines, the glands of the membranous stomach are in full development, and capable of digesting vegetable aliment. Then, and only then, therefore, as a rule, may vegetable food be given, and consequently weaning may be tried, if necessary. But even in this case the most easily digestible only should be administered, as a beginning; and it is best to continue also, in great measure, the animal milks in combination.

Individual cases may, of course, form exceptions. I have alluded to some of these before; and it is clear, if development is earlier in some, so we may conclude that these could bear vegetable food at an earlier date.

CHAPTER VII.

ON THE METHOD OF BRINGING UP CHILDREN BY HAND.—ADVAN-
TAGE OF ALLOWING CHILDREN TO SUCKLE ANIMALS DIRECTLY
—THE VOLATILE PRINCIPLES OF MILK ARE THUS NOT LOST.—
DIFFICULTIES IN CONVEYING MILK.—ERROR IN OUR FOUNDLING
HOSPITALS.

HAVING now dwelt upon that class of cases where the mother is either able, or can be made able to suckle her own child, we pass on to the second inquiry referred to, viz.—If she be not able to suckle the child at all, certain principles ought to be observed in feeding it, whether the artificial food given be animal milks or something more distinctly artificial, leaving the employment of a wet-nurse as a *pis aller.*

In those cases where we are compelled to bring up a child by hand, there is the greatest need of care and judgment. Prior to eight months this difficulty is considerably enhanced.* After that period teeth are generally present, the anatomical conformation of the alimentary canal is well nigh

---

* Page 345, 71 and seq.

A A

completed, and the child is enabled to digest even vegetable materials. But in the earlier periods, and particularly in the first three months of existence, the danger of death under artificial feeding is very great, as most of the tables before referred to prove.* This is especially true for illegitimate children.

In a table drawn out by Mr. Acton in his paper before quoted, the chance of death at this period amongst illegitimate children, such children being generally brought up by hand, is about one-third of all the deaths in the year: thus out of 326 children, 31 died under 1 week, 45 above 1 week and under 1 month, 110 under 3 months, 74 under 6 months, 27 under 9 months, 39 under 1 year.

Now I believe that no treatment can be safely recommended in these cases, which can bear any comparison with that which experience has proved to be most successful in other countries : I allude to the direct suckling of the child from the breast of some other animal, as for instance the goat, to which I have already referred.† Besides it is the most natural. This itself is no small advantage. But it also does away with the necessity of an experienced nurse to prepare the child's food *secundum artem*, so that it shall not disagree.

---

* Page 54, and Appendix A.   † Page 283.

Lastly, no improper practices of the animal are likely to endanger the safety of the child, which, after suckling a short time, it will come to love and protect as its own offspring. Some precautions, however, are necessary at first, as a child may be injured by the violence of the movements of the untrained animal. For instance, it is difficult to admit the prudence of allowing a child to suck a mare, and even with some cows, such a proceeding would be highly hazardous. The most natural way would be to select a cow, known for her gentle disposition, and then if the child were not held by a person to the udder, it might be placed on a raised bed, which would stand in front of the cow's hind legs, so that she would be prevented from moving. The nipple might be taken hold of, and thus the child be fed directly from the breast. The udder, however, of the cow would be too large for a small child to suck, and therefore, speaking practically, a goat would be the animal selected. The goat could be easily overpowered and tied down, its feet enveloped in some cloth, and the child, till such time as the goat became accustomed to the plan and allowed it to be done without hindrance, could be safely allowed to suck the udder directly. If the cow be preferred, it appears prudent to milk the cow at some place as near the child as possible, and as often as the child requires it. The cow should then and there be milked, and the milk at once conveyed into a proper feeding bottle, and the child allowed to suck from it in the ordinary way.

Undoubtedly, the plan has experience to recommend it. But more than this; I have already shown, pp. 269 and 277, that by properly feeding these animals we may obtain from them, as well as from cows, a milk which shall so closely resemble human milk as scarcely to be distinguishable from it even by chemical examination. The particular disadvantage which attaches to the employment of milk as it is usually obtained from cows, even when free from adulteration, is thus obviated. Very fresh milk undoubtedly agrees best with children.

Now it has occurred to me more than once that the explanation may be possibly given, namely, that the milk when warm, precisely as the blood, loses by evaporation some vital volatile principle, and is thus rendered more difficult of digestion. In confirmation of this view it may be stated, that the existence of such volatile principles, as I have before stated, *vide supra*, p. 233, has been proved incontrovertibly by the experiments of Parmentier and Deyeux, although unfortunately their chemical composition has not been made out. With the intention of making this out, they distilled frequently several specimens of milk. Speaking of the distilled product they remark: "It would be a mistake to condemn the distilled water of milk as simply water. Its smell, taste, and especially the ready manner in which it is changed by exposure, prove evidently that it holds in solution one or many substances. But what are these substances? is it a ferment which, like cerealin or pepsine, aids its digestion?" "This is indeed a difficult problem to solve. All that is possible at present to say is, that these substances are easily decomposed, since we find their remains in the water which contained them; they are those remains which affect the transparency of this fluid, and give it that viscosity and putrid odour which it acquires after a time."

Messrs. Parmentier and Deyeux believe this product to be analogous to those obtained by the distillation of muscle, urine, blood, lymph, and albumen, which also as readily decompose. These volatile principles are occasionally affected by the aliment previously taken; particularly by some of an aromatic character, though not by all these: but they are, nevertheless, always present, and obtainable from milk. Ferris proved that ammonia constituted no part of these principles, nor was it evolved during any period of its decomposition.

So far, however, it may be conceded, that there are some volatile principles which escape from milk during exposure to the air. We have an analogous example in the case of the blood. Where blood is first drawn it is perfectly fluid, and could be safely injected into the veins of another animal of the same species. If, however, it is allowed to remain for a few minutes aside, it coagulates, separating into clot and serum. Dr. W. B. Richardson has shown that this change depends upon the escape of ammonia, which holds the fibrin in solution. Now it is a remarkable fact, that new milk has a much stronger odour *sui generis* when first drawn than after it has been kept for a time and is cool.

Moreover, we are all aware (more particularly in reference to cow's milk, although the same truth applies in a lesser degree to other kinds of milk) that exposure to air causes it to become acid, from lactic acid fermentation; and this, as before seen, is one of the causes of the diarrhœa and other abdominal discomforts so commonly observed among children.

On this supposition two popular customs may be explained. First, that boiled milk does not agree so well with children as milk which has not undergone this process, because the volatile principle, whatever it be, has been expelled by the boiling. Secondly, and no doubt, also, this is the reason why, when ass's milk is ordered, the animal is brought to the door and usually milked immediately before the milk is taken. As in the case of the blood, which when coagulated may be said to have lost its vitality, so it may be with the milk. It can, therefore, be no matter of wonder, that as milk is usually obtained in towns, even when it is perfectly unadulterated, yet by reason of the necessary exposure to which it must have been submitted, it so commonly disagrees with children; while in the country, where it is usually given very soon after it has been drawn, it agrees so well.

There is another reason also why milk as usually obtained in towns should be unwholesome. It is a matter of common observation, that there is much difficulty in bringing milk by the railways into London, the very agitation of it causing it to be decomposed, and tending to the production of butter and buttermilk. To obviate this inconvenience, all sorts of methods (and some of these are very ingenious) to prevent agitation have been adopted. Still it must be obvious, that even the transport of cold milk in a cart some two or three miles only must be attended with this alteration of the intimate chemical union of its elements, and particularly so, as I have before stated, when the milk has been previously watered, which circumstance favours the separation of the cream. The objection is not a solid one which would deny that milk can be so deteriorated because it

is nevertheless occasionally found to be *nutritious*
to a child. The ordinary black pudding, and
even meat, are nutritious ; and in both these cases
change, by which all volatile products have
been expelled, has taken place. But adults have
powers which infants may not possess of *assimi-
lating* these substances. The same is true of
milk.

Some children may also have a stronger digestion than others. But as a rule,—and precisely
as they have very little power of generating heat,
while adults have a good deal,—so to children
these volatile principles may be essential to the
requirements of their organism, while to adults
and to some stronger children they may be super-
fluous. Whatever be the cause the fact is incontrovertible—the newer the milk is the better it is
for the child ; and it points most distinctly to the
absolute necessity of allowing the milk to remain
as short a time as possible exposed to the air before it is given to the child ; and therefore is
evidence of the immense advantage which would
accrue by allowing all infants to take the milk
directly from the nipple of the animal. Acting
under the knowledge of these difficulties, whenever a child is being brought up by hand, and it
is practicable, I always recommend that the cow,
like the ass, should be brought to the door, and
then and there milked, and the milk in its fresh

state at once given to the child. It is remarkable how well some children will thrive under this mode of procedure, when other means have failed.

And here I may take the opportunity of replying to a question that has been asked me, as to the best mode of bringing up children on a large scale by hand; in other words, what is the system which I would recommend to a foundling hospital. This depends upon several conditions:—

1. I have shown that the mortality of children in towns is much greater than that in the country (pp. 42-3). Therefore, foundling hospitals should be built in the country.

2. The children should not be too closely congregated—hence the separate rooms should be numerous (p. 35), and they should have proper exercise (p. 35 and p. 50).

3. Those animals which produce milk being generally not only more healthy, but producing a richer milk, and being tamer, when living at the sea-side, the country station should, if possible, be a watering-place. Add to this, that as the air is always purer, and more antiscrofulous, struma, a malady to which hand-fed children are peculiarly obnoxious, may be avoided.

4. As by a particular kind of food (p. 269 and 277), a milk may be produced in the cow and goat.

which shall come to resemble very closely woman's milk, the animals should be fed according
to rule. Ass's milk might be tried also, to enable
us to judge of the effects produced (p. 283).

5. Means should be taken to feed the child
upon milk directly from the animal, or given to
the child at the earliest possible moment after
milking.

6. These animals, the goats and asses for instance, might be used to give the children such
change of air in vehicles as might be found
desirable.

7. By well regulated railway arrangement, the
transmission might be effected safely, somewhat
upon the same principle as at Lyons (p. 22), so
that the mortality might be positively diminished
by the journey (p. 47).

8. If such measures were taken, and every
facility was given to admit of the reception of infants, infanticide would soon cease to be the
reproach of this christian country, and many
souls would be added to the population.

9. The large and ample funds of our foundling
hospitals would no longer save mere hundreds,
but in cheaper, larger, and more healthy premises,
in a pure and country air, thousands would live
to bless the day of their reception in them.

If the conclusions come to above are correct,
they justify the belief that the means hitherto

taken in these institutions for the preservation of life, have been always too partial, often erroneous. They point out in unmistakable terms the importance of establishing our foundling hospitals upon a totally different principle. What advantage would accrue to large towns, if foundling hospitals and other institutions in which children are brought up were to adopt these simple common-sense principles, and so bring up the children committed to their care! How many parents would thus have the comfort of rearing children instead of laying them in their cold graves! How many thousands of infants, slowly and certainly, however unintentionally, are killed by injudicious feeding in workhouses! How many women—now writhing under the gnawing pangs of remorse, who might have sent their children to such institutions had they existed, at a cost quite commensurate with their small means—might have been still happy in the non-commission of infanticide! And in how many homes would the example of vice rewarded as an inducement to further crime have been obviated!

The question is, too, important as a means of saving the lives of thousands who might hereafter prove useful and ornamental members of society, and it ought to be taken up by the State.

The late Emperor Napoleon was a great friend to the establishment of foundling hospitals. He hoped in this manner to have a nursery for his future armies. But the Emperor Napoleon did not understand how to bring up the foundlings, and the result was that, like our own, his foundling hospitals* became charnel-houses for the dead. Now, however, that we are better acquainted with the conditions of infant life, why should not his principle be borne in mind and acted upon, if not for our armies, at least for the sake of humanity.

It is an encouraging symptom in the opinions of the day, that the subject of bringing up children by hand, and that more judiciously, is beginning to occupy the particular attention of the public and the profession. Let us hope we are on the eve of better things, and that we may, please God, rid ourselves as a nation from bad customs and malpractices, which not only diminish our numbers, but are both cruel and unchristian.

---

* *Vide supra*, p. 45.

PART IV.

CHAPTER I.

GENERAL REMARKS ON PREVALENCE OF ABDOMINAL DISEASES.—
DEFECTIVE ASSIMILATION.—FORMS OF DISEASE—THREE STAGES
—MALIGNANT VARIETY—POST-MORTEM APPEARANCES—NATURE
OF THE DISEASE.—PRINCIPLES OF TREATMENT.—THE DIETETIC
MEANS OF ENSURING DIGESTION OF NITROGENOUS, FATTY, AND
SACCHARINE ALIMENTS—NEED OF PANCREATIC JUICE.—VEGE-
TABLE ALIMENTS.—MINERAL ALIMENTS—WATER; LIME WATER.—
ADVANTAGES FROM THE COMBINATION OF MILKS—PRECAUTIONS
NECESSARY IN USING.—INDIA-RUBBER NIPPLES—ADVANTAGES OF
USING FOR A TIME OTHER ANIMAL MILKS.

In the first part we had occasion to speak of the
great number of cases of abdominal disease, which
proved fatal to children. Taking the children
under 1,* the number of deaths from developmental diseases are 70·6 per cent. to all deaths,
and inclusive of the several diseases 51·4 per
cent. to all deaths; and the accounts from the
Manchester Hospital for children 79 per cent. of
the deaths occurred to children under 2 years,
and were due to diseases arising from defective
or faulty nutrition.

---

* See Appendix A.

In the third Report of the Children's Hospital, in reference to the table of diseases treated, Dr. Whitehead remarks : " The most important item in the preceding tables is undoubtedly that which represents disorders of the abdominal organs, for although the number (1116) of these stands below that representing chest affections, the first three groups, developmental disorders, rachitis, and constitutional debility, and probably also some cutaneous affections, may be considered as belonging to the same category, as they frequently owe their origin to the same causes, namely—faulty nursing, erroneous diet, uncleanness, impure air, and unhealthy locality. Thus considered, the number of gastro-intestinal or digestive and assimilative disorders will exceed that representing those of the chest, large as it is, by more than 700. I exclude dyscrasic affections, some of which may be considered to have a similar origin ; but should the last-named be taken into account in this sense, they would swell considerably the number of the class of diseases, by far the most destructive of life to infancy, which owe their origin to causes susceptible of great mitigation if not entire removal by hygienic measures."*

Upon the subject of these several diseases *in*

---

* Third Report, p. 66.

detail it is not my intention to dwell here; I may refer to one or two of them in the sequel. I think it better to consider now more fully the subject of *defective assimilation* as a general morbid state brought on by injudicious feeding, and because it is doubtless the very *"fons et origo"* of the several diseases above referred to, and of many others closely allied to them. For the same reason the term defective assimilation will be made use of in lieu of that which is more usually employed, *atrophy* or *marasmus*, which is only a very characteristic form in which it frequently occurs.

In the third Clinical Report of the Manchester Hospital for Children(p. 69), Mr. Whitehead gives the following opinion, which is very confirmatory of my own on this disease; "almost invariably it may be traced to bad nursing, erroneous diet, impure air, or want of cleanliness. I believe it to be entirely preventible by proper hygienic measures, as it scarcely ever occurs in the children of attentive and thrifty mothers. This is a most serious malady and not of uncommon occurrence, as 178 cases of decided form were treated, of which number 50 (or 29 per cent.) died." So serious an affection should be most closely watched; it comes on so treacherously that it needs all the intelligence of a medical man to detect it, particularly in its first stage; for when once it has reached its second stage in many cases, but almost always when it has reached its third, then it is, so far as I know, perfectly incurable. I do not include, however, those cases of atrophy arising from simple tuberculosis and syphilis. I believe that both these varieties, the latter very frequently, are curable; but I wish exclusively to confine myself to those cases of atrophy arising from defective assimilation.

Causes.—The *predisposing* causes of this disease are a hereditary tubercular taint, previous debilitating disease, but more especially the sequelæ of exanthemata. The *exciting* causes are those previously enumerated, viz., injudicious food, bad air, want of cleanliness. These causes appear to be so powerful in their operation for evil that district registrars often call attention to them. Thus, in one of the reports of the registrar, in November, 1859, we read—"In the East Wymer sub-district, the large number of deaths (18) from atrophy, seems, on inquiry, to depend upon improper food, from the mothers not suckling their children, as they say it would interfere too much with their work."* But even the healthiest children may become subject to the malady, especially when they are deprived of breast-milk *in the earliest periods*, and are fed indiscreetly. From my own

---

* *Medical Times*, November 1859, p. 542.

experience I should also gather that one of the most powerful causes of its production, is that peculiar atmosphere which is invariably developed when young children are congregated together in any large number.

Forms of the Disease.—In order to describe the disease more conveniently, I shall divide it into three stages. The 1st, or premonitory; the 2nd, or emaciative; the 3rd, or exhaustive.

First Stage. The child may appear at times to be in ordinary health, and its spirits may be good; more frequently, however, it is unusually peevish and irritable by fits and starts, apparently without reason; the flesh feels flabby, and loses that silky texture so common in young children; it will frequently throw up its food, which then smells intensely acid; its appetite is not good; its sleep is disturbed. There may be constipation of the bowels; the motions when passed are like clay, with white lumps in them.

In the *second stage* all these symptoms are increased in intensity; there is more decided irritation of the intestinal canal; vomiting may now be of frequent occurrence, and there may be diarrhœa, the motions being very green, intensely offensive, and very acid, so as often to excoriate the fundament and surrounding parts, —the emaciation is now more rapid, the eye assumes a peculiarly bright expression, and the

B B

child looks aged; sometimes there is no diarrhœa, but the process of emaciation continues,
and the motions arc replete with undigested
matters.

The *third stage* is but a further development of
all the symptoms already enumerated; the child's
appetite is now voracious to a degree; nothing
seems to satisfy it, but all the food it takes does
it no good.   Aphthæ now appear on the mouth,
which gradually extend down the alimentary canal.
If there be diarrhœa present it proves perfectly
unmanageable.   Thirty and forty motions daily
are not of uncommon occurrence, and these appear to be nothing else but undigested food;
the emaciation becomes perfectly frightful in the
course of a few hours—the child has the look of
a wrinkled old man in every part of its body; the
eyes possess an unnatural brightness, and seem
to project out of their sockets.   It is voracious to
the last, so long as it has strength to take food;
it is sleepless, constantly whining and crying for
more; it loses its flesh more and more, till it
dies in the last stage of inanition.

When the disease assumes this aphthous character, especially if a number of children be
congregated together, so that an infantile hospital atmosphere pervades the apartment, it is
apt to assume a contagious character, and become
exceedingly malignant; so much so, that if the

same towel or the same artificial nipple be employed by another child, it will catch the disease. Children previously quite healthy will become affected by the disorder, which will speedily pass on in most cases to a fatal issue. The affection does not confine itself to the alimentary mucous membrane; sometimes it is so fearfully contagious that no measures of precaution prevent its extension to other mucous membranes.

On one occasion, in a nursery where the disease broke out, two of the adult girls in attendance became affected with these aphthæ on the conjunctiva, having much the appearance of scrofulous ophthalmia, only the ulcers were more lengthened, and there was no photophobia. Chloride of lime was largely used in the rooms; the whole walls were washed with a solution of it. The same spoon was never used for another child, and was always washed after use in a solution of chloride of lime. A separate nipple was kept for each child. Still the disease often recurred, and proved equally contagious. These children ate enormously, but got thinner and thinner, till at last they died, as I have before said, with all the symptoms of inanition.

Where diarrhœa is not present the illness may extend over a period of several weeks. But the symptoms are analogous, and as certain to be developed, only more gradually so. It is singular, even in such cases, how the little shrivelled old-looking child will sometimes smile at you, particularly after a meal. It is, alas, but a temporary sunbeam in the midst of the general wreck; no quantity of food given, not even cod-liver oil, will do any good, however assiduous and varied the trials made.

Sometimes the disease having reached the second stage, or while yet in the first stage, does not pass on to the third, that is, the *primary* assimilation is defective only, but not entirely prevented. *Tuberculosis*, with other developmental disorders, then makes its appearance, generally as *tabes mesenterica*, more rarely as *phthisis*. By far the most common of the diseases it gives rise to is *anœmia*, with more or less of *rachitism*, a disease graphically described by Dr. Jenner, as produced by whatever is favourable to the production of watery blood, viz.—impure air constantly breathed, food insufficient in quantity, or defective in quality, deficient light, want of cleanliness. Painful as these latter complications are to behold, they exhibit, nevertheless, a fortunate phase in the original disease, because, under proper treatment, they are comparatively manageable, whereas defective assimilation, in the third stage, is very seldom, if ever, cured.

The *Post-mortem Appearances* present different

peculiarities : 1st, in those who have died from diarrhœa, as a complication; and 2nd, in those in which this last has not occurred. In both varieties there is great emaciation, scarcely any fat remaining; the cellular tissue is very scanty, and the muscular tissue much wasted. In the variety where diarrhœa has existed, the alimentary canal from its beginning to its termination, is lined with red patches and aphthæ; these vary in size from the size of a pin's head to that of a bean. And, as has been shown, these, after a time, become more or less filled with the *oïdium albicans*. In addition, Peyer's glands are much reddened and swollen. Sometimes there are no aphthæ, but the mucous membrane from below the liver is intensely reddened with a bloody and intensely acid mucous exudation upon its surface. In those cases where there is no diarrhœa the mucous membrane of the alimentary tract is pale, but Peyer's glands are very much swollen, and project from the mucous membrane as round patches about 3 or 4 lines broad by 10 or 12 long, apparently filled with exudation, and precisely resembling those enlarged Peyer's glands found in cases of Asiatic cholera.

Nature of the Disease.—In its worst forms, it is the power of *primary assimilation*, or digestion in the alimentary tract only which is lost, while that of *secondary assimilation*, or the absorption and appropriation of assimilable matters, if present, may still be effected. It is, therefore, manifest that ordinary dieting will never suffice to restore the child. Starchy and vegetable matters, which are so generally prescribed and taken, should not be given. These substances, when digested, are first converted into sugar, and subsequently into fat. But in children affected with this disease they are not in any way convertible into this substance.

That this is the fact was before shown (p. 325); M. Guillot, of Paris, having proved that the starchy matters of the aliments taken by infants whom it was wished to bring up by hand, and who died, were found unchanged throughout the alimentary tract. This was beautifully proved by the iodine test. How far *sugar* is or is not in any measure digested in such cases remains for future inquiry. It is probable, however, that as *glucose* it is occasionally assimilated. The albuminous matters, particularly the casein and oily substances, do not appear to be digested any better. The milk taken passes away by the bowels in many instances only curdled, but otherwise unchanged. Now this is a state of things which is peculiar to this disease. It does not occur in other analogous atrophies (in infants) at least, to the same extent. It comes, in fact, to resemble some cases of *senile atrophy* in cancerous subjects, especially where the pancreas is affected with the disease. It is true we often find among little children considerable gastric irritation and anæmia present. But in all assimilation or digestion are, to a certain extent, possible. In the cases, however, now under consideration it is not so. Even the attempt to feed them on breast-milk has been made and has failed. They do not seem either able or willing to take it. In Dr. Whitehead's cases the chief measures employed were improved diet and cleanliness, assisted by cod-liver oil and chalybeates. I confess, however, that for my part, except in the first stage and more rarely in the second, I have never seen any of these measures do permanent good, at least in the third stage.

But, secondly, if the power of digestion in primary assimilation is lost, that of the appropriation, or the absorption, of digested matters, or *secondary* assimilation, appears to be present. The faculty remains only in abeyance from want of digested matters to take up; because, first, many poisons are capable of absorption; and, secondly, from the continued absorption of the child's own fat and cellular tissue it is manifest secondary assimilation is carried on.

Principles of Treatment.—The foregoing remarks necessarily lead to the question as to the modes of treatment to be adopted; and this may be considered under three heads :—I. The *dietetic*, which will involve the consideration of the means to be adopted for ensuring the readier digestion of (*a*) albuminous, (*b*) fatty, and (*c*) water, and some mineral aliments.   II. *The Hygienic*, including the preventive rules to be observed in the nursery.   III. *The Medicinal* treatment.

I. The *dietetic* treatment, and first, as regards the albuminous substances.   As primary assimilation only is defective, it is clear that if we could supply a child with food which has already undergone this process, *i. e.* already digested, we should be giving that food most fitted for its wants. The food would have simply to pass through the alimentary canal, not for digestion but for simple absorption.   The child's powers until it is stronger would not be overtaxed, while secondary assimilation would go on under the most favourable circumstances.   We have already shown, when speaking of animal substitutes for human milk (*vide* p. 302), that this can be done by *artificial gastric juice*.   In this manner milk or meat already digested may be given.   In the first case the *casein*, and in the second the *albumen*, are supplied to the child in a condition in which either can be readily assimilated.

With the same intention, the essence of rennet, as it is called, which is merely a concentrated solution of the mucous membrane of the calf, may be used as an adjunct in the food given. The *" liquor pepsinis"* fulfils the same indication. Both contain in a concentrated state the active principle of gastric juice, and so *will* facilitate primary assimilation where, by reason of want of power in the juices secreted by the child itself, ordinary food given as such would not be digestible.

With this intent, Mr. Joulin,* in a paper on the employment of Pepsine in the Inanition of new-born children, relates some experiments which he conducted.

' That gentleman observed, that on several occasions he had lost children from congenital weakness. Death could not be traced to disease of any one viscus ; the entire system seemed to suffer. Respiration became in some degree impeded, but nutrition seemed to be chiefly interfered with. Twice the symptoms were well marked, the respiration was, if not vigorously, at least regularly performed, the voice was sonorous, and screams enduring. But the insufficient nutrition effected did not supply the system with materials adequate to the support of life.

One case was that of a very small, wrinkled, exceedingly emaciated child, four days old, yet presenting almost the appearance of decrepitude.

---

* *Moniteur des Sciences.—Journal de Méd. et de Chemie Pratique,* August 1861 : Ranking's *Half-Yearly Abstract,* vol. xxxiv, p. 266.

lt weighed only 3½ lbs. Troy. The voice was weak and distinct, and respiration not obstructed. The mother was an excellent nurse; but, although the infant took the breast readily, he constantly threw up every meal. What passed through the bowels was *unchanged*, although slightly tinged with bile. Diarrhœa was also present. Syrup of poppies, and blistering on the epigastric region were tried without good result. Emaciation was on the increase ; the child was, in fact, dying.

At this stage, M. Joulin ordered 15 grains of Wasmanoz pepsine to be divided into ten powders. One powder to be given mixed with a few drops of sugar and water, and introduced with a little of the mother's milk into the mouth of the child, who had now scarcely strength to take the breast. This remedy was begun on the 8th May, 1859. The condition of the child continued stationary up to the 11th, when the diarrhœa ceased, and the child appeared much stronger. By the 20th, all vomiting and diarrhœa had ceased. The remedy was continued till the 30th, when the child was quite well, and in two years became a fine vigorous little fellow. This is a case which speaks strongly to the convictions. If, at so early a period of life, when vitality and digestion were so weak, the artificial pepsine effected a cure, *à fortiori* will it be likely to do so in the case of older children ; and so I have found it in practice. The digestive powers are thus assisted, and food, which was before useless, because undigested, readily becomes assimilated.

Secondly, as regards *Fatty matters.*—For these a different digestive juice is required. But this may be supplied in three ways. 1stly. By an artificial pancreatic juice. 2ndly, by supplying fatty matters as fatty acids. 3rdly, by the admixture of phosphate of soda with the food. By either of these processes we may supply the child with a fatty aliment, which (like the albuminous matters already digested in gastric juice) may be taken up by the lacteals and absorbed into the system.

1st. *By an artificial pancreatic juice.*—Bernard showed that, if fatty matters are taken by animals in whom the pancreatic gland (or sweetbread) is diseased, they will pass through the bowels unchanged. The same is observed when this organ is cancerous, or so diseased even in man, that the secretion from it does not reach the intestines. The fatty matters are not assimilated. It would hence appear probable upon a principle analogous to that of the former case and as before seen,* that if an artificial pancreatic juice could be prepared, we should place the child in the position most favourable for the absorption and

---

* Page 303.

secondary assimilation of fatty matters. The experiments of Bernard, however, are too exclusive. It cannot be denied that one of the uses of pancreatic fluid is to emulsify fats so as to permit of their absorption and assimilation ,in the blood. But Frerichs, Lehmann, Leng,* and others, have shown that this transformation will occur in cases where the pancreatic secretion is artificially kept away from the intestines. Again, a mixture of the pancreatic fluid with bile and the ordinary intestinal juices effects this change far more readily. All this proves that the artificial juice required is something more than purely artificial pancreatic juice ; but practically this would be very difficult to obtain, and, if obtained, to keep fresh for use.

The advantages to be derived from the use of such a juice appear to be still more important when we come to consider some of its other properties upon aliments in primary digestion. First, it is not only a solvent of fatty matter, but also as powerful an agent in converting *starchy* matters into *sugar*, although, as in the former case, it does so more readily when in connexion with the other *intestinal juices* and *bile*. Secondly, it would appear to be especially necessary in the case of very young infants (and particularly in

---

* Carpenter's *Physiology*, p. 431.

those to whom starchy matters are given); as in infants under two months there is actually no saliva secreted to compensate for any defect in the pancreatic juice. And lastly, because it is now evident from the experiments of Drs. Corvisart, Brinton, and Harley, that under particular circumstances the pancreatic juice does exert a solvent or digestive influence even upon albuminous matters. Unfortunately, however, we have not yet accurate knowledge enough to prepare this artificial juice; nor has any chemist prepared pancreatic compounds analogous to the *essence of rennet*, or *liquor pepsinis*, for convenient use. The price also of sweetbread in large towns is an additional difficulty in the way. It is to be hoped, however, the desideratum being known, that some means may be devised by which it may be procured, so as to admit of convenient employment in cases like those under consideration. Dr. Harley* has, indeed, recommended *pancreatine*, the active principle of the pancreatic fluid, as a remedy in weak digestion, and he believed he had been able to procure it sufficiently pure; but it is not to be had as yet in the London markets.

Secondly. Another way in which this emulsion of fat can be accomplished, is by giving the pa-

---

* *British Medical Journal*, October 1858.

tient, not fat, properly so called, but the *fatty acids* of which they are composed, and which are very readily absorbed into the system. The good effects of cod-liver oil are probably in some measure due to the excess of fatty acid present. So, also, those of butter. It is indeed a matter of popular observation, that many children grow fat upon bread and butter. They appear to thrive on it when other means fail. This good effect cannot be due singly to the bread, for reasons before stated,* but to the free acid which is also in excess in butter. The same explanation will apply to the good effects of cream on some children. Except, however, in the three instances here mentioned, fatty acids, as such, in anything like a reasonable quantity and at moderate prices, cannot be procured. There are, of course, difficulties which prevent their employment on a large scale, and limit experience.

The third method, upon the whole, is at present the most practicable. I have already alluded to the peculiar property which phosphate of soda has in emulsifying fats.† This is a salt which is readily obtained, and therefore very readily mixed with the food supplied to children. When the matters given are of a vegetable nature, and whenever the case is one which justifies their

---

* *Vide supra*, p. 328, *et seq.*   † *Vide supra*, p. 250.

employment, *cerealin* is the substance to be given instead of *pepsin,* for the reasons before stated (p. 333). In practice, the difficulty is to obtain it as a powder, and ready prepared. Here, therefore, bran-tea, which is especially rich in cerealin, may be given. A strong solution may be prepared by filling up with lukewarm water a tumbler already half filled with *wheat-bran,* stirring very freely for half an hour, and straining through a coarse sieve. From one to two tablespoonfuls of this bran-tea should be added to the vegetable food, and its digestion will be ensured.

3rd. Water, and the mineral alimentary matters, or medicaments essential to the proper assimilation of the constituents of the class of aliments before mentioned, should be also given.

The most important of these is water, and this should most certainly be good of its kind. Usually, where milk and water are given, it is the warm or boiling water which is added to the milk. I have already pointed out the disadvantage of boiling or even warming the milk by the fire. In most places where the water used is moderately good, the very act of boiling the water before use, tends to destroy any active ferment contained it; and as the lime generally held in solution in it is thrown down in the process of boiling, a sort of artificial filtration has taken place, and the impurities of the water are deposited with the falling particles of the lime. Occasionally, however, and this is especially the case where rainwater is used, even after boiling, its colour shows it contains many impurities. It is wise, therefore, and especially if the water used be lukewarm and not boiling, to select water that has been properly filtered through charcoal, which has the peculiar property of destroying all smell and impure matters. For the same reason, when water is given to children as an ordinary drink or mixed with their milk, it should always be filtered or boiled previously. It is for this last reason that toast or barleywater are to be preferred to ordinary water.

This is not a mere refinement. I have seen carelessness in this respect lead to fatal results. During cholera seasons, impure water, the chief *nidus* for cholera ferment, will often produce the disease. The same is true for typhoid fever. But even under more particular circumstances the same unhappy effect may be observed. I remember full well the deaths of two infants from drinking impure water, in a northern watering place. Here a lazy servant, to save herself the longer walk towards a well of good water, was content to take the less pure water in the neighbourhood, which, although apparently pure looking, was mixed with sewage matter, and thus proved fatal to them both.

We have before seen that in many of these cases of defective assimilation there appears to be an excess of acid in the alimentary canal. Hence the advantage of keeping test-paper (p. 397) and galactometers (p. 313) in the nursery. These should be always at hand to enable us at the onset of any untoward symptoms which may seize the child, to determine how far the milk supplied may be regarded as the cause of the attack. The excess of acid is, during life, evidenced by the constant craving appetite of these little ones; and the *post-mortem* appearances before referred to, prove it unmistakeably. It therefore forms an essential part in the treatment of such cases to administer alkalies to neutralize this excess. It is for this reason that *limewater* is oftentimes so efficacious. But *lime* has also other peculiarities, to which I have before alluded (p. 258); *carbonate* of *lime* is insoluble in the blood except there be excess of carbonic acid; and phosphate of lime increases the power of the blood to contain carbonic acid in excess.

On the other hand, an excess of lime is also useful to allow of the formation of biphosphate of lime, which, from the experiments of Blondlet, appears to be the acid principle of the gastric juice.*　　The great use of lime-salts in providing material for the muscular and bony structures, is a strong reason for giving them in combination with the alimentary matters supplied.　The uses of chloride of potassium as a solvent of carbonate of lime have been already insisted upon, and need not be again referred to.†

For these reasons, wherever children are brought up by hand, large quantities of lime-water, sugar of milk, and dillwater are required. It is well, therefore, to keep these in large bottles on a shelf ready for use, and these may be always kept in a state of preparation.　If there be any difficulty in obtaining the limewater from a chemist as often as required, it may be prepared in the following manner, and will generally be found to suit for all practical purposes :—

Let a quantity of pure quicklime, say four or five lumps about the size of a lump of sugar, be placed in a large bottle; let this be filled with distilled water, or, if this cannot be got, with water that has been boiled or filtered; the whole well stoppered.　A small quantity of the lime, about 12 grains, at the ordinary temperature, of 60° Fahr., will be taken up.　If allowed to stand, and filtered when required through a piece of calico, we have for all purposes tolerably good

---

* *Journal de Phys.*, April 1858.　　† Page 261.

limewater. As fast as a quantity has been taken out from the large bottle, it should be filled up with fresh water till again required. In this way we have a continual supply. It needs only that the quantity taken out and filtered should be also kept in a well-stoppered bottle; else it is apt to be decomposed by absorption of the carbonic acid of the air, and becomes converted into chalk, and thus gives rise to constipation of the bowels.

The coexistence of flatus with considerable abdominal pain, although in part relieved by the limewater, still points to the necessity of administering some carminative. It is one of the great advantages which Mrs. Wells's vegeto-animal food possesses over most of those ingredients usually given to children, that it contains in its composition some kind of carminative to supply this desideratum. *Dill-oil* is the carminative usually selected for a child,—to use the nurse's expression,—" to disperse the wind;" and as a rule, it is advantageous to give small quantities of *dill-water* in the regular food the child takes, in quantities varying from one to two teaspoonfuls. Many other of the non-poisonous essential oils, such as carraway, peppermint, mint, cloves, cajeput, etc., would answer as well: and dill has one disadvantage, that it is not very miscible with water, requiring that the herb should be directly distilled with water. In small country places, where chemists are not always near, and occasionally not very abundant in their supplies, it is often difficult to procure dill-water in good condition. To remedy this disadvantage, the London College recommend the oil to be rubbed with magnesia first, and then with distilled water. The objection to this mode of preparation is, that the solution is somewhat milky, and portions of the oil, not taken up, float upon its surface. The same is true if the oil is rubbed up with sugar. The proportions to be used are one drop to three grains of magnesia or sugar, and one ounce of water.

In practice, however, as we use limewater, I have found it of advantage to mix the dill-oil with the limewater at once. The quantity required, one drop per ounce, is very readily taken up, and mixes well. A little boiled milk, about two teaspoonfuls, will also readily mix with it, and this small quantity may at any time be mixed with the child's ordinary food without doing harm. The same facility in after admixtures of the dill-oil with water, obtains if we rub up the oil with quicklime directly instead of magnesia.

Another excellent carminative is *wine*. It is a remarkable fact, that many children who have by injudicious artificial food been brought to that state that they cannot digest fatty, albuminous, or starchy matters, or at least do so very imperfectly, appear to be capable of digesting alcoholic substances. Wine whey, made by pouring a wineglassful of good sherry or port into two wineglassfuls of boiling milk, is a convenient form. The little creatures will suck it with great glee, and under its influence they are seen to thrive daily. As they take it the pain from flatus disappears. The wind breaks upwards at once, and the child, previously in great pain, is quiet, and soon falls into a quiet sleep. The wine-whey should not, however, be given extensively, and as a substitute for the ordinary milk food supplied. One meal in the twenty-four hours of this wine-whey will suffice, and the quantity given at a time should not exceed one wineglass. I shall, however, again have to refer to the use of wine.

In the great majority of cases, the readiest method of giving children the required alimentary principles is by using fresh milk, which has the advantage, before spoken of, of not only supplying the proper azotized and combustible, but the mineral ingredients in requisite quantities, and particularly the volatile principles. An exclusive restriction to fresh milk, however, will not suffice, except in cases where we have to deal with partial defective assimilation only. The other means of treatment previously recommended must be combined.

I have before maintained that the popular pre-judice, that it is dangerous to combine two milks, is founded on erroneous conclusions.

And looking to the immediate preservative in-fluence of breast-milk in preventing the mortality of infants, it is at once obvious that wherever it can be done it should be supplied, if not exclu-sively, at least in as large a measure as possible. If the child has not lost the faculty of *sucking,* the difficulty is comparatively small, because all children prefer the sweet taste of human milk to that of milk from any other animal; and when a wet-nurse for the exclusive use of such a child cannot be provided (and I have already strongly protested against hired wet-nurses), a married woman suckling another child may often be found to give it a morning and an evening meal, and this without detriment to her own child. But if the measures and precautions given above, when speaking of defective lactation,* be taken, nearly all mothers may be so acted upon by ga-lactagogues as to supply a very fair quantum of milk, thus obviating most, if not all, the disad-vantages of exclusive hand-feeding. This is one of the reasons why it is so wrong in those who take charge of children to attempt to bring them up by the *spoon* and not by the *bottle* with an

---

* Part iv, chap. ii. and iii.

artificial nipple attached. The faculty of sucking once lost in a child is seldom, if ever, regained; and thus if an emergency occur when, from the child's state of health, breast-milk would be desirable, the difficulties in its administration are materially increased.

For the same reason the employment of the breast-shaped bottle (p. 83), to be placed in the usual position of a woman's breast, by whatsoever nurse the child may be fed, is to be preferred. When, however, the child has lost the faculty of sucking, there is great difficulty in giving it the breast-milk. It may be milked into the child's mouth; but this process often fatigues both child and mother. The woman has to acquire the faculty of being milked just as any other milch animal. But when this has been done, the milk being collected in a cup may be subsequently given to the child whose natural instincts have been so completely perverted, either by the use of a small indiarubber bottle-syringe, by which it can be squirted into the child's mouth at successive jets, or by the spoon.

I might, however, remark, *en passant*, that although it is undeniable that infants do lose the power of suction, and that once lost it is not again acquired at that early age, yet we should be cautious before we conclude that a child does not suck. A babe exhausted by defective assimi-

lation has but little muscular power. Now that
India-rubber nipples are so commonly used many
are made so stiff and resistent that the child cannot suck with them. After a very ineffective
attempt it falls back, and the conclusion is at
once come to that the child cannot suck. But it
is not so. Better by far use the old-fashioned
cowteat with all its disadvantages than one of
these unyielding nipples. There is another disadvantage even if the child be strong enough to
use it. In the effort required he sucks in a
quantity of air with the milk, and hence suffers
subsequently from flatulence. That this is the
case we can very readily convince ourselves. If
a closed bottle be examined as a child sucks, it
will be found that bubbles of air enter into the
bottle, apparently from the child's mouth, as
the milk is sucked in, in rapid succession. The
nipple then may be said to act properly. It is not
so if it be too stiff: the bubbles are few and
far between, but it sucks air. An excellent
nipple, which I have seen used, is that invented
by Mr. Cooper, of Oxford Street. This is very
yielding, and, moreover, enables a proper regu-
lation of a copious or smaller flow of milk into the
child's mouth, according to its age, by a stop-cock
provided at the inner end, which drops down to
the bottom of the bottle; and so, if the artificial
nipple plays well, no air can be taken in.

More recently, another kind of India-rubber nipple has been made. Instead of being provided with only one hole, it has several, and these are rather slits than actual openings, so that a kind of valvular action is kept up. The nipple in this manner comes more closely to resemble the cow's teat. The flow comes more readily, and is more easily checked if too copious.

More important, however, than even the choice of a nipple, is the state of it. Every article employed should be kept in the most scrupulous cleanliness. Nothing is so essential to success, especially if the child is in any way brought up by hand. Next to actual neglect of the child, error in this particular is the greatest sin which a nurse can commit. And, fortunately, most nurses of any pretensions will attend to the outward and inward cleanliness of the pots, cups, pans, spoons, etc., used. It is, however, chiefly in the cleanliness of the teat used that there is fear of inattention. It should always be placed in lime-water after use, and not only wiped outside before used, but sponged out inside. Curdled milk in a sour state may sometimes accumulate at the upper end of the nipple. An excellent because simple, way of doing this is to fasten a piece of sponge or flannel to the end of a short stick, by which the inside of the nipple can be, as it were, mopped clean. It is most important that

in any place where more than one child is fed
from a bottle, each child should have its own
teat. The indifferent use of these is sometimes very injurious. I have seen, in a public
institution, a whole ward infected with malignant
thrush by one child, where a careless nurse, wise
in her own conceit, had thought fit to disregard
the medical directions given.

When human milk cannot be procured, or,
if obtained, does not agree, it often happens
that another animal's milk, whether taken simply
or combined with the food, will effect a complete recovery. Thus ass's, goat's, or mare's
milk may be given; care being always taken,
that, as in the case of human milk, these milks
should be perfectly fresh. Indeed, in defective
assimilation we frequently find, that when the
milk of one of these animals is given, it seems
to supply some ingredient which was needed
in the child's organism, although we are unable to define the principle more exactly, and
which the human milk before given did not contain. The following examples will illustrate my
meaning :—

Mrs. P——, being much annoyed with a wet-
nurse whom she had in her service, was at last
compelled to part with her. Being aware that
a friend in the neighbourhoood was possessed
of a goat, it was asked for to supply the wet-

nurse's place. The child took to the goat at once, and the poor thing after a short time would run up the stairs when she was loosed for the purpose of supplying a meal, and the child would suck the goat like a young kid. Mrs. P——, in reference to this case of her own child, makes the following very pertinent remarks :—" I had no particular reason for selecting this mode of nourishment, but that it presented itself at the time, and I considered it approached nearer cow's milk than that of any other animal, and therefore contained more of the elements of nutrition than human or ass's milk." The little boy did at any rate exceedingly well under this treatment.

The husband of this lady, a medical man at Gravesend, had under his care a child who was treated by mare's milk, and cured in like manner. " The little babe was six weeks old when he was sent for. It was reduced to a shadow by diarrhœa. Ass's milk had been tried, as also that of one of the father's best cows. As the father was himself a farmer we cannot doubt that this cow's milk was the best of its kind; still the child wasted away. One day, when putting up his horse in the stable, he saw a foal sucking its mother, when it occurred to him to recommend the foal to be weaned, and the mare's milk given to the child. The effect was magical. The child completely recovered, and is now five years old, and as fine a boy as the most fastidious parent could desire to see."

A child under my care, although suckled by a wet-nurse, whose milk on examination appeared to be good, was seized with diarrhœa. Nothing could control this. Ass's milk was now given. It perfectly succeeded for a few days. However, as the good effect did not persist, another wet-nurse was procured, and the child did well.

A medical man of eminence in this town informed me he had brought up, almost exclusively upon ass's milk, his own sickly child, this milk restoring it completely to health. It was not done, however, at a cost under forty pounds. Thus the expense of this remedy in towns is a serious objection to its employment. Except this last example, however, I have never heard of ass's milk sufficing of itself to restore a child, its good effects soon wearing away, and rendering, after a period of a few days, the employment of other food necessary. The question must be looked upon as still open to further experiment.

The above few examples, however, are numerous enough to show that in some cases of defective assimilation we may occasionally employ very unusual modes of alimentation with perfect success.

CHAPTER II.

DIETETIC TREATMENT, CONTINUED.—OF THE NATURE OF ALIMENTS
TO BE GIVEN, AND THE MODE OF THEIR ADMINISTRATION.—
COW'S MILK, ADJUNCTS TO.—NECESSITY OF USING TEST-PAPER.—
HOW SOME KINDS OF DIARRHŒA WHICH SUPERVENE ARE TO BE
TREATED.—THE EXHIBITION OF SOUPS.—RAW MEAT.—DR. LEVE-
RET'S CASES.—EXAMPLES OCCURRING IN DR. MORRIS'S PRACTICE.
—ANALOGOUS EXPERIMENTS WITH ADULTS.—UNDERDONE MEAT.
CASES.—VEGETABLE REMEDIES TO BE CONJOINED. — FREQUENCY
OF FEEDING.

In the previous chapter we have chiefly referred
to those agents, not necessarily aliments, but
which by their solvent action upon articles of
food given at the same time tend to nourish a
child.

We must now speak as to the kinds of artificial
food to be given. In early months, for the reasons
before assigned, it should be exclusively animal.
We should always endeavour to obtain milk from
a cow at grass, because it is more likely to be
wholesome, and the disposition to fermentation
is less. This milk should be given to the child
in a diluted state, *i. e.* in the proportion of one or
two pints of water to one of milk, according to
the age of the child, diminishing of course the

amount of water as the child becomes older. If the cow's milk be already diluted with two parts of water, sugar also should be added in the proportion of one to two drachms to every pint. If, however, there be only one part of water, and the milk is pure, the amount of sugar contained is already about 24 per 1000, the normal proportion of human milk, and it need not be therefore increased. This proportion is calculated on the latest analyses of milk, and will in practice be found to agree very well with most children.

At the onset, here we meet with two classes of objectors. Curious enough, they contradict one another. First. That such a mixture will produce diarrhœa. Second. That it will produce constipation.

1st. Some practitioners have told me that such a mixture is very apt to produce diarrhœa, and as lately as 1861, M. Dubois points it out as an evil arising from the administration of spoon meat to children who also take the bottle. "The Editor of the *Journal of Practical Medicine and Surgery*, after commenting upon the fact that a new-born infant, in one of M. Dubois's wards, passed green motions every morning, and yellow natural motions every evening," he proceeds to say : "This fact is one of daily occurrence in the lying-in hospitals, and is referable

---

* April 1861.

to mixed alimentation. An infant is, during the day, nursed by its mother, and passes yellow and homogeneous excrement. At night a more or less adulterated milk is administered liberally with the sucking bottle to prevent its crying. In the morning the motions are green, colic is present, and the anus red. This returns regularly day after day, and often induces fatal enteritis. In hospital the number of wet-nurses is too small— a circumstance accounting for the defective feeding, which M. Dubois has often noticed and regretted; but the same fact is likewise observed, from other reasons, in private practice. The opinion is too generally prevalent that children may be brought up by hand as well as by the breast. This method may, sometimes, it is true, be successful, but only in families in an easy position, and under quite exceptional hygienic circumstances, etc."*

The second opinion is so general that it scarcely needs comment, and more than once it has been urged to me as one of the chief objections to bringing up a child by hand, as it necessitates also such a quantity of purgative medicine to be administered.

Opinions of so contradictory a nature require comment. The explanation is, that if we place a

---

* Ranking's *Retrospect*, vol. xxxiii, p. 256.

child in impure air and give it bad milk, whether the maternal milk or that obtained from the cow be at fault, we must expect diarrhœa and other evidences of defective assimilation. It is not the mixture which is injurious, but that one, it may be both, the milks employed, are bad of their kind.

Again, if the hygienic conditions maintained are good, and the milk of good quality, experience shows that the admixture of two milks, so far from being injurious, may prove very beneficial. I do not find, as a rule, under artificial feeding judiciously carried out, whether with or without maternal milk, that the bowels suffer; or, if they do, whether from constipation or diarrhœa, that they cannot generally be properly regulated. Such disorders will occur, however, in the healthiest child, whether artificially fed or suckled. One thing I am particular about. Wherever it can be done I never give ordinary sugar, but always *sugar of milk*. This may appear inconsistent. But sugar of milk will often check diarrhœa, as I have before stated, and I cannot too strongly recommend its employment in preference to ordinary sugar in these cases; and, more than this, sugar of milk, which, as it is usually sold, contains all the salts of milk in solution, and when substituted for the ordinary white sugar, it often not only stops excessive purging,*

---

* Page 317.

but keeps the bowels regular. This constipative effect can be besides, if need be, more directly removed by the addition of a little carbonate of magnesia, in the same way as phosphate of soda is added in that variety of baked flour food to which I have before referred (p. 342), and, indeed, most writers on children's diseases, agree in recommending this salt, as the antacid substitute for limewater in all cases where the bowels are not sufficiently relaxed.

Lastly, to every pint of artificial food prepared, from an ounce to an ounce and a-half of limewater should be added to neutralise the amount of acidity present. This amount may be generally determined either by testing the milk with litmus paper, or more accurately by the symptoms observed in the child.

To ensure the proper examination of the milk, I think in every nursery where children are brought up by hand there should be *test-paper* kept, very slightly reddened, and some slightly made blue. If the former is turned blue when dipped in the milk, the milk is *alkaline*, and very little limewater is needed. But if not affected, or if it be more intensely reddened, then the blue litmus paper should be dipped into the milk, and this last will of necessity become reddened. In these cases there is excess of acid present; limewater, therefore, should be added in larger quan-

D D

tities to neutralise this. The moment the litmus that was reddened has resumed its natural blue colour enough limewater has been added. In practice it will be found that two to four teaspoonfuls of limewater to the half-pint will suffice, and even be more than sufficient; but this excess, for the purposes of the growth of the child's bones and teeth, is desirable.

But I have said the presence of excess of acid may be more accurately determined by the *symptoms*. These are frequent hiccough, and apparent griping, especially after food, as evinced by an occasional cry, and it may be drawing up of the legs. A loose motion generally follows, the colour tending to the green. There is also very generally vomiting present, and the ejected matters have an intensely acid odour. These are premonitory symptoms, which, if not attended to, will often pass on to diarrhœa. In these cases limewater in excess is indicated, and the proportion may be increased to two tablespoonfuls to the half-pint, and even more.

All admixtures of vegetable matters at early periods are contrary to nature, and, except in disease, they should be avoided, or given only as correctives of bad milk. I have already alluded to the manner of estimating and correcting inferior kinds of milk (p. 312 *et seq.*), by arrowroot, tea, and cream. Occasionally, where the diarrhœa is very obstinate, rice-water may be substituted for ordinary water, as the diluting medium, together with the proper medicinal remedies to be just now mentioned. These are circumstances which, when they occur, are very apt to dishearten a parent, and the difficulty is usually met by at once flying to a wet-nurse. But I am certain this is often done prematurely. It is rare that a judicious treatment will be found to fail. The most distressing symptoms present besides the diarrhœa are the great apparent weakness, and the pain, accompanied with sleeplessness, observed in the child. If the suffering child is treated in time, these symptoms will seldom attain to any very great amount, but in no disease is the old adage more truly verified than in this affection, "One stitch in time saves nine." Unfortunately, however, these cases are often neglected. In the better classes of life the child is usually at once given to a wet-nurse. Too often, however, it cannot suck the breast from sheer weakness, and except the milk is milked into its mouth, even with a wet-nurse no good can be expected. Where a wet-nurse cannot be got, the child usually dies, as much from want of judgment in those who take charge of it as from exhaustion. Food of various kinds, which it cannot digest, and that very frequently and in large quantities, is forced into the child's stomach. The diarrhœa is increased, and death usually follows.

Now the secret in these cases is to feed the child, little and often, and to give wine in comparatively large quantities. Half a teaspoonful of milk, prepared and corrected as before said, given every quarter or half an hour; wine and water, or better still, wine whey (made with one part of wine to two of boiled milk, p. 385), will often do marvels. I have seen a child so weakened and reduced by diarrhœa (in this case induced, however, by a wet-nurse's milk), that it could only take its food by a feather, for nearly eight hours, all the while looking more dead than alive, blanched, and pallid to a degree, and yet make a perfect recovery. Wine whey, indeed, is here our sheet anchor. Where children are older the same good results follow the use of Hogarth's essence of beef, given almost undiluted. I have now seen so many similar cases, and so apparently hopeless, recover, that I never give up a child, and I am thankful to say that, under Providence, I have been the means of saving life upon more than one occasion by adopting this plan perseveringly.

These extreme examples are, however, comparatively rare. If due attention be paid in providing a child with a proper quantum of good food, fresh air, and exercise, particularly if it be fed at regular hours—when very young, say every two or three hours; and three times a-day and once at night only, after it is four years old —we may then safely hope serious complications will be avoided.

Now and then, however, not only is diarrhœa present, and intense debility, but the stomach is very irritable; no kind of food can be kept down, particularly milk, not even wine whey; and those substances, perhaps, which have hitherto best agreed with the child, cannot now be borne. The aliments to be given in these cases are two: —*Good black tea* mixed with milk, which last should be given only in sparing quantities and *raw meat.*

Tea, for the reasons before stated (p. 342), comes to resemble very closely beef-tea, and as such may be looked upon as a very good substitute. While it dilutes the milk, which in the cases we are now considering appears to be too rich for children, it facilitates the digestion of the smaller quantity of milk now given, and itself sustains the strength of the little child, retarding the waste of the body. The small quantity of sulphate of copper which it contains seems to act as an astringent, and as it often does in the adult after an attack of sea-sickness, it allays the nausea also.

The following case, stated succinctly, is an example of this kind. A little child, aged about one year, of delicate constitution, hearty neverthe-

less, and who, from the age of 4 months, had
been brought up by hand—on milk and water at
first; subsequently milk only, corrected by limewater and sugar of milk—was suddenly seized
with vomiting; the moment it took its milk, of
which it always partook with its usual avidity, it
became sick. Diarrhœa also supervened, the
motions passed were unchanged food, the child
became weak and emaciated, and appeared to be
losing flesh every day. My colleague, Dr. Savage,
being called into consultation, recommended that
pure milk should be discontinued, and from two
to three parts of weakish infusion of black tea
to one of milk should be given to it. No other
treatment was ordered, but this sufficed to restore
the functions to their normal condition. In this
case the child was not bilious, and the milk was
exceedingly good. The simple fact was, it could
no longer digest pure milk.

2. The other aliment which proves so beneficial
in this state of stomach, is *raw-meat*. I have already
alluded to it (p. 304). Raw meat contains in its
composition, besides the nitrogenous fibrin, also
an abundance of phosphoric acid and chloride
of potassium; and thus, for the reasons before
stated, it contains two elements of great importance to a growing infant. The small bulk which
it occupies also renders it, because at the same
time intensely nutritious and exceedingly digest-

ible, of the greatest value. Dr. Leverett tells us one or two mouthfuls are enough for a repast. It has the same advantage over cooked meat which raw albumen of egg has over that which is boiled hard. The juice of flesh contains, among its other ingredients, albumen, and the colouring matter of the blood; the former coagulates at a temperature of 133° Fahr., the latter at a temperature of between 158° and 165°. When these principles are coagulated they are very much more difficult of digestion. Indeed, many persons, even among adults, cannot digest them at all, and suffer intense pain after food, particularly after eating cooked meat. Hence the advantage of giving raw meat to weak persons and to dyspeptic individuals. But this is not all. Raw meat often settles the stomach and alimentary canal, when all else which is taken is rejected by vomiting. Indeed, so general is its utility, that after some years of experience I have come to regard it as one of the best and surest remedies which we possess in such cases.

I prefer, however, first giving the experience of Dr. Morris to my own, lest I should be regarded as too much of an enthusiast in its favour. "The first cases to which Dr. Morris (before referred to, p. 176) gave the raw meat, were two little German brothers, five and six years of age, who had been much reduced by long neglected

intermittent fever. Soon after their admission
to the hospital the fever had yielded to quinine,
but an obstinate diarrhœa had resisted all the
ordinary modes of treatment, and they had been
reduced almost to skeletons. Just then Dr.
Morris came on duty, and commenced at once
the use of *raw meat.* The children soon began
to improve, and in less than a fortnight the little
fellows who had been so recently too weak to sit
up in bed, were playing in the wards with the
other convalescents. About this time *cancrum
oris* made its appearance in the hospital. Many
were attacked, and amongst others the younger
of our little Germans; yet, notwithstanding the
unfavourable state arising from his previously reduced condition, he recovered under the use of
raw beef and the topical application of nitrate of
silver.

Dr. Morris's next case was a child two years
old, suffering from hereditary syphilis. He was
a miserable-looking object. Death, which seemed
of all things the most desirable for him, had
been warded off for some days by the free use of
brandy. Raw beef was prescribed, but almost
without hopes of benefit. It was given in brandy,
for which he had a greater relish than for anything else. In a week there was a change for
the better. As soon as possible iodide of potassium was administered, in order to eradicate, if

possible, the constitutional taint. The brandy, of which it was positively said he took two ounces daily, was gradually decreased in amount, and when we last saw him, after the treatment had been continued for some two or three months, he was fat and hearty."*

I select these cases from many others to which Dr. Morris gave raw beef, because they show, in the most convincing manner, the beneficial effects of this remedy. Dr. Morris prescribed it whenever the system was exhausted by previous disease or inanition. Generally he used it with marked benefit.

I may now, perhaps, with less risk of being found fault with, relate two cases which, amongst many others, occurred in my own practice. A little child, aged about eight months, was reduced, while yet sucking its mother, to a state of extreme debility. Bronchitis was present. It lay on its back unable to sit up, much emaciated, and in a semi-conscious state, moaning occasionally, but otherwise showing but faint indications of life. The mother's breast was milked into its mouth, and wine given. The child rallied a little, but still not to any great degree. Raw beef was now given. In two or three days it was able to sit up, and was convalescent in a week.

---

* *Dublin Medical Press*, May 9, 1860.

A second case was that of a young babe, who had been brought up by hand, and was affected with jaundice, and excessively weak. Mercury and wine were given, but the latter seemed only to have a partial effect, and the former seemed to produce so much weakness that it could not be persisted in, except in excessively minute doses. Raw meat was now given. The child did not appear to relish it, but it was persisted in for two days. This period, however, sufficed. The child was enabled on the second day to sit up for several hours, and gradually recovered. These cases, together with others, are sufficient to show what a valuable remedy we have in raw meat in cases of debility and inanition.

If we notice the operation of this remedy when occasionally given to adults, we learn much which is particularly instructive when applied to infants. With this view, the mention of a few cases may prove interesting. There is at first a difficulty in giving it to an adult, which, judging from my experience, does not apply to children. In the former, Dr. Leverett says, " the difficulty is to overcome the natural repugnance at eating raw flesh. M. Trousseau, however, declares the disgust may be overcome even in the case of the most fastidious and delicate ladies. He told us of one to whom he gave it. At first she took it, he said, with loathing and aversion, soon with ease, and before long she ate it voraciously."*

I have noticed this last effect myself among adults. A grown girl actually assured me that she had been taught by her father to eat a raw steak, and the idea seemed in itself to give her a relish. With her it amounted quite to an unnatural and repulsive fondness.

And after all, reasoning without prejudice, this predilection for raw food is not so unusual as we believe. It is traceable among those even who eat *cooked* meat. Some persons very much prefer *under-done* meat. They, moreover, find by experience it agrees best with them. This preference is so little exceptional, that where it occurs we may fairly conclude it is instinctive. The absolute difference, therefore, between persons who take *very under-done* meat, and those who take *raw* food is more one of degree, than of kind.

In another case, where the patient had gastrodynia, and could retain nothing upon her stomach, so that anæmia and intense debility were present, raw beef scraped and spread between two pieces of thin bread-and-butter effected a cure. The idea of eating raw meat at first was very repugnant to her feelings, but it wore off very soon.

---

* *Ibid.*

Dr. Leverett, before quoted, tells us "Dr. Morris was equally successful with raw meat among adults. In an adjoining ward was a man suffering from chronic diarrhœa. He had *run the gauntlet of treatment* for diarrhœa without relief; for if better under one plan of treatment one day, he was worse the next. There was no physical sign of consumption, though the obstinate diarrhœa gave ground for suspecting such a condition. Raw beef was working wonders in the children's department—why should it not be tried for him? It was given, and in less than two months the man left the hospital cured. Raw beef had saved his life. Two summers since, while in Paris, Dr. Leverett saw a precisely similar case of supposed tuberculosis of the mesenteric glands, in the service of M. Trousseau at the Hotel Dieu. The result was, however, different, for the patient died. The autopsy showed no trace of tuberculosis: and M. Trousseau, in lecturing afterwards on the case to the class, expressed great regret at not having given raw beef. He had done, he said, everything else; and added, that he would never let such another case die in his hands without giving raw beef. He believes the remedy invaluable."

"In 1856," continues Dr. Leverett, "while Resident Physician in the Episcopal Hospital, Philadelphia, the various visiting physicians allowed me to administer raw beef in a number of cases, in many with a decided benefit. In one case of chronic dyspepsia, with great irritability of the stomach, it was retained, when almost everything else was rejected. In the later stages of typhoid fever it proved a valuable article of diet, as I should have mentioned that it did at the Philadelphia Hospital. I found that it could be rendered palatable to adults if sprinkled with salt and allspice, and spread on a thin slice of bread, or between two slices, as a sandwich. I recollect none to whom it was given who did not soon learn to take it at least without dislike. Of the cases to which it was then given I will give an account of but one. It was that of a little girl to which my colleague, Dr. Hopkins, and myself, were called. We found her suffering from the sequelæ of scarlatina. Her parents had a few days previously laid two of their children in the grave from the same complaint. The life of this their last was despaired of. We found her a pitiful-looking object. She was only 1 year old, but appeared an old woman. She was extremely emaciated, her skin hanging on her bones. She had large bed-sores, a hard tumour of the right parotid, and a fluctuating tumour on the left wrist. She was moaning or crying almost incessantly with pain. The case seemed, as it had been decided, desperate. We determined to give quinine in small doses as a tonic, and raw beef as an article of diet. We made anodyne applications to the tumour of the wrist, the principal source of pain, and painted the tumour of the parotid with tincture of iodine. She soon showed some improvement. When she became tired of raw beef we had it boiled, but so slightly as to cook merely the surface; then we changed to mutton, and soon returned to raw beef. She gradually recovered, and was eventually restored to perfect health."*

When everything else had failed I have given raw meat to little sucklings, infants so young that I could not put the pulp of the raw beef even in small pieces upon the tongue, because they had not the sense to swallow it down. However, a piece of raw beef, thinnish, of a certain length, was put into the child's mouth. Suction at once was induced, till the meat became diminished in size, and colourless as fish. It is remarkable how soon the diarrhœa and gastric symptoms ameliorated in character, and how the strength of the little invalid improved. Remedies previously inert now began to take effect, and in a short time the natural food was resumed.

When a child is so weak or so young that the raw meat cannot be sucked, then *raw meat juice*,

---

* *Dublin Medical Press*, May 9, 1860.

made with lukewarm water, in the way before specified, may be substituted.

By means of a small india-rubber hollowed ball, or bottle, with a jet attached to it, it can be introduced within the mouth, and squirted, in very small quantities, about a tea-spoonful at a time, down the throat. As it reaches in this manner to the first part of the pharynx, even in cases of extreme weakness it is involuntarily swallowed, and so the child obtains nourishment and is able to rally. I have kept children alive in this way for days, when weakened to that degree, or so affected with disease about the mouth that they could not suck, as, for instance, in cancrum oris, bad aphthous spots, etc. We can also readily see how the same instrument may be employed to administer wine whey, etc.

In the treatment of all cases in which the raw meat or raw meat juice is employed, it is manifest that there must be great disadvantage if the meat supplied be in any way tainted, or affected with parasites, as instanced at p. 307 *et seq.* We have in raw meat a first-rate remedy, but it must be good meat of its kind to act well.

If, however, a child has teeth, which, as I have before stated, is an indication that those physiological changes which are essential to the digestion of vegetable matters have taken place, then vegetable matter may be usefully combined with the food which is given to the child. Of these several preparations have been from time to time recommended, and used with advantage. Thus we hear of " Hards' farinaceous food," of baked flour, tops and bottoms, biscuit-powder, and a variety of other aliments of that kind. In my own practice, without denying that with some children these substances will prove occasionally very useful, I have generally limited myself to the employment of three substances : "Mrs. Wells' Vegeto-Animal Food," "Robb's Biscuits," and " lentil powder ;" and among breads, pure home-baked, the aerated or unfermented bread. I have already spoken of these several substances in a former chapter.*

In the first, we have many of the ingredients which exist normally in milk, namely, the sugar of milk and the salts. In lentils, we have the nitrogenous principle present identical with the *casein* of milk; and so the change from purely animal milks to these compounds is more gradual, and more likely to agree with the child. In the success which follows the employment of Robb's biscuits the same analogy cannot be traced, but there certainly is something in their composition which proves particularly fattening and wholesome to children. If the meals given

---

* Page 328, *et seq.*

be properly regulated, and due attention be especially paid to the state of the bowels, we have every reason to anticipate that the plan followed will be attended with success. Dill or cinnamon water, as occasional carminatives, should be given, particularly with Robb's biscuit and lentil powder, etc.; and it should not be forgotten that lentil powder is occasionally purgative, for which reason it should be watched, and not continued too long if it be too active in this respect.

We have, lastly, to consider the simple yet important question—How often should a child be fed? In extreme infancy, for the first two months or so, it may be wise to give them their food every two hours. As soon, however, as it can be done, the child should be taught to suckle or feed at regular hours—every three or four hours—and then to sleep, if need be, after it. But I am a very great advocate for teaching a child another good habit, and that is to take its food at night as seldom as possible. I like to teach the child to take its food four times in the day, but once only at night. It is better both for mother and child. It gives the child an opportunity of having a longer night's sleep, and affords the stomach also a longer period of rest. It is certain it is more healthful for a suckling mother because she sleeps better, and besides it makes a nurse more contented. A very little firm manage-

E E

ment will suffice for this. It only needs to be gradually done. Otherwise babies are very apt to get into the bad habit of sleeping all day and waking all night, to the immense annoyance of nurses as well as parents.

CHAPTER III.

HYGIENIC AND PREVENTIVE TREATMENT OF DEFECTIVE ASSIMILA-
TION IN THE APPOINTMENTS OF A WELL-REGULATED NURSERY.
—EXTENT AND VENTILATION OF A NURSERY.—CLEANLINESS OF
A NURSERY.—IMPROPRIETY OF KEEPING DIRTY LINEN IN THEM.
—TEMPERATURE.—CURTAINS.—ABLUTIONS.—WARMTH OF WATER
AND VARIETY OF SOAPS.—EXERCISE, CLOTHING, PERAMBULATORS.
—EARLY RISING AND GOING TO BED.—EXTERNAL LIGHT.—CLEAN-
LINESS OF WET-NURSE.

Second. The hygienic treatment involves the
question of the appointments of a well regulated
nursery. This last is all important, if we wish to
bring up healthy children. Moreover, it is also
the best preventive treatment against the occurrence of defective assimilation in those liable to
it, and as such needs especial discussion at this
point of our inquiry.

Wherever it is practicable, the child should
not be confined to one room, except in illness.
A night nursery, as well as a day nursery, should
be provided. This very change of air has a wholesome tendency. The sleeping room should not
be too small; six hundred cubic inches is the least
that can be safely given to an adult; a child re-

quires at least four hundred. Although smaller in bulk, its respirations are more rapid; and it sinks more readily under the influence of a deleterious atmosphere. The confined air of towns is, as a rule, made worse by the closeness in which rooms are kept. The absence of confinement in country places is one of the reasons why they are so much more healthy. A child must not be allowed to breathe his own expired air over and over again. In the long run, with unusual delicateness, scrofula or consumption of some kind will be surely developed.

The large size of the room, although it will make this less possible, will not always suffice; the ventilation must also be good; a burning fire which can be borne in winter assists in the purification of the air of a room, but does not do enough; and in summer, it cannot be tolerated. The simplest and most effective ventilation with which I am acquainted, is effected by perforated zinc plates in the walls on a level with the ceiling. These may be arranged in two ways, either when the tops of the windows reach to the ceiling, at the top of the window, so constructed as to admit of the closing the window to a greater or less extent, and to increase or diminish at will the entrance of air. The zinc plates should extend completely across the top of the window, and descend to from four to six inches;

or, secondly, the zinc plates may be placed between the windows, and in this case should be usually from about one to two feet long, by six inches broad. This second plan has an advantage, as two plates, the perforations of one of which are larger than the other may be used. The larger being placed externally, the smaller internally, and so all draught is obviated. When winter occurs, the inner one is always kept in, and in very cold weather may be closed in part. In summer it may be removed altogether. Wherever these plates are placed, however, it is imperative, that in the portion of the wall opposite to them, similar plates should be placed, over the doors and opposite windows in the adjoining rooms, if they are separate, so that a free current of air may pass along the ceilings, and no draughts descend upon the children. This system can be most advantageously carried out in the case of entire houses, in every room; only in this case it is well to have a similar draught to proceed from the bottom of the house to the skylight above, both the places where the air enters and passes out, being also guarded by perforated zinc plates. It is this plan which has been so satisfactorily carried out at the Cripples' Home and the Samaritan Hospital, in London.

There are some practices kept up in most nurseries, which are most detrimental. One is the *drying of napkins* by the fire-place. Indeed, nursery-guards with a double rim round them, are made and sold with this very object. Independently of the dampness thereby induced, as they are often not washed at all, and in many cases only rinsed out in water, the urinous odour given out is intensely unwholesome and offensive. Not only is ammonia emitted, but perhaps cyanate of ammonia, a poison, and so an atmosphere may be generated which will prove highly injurious.

But more than this, I have known several instances, and, indeed, among wealthy families, where the ordinary unclean napkins or utensils are left an undue time, sometimes hours, in the nursery; or, what is more usual, as it saves the nurse a little trouble, they are not at once removed to a distant part, but placed outside the nursery door, to poison the surrounding atmosphere, and to foul the air in the nursery the moment the doors are open. It cannot be supposed but what such a course of misconduct must prove very injurious to children. That very atmosphere so fatal to infants before spoken of (p. 35), is at once generated and maintained. It is extraordinary, however, how all these contingencies may be removed by a very simple procedure. If chloride of lime be used in the proportion of four ounces to the quart bottle of water and well shaken, and about a tablespoonful of this solution placed in the chamber before used by the child, there will be no odour generated. Moreover, if the same quantity be placed in a utensil already containing urine, free chlorine is given out by mutual decomposition, and all odour is at once destroyed. All other soiled napkins should be removed at once in a yard or to a distance, so that the air should in no way be contaminated.

The *temperature* of a nursery should not be under 65°, when the children are very young, and it may be one or two degrees above that. When they have reached the age of one, 60° is sufficient.

Curtains to beds are in every way to be condemned; they should never be tolerated. They tend to annul all ventilation in the bed; they oblige the child to breathe the air already expired over and over again, and tend to make it particularly obnoxious to cold. If it is believed that a draft comes from a door or window, a screen is the proper thing to ward it off; in this way ventilation is modified, not arrested. Upon the same principle, caps, however becoming, should be avoided in the house. They render the head, supposed so likely to suffer from exposure, more obnoxious to cold. A child's head is either in such constant perspiration that, if the cap be removed at any time, it may catch cold, or if the temperature falls it suffers, because the ordinary

covering does not suffice. I believe that hydrocephalus, or water on the brain, is often due to
imprudences in this respect. Infants should be
blue-coat boys, at least in their nurseries. There
is another advantage. Exposure of the head pro-
motes the growth of hair, and makes it stronger
when it does grow.

A child should be early accustomed to *cold
water*. Except in extreme infancy, when tepid
water only would be safe, a morning cold sluicing,
from the head downwards, is most beneficial. It
will suffice at night to use lukewarm or warmish
water for the purposes of cleanliness. Of course
this general statement in no way precludes other
local ablutions, if necessary. The custom, however, which obtains in some families of washing the child with warm water in the morning,
sometimes of the temperature of 100° Fahr., is, I
think, highly reprehensible. Instead of being a
hurried process, as it is sure to be when cold water
is used, the heat, agreeable by practice to the
child, leads the nurse to prolong the operation,
and so the child comes out of the bath, not only
feeling weaker, but extremely liable to catch cold
on exposure to any vicissitude of temperature.
Now, the exhilarating and bracing effect produced,
is one of the advantages of a cold bath, and it is as
true, if not more so for the infant, as it is for the
adult. It is a matter of daily observation that
persons accustomed to take colds continually,

have entirely lost the habit of using a cold-water bath every morning. It fortifies the system, keeps the body in a healthy glow, and enables it to resist with better success the alternations of hot and cold. Moreover, it is an excellent preservative against chilblains and chapped hands, so often a source of discomfort to our little ones.

Of the use of *powder*, I can only speak in commendatory terms. It is well calculated to prevent chaps and excoriations. For the same purpose some oily inunctions will be found efficacious to affected parts, such as sweet oil, cold cream, etc. Glycerine rubbed in occasionally, will do much good, unless the chapping be extensive, when, although curative it gives great pain, and is then too much an object of dread to sensitive infants to be persisted in. In these cases, honey is the best application, and should be used at night and washed off in the morning.

Much is said in the present day as to the injurious effects of certain *soaps*, more especially the ordinary whity-brown used for all domestic purposes, which is alleged to irritate the skin, and otherwise promote chapping. I believe this is all a mistake ; no soap is so effective for the purposes of cleanliness, and if the superior kinds are used, in which there is not an excess of soda, it is the best; indeed, the very chapping between the legs and under the arms, so common in children, is often cured by washing the parts over with this soap. I think it cruel, however, to allow the face and eyes to be washed over with it in the coarse and rough way in which I have often seen it done. The nurses have almost appeared to me to take a sort of morbid delight in its employment in this way. Even to an adult, soap in the eyes is a very painful ordeal to go through; in the end it inevitably produces chronic, sometimes acute, ophthalmia. I think, therefore, children should be spared this barbarity, and the eyes, at least, carefully avoided.

In the above remarks, it is in no way my intention to forbid the use of scented soaps, and especially glycerine soap, for the purposes of ablution to those who prefer them, but to show that they have no advantages in most cases. So, I think, a piece of soft flannel is more effective and should be preferred, except in the case of very young children, to the sponge, as both more cleanly and likely to produce a healthy glow after its employment upon the skin.

Every child should, as far as practicable, take *daily exercise.* Fresh air is everything to a child. I believe the healthy look of many of the ragged boys and girls who crowd our dirty alleys and courts even in London, is due to this one contingency. Certainly, their food and raiment and habitations are not, as a rule, calculated to benefit their health. The good sanitary condition of many of the inmates of the ragged, dirty, Irish cabins is, probably, in measure also due to their constant daily open-air exercise and insolation. I do not mean to say that a child should go out in very foggy or damp weather, or when it is intensely cold, particularly during an east wind; but, even in such days, a ten minutes run, if the child be warmly clad, and especially dry footed, will do much good. It is the late hours at which children are kept out, which are so injurious. Even in London, between ten and two, it is rarely that a few minutes of bright weather may not be found and taken advantage of. In the summer, if damp on the one hand, and the meridian sun on the other, be avoided, and if, especially the head is kept well guarded from the sun's rays, the longer a child is out in the open air the better.

But, here I must lay great stress upon this *protection of the head.* I believe even in the North, but certainly in Southern England, exposure to the sun is a frequent cause of cerebral disease, even though the heat borne may not amount to a " coup de soleil." This is especially the case with very young infants, in whom it should be remembered that the opening in the fontanelle has not yet been closed. I have seen indiscretion in this respect often give rise to cerebral congestion, in some cases to water on the brain, convulsions, or permanent idiocy.

One word about *perambulators*. They have been severely condemned, I think unwisely. It is alleged that they enable nurses to attend to their own pleasures either in idle reading, or companionship with followers. This is true. I have seen it over and over again in our London Parks, and at the sea-side. So also the child will fall asleep in them, and catch cold if the weather be unpropitious.

But, on the other hand, it is not the use of a *perambulator* that makes such a nurse unworthy of confidence. Such a person would probably err even if she did not use one. Then it is some-times positively cruel to compel a nurse to carry an unusually heavy child. She will either sit down on a bench, where a child is equally liable to catch cold, or will shorten the period allotted for the child's exercise. Again, some children are too fond of walking, and do so before their skeleton is in a fit condition; hence, if rickets be present, deformity, most frequently for life, is the result. This is avoided by using a perambulator. If a child be asleep it is easy to return home. Let us remember that we should not work a willing nurse, any more than a willing horse, too severely; and if the child be warmly clad, the advantages of the perambulator far outbalance its disadvantages. In very cold weather a warm bottle and a rug can be placed in the carriage, and so the child may be kept warm. This is often not possible when a short-coated child is carried. The legs are exposed and often become very cold. Nor does the use of the perambulator necessarily preclude moderate walking exercise. It merely allows of rest both to the nurse and child, and when the ground under foot is wet, the child at least remains dry.

As to the use of *clothing*. A child should be kept warm, especially in its feet. Damp feet are always more likely to injure a child than exposure to almost any other kind of cold. But the amount of clothing should be regulated with the season and the day. Habitually, therefore, in every-day practice, it is well to inquire and satisfy oneself as to the kind of day, and regulate the dress accordingly.

As with adults, so with very young children, *early to bed and early to rise,* must be the maxim. No child under 10 should be out of his bed after eight at night, and none under 5 after six or seven. It is not, however, in this particular that parents usually err. It is in the hour of rising. It is a common prejudice to say a child needs sleep, and so he is left in bed till nine or even later in the morning. I think, except in the case of very young children (of 2 to 3 years old), this is a mistake. Too much sleep is apt to produce a certain amount of cerebral congestion. The erect or semi-erect position is as necessary for a child as the recumbent. In a weak child, the latter may produce passive congestion of all the lower parts of the body. We have seen its injurious influence so well described by M. Hervieux (p. 49). If the child needs sleep, it is better to let it have a mid-day *siesta*. The alternation will have done good. Seven in the morning is not too early for a child over 2 years old, who has retired at seven the previous night to sleep.

Moreover, it teaches a child from early life a good habit. Our fondness of the bed of a morning is very often a sin which those who have brought us up have to answer for rather than ourselves. Besides, it is to be borne in mind that the morning air is always purer than night air. It is richer in oxygen; and during summer, it is even in London most refreshing. I make it a rule to give a child a crust of bread every summer morning, and if he be not too young, to send him out for a run, for a few minutes or longer as the case may be, before breakfast. Except in damp weather it will be found a healthy plan, and one to which children who have once enjoyed it always look forward with pleasure.

I believe it is imperative that a nursery should be *freely accessible to external light*. There is, to speak socially, always a cheerfulness in bright light, which keeps up the spirits of the child, as the night from an opposite effect produces sleep. We have already shewn (p. 66) that the absence of light tends to retard growth, if it does not in some cases absolutely stop it, and the pasty-white, cachectic face is almost always a characteristic of it. For this reason, a sombre dark nursery is to be avoided.

In like manner, the experiments of Stark, before alluded to (p. 69), prove that dark tints or colours absorb odours, another reason why they should not be used. Let the papers be, therefore, bright and cheerful, but let us not fly to the opposite extreme. Green appears, from the entire aspect of nature, to be the favourite colour, and it is certainly that which is most agreeable and soothing to the eye. But a large number of the green coloured papers, and certainly the cheaper varieties, are arsenical; the emanations and sweepings therefrom are poisonous. Such kinds of papers should, therefore, be banished from nurseries altogether. If used at all, they should be well varnished over. After all, plain whitewashing above, and painted skirtings, appear to be the most rational kind of decorations. The yellow colour is also unhealthy. It prevents the admission of the chemical rays of light, and is hurtful to animals as well as to plants.

I need not add that if the strictest regard to cleanliness applies to the child as well as the articles used for its food, so regard should be had to the *cleanliness of the wet-nurse*. If it be the mother who suckles her child, in our ranks of life, such a remark would be libellous. Such precautions are, however, necessary with *hired* wet-nurses. Their breasts, especially the nipples, should be kept very clean to obviate the disadvantages of animalcular formations before referred to (p. 196). A conscientious mother is bound to be a very close observer of the wet-nurse she employs. Irregularity of conduct, the occurrence of the catamenia, a deficiency of milk, are often thus discovered in time, and a great deal of future mischief to the child is thus prevented.

I am not one of those who would discourage plentiful ablutions even for a wet-nurse. Indeed, a sea bath may be allowed in summer if the breast is carefully dried and kept warm subsequently. As cleanliness is a great element of health, so it can only lead to an amelioration both in the quantity and quality of the milk. I do not say that in every case a sea bath is desirable, but in very many. The woman should not, however, be allowed to stay long enough to become cold. In and out the sea is all that is necessary, followed by an energetic rubbing all over the body to ensure the occurrence of the glow.

CHAPTER IV.

THE medicinal treatment of defective assimilation is very difficult; and mostly unsatisfactory.
In the milder cases, simple attention to the food
is the best means of overcoming the disease.
The occasional use of carminatives, and a half
teaspoonsful of castor oil, if needed, with small
doses of alkalies, will often remove all irritability
of the alimentary canal. Cod-liver oil, in teaspoonful doses, is almost always beneficial: if
there be much acidity, one or two drops of liquor
potassæ mixed with it, or more according to the
age of the child, is readily taken. This oily mixture should always be given after meals. Sometimes, where there is reason to suspect indigestion, it is well to combine the oil with half to one
teaspoonful of the essence of rennet, and this may
be followed with much advantage. In more severe
cases, however, and if diarrhœa be present, the

F F

best remedy is, without doubt, the *nitrate of silver*, in doses from 1-16th to 1-8th of a grain: sometimes the sulphate of copper in similar doses proves effective. I cannot say that I have found that much dependence can be placed on most of the usual remedies recommended, such as catechu, logwood, chalk mixture, or opium, except as adjuncts, just as rice-water or arrowroot act. They do very little good; the latter is chiefly beneficial in checking pain. Yet anodynes are certainly sometimes useful. I know that, as a rule, they are condemned; but where a child cannot have sleep, and cannot rest without them, they are imperatively called for. The nervous child is over-excited, it needs to be calmed; but two to five drops of tincture of henbane, in about a teaspoonful of dill water, at night, will suffice. It is remarkable how, after a week or ten days, the child sleeps normally, and no longer needs it. As a temporary remedy anodynes, therefore, must be deemed very useful. Opium is more certain, but it is also a much more dangerous remedy to give to children. I have seen two children killed by it. In one case, one drop of laudanum was fatal. But in quarter-drop doses, gradually increased and carefully watched, these unfortunate results can be usually avoided.

Defective assimilation is sometimes accompanied by feverish excitement, which usually comes on at night, and is no doubt due in great measure to the gastric irritation. It is in such cases that external inunctions of oily or lardaceous substances are so effective. The *rationale* of the operation of these substances is not yet entirely explained, but of the fact there can be no doubt.

If a child's skin be burning from fever, so as to be actually unpleasant to touch from its heat, the other ordinary symptoms of anorexia—viz., restlessness, sleeplessness, rapid pulse, thirst, debility—will also be surely present, and the emaciation induced will be extreme. Debility will soon come on to an alarming degree, particularly if diarrhœa be present, and death will soon close the child's sufferings. In such an exhausted state the use of antiphlogistic remedies, such as calomel or antimony, are clearly contraindicated. Now these are precisely the cases in which external inunctions with oily matters, as first recommended by Mr. William Taylor, of St. John Street Road,* do so much good. If a child so affected be completely rubbed over with a mixture of suet and sweet oil (a certain amount of consistency being necessary to allow it to remain upon the body), in about three hours time, or even before, the skin will be found to have

---

* In a Paper read before the Medical Society of London.

cooled and become soft; the anorexia present will have disappeared, and often a quiet, comfortable sleep will follow. The child is left in this state, and the next morning may be washed in a warm bath. Two or three applications of these inunctions generally effect a cure of the feverish excitement, and the irritation of the alimentary canal is usually at the same time greatly benefited.

I have said the *rationale* of this mode of cure is not so clear; it may, however, be the following, to which I have also elsewhere referred. There is probably in all animals, particularly young animals, a certain amount of cutaneous respiration, *i. e.* some action between the oxygen of the atmosphere and the capillaries of the skin. The way in which this process is carried on I do not presume to explain.* If, however, this external communication with the oxygen of the air be cut off—which may be done by rubbing over the body with an impervious varnish, as has been done by experiment upon animals—the temperature falls several degrees. Thus Becquerel and Breschet† found the temperature of rabbits, first shaved, and then covered with a varnish, fall in an hour from 100° to 76°; in another rabbit to 69½°.

The experiments of Dr. Fourcault prove that

---

* Vide *Essay on Pneumonia*, by the Author, p. 38.
† *Comptes Rendus*, Oct. 1841. Carpenter's *Physiology*, p. 646.

the application of this varnish produces what he calls "cutaneous asphyxia, which is marked by imperfect arterialization of the blood, and a considerable fall of temperature, and which, as it produces death in the lower animals, would probably do so in man."* Certainly fish absorb oxygen and exhale carbonic acid, not merely with their gills, but the whole surface of their body, so long as surrounded with water impregnated with air. Embryos of birds and insects do the same. So also the development of the egg is stopped, in warm water (which is necessarily deprived of air), and in irrespirable gases.

This has been proved by Viborg and confirmed by Schwann. These experiments, we may say with Carpenter,† "place in a very striking point of view the importance of the cutaneous surface as a respiratory organ, even in the higher animals." The fall of temperature during perspiration is usually attributed to the cold produced by evaporation. But looking to the oily character of the sebaceous exudation on the skin, and the greasy character of the perspiration in some persons, it may be a question whether this natural oily covering does not contribute equally with the evaporation of the watery matters of the perspiration, to produce the cool-

---

* Carpenter's *Physiology*, p. 632.   † *Ibid.*, p. 646.

ness of the skin observed under these circumstances.

There is another way, however (and this is especially true for chronic cases), in which inunctions do good. Dr. Simpson, of Edinburgh, has
shown the good results of external inunction of
cod-liver oil in those cases where the remedy could
not be taken in the ordinary way. In some cases
of defective assimilation, there is, together with
the emaciation present, occasionally hectic fever.
Thus, if children thus affected be rubbed with
the cod-liver oil, both symptoms often disappear,
and there is much amendment in the symptoms.

Dr. H. Wright has informed me of a case of a
little girl in whom dyspepsia, with emaciation to
a great extent, was present, and in which he
effected a cure by *milk baths*. I presume in this
case, as in the former instance, there was absorption of the nutritive and fatty matters through
the skin, which could not be digested in the
ordinary manner when taken by the mouth, and
so recovery resulted.

This same advantage may be sometimes gained
by nutritive injections. Aliment in a fluid state
is often readily absorbed in this way, as in the
sad examples of adult persons, intent on suicide,
and who have cut their throats. In these persons, swallowing in the ordinary way has become
impossible, yet they have been kept alive for six

weeks by these injections. The same is true for cases where, from disease of the stomach, food could not be swallowed without provoking vomiting. Life in this manner has been prolonged till the irritation of the stomach has subsided, and food could be again taken in the ordinary way. Even cod-liver oil may be absorbed if given in an injection. Persons who have so taken it have complained to me of feeling the taste of it in their mouths for hours after. This is equally true as regards young children.

Lastly, I may notice the treatment of those aphthous exudations which so often accompany defective assimilation. The *mild form* will generally yield to borax and honey, weak solutions of alum, and the other remedies employed ordinarily in thrush. The other variety, the *malignant* or *contagious*, is a much more serious affection. It more closely resembles *diphtheria*, and requires an analogous treatment. Generally wine whey, or wine, should be freely given. As local applications, the only remedies which in my hands have cured have been, first, a weak solution of nitrate of silver, applied by means of a sponge all over the affected parts, twice or three times a day. Secondly, the tincture of sesquichloride of iron, in strength varying from one part of the tincture in from seven parts to an equal quantity of water. In cases where the throat or nasal mucous membranes are covered with these aphthæ, I have used a fine syringe, and injected sparingly, either down the throat or up the nasal cavity, the weaker solution. Whether the cure be due to the presence of *free chlorine*, to the *free hydrochloric acid*, or to the *astringent local effect*, I know not, but the aphthous exudation has got well. Such local and general treatment, however, must not supersede the hygienic, before referred to. Pure air, isolation, the free use of disinfectants, and scrupulous cleanliness, are also needed; in fact, every measure is to be taken which will in any way prevent the development of that infantile hospital atmosphere which I have already spoken of, and which is always observed wheresoever many children are congregated together, and is invariably deadly in its effects.

I have dwelt thus long upon the subject of defective assimilation, because I believe this morbid condition is, so to speak, the parent of those several rachitic, tubercular, developmental, and other fatal disorders which so commonly occur among older children. A due attention, therefore, to it, in its causes and prevention as well as treatment, will be the means of saving life and preserving health. If due regard be had, not only to the condition of the child, but also to that of the mother, I think we may safely hope for the most fortunate results.

Having so far considered the disease which I think is the origin of most of those distressing ailments which are commonly met with in children, it may not be out of place to make a few remarks on the subject of rickets and scrofula.

From the most careful experiments, it appears that *rickets* is generally dependent upon the weakly health of the suckling mother. Thus, Dr. Jenner states, "whatever renders her delicate, whatever depresses her powers of forming good blood, that tends to induce rickets in the offspring. Of the influence of the father, I am very sceptical. Of this much I am sure, that where the mother is in delicate health in a state of which anæmia and general want of power form the prominent features, without being the subject of disease usually so called; there the children are often, in a very decided degree, rickety, and that although the father is in robust health, and the hygienic conditions in which the children are placed, are most favourable. On the other hand, I know no case (though I do not deny there may be such) in which the mother being robust, the hygienic conditions favourable, and the father delicate, the children have proved rickety."

" Phthisical parents are no more likely to have rickety children than are non-phthisical parents. Nay, the facts contained in a table made for me

by my friend, Dr. Edwards, some years ago resident at this hospital, and now Physician to the
Consumption Hospital, at the East of London,
render it probable that they are even less likely.
It is very common the first or the two or the
three first-born children to be free from any signs
of rickets, and yet for every subsequent child to
be rickety. Again, if a woman have one rickety
child, in the large majority of cases all her subsequent offspring will be rickety. The explanation of this fact is, that among the poor the
parents are generally worse fed, worse clothed,
and worse lodged the larger the number of their
children; the man's wages remain stationary, the
calls on his means are increased. And, among
the rich and poor, the larger the number of children, the more has the mother's constitutional
strength been taxed, and the more likely is she
to have lost in general power."*

I have introduced this passage in full because
it so entirely agrees with my own experience,
and so readily points out the curative measures
to be employed. If a woman be weak, the more
need of assisting her by giving the child artificial
food besides the breast-milk, as well as by putting her under proper tonic treatment herself.

. * *On the Causes of Rickets*, by Dr. Jenner, *Med. Times and
Gazette*, May 12, 1861; Ranking's *Half-Yearly Abstract*, vol. xxxii,
p. 52.

In this way, you allow her to supply her offspring with better milk, and by enabling her to nurse longer, you put her in a condition in which she is less likely to bear children fast. It is the duty of a medical man to point out to a mother who has children fast, that she is probably preparing herself to witness, in the sequel of her history, her children deformed. I make this statement advisedly. I have met with women, and even in the better classes of life, who seem to take a pride in the frequency of, and small intervening periods between, their confinements. The result has been in the long run, rickety or badly developed children. To effect this, they suckle their children for only a limited period, because then they believe their chances of becoming again *enceinte* greater. I hesitate not to say that if a mother is able to do it, and her strength allows of it, she ought to suckle her child for at least twelve months. Drs. Merei and Whitehead's tables prove this. A child should not be weaned, if possible, till it has teeth, and then only if the mother suffers from suckling. Even then, she may be assisted by also feeding the child.

There is one point in connexion with the origin of this disease, insisted upon by Dr. Tilbury Fox, and before noticed, to be borne in mind, namely, that rickets generally occur in the children of women who have repeatedly menstruated during lactation, and that those cases in which rickets were not present are those in which children were also artificially fed. If this opinion be correct, it also points out the advantage of combining artificial food in these cases with the mother's breast milk.

The disease may be divided into three stages : —1. Where we have, besides the general weakness of the child present, abnormal excretions, highly offensive and dark, enlarged ankles and wrists, but no actual deformity or bending of the long bones. These form by far the larger proportion of cases. 2. Those in which all the above mentioned symptoms are more marked, the long bones especially somewhat bent; ossification generally retarded. Lastly, and these are less numerous cases, where the disease has gone on to produce actual deformity, and, in some cases, become actually crippled.

And here it may be important to notice, that deformities are for the most part *acquired*, and that during the first year of life,—not congenital. In the only table setting this forth from the Lying-in Hospital, Dublin, out of 13,933 births, 19 males and 28 females, *i. e.* 47, or 3·4 per 1000, were born deformed in some way ; of which 11, or ·7 per 1000, were affected with club-foot or deformity of the lower extremities ; 2, or ·14 per 1000, with deformity of upper extremity ; and 6, or ·42 per 1000, with spina bifida. Ten died, or ·70 per 1000, during their residence in the hospital, *i. e.* about one month, or at the rate of 8·40 per 1000 in the year.

Upon the same scale, in the year 1860, out of 684,048 births in England, we should have had 2,302 children born deformed, out of which number 19·3 would have died in the year. The Registrar-General's returns, however, state the number of children, under one year old, dying from malformations and deformities, to be, not 19·3, but 8,726 for the year. These deformities appear for the most part to be of the same class as those occurring in the Lying-in Hospital, but in addition include, doubtless, malformations produced by rickets. Thus, in round numbers, it is probable that over 39,000 deformed children existed that year, under one year old, in England, of which number some 37,000 had become deformed during the year, *i. e.* about 1 in 18, or 54 per 1000. Mr. Holmes Coote has estimated to me the proportion of cripples, congenitally deformed, which present themselves at the Orthopædic Hospital, to those which have become so, as 1 in 13. Even admitting the numbers to be somewhat exaggerated, yet they are high enough to prove that the negligence displayed by those who have the care of children in bringing them up, and in feeding them, is most gross and reprehensible, and to an extent that appears scarcely credible.

Rickets, especially in its first and second stages, is curable, and even in the third may be greatly benefited, although sometimes the deformity cannot be removed. Everything that tends to improve the general health, such as good food and good air, is necessary. The remedies are iron, cod-liver oil, and lime. The best preparation of iron in this disease that I am acquainted with, is the superphosphates of iron and lime combined. The salt actually deficient in the bones is the phosphate of lime, and this is in this way directly supplied to the system. Experience has also shewn that cod-liver oil has a most beneficial effect.

Tuberculosis, the deposit or circulation of tubercular matter in the blood, shows itself generally among infants in four forms. 1. General scrofula. 2. Consumption of the lungs. 3. Tabes mesenterica or consumption of the bowels. 4. Tubercular meningitis, generally accompanied with water on the brain. I have annexed for convenience the per centage proportion of deaths from these causes, as compared to the deaths from all specified causes, from which it will appear that the deaths from consumption of the lungs, as well as from scrofula, properly so called, are rare.*

Consumption, properly so called, and so fatal in adults, is with children under five, a comparatively rare form of disease. Mesenteric disease, or consumption of the bowels, on the other hand, is the most common, and next to it disease of the brain; but as the terms hydrocephalus and brain disease here spoken of may include diseases other than tubercular of that organ, this last is probably exaggerated.

I have already described the scrofulous temperament (p. 240), and there is no doubt that the deposits which in some cases occur in the neck and secreting glands, are identical with those which occur in mesenteric disease. These patients are also peculiarly liable to that variety of ophthalmia so common among the ill-fed children of the poor. Except that scrofula is hereditary, whereas rickets are not, the causes are identical. Impure air, especially air that has been breathed over and over again, defective

---

* Proportion of deaths from scrofula, phthisis, tabes, hydrocephalus, and brain disease, to deaths each class, all specified diseases :—

	Each disease. Deaths, all ages.		Deaths under 1.		Deaths under 5.
Scrofula	100	...	13·0	...	29·8
Phthisis	100	...	1·8	...	5·2
Tabes Mesenteria	100	...	42·6	...	81·1
Hydrocephalus and brain disease	100	...	25·7	...	58·5

hygiene, want of light, cleanliness, and good food, are, without doubt, the causes which, either singly or unitedly, lead to its production.

Essentially, however, and in the better ranks of life, it is chiefly attributable to two causes in operation, excluding always hereditary taint, that we have to ascribe its development. One is, the overcrowding of children together. Experiment has shewn that if an animal be kept confined in a barrel or closed box so that the air supplied is always more or less vitiated by the carbonic acid which it expires, however well fed that animal may be, tubercle will be developed in about three months. And so it is with many of the spoiled children of the wealthy. The hot and ill ventilated rooms, and the massive curtains with which they are surrounded, effect as much evil as the small and close rooms of the poor. But it is chiefly by the sweets and bonbons with which they are spoilt, as well as the starchy aliments with which they are fed, that the strumous development is ensured. We have already seen the effect of an excess of saccharine food in the production of strumous ophthalmia. Add to this, that the bad and vitiated tastes induced by this species of pampering, prevent them from relishing proper and wholesome food when it is given to them.

I had occasion to speak before of the brewers'

mash given to cows, and how readily it depraved their appetites, and ultimately led to the development of ulcerative disease among them, and so it is in this case. The quality of the blood is deteriorated, and the several diseases of tubercular character are developed. A sugary diet besides leads to the production of worms, a source of much dyspeptic distress to children, sometimes of convulsions.

Common sense points out the wickedness and absurdity of many practices even now-a-days carried on and maintained by many who ought to know better; and certain it is, that parents and those who take care of children often treat these tender little ones, as they would not think of treating their pet animals, favourite dogs, or horses of value; and surely that sweet and lovely thing we know a babe to be, is worth many animals, however costly and valuable.

In conclusion, if by what I have said I may, under Providence, be the means of saving the life even but of a single child, and of making but one sorrowing mother, or one grieving father happy again, I shall be thankful, and shall consider I have not written in vain. Yet this is not all I have desired to accomplish. I have wished to call the attention of the community to the subject of infant feeding, as one fraught with difficulties and social evils of no ordinary kind, and calling loudly for more care, and even for legislative enactments. The food of our little ones must not be adulterated or poisoned. Our foundling hospitals must be regulated by wiser laws; the encouragements now given to crime must be repressed; and parents who by their ignorance prove themselves unworthy to care for their children, must be taught their responsibility. This is a noble work for philanthropists of both sexes; it is, moreover, to its full extent a Christian work; and blessed shall they be who perform it. "Insomuch as ye have done it unto one of the least of these, my brethren, ye have done it unto me."

APPENDIX A.

Specified Causes of Deaths in all England, 1860, reduced to a Scale of 100.
Also each Class, upon a Scale of 100.

CLASSES.

	All Ages.	Under 1.	1 Year.	2 Years.	Under 5.	To 100 bir. dths per cent. ages under 1.
All Specified Diseases.	100	23·9	7·9	3·6	36·7	**14·3**
ZYMOTIC DISEASES.	**75849**	**17235**	**12203**	**7369**	**46261**	2·5
To 100 all specified deaths.	18·3	4·1	2·9	1·7	9·2	
To 100 each class.	100	22·7	16·	9·7	61·	
CONSTITUTNL. DISEASES.	**82088**	**6326**	**4224**	**1930**	**14357**	·9
To 100 all specified deaths.	19·8	1·5	1·	·4	3·4	
To 100 each class.	100	7·7	5·1	2·3	17·4	
LOCAL DISEASES.	**171037**	**42598**	**12126**	**4633**	**63432**	6·2
To 100 all specified deaths.	41·3	10·2	2·9	1·1	15·3	
To 100 each class.	100	24·8	7·1	2·7	37·8	
DEVELOPMENTAL DISEASES	**70311**	**29682**	**3708**	**770**	**34631**	4·3
To 100 all specified diseases.	16·9	4·7	·9	·1	8·8	
To 100 each class.	100	27·8	5·2	1·09	49·2	
VIOLENT DISEASES.	**14775**	**1354**	**666**	**613**	**2597**	·1
To 100 all specified diseases.	3.5	·3	·1	·1	·6	
To 100 each class.	100	9·1	4·5	4.	17·4	—— 14

ORDERS.

No. 1.   ZYMOTIC DISEASES.

	All Ages.	Under 1.	1 Year.	2 Years.	Under 5.	To100 bir. dths per cent. ages under 1.
1. MIASMATIC.	**71304**	**14514**	**12049**	**7306**	**43161**	2·1
To 100 all specified deaths.	17·4	3·5	2·9	1·7	10·4	
To 100 each Order.	100	20·3	16·9	10·2	60·5	
2. ENTHETIC.	**1252**	**768**	**48**	**7**	**820**	·1
To 100 all specified deaths.	·3	0·1	·01	·001	·1	
To 100 each Order.	100	61·3	3·8	·5	65·4	
3. DIETIC.	**2206**	**851**	**51**	**17**	**1136**	·1
To 100 all specified deaths.	·5	·2	·01	·003	·3	
To 100 each Order.	100	34·	2·3	·7	51·5	
4. PARASITIC.	**1087**	**902**	**55**	**39**	**1038**	·1
To 100 all specified deaths.	·2	·2	·01	·006	·2	
To 100 each Order.	100	82·	5·	3·6	94·8	—— 2·4

G G

No. 2. CONSTITUTIONAL DISEASES.

	All Ages.	Under 1.	1 Year.	2 Years.	Under 5.	To100 bir. dths. per cent. ages under 1.
DIATHETIC.	16404	350	186	122	434	·04
To 100 all specified deaths.	3·9	·08	·04	·03	·01	
To 100 each Order.	100	2·1	·11	·7	2·6	
TUBERCULAR.	65684	5966	4038	1858	13523	·8
To 100 all specified deaths.	15·8	1·4	0·9	·4	3·2	
To 100 each Order.	100	9·8	6·1	2·2	20·5	·84

No. 3. LOCAL DISEASES.

	All Ages.	Under 1.	1 Year.	2 Years.	Under 5.	To100 bir. dths per cent. ages under 1.
1. DIS. OF NERVOUS SYSTEM.	55577	21047	3217	1377	27870	3·
To 100 all specified diseases.	13·4	5 08	·7	·03	6·4	
To 100 each Order.	100	37·8	5·7	2·4	50.1	
2. DIS. ORG. OF CIRCULATION.	18758	105	49	33	259	·01
To 100 all specified diseases.	4 5	·02	·01	·005	·06	
To 100 each Order.	100	·5	·2	·2	1·3	
3. DIS. ORG. OF RESPIRAT.	684048	17804	8306	1910	31370	2·6
To 100 all specified diseases.	16·7	4·08	2	·4	7·8	
To 100 each Order.	100	26·2	12·1	2·8	47·3	
4. DIS. ORG. OF DIGESTION.	19718	2178	409	229	3106	·3
To 100 all specified deaths.	4·6	·5	·09	·05	·7	
To 100 each Order.	100	11·	2·	1·1	15·7	
5. DIS. OF URINARY ORGANS.	4990	37	44	30	168	·005
To 100 all specified deaths.	1·2	·006	·01	·005	·04	
To 100 each Order.	100	·7	·8	·6	3·4	
6. DIS. ORG. OF GENERATION.	1068	6	6	1	15	·0008
To all specified deaths.	100 2	—	—	—	·008	
To 100 each Order.	100	·5	·5	—	1·4	
7. DIS. ORG. OF LOCOMOTION.	1466	44	32	24	168	·006
To 100 all specified deaths.	·3	·01	·006	·003	·04	
To 100 each Order.	100	3·	2·1	2·2	11·	
8. DIS. INTEGUMENT. SYST.	1002	377	63	24	476	·05
To 100 all specified deaths.	·2	·09	·012	·003	·1	
To 100 each Order.	100	37·6	6·2	2·3	47·5	6·118

No. 4. DEVELOPMENTAL DISEASES.

	All Ages.	Under 1.	1 Year.	2 Years.	Under 5.	To 100 bir. dths. per cent. ages under 1.
CONGENITAL MALFORM. Developml. dis. of Children.	**12706**	**10688**	**1811**	**176**	**12688**	**1·5**
To 100 all specified deaths.	3·06	2·5	·4	·04	3·06	
To 100 each Order.	100	82·5	14·3	9·3	99·	
DISEASES OF NUTRITION.	**26930**	**18994**	**1997**	**594**	**21943**	**2·7**
To 100 all specified deaths.	6·5	4·5	·4	·1	5·3	
To 100 each Order.	100	70·6	7·3	2·2	81·9	
						4·2

No. 5. VIOLENT DISEASES.

	All Ages.	Under 1.	1 Year.	2 Years.	Under 5.	To 100 bir. dths. per cent. ages under 1.
ACCIDENT OR NEGLECT.	**12991**	**1147**	**660**	**508**	**3379**	**·01**
To 100 all specified causes.	3·1	·2	·1	·1	·8	
To 100 each Order.	100	8·8	5·1	3·9	26·	
HOMICIDE.	**377**	**206**	**2**	**5**	**216**	**·03**
To 100 all specified causes.	·07	·04	—	—	·05	
To 100 each Order.	100	54·7	·5	13·	57·2	—
SUDDEN DEATHS, CAUSES NOT KNOWN.	**2894**	**770**	**60**	**40**	**907**	**·01**
To 100 all specified deaths.	·6	·01	·011	·006	·2	
To 100 each order.	100	26·6	2·7	1·3	31·7	·05

Deaths, all England, from some Diseases more or less produced by errors of diet and bad food.

Disease.	All Ages.	Under 1.	1 Year.	2 Years.	Under 5.	Deaths under 1 to 100 births.
DYSENTERY.	1156	167	88	43	427	·02
To 100 all specified deaths.	·2	·04	·02	·01	·1	
To 100 each disease.	100	14 4	7·5	3·7	36·8	
DIARRHŒA.	9702	5067	1400	299	6913	·7
To 100 all specified deaths.	2·3	1·2	·3	—	1·6	
To 100 each disease.	100	52 2	14·4	3·0	71.1	
PRIVATION.	68	3	1	1	6	—
To 100 all specified deaths.	·012	—	—	—	—	
To 100 each disease.	100	4·4	1·4	1·4	8·8	
WANT OF BREAST-MILK.	1002	992	10	—	1002	·1
To 100 all specified deaths.	·2	·2	—	—	·2	
To 100 each disease.	100	99·	·9	—	100	
TABES MESENTERICA.	4680	2007	1060	458	3810	·2
To 100 all specified deaths.	1·1	·4	·2	·1	.9	
To 100 each disease.	100	42·6	22·6	9·3	81·1	
CONVULSIONS.	25205	20796	2437	911	24769	3·4
To 100 all specified deaths.	6·	5·	·5	·2	5·9	
To 100 each disease.	100	82 1	9·6	3·6	98·2	
TEETHING.	3896	1962	1768	152	3895	·2
To 100 all specified deaths.	9·	·4	·4	·03	·9	
To 100 each disease.	100	50·3	43·	3·1	99·9	
THRUSH.	920	881	27	6	917	·1
To 100 all specified deaths.	·2	·2	·003	—	·2	
To 100 each disease.	100	95·6	2·9	·9	99·6	
						4·72
TOT. INCLUD. DIGEST. ORG., DIETETIC, & PARASITIC.	69640	35806				10·1
	16·8	8 5				
	100	51·4				

FROM VIOLENT DEATHS.

Disease.	All Ages.	Under 1.	1 Year.	2 Years.	Under 5.	Deaths under 1 to 100 births.
POISON.	240	74	14	9	106	·01
To 100 all specified deaths.	·05	·01	—	—	·02	
To 100 each disease.	100	30·8	5·8	3·7	44·1	
SUFFOCATION.	1061	760	38	14	834	·1
To 100 all specified deaths.	·2	·1	·005	—	·02	
To 100 each disease.	100	71·6	3·6	1·3	78·6	
HOMICIDE.	377	206	2	5	216	·03
To 100 all specified deaths.	·09	·04	—	—	·05	
To 100 each disease.	100	54·3	·5	1·3	57·2	
THE THREE TOGETHER.	1678	1030	54	28	1156	·14
To 100 all specified deaths.	·45	·2	·01	·003	·2	
To 100 each disease.	100	61·5	3·2	1·6	68·8	
WITH PRIVATION.	1746	1033				

APPENDIX B.

Mortality in Foundling Hospitals in different parts of the World.

	Per cent.		Period.
Dublin	91		
Marseilles	90		
St. Petersburgh	40		Close of
Florence	40		last
Barcelona	60		century.
Paris	80		
All France	60		1824
„	75		1818
Dublin	48·7		1750-60
Paris	50		1838
Mean	63·4		

Mortality of Foundlings in the Departments of France in regard to the totality of their number.

(a) Departments showing the highest rate of mortality.	Per cent.	(b) Departments showing the lowest rate of mortality.	Per cent.
East Pyrénées	} 33·3 to 50	Haute-Sâone	0
Seine-Inférieure		Haute-Garonne	} 2·2 to 2·5
Gironde		Haut-Rhin	
Loiret	} 25 to 33·3	Jura	} 2·5 to 3·3
Seine-et-Marne		Hautes-Pyrénées	
Aube		Ardèche	
Cantal		Finisterre	} 3·3 to 4
Cher		Moselle	
Côte-d'Or	} 20 to 25	Vosges	
Ile-et-Vilaine		Gers	
Loire-Inférieure		Lot-et-Garonne	} 3·3 to 5
Seine		Nièvre	
		Basse-Pyrénées	
		Bas-Rhin	
Mean	26.5	Mean	3·6

Mortal. of Found. in France in regard to the number of Expositions.

Highest.	Per cent.	Lowest.	Per cent.
Basse-Alpes	83·3	Haute-Saône	0
Loire-Inférieure		Haut-Rhin	5·6
Loiret		Vosges	6·3
Seine-Inférieure	} 76·9	Moselle	11·3
Vaucluse		Ponts	13·
Ardéche		Finisterre	15·8
Aude		Ariège	15·9
Aveyron		Hautes-Pyrénées	16·3
Cher	} 71·4	Jura	17·4
Gers		Nièvre	17·5
Gironde		Bas-Rhin	17·8
Ile-et-Vilaine		Haute-Garonne	18·4
Manche	} 60	Lot-et-Garonne	19·2
Seine			
Mean	72·4	Mean	13·4

APPENDIX C.

Infant Mortality in Brighton.

Fifty cases taken from the books of the Registrars of the several districts, showing the age of each child, the cause of death as *certified*, with additional information obtained by personal inquiry into the method of feeding, etc.

1. Girl: aged 4 months. Died suddenly in a fit. Coroner's inquest. Fed on boiled French roll given with a spoon; very little breast-milk. Fed freely.

2. Boy; aged 9 months. Died of bronchitis and convulsions. Fed on boiled rice and sago, and the breast. A fat, heavy child.

3. Boy; aged 8 months. Died in a convulsive fit. Coroner's inquest. Alleged cause, teething. Fed upon tea and *muffin* heartily the night before it died. Always ate heartily, and had also breast-milk. Was a very thin and puny child.

4. Girl; aged 7 months. Died of diarrhœa (during dentition). Fed partly from breast, partly with boiled milk.

5. Boy; aged 5 weeks. Died of diarrhœa. Fed partly from breast, partly with boiled milk.

6. Boy; aged 8 months. Died of hooping-cough. Fed entirely from mother's breast.

7. Girl; aged 2 months. Died from want of breast-milk. The mother died when the child was five weeks old. It was weakly from birth, and did not thrive upon the food given. The bottle was not tried.

8. Girl; aged 6 weeks. Died of bronchitis and convulsions. Death sudden. The mother says it had nothing but the breast as food; and no drug or medicine except given by a medical man.

9. Boy; aged 6 months. Died of hooping-cough and convulsions. Had breast-milk the first four months: then bread and water food sweetened.

10. Girl; aged 3 months. Died of marasmus. The mother, not having sufficient breast-milk, tried bread and milk, and then milk and water, without success.

11. Boy; aged 9 months. Died of mesenteric disease. The child was weaned suddenly, and fed without judgment.

12. Girl; aged 3 months. Died of convulsions. Fed entirely from mother's breast.

13. Boy; aged 5 weeks. Died of bronchitis. — Had boiled bread food and the mother's breast.

14. Boy; aged 9 months. Died of diarrhœa and convulsions. — Was suckled by its mother till three months old; then put out to dry nurse, and fed with milk sop, arrow-root, beef-tea, mutton-broth, etc.

15. Child; aged 3 months. Died of convulsions. — Fed entirely from mother's breast.

16. Girl; aged 4 months. Died of marasmus. — Fed entirely from mother's breast.

17. Girl; aged 4 months. Died of diarrhœa and convulsions. — Partly fed from breast; also with all kinds of food, which the stomach rejected. "Delicate from birth."

18. Boy; aged 3 months. Died of diarrhœa. — Partly suckled; also had boiled French roll.

19. Boy; aged 5 months. Died of atrophy. — Had arrow-root—probably insufficient in quantity.

20. Girl; aged 4 weeks. Died of convulsions. — Fed on mother's breast and arrow-root. Mother says it was an "eight months' child."

21. Boy: aged 10 months. Died of convulsions. — Mother's breast, and boiled French roll.

22. Child; aged 9 months. Died of convulsions. — Weaned at three months; then fed chiefly on gruel. Ailing from birth. Mother sickly.

23. Girl; aged 10 months. Died during dentition. — Nursed entirely from mother's breast.

24. Girl; aged 3 months. Coroner's inquest: verdict "affection of brain from overloading the stomach." — Two cups of arrow-root, milk and water, in addition to breast-milk, within a very short time.

25. Girl; aged 6 months. Coroner's inquest: verdict "accidental death." No blame attached to nurse. — Suffocated by being overlaid by the wet nurse, a heavy sleeper. She was questioned as to taking any extra drink herself, or giving any narcotic to the child, which was often very restless.

26. Girl; aged 4 months. Died of marasmus. — Weaned at eight weeks; then fed on arrow-root and boiled bread. "Pined to a skeleton."

27. Boy; aged 8 months. Died of diarrhœa. — Born a fine healthy child; lost its mother in the first month; was put out to dry nurse, and shockingly neglected; removed to care of another person when $7\frac{1}{2}$ months old; lived 13 days in a state resulting from starvation and disease. No coroner's inquest.

28. Boy; aged 4 months. Died of phthisis. — Partly suckled; partly fed. Constitutionally delicate.

29. Boy; aged 1 year. Died of phthisis and convulsions. — Ditto, ditto.

The father of these two children (28 and 29) died of consumption; all three deaths occurred within a week or two.

30. Girl; aged 11 months. Died (as alleged) of constitutional debility. Died in a fit of convulsions. — Partly suckled by mother, partly fed, for six months: a pint of thick food three or four times a day. After six months was put out to dry nurse; fed with bun and milk and gruel a few minutes before it died. Probably a case of overfeeding.

31. Child; aged 9 months. Died of bronchitis. — Suckled entirely by the mother.

32. Girl; aged 1 year. Died of hooping-cough. — Weaned at ten days old; fed on arrow-root and gruel.

33. Child; aged 6 months. Died of choleraic dysentery. — Weaned *suddenly* three weeks before death; fed on bread and milk.

34. Boy; aged 3 weeks. Died of "exhaustion of vital powers." — Suckled by a wet nurse; but fed also on rolls and cow's milk.

35. Girl; aged 9 months. Died of hooping-cough and pneumonia. — Suckled entirely by the mother.

36. Boy; aged 6 months. Died of convulsions. — One of twins; suckled by the mother; also fed on prepared barley. Ailing from birth.

37. Boy; aged 3 months. Died of hooping-cough. — Suckled by the mother.

38. Child; aged 1 month. Died of "constitutional weakness." — Suckled entirely by the mother.

39. Boy; aged 1 month. Died of "diseased stomach." — Fed on cow's milk and water.

40. Girl; aged 8 months. Died in dentition. — Fed on the mother's breast.

41. Child; aged 9 months. Died of bronchitis. — Brought up by hand, on new milk and tops and bottoms.

42. Girl; aged 6 months. Died of pneumonia. — Fed partly from breast, partly with biscuit powder and cow's milk.

43. Girl; aged 7 months. Died of convulsions during dentition. — Fed entirely on cow's milk and water. Dentition unusually early; ten or twelve teeth in seven months.

44. Boy; aged 5 months. Died of hooping-cough and convulsions. — Fed partly from mother's breast; also on bread sop.

45. Child; aged 1 year. Died of hydrocephalus.

Always fed a great deal (the mother having difficulty in suckling). When weaned, had anything (*i. e.* everything). Convulsions came on with teething. Treatment consisted of blister to top of head, mustard to the back of the legs and neck, and leeches to the temples.

46. Boy; aged 1 year. Died of convulsions.

Partly fed from mother's breast; also with boiled bread.

47. Girl; aged 2 months. Died of diarrhœa.

Very little breast-milk; had baked flour and biscuits boiled.

48. Child: aged 5 months. Coroner's inquest: verdict " overfeeding."

49. Child; aged 7 months. Coroner's inquest: verdict " overfeeding."

These cases happened together in the same house. The child of a wet nurse, and her nurseling, were fed on a hearty supper of bread food; and were found dead at 4 A.M.

50. Child: aged 4 months. Coroner's inquest: verdict " overfeeding."

A similar case to the preceding two.

APPENDIX D.

Mortality in early months, Parts of England, 1842, compared to Births.

PLACE.	Births.	$\frac{0}{1}$	$\frac{1}{2}$	$\frac{2}{3}$	$\frac{3}{6}$	$\frac{6}{9}$	$\frac{9}{12}$	Under 1 Year.
England	517739	24353	9059	6543	14913	12408	11428	78704
	100	4·7	1·7	1·2	2·8	2·3	2·2	15·2
London	60240	2102	1116	838	2034	1700	1548	9438
	100	3.4	1·8	1·3	3·3	2·6	2·5	15·6
Oxfordshire	5145	244	93	72	183	121	118	781
	100	4.7	1·7	1·4	2·5	2·3	2·2	15·1
Cambridge	5979	325	111	84	105	145	106	976
	100	5·4	1·8	1·4	1·7	2·4	1·7	16·3
Durham	12058	719	219	151	323	277	253	1942
	100	5.9	1·8	1·2	2·7	2·2	2·	16·1
Monmouth	4910	192	97	62	142	113	119	727
	100	3·9	1·9	1·2	2·9	2·3	2·4	14.8
South Wales	16836	646	241	173	330	268	258	1916
	100	3·8	1·3	1·	1·9	1.6	1·5	11·3
North Wales	10693	407	144	116	195	140	150	1153
	100	3·8	1·4	1·	1·8	1·3	1·4	10·7
Norfolk	12271	693	265	180	417	297	214	2066
	100	5·6	2·1	1·4	3·3	2·4	1·6	16·8
Kent, extra metropolitan, except Greenwich	14326	629	238	188	431	352	286	2124
	100	5·	1·6	1·3	3·	2·5	1·9	14·7
Surrey, extra metropolitan	6233	227	81	69	142	132	105	756
	100	3·6	1·2	1·1	2·2	2·1	1.6	12·1
Dorsetshire	5163	169	59	48	147	113	108	709
	100	3·2	1·1	·9	2·8	2·1	2·	13·5
Yorkshire, W. Riding	40165	2428	702	464	1025	913	974	6506
	100	6·04	1·7	1·1	2·17	2·	2·4	16.
Yorkshire, E. Riding	7284	448	83	117	255	181	132	1316
	100	6·06	1·1	1·7	3·4	2·4	1·7	17·8
Yorkshire, N. Riding	5646	313	80	59	131	88	90	761
	100	5·5	1·4	1·6	2·3	1·5	1·5	13·5
Lancashire	64596	3379	1417	1015	2361	2220	2213	12605
	100	5.07	2·1	1·5	3·6	3·4	2·4	19·4
Devonshire	15444	484	180	133	332	325	259	1716
	100	3·1	1·1	·85	2.1	2·1	1·6	11·6
Rutlandshire	738	35	11	16	16	16	4	98
	100	4·7	1·5	2·1	2·1	2·1	·5	13·2

APPENDIX E.

Table calculated upon the Population Tables of 1851, compared to Deaths for the several ages under one year, shewing also the proportionate Mortality per cent.

Place.			Mth. 1.	Mth. 2.	Mth. 3.	Mnths 4 to 6.	Mnths 7 to 9.	Mrths 10 & 11	Under 1 Year.
ULSTER.									
Rural districts	Births, 1851	36966							
	Deaths, 1850	—	609	223	233	417	351	151	2185
	Propor. per ct.	—	2·1	·6	·7	1·1	·9	·4	5·9
Civic districts	Births, 1851	7431							
	Deaths, 1850	—	276	55	82	153	186	109	861
	Propor. per ct.	—	3·7	·7	1·1	2·	2·5	1·5	11·5
CONNAUGHT.									
Rural districts	Births, 1851	19695							
	Deaths, 1850	—	62ʳ	166	239	393	235	63	1624
	Propor. per ct.	—	3·1	·8	1·2	1·9	1·2	·3	8 2
Civic districts	Births, 1851	1868							
	Deaths, 1850	—	103	25	26	55	38	20	267
	Propor. per ct.	—	5·5	1·3	1.3	1·8	2·	1·	14·2
LEINSTER.									
Rural districts	Births, 1851	23897							
	Deaths, 1850	—	805	170	187	353	578	182	1624
	Propor. per ct.	—	3·5	·7	0·8	1·4	1·2	·8	9·0
Civic districts	Births, 1851	12490							
	Deaths, 1850	—	581	153	134	370	376	184	1798
	Propor. per ct	—	4·6	1·2	1·	2·8	3·	1·4	14·4
MUNSTER.									
Rural districts	Births, 1851	27380							
	Deaths, 1850	—	920	373	343	604	446	160	2856
	Propor. per ct.	—	3·3	1·3	1·2	2·1	1·6	·6	10·4
Civic districts	Births, 1851	9359							
	Deaths, 1850	—	435	103	132	257	261	117	1316
	Propor. per ct.	—	4·6	1·1	1·4	2·8	2·8	1·2	14.
ALL IRELAND.									
Rural districts	Births, 1851	107918							
	Deaths, 1850	—	3167	832	1002	1779	1416	559	8699
	Propor. per ct.	—	2·9	·7	·9	1·6	1.3	·5	8·
Civic districts	Births, 1851	31343							
	Deaths, 1850	—	1395	336	774	846	861	428	4640
	Propor. per ct.	—	4·4	1·	2·4	2·6	2·7	1·3	14·8

* The above results have been obtained by an approximative calculation made on the Returns of Population and Deaths for Ireland, the table of which was given in my last edition. Take for instance the ages, 1 year and under. There were living in rural districts in 1851 103,569 persons; therefore, all these were born within the year 1851. Also, 8,699 persons died under 1 year old, but some of these were born before the year 1851. Hence the births during 1851 were greater than 103,569, and less than 112,268, mean, 107,918; while the deaths were 3,167, *i. e.* 2·9 per cent. Again, in the civic districts the births were greater than 29,023, and less than 33,663, mean, 31,343, and the deaths 1,395, equal to 4·4 per cent.; and so on for other ages.

APPENDIX F.

GENERAL RULES.

(*a.*) No vegetable food, particularly arrowroot, should be given to any child *without teeth*, except by special order from the medical man. If teeth be present, it may occasionally be given.

(*b.*) If the milk be poor in quality, the animal food under Section No. III may be given to children under six months, and under Section No. II to those under three months.

A.—ANIMAL FOOD.

DIET FOR INFANTS WITHOUT TEETH.

I.—*Under Three Months.*

Take of milk and water, of each four oz.; sugar of milk, one drachm; lime water, two teaspoonfuls. Mix.

II.—*Under Six Months.*

(*a.*) Take of milk, six oz.; sugar of milk, one and a half drachm; water, two oz.; limewater, one tablespoonful. Mix.

If the above disagree.

(*b.*) *Substitute for Whey.* (Mr. Turner's.)
Dissolve one oz. of sugar of milk in three-quarters of a pint of water, at a temperature of 160 deg. Fahr. Mix with an equal quantity of good cow's milk.

(*c.*) *Milk Whey.* (Mr. Lobb's.)
Set aside half a pint of new milk, to allow the cream to separate. When this has taken place, take the skim milk left, add half a teaspoonful of prepared rennet, and heat over the fire up to 160 deg.

Fahr., until the *curd* has separated. Filter through a coarse sieve; add to the whey, in summer three drachms, in winter, three drachms and a half of sugar of milk, and limewater one table-spoonful.

III.—*Infants under Nine Months.*

(*a.*) Take of pure milk, half a pint; sugar (of milk), two drachms; limewater, one tablespoonful.

(*b.*) Prepare Mr. Lobb's Whey, with fifteen drops only of pre-pared rennet instead of thirty.

B.—VEGETABLE FOOD.

DIET FOR INFANTS ABOVE EIGHT MONTHS, IF POSSESSING TEETH.

I.—*Vegeto-Animal Food.* (Mrs. Wells's).*

(This consists of baked flour, sugar of milk, and a little carmi-native or spice.) Take about a dessertspoonful, make up into a paste with cold water, add from two to three tablespoonfuls of boiling water, then mix the whole with a quarter of a pint of milk raised to a temperature of 160 deg. Fahr. Finally, add one table-spoonful of limewater.

II.—*Lentil Food.*

Prepare in the same way as above with lentil powder.

III.—*Yorkshire Food.*

Take of baked flour, three pounds; phosphate of soda, one ounce and a half; carbonate of magnesia, a quarter of an ounce. Mix. Take three teaspoonfuls of the food, and add water and milk as in preparation of vegeto-animal food.

IV.—*Bread Sop.*

Take four ounces of stale home-baked or aerated bread, break it up in small pieces, add boiling water enough to soak it, mash it up completely. Add gradually milk raised to a temperature of 130 deg. Fahr., stirring up all the while with a spoon. Pass through a coarse sieve.

N.B.—Robb's biscuits, or tops and bottoms, may be substituted for the bread.

---

* To be had at Mr. Greenish's, 20, New St. Dorset Square.

C.—ADDITIONAL FOODS FOR WEAKLY CHILDREN.

TO BE GIVEN ONLY UNDER MEDICAL DIRECTION.

I.—*Wine Whey.*

Boil two wineglasses of milk, and add a wineglass of sherry or port wine. Strain, and add a wineglass of warm water; one meal of this may be given once or twice a day.

II.—*Hogarth's Essence of Meat.*

One teaspoonful in its natural state, with from one to eight tea-spoonfuls of water, three or four times in the day.

III.—*Liebig's Beef Tea.*

Take half a pound of the best raw beef, mince it up in very small pieces, place it in a tall jar, add three-quarters of a pint of cold water, cover it, and let it stand in a cool place for twelve hours. Strain now through a coarse sieve. Next add three des-sertspoonfuls of limewater. Heat it gently to a temperature not exceeding 130 deg. If need be, it may be thickened by a little gruel, arrowroot, or flour; a wineglass should be given two or three times a day.

IV.—*Raw Meat.*

In cases of excessive weakness, with or without diarrhœa, *raw meat* may be given.

Take a piece of the best lean rump-steak, scrape it with a knife so as to reduce it to a pulp. Dose,—one teaspoonful, spread over two very thin slices of bread and butter (where the infants have teeth): in other cases, sweetened with sugar: seasoned with salt, or a little cinnamon, or carraway powder; or even in its natural state. Three times a day, gradually increasing the dose.

V.—*Raw Meat Juice.*

Take of the best gravy meat, or rumpsteak, a certain quantity, say as much as will fill half a tumbler. Cut it in very minute pieces, so as to make the finest possible mince of it, as fine as cut-up spinach. Put this in a tumbler. If there is time to wait, add cold water to it, enough to cover the meat when mixed up with it. Stir up frequently, from time to time. At the end of three or four hours the supernatant water will have the colour of blood, the meat will have become white as fish. Strain through a coarse sieve; drink cold, about a wineglass to two wineglasses three times a day.

If the raw meat-juice is required in a hurry, water, a little better than lukewarm, but not above 130 deg. Fahr., may be used. If stirred up for about half an hour and strained as before, it may be given with advantage. Boiling will, in either case, throw down half the dissolved nutritious matters. Wine or brandy will have the same effect.

VI.—*Medicinal.*

In scrofulous cases, give cod-liver oil in teaspoonful doses; the syrups either of the iodide or superphosphate of iron, or of the superphosphate of iron and lime in doses of from ten to twenty drops. Twice a day.

APPENDIX G.

A remedy which I suppose bears some similarity to shellfish was in great vogue among the ancients. I allude to *earthworms*. It is one, however, which is not likely to take with the British public. I am, nevertheless, bound to mention it. Aetius, in his *Tetrabiblos* (serm. iv, chap. 33), thus alludes to them: "Take about five or seven worms of fishermen, which are found in the mud of rivers (and are called *lumbrici*), bruise them, and add to them boiled dates, and mix them altogether. Give this compound in beer to the woman upon an empty stomach daily, and in about ten days you will be surprised at the quantity and excellence of the milk found." The author of *Gynæciorum* also recommends their exhibition ! ! !*

---

* Lumbricorum vivorum. Scrup. ij. tere et cum mellis cyathis ij. bibat, ut non cognoscat.* He also recommends their exhibition boiled in milk and honeywine, as a remedy most efficacious in inducing an abundant secretion of milk.

---

* Lumbricus terrestris, officinalis, or earthworm, is so well known that I need not explain its figure. In its use it proves very diaphoretic, diuretic, and anodyne. It is a discutient and emollient. It is good in apoplectic cases, and where the muscles and nerves are affected; in the great dropsy, the colick, and in the scurvy it has been used with great success."—(R. Bradley, F.R.S., *Lecture on Materia Medica*, 1730.)

T. RICHARDS, 37 GREAT QUEEN STREET, W.C.

www.ingramcontent.com/pod-product-compliance
Lightning Source LLC
Chambersburg PA
CBHW021323110726
47900CB00005B/1333